jarrettsville

jarrettsville

a novel by
cornelia nixon

COUNTERPOINT
BERKELEY

Library of Congress Cataloging-in-Publication Data is available.

ISBN: 978-1-58243-512-1

Cover design by Gerilyn Attebery
Interior design by Megan Jones Design
Printed in the United States of America

COUNTERPOINT
2117 Fourth Street
Suite D
Berkeley, CA 94710

www.counterpointpress.com

Distributed by Publishers Group West

10 9 8 7 6 5 4 3 2 1

In memory of my mother, Jean Cairnes Nixon Blickman

contents

JARRETTSVILLE TOWN CENTER

Scale: Approximately 100 yards to one inch

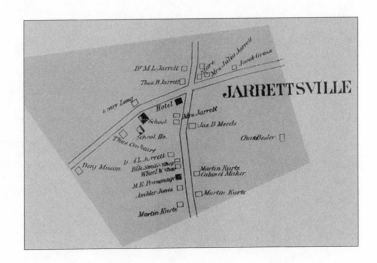

JARRETTSVILLE, MARYLAND

Scale: Approximately 2⅜ inches to one mile

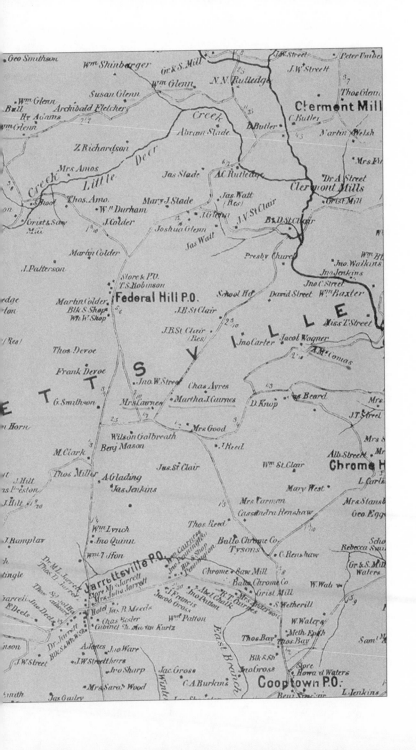

I.

Fourth Anniversary of the Confederate Surrender at Appomattox

APRIL 10, 1869

Martin Jarrett, M.D.
Confederate States Army Veteran

My house was right across the road from the hotel, and I heard the shots. At first I thought it was the usual high spirits, the Yanks congratulating themselves all over again. Every damn year since Lee betrayed us all and signed the truce, they got themselves up like peacocks, plumed hats, gold braid, and swords they did not know how to use, and pranced around a meadow for the ladies to admire. Then they would repair to the hotel that I was cursed to live too near and pour whiskey down their gullets all night long. They got so full of themselves, they would sing weepy battle hymns and lie about the glory they had shed. I could hear them perfectly.

"Wish we could rout out Johnny Reb again!"

"By gad, we'd kill us a bunch more of them yellow-bellied sapsuckers this time!"

Every one of those fools had a pistol in his pocket, and I sometimes had to patch up one or two. The guns could go off *inside* a pocket and hit a knee or worse. Last year some ignorant young lout shot his own pecker off, and I imagine he's regretted that.

Not that all Yanks were idiots. My own brother Jimmy followed his conscience, or so he said, when he enlisted as surgeon for the Union side. I did the same for General Lee, and I supposed in some way we cancelled each other out.

One day at Manassas, however, I was damn glad he had gone with McClellan's mighty league, "Army of the Potomac," as they styled themselves. The Rebel line had broken and let through a nasty band of rough-handed gents in blue, who surrounded my tent, snatched me away, and locked me in a barn that reeked of pigs. But they happened to be from my brother's regiment, and in the middle of that pitch-black night he cut the chain on the loft door and let me out. He even smuggled me some Yankee bacon and a flask, both much appreciated as I slunk through Virginia bogs, trying to find my own army again.

Tonight I felt at least as outnumbered as I had then as I put my horse into the barn and listened to the mob across the way. I was exhausted, having delivered a woman of a hefty boy she could not squeeze out through her narrow hips. I had to use the forceps, always a tricky business, and she screamed so loud she broke her own eardrum. But I had made it home, and when I heard the *pop-pop-pop*, I hoped it was just bullets wasted on the ceiling or the sky.

But now the crowd roar ceased, and voices shouted, "RUN! RUN!"

I stepped out of the barn and saw a gun-flash in the dusk, on the dark porch of the hotel, not straight up but aimed level, and a man fell backwards off the rail and hit the ground. Men were leaping off the porch, crouching or flattening along the ground, shouting incoherently.

A dark figure moved quickly, lightly, down the steps into the yard, and I thought I saw a skirt. Was that a *woman* with a gun? She stood over the downed man, her arm pointed straight at him as the gun flashed two more times. I snatched my bag and ran across the road, hesitating not one second, though I knew she might shoot me, too.

Nearby a young man's voice bellowed like an abandoned calf.

"Come on here and get on your horse! Come on here and get on your horse!"

The lady dropped the gun, sat down in the dirt, and took the man's head on her lap. She cradled him, crooning and quivering with sobs. Quickly I knelt by them.

"Bring a lantern!" I commanded no one in particular, and no one moved.

Blood pumped straight up from the man's aorta like an ornamental fountain, and when I put my fingers in the hole, made by about three bullets entering on top of each other, I knew he did not stand a chance. The hole in back, where they exited, would be larger, his lifeblood draining straight into the ground.

When someone finally brought a light, the crimson torrent was subsiding to an ooze, and it soon stopped. Dark heart's blood pooled in the center of his chest, glistening, starting to congeal. I worked fast, trying to pump his heart. I knew it was too late, but I was duty-bound to try, and it was a while before I glanced up at his face.

I could not quite place the man, but when my eyes lifted briefly, I saw the woman holding him was Martha Cairnes—my Martha, I had once thought, my Martha Jane, before she threw herself away on a Yankee bastard, son of a thieving Abolitionist who helped steal contraband. I supposed this could be he. The wounds showed that she had spared his face but aimed to hit his heart. She was a crack shot and could have picked one button off his coat and never nicked the skin, if she had wanted to. I still felt some tenderness for her, though I was lately married to a sweet young girl, a paragon of purity. On the whole, I felt I had been spared a world of trouble when Martha Jane did not choose me.

About fifty men hung over the porch rail, gaping, and a few had lost their dinners, filling the air with the acid smell of vomit laced with whiskey.

And whoever was bellowing had not desisted yet.

"Come on here and get on your horse! Come on here and get on your horse!"

It sounded like her yellow-bellied brother, Richard—no doubt terrified some Yank would shoot him just for being there, when his sister was so brave and had risked everything.

I reached up and closed the dead man's eyes, and Martha wailed. Misgiving slid below me like a bank of sand. When the men around us got over their immobility, would they take her life in their own hands?

I fixed her with my eyes and used my stern physician's bark. "Go on now. GO!"

She did not move, and I glanced around for someone who might take her from the reach of all these armed and drunken men.

My youngest brother, Josh, stood not far off, shaking so hard I thought he might fall down. He was skittish and could never pay attention long enough to take much in.

"Damn!" he kept saying, like it was the only word he knew. "Damn! Damn!"

"Josh," I called. "Come here and help Miss Cairnes get to her horse."

But her cousin George Andrew was there already, and he tried to lift her up.

"Come away now, dear," he said gently. "Come away with me."

I lifted the bloody head off of her lap so she could stand, but she did not.

Fixing my eyes on George Andrew, I could hear the fear in my own voice. "Tell her not to say a word of this to anyone. You neither. They'll find out soon enough."

It took Josh and G. A. both to lift her up, and she sobbed like her heart was being torn out of her chest. But in a moment she was gone, and I heard two horses gallop off.

It took a while to get any man to come in close enough to help me tote the body in.

"Come on, gunshot wounds are not contagious. Lend a hand."

Finally, two young men came down, saucer-eyed with fear. The dead man was not tall, but his bones were big, and as a dead weight, any man is heavy. I let the others pick up his extremities and assigned myself his messy torso, the still-warm, sticky blood soon gluing me to him. There was a gun in his pocket, and it pressed into my forearm as we lugged him up the stairs. He would not need it anymore, so I let it drop onto the porch.

The crowd of Yanks parted, gasping, as we staggered through the door to the saloon.

Tom Street, the innkeeper, cleared glasses from the bar. "Here. Lay him out right here."

"It'll make a mess," I warned, but he shook his head.

"Doesn't matter. Put him here."

At times like this I wished I was a Romanist. Priests were never at a loss for words, and if there had been one here, he would have said a solemn benediction. Just fifteen minutes had passed since this body was a man, who like all men had noble capabilities, whatever use he made of them. And now he was no better than a side of beef. Soon the worst indignities of death would start: eruptions of gas and noxious ooze, the stiffening. Mrs. Street bustled to help me lay him out, close his mouth and tie his chin with string, put pennies on his lids, mop up the blood.

I did the best I could, crossing his hands over the crater in his chest, not quite saying a prayer, because he was a Yankee after all.

Joshua Jarrett
Youth

I WAS A GROWN MAN, eighteen years old, but I ain't never seen the like, nor did I ever expect to again in my whole life. A woman, a frail girl, pretty, too, popping off a man with a six-shooter! Damn! I could not get over it, no matter how I tried.

And now she was galloping so fast, I kept losing her in the dark. G. A. had ordered me to follow her, gimme his horse and his Colt's, too. Told me to protect her with my life. I was trying to do that, but damn! She was fast!

Panting in the cold air, riding so hard I thought I might pass out, I could see her dimly as she bolted past the turn to her own place. Where was she headed? Some of those Yanks back there would want to string her up. It warn't safe out here a-tall!

"Miss Cairnes!" I called. "Hold on! Wait up!"

At the fork for Cooptown and Bel Air, she careered south, and I spurred George Andrew's horse to catch her up. This time I got close enough, so she heard me, and she stopped and whirled around. I thundered up so fast, I overshot and had to turn around.

"Please arrest me now!" she cried, her pale face glowing in the blue dark. Her horse was white-eyed from the gallop, keyed up, dancing and clinking under her. Mine was, too, and I could barely hold it as my voice cracked shrill.

"I saw it all! I never thought to see the like!"

"Then arrest me, please," she cried and held both her slender wrists toward me.

"I'm not the sheriff, miss. Don't you know me? Josh Jarrett, Martin's brother. You know me. George Andrew told me to chase after you. This here's his horse."

She was panting, out of breath. "I don't need you. But tell me quickly, have they left him on the ground?"

What was she on about? She sounded horrified, like cold dirt could hurt him now.

"Reckon he better get used to it, since he'll be under it before too long. What a piece of work you did! Plugged him on the first try, you did, by gum. Next two went wild, and I expect they'll find them in the eaves or maybe in the roof. But your aim was true on those last two! I saw it plain. But they were shot in a dead man. Your brother could not have done it half so good. Richard's afraid of him, you know. But you took care of that!"

My horse shied away from her excited mare, and I reined it back around.

She spoke slowly, carefully, like to an idiot. "Josh, tell me quick. Did they carry him into the hotel?"

I could only gape at her. "Don't know. George Andrew said I ought to go with you, and he give me his horse. His gun, too." I flourished it to show her, the long barrel glinting blue.

Without another word she turned and galloped off.

"Hold on, now!" I yelled. "Hold on! You got to wait!"

It took a second, but I got the horse to take off after her. She didn't answer, only rode, and I had no choice but to try to catch her reins and run her off the road.

My horse crashed into hers, and we both shot off into a crackling field of old cornstalks. Her horse snorted and threw its head, but it couldn't get away from me.

She yanked at the reins. "Let go! This is none of your affair. I've got to find the sheriff!"

"Sheriff won't be round this time of night, no how. They had a parade in Bel Air, too, you know. Come on, Miss C., got to get you safe home. Your lane's back this way. You missed the turn. But God be praised, that's all you missed this night."

I kept a tight hold on the mare's reins and spurred my horse. Both mounts exploded north, hers taking off beside mine like a greyhound. I herded her straight to Richard's lane and barely made the turn, we were on so fast. But we galloped right down it to the house.

I hopped down and hauled her from the saddle like a bundle, carried her up the porch steps, and set her down.

"George Andrew said I got to see you go inside the house and stay here and guard you with this gun. Now, go on in. Don't you say a word of what you did. Not to no one."

I crossed my arms and stood foursquare, tall as I could, until she went inside.

ALEX MCCOMAS
United States Army Veteran

I DID NOT GO to the parade. I had hated army life, which was like living in a pigsty in the snow, and I had left a little earlier than was quite legal, a fact my family did not know, but someone at the celebration might. No, I had spent the last months of my enlistment productively, learning dairy farming from an old man in Ohio, which is where I went missing. I spent the Appomattox anniversary productively as well, helped not one but *two* cows calve and used the cultivator on my mother's fields, where I now grew hay. After a pleasant supper with my wife, I read the papers at the table, enjoying the warm fire nearby, while she took the children upstairs to prepare for bed.

I was not expecting anyone, so I was surprised to hear fast hoofbeats in the lane, two horses or more, and in a hurry, which was odd for this time of evening. A moment later my wife's brother, George Andrew, burst in our front door without knocking. He looked pale and shaken, and right away I tried to kid him out of it. He was a big kidder himself.

"Too late for supper again, poor fellow!" I called without getting up. "Afraid we polished off every last scrap. Might scare up a crust of bread and water. Bread and water, that's your favorite, right? You seen a ghost or what?"

He came toward me and took hold of my shoulder, and I felt him shake. "Your brother has been shot. He rode in the parade, and he was shot. I think he's dead."

I heard only a few syllables of this, refusing to take it in.

"Can't be," I said reasonably. "He's up in Pennsylvania. Hasn't ridden down this way for months. Must be someone else."

George Andrew closed his eyes and shook his head. "I wish that were true, but it's not, and you'll believe me when I tell you who did it. It was my cousin Martha. She shot him more than one time in the heart."

I leapt to my feet, wanting to punch him in the jaw. But he was not the murderer, only her cousin, and my wife would never have forgiven me. He was her kid brother, the only son in a big family, and his seven sisters all revered him like he was the second coming of the Lord.

Instead I left him there and walked away, out to the barn. I got my gun, got on my horse, and rode pell-mell to the hotel, not sure who I meant to kill, but it would be someone.

The sight in the bar was sickening, silent white-faced men standing and staring at my dead brother laid out on the bar like a bad drunk, a bloody hole in his chest big as my fist. It was indecent, and to keep from throwing up, I started to shout.

"Stop staring at him! Don't just stand there, clean up the blood! Where is that vile woman? Someone get the sheriff, now! You, Jarrett! Did you even try to save him? Why couldn't he have a damn Federal physician at least? God, can you tell me that? You should all be arrested, every one of you! Did you even try to take away her gun? Won't someone at least clean him up? His mother should not have to look at him like this! Where the hell is the sheriff?"

I went on in that vein awhile, until Tom Street put a glass of whiskey in my hand.

"Toss that off straight. Sheriff won't be round tonight and maybe not by morning either. Tomorrow's Sunday. Don't you worry, he'll hear about it soon enough, and he'll see justice is done. Here." He handed me my brother's pistol and shook his head.

"He never even took that out."

He got another whiskey, and I swallowed that one whole as well. It turned hatred into tears, and I wanted to weep like a woman. Wasn't it enough that someone cracked our father's head open and trampled on him with a horse? Our father always told us we must turn the other cheek. But I knew the other cheek could be murdered, too. My father had been killed, and now my brother. I had no cheeks left to turn.

The barkeep's wife had two men carry him upstairs, and she cut away his uniform to wash him properly. Another militiaman took off his own uniform and gave it to her to put on him. It was too big, and it had gaudy gold epaulets and gold on the pants, stuff my brother would have ridiculed. But at least our mother would not have to see the wounds, and we could bury him in it.

The thought of another cold grave gaping in the ground sent me downstairs for a third whiskey. He was not in Pennsylvania. He was dead. Dead like our father. Dead like Abraham Lincoln or Jesus Christ.

All right, my brother was no saint. You don't get challenged to a duel at age sixteen by a wronged husband if you're a saint.

But it must be said: My brother's incautious dealings with women were his only failing. He had stayed at home to help our father, while most men got to go out courting, marry the girl they wanted, and take her to bed on their own farms. Could you really blame a bachelor for having secret women? A grown man has needs.

But he never complained about that or anything, though our father was not an easy man to work for, anything but. Our father never praised us, only noticed when we did something wrong. After the duel incident, he had asked my brother to explain, and when he would not (to spare the lady's reputation, I suppose), our father sent him out to shovel shit out of the pit of the latrine and bury it, a hateful task. But my brother did not complain even about that, though he had to leave his clothes up in the barn and scrub himself repeatedly with cold water and hard soap before our mother would let him in the house.

Now he was cold clay and washed for the last time. Someone brought a wagon, and Dr. Jarrett and two men loaded him in, everyone silent and respectful now. Slow as a dirge, Jarrett walked the wagon horse to my mother's house, my horse walking alongside. I had my brother's pistol and my own crossed in my belt, and I was itching for the chance to use them both.

We carried him into my mother's house, and she fainted at the sight of him, as did our youngest sister, who was delicate. My aunt and other sisters screamed and wept. But they got the dining room table cleared, and we laid him out properly.

Jarrett offered to give sleeping powders to my poor weeping mother and sisters, and I had no choice but to trust him, wretched traitor though he was. But I sat up with them awhile after they slept to make sure he had not poisoned them.

I had never hated anyone, not specifically at least. Our father had raised us all to hate slave-owners in general, along with the criminals of the Confederacy, Jefferson Davis and his lot, though I knew them only from their photos in the papers. Hating from a distance is a different thing and much more calm.

But now I hated Martha Cairnes with a hatred that was quite particular. I was not sure I could let her live, and for that reason I left both guns with my mother and took myself home.

Mrs. Ayres
Farmer's Wife

I WAS AT THE woodstove, getting supper on for Mr. Ayres. He would be coming down directly from the barn and liked his supper hot. He was always cross unless I had it ready from the second he sat down. I used to hate that, but after thirty years of matrimony, well, it wears a person down. Some things you just got used to, I guess.

I heard a knock on the screen door and knew it must be someone else, a neighbor dropping in, looked like. Sure enough, it was Martha Cairnes, from the next farm south, poor girl. She had been a good friend to my daughter when they were both growing up, but I did not suppose they had seen each other much lately. My girl had married right well and had a fine place of her own and two little sons, though she was hoping for a girl next time to help around the house. Folks used to say that she was plain, and they always made out Martha Jane to be the prettiest girl around. Everyone thought she would make a good match. Well, it showed you how much some folks knew.

Of course it was a shame how things had gone for Martha Jane. The things folks said about her, shaw! A person hardly knew what she should think. Well, you never knew about some people, did you? The Cairnes family, so proud, with their big farms and tall white houses, look at them now. But I was a Christian, and I tried to keep an open mind. So I opened the door to her.

"Hello, my dear. Is everything all right? And what a nice suit that is. Such a good blue. I like a good blue, don't you? Come in and rest your feet."

I did not mention what I really meant, that she had kept her girlish figure despite everything. That's what made the suit look well on her. My girl Mary never managed that, what with cooking all the time and getting with child again so fast. Living in the kitchen, that'll make you fat. I went back to turn the bacon browning on the stove.

Next time I thought to glance at her, she was still standing up, holding onto the back of a chair with a tight grip. She looked like she had been crying and was maybe crying now.

"Why, Martha Jane. Whatever is the matter, dear? Won't you sit down?"

She seemed to collect herself. "I've come to speak to Asbury. Is he at home?"

Asbury was our younger son, and he had stayed with us to help his father out around the place, dear child. But today of course he had gone out for the parade.

"He's still to town, but he should be along right soon for supper. Are you all right, dear?"

"Yes," she said softly and seemed to waver as she stood.

I put the bacon on a plate to drain and set it in the oven with the biscuits so it would stay hot. I threw some extra lard into the bacon pan, and when it was hot, I dropped in the balls of apple dough I had already made for fritters. That was Mr. Ayres's favorite treat of a Saturday night. I moved the coffee kettle to the hottest spot on the stove because he liked his coffee piping and didn't mind a little burn.

"Did you eat already, dear?" I thought to ask her, since there really was enough.

She nodded and looked at me, her eyes shining too bright. "How nice it is in here."

I wondered if she had fever and went to feel her forehead, but it was cool enough.

"Do sit and rest your feet," I said again, and finally she sat on a hard chair.

I tried to cheer her up. "It's not always so nice in here. There's the rheumatism in the cold, unless you have good fires. I like a good fire of an evening, don't you? It's comforting."

I went on to tell her about my Mary, how well she was and what fine boys she had and that she was expecting a third child, a girl this time, she hoped. Sometimes I paused a little, hoping Martha Jane would say something. But she just said "yes" and "oh," and I gave up expecting company from her.

Boots stamped outside the door, and Mr. Ayres came in, bringing in the evening chill. He had on a threadbare sweater I sometimes tried to take away from him, it was such a disgrace, but he refused to give it up, said he was attached to it. He hung up his old hat, and his poor bald head shone white in the lamplight. But his face was brown and cracked from a long life out of doors.

With a start he seemed to notice our visitor. "Why, neighbor, what has troubled you, to call this time of night?"

She blinked quickly. "Why, hello, Mr. Ayres. Is Asbury with you? I've only come to speak to him about a particular matter."

I could not help it—I bristled at the airs she took. A particular matter? Why couldn't she speak like anyone? But Mr. Ayres was generous to a fault, and he spoke to her kindly.

"Well, that ye may, I'm sure. He's overdue for his supper."

He gave a quick glance toward the stove as if to make sure food was coming, and when I set the plate in front of him, he hunched over it and ate like I had starved him for a week.

Martha stayed on at the table, and I went on trying to get her into conversation. I asked about her mother and Richard. But all she said was, "Both quite well."

"And your brother has a wife now, doesn't he?"

This subject seemed to distress her, though I did not know why it should, really. Her brother had married a fine young lady, a Nelson, one of her cousins, and he had built a house across the lane from his mother's place. But Martha had tears sliding down her cheeks, and she did not even brush them off.

Mr. Ayres finished his supper and drank his milk. "Has he got the house finished? I should look in on him and see if he needs help. Is he going to dig himself another well?"

"Why, I'm not sure," she said, taking a jagged breath. But that was all.

"Don't expect he'll have much trouble in that spot, what with the hill and all. Well, I'll be off," he said and clumped with weary steps to the stairs. I heard them creak as he climbed up.

He would need help with his boots, now that the rheumatism had gotten in his hands.

"You'll excuse me, I'm sure," I said to Martha and took off my apron.

But I heard hooves hitting in the lane and turned to fill another plate. "That'll be Asbury. I'll leave you with him for a bit, if you don't mind."

I got all the way upstairs and had pulled off one of Mr. Ayres's boots, when I heard shouting downstairs. Mr. Ayres and I both lifted our heads to listen. It sounded like Asbury.

"You better go see what that's about," Mr. Ayres said wearily. Lifting his shaggy eyebrows, he gave me a look that said neighbors who showed up at bedtime were quite rude.

"After I get the other boot." I reached for it, but the shouting got louder.

"Best go now," he said.

Going down the stairs was harder now than going up. My knees hurt every time one of them had to take all of my weight, and it was a while before I got down.

Now I started to make out what Asbury was shouting.

"M-m-mother!" he bawled.

Martha was on her feet again, and she said something shrill I could not make out.

Asbury was stuttering so bad, he almost couldn't get it out. "Wh-wh-what does it matter? G-g-good God! You sh-shot him d-d-down just like a hog!"

I rushed into the kitchen fast as I could go. "What's that you're saying, son?"

His cheeks flushed red—he had not come all the way into the kitchen, one foot still on the stoop outside, and he seemed to swell to fill the doorway, vessels bulging in his face. He pointed a thick hand at Martha.

"She sh-shot a man not an hour since. I s-saw it all at the hotel. She sh-shot him and she sh-shot him and she sh-shot him d-dead!"

Martha raised her voice, face flushed. "I've only come to ask you if they carried him inside. Is he inside or still on the cold ground? Tell me quickly, and I will be gone."

I gaped at her, terrified, and whirled around and clattered back upstairs, calling for Mr. Ayres. When I told him what Asbury had said, he stared at me like I had gone mad.

In a second he had thudded down the stairs in one boot, shaking the house frame, me after him. "What? What's that you're telling, son?" my husband cried.

"She's a m-m-murderer. She k-k-killed a m-man not an hour since. I t-tell you, he's lying d-dead at the hotel!"

Mr. Ayres took hold of Martha's arms and shoved her back into the chair. He did not turn to look at Asbury. "Son, run to Mrs. Cairnes and tell her she's got to come and take her daughter home. Take the horse and be quick. The officers will look for her, and when they find she isn't there, they'll come here, and we don't want them. We've done nothing wrong. Now, you go on."

The screen door banged, and Asbury was gone.

"Forgive me," Martha said. "I'll just walk back the way I came."

I wanted to slap her for having sat by me so calm, not letting on!

Mr. Ayres held up his big hand and blocked the door. "No, you won't. I'll keep you here until your mother comes. I have a thing or two to say to her about all this, young lady!"

None of us spoke after that, and it felt like an hour before Richard and George Andrew Cairnes burst in. Richard moved in jerks and coughed, and even George Andrew's solemn face looked wild as they stepped to either side of Martha and faced us.

"Where is your mother?" Mr. Ayres demanded, standing back.

Richard coughed and choked but sounded pleased. "She's gone to bed. She fainted in a heap when Asbury told her."

Abruptly Martha turned and walked out the door, and George Andrew and Richard tumbled after, barely keeping up. They must have brought horses. I could hear the bridles clinking in the dark, and one horse sighed, flapping its nostrils.

Martha's voice rose clear and strong through the screen door. She was still on about the man she killed. "Richard! Have they taken him into the house?"

Richard snorted in the dark. "Taken who? He's gone to his reward. It was in fine style, too, you did the thing. You didn't mince a word. Just *blam*! You put the fear of God into those Yankee saps, I'll tell you that."

"But what of him? Will he live?" she cried shrilly. "Have they taken him inside?"

For a minute I almost felt sorry for her, poor mad wight.

Richard's voice was hoarse with impatience. "Oh, calm yourself, woman. We have to figure where we're going to hide you. What do you think, G. A.? Baltimore?"

"What about the Baileys' in Virginia?"

"Yes, that's first-rate," said Richard. "We can set off in the morning."

Martha must have started to walk back alone in the pitch black, because they both cried out. "Hey! Come get on your horse!"

Mr. Ayres had had enough. He flung the door open. "Go home now and leave us be!"

"Yes, sir," Richard called.

But as they walked their horses off, I heard Richard laugh and crow.

"Not one of those damn Yanks will sleep tonight!"

II.

Martha Jane Cairnes

1865

SATURDAY, APRIL 15, 1865, dawned fine, yellow sun and leaves beginning to unfurl, and I decided it was time to take the legless man onto my back. Not a man really, more of a boy, sixteen, but still a Rebel soldier, one of Jubal Early's men, who was marched up from his home in Horse Pasture, Virginia, wounded, and left for dead. He had been well enough to travel for some months, but with no safe way to get across the Union lines. Virginia had seen the worst, parts of it burned to ashpit, and the things you heard had happened there did not bear thinking of—twenty acres of dead Rebels left unburied at Fort Harrison, small boys caught spying and dragged behind horses till their heads came off, and how many hundred thousand men put in the ground?

But thank God the truce was signed six days ago, and General Grant had said the Rebels might go home. A few generals were still fighting farther south. But a neighbor had promised to get the boy as far as Baltimore and on the train, and he planned to leave today.

I dressed the boy in one of my father's suits, the legs stitched closed, and my father's second-best hat, though it was too big and rested on his ears. I was supposed to wait for help to get him to the cart, but with no men on the place, there were just some things you had to do yourself.

"There now, Mr. Bailey, you climb on," I said and turned my back to him as he sat on the bed. "Go on, grab me around the neck like I'm a sack of oats."

"Don't want to hurt you, Miss," he said and clasped me tight.

I staggered to my feet, grasping his arms to stop them from choking me. A man's weight is all above the legs, and he hung like the anchor of an iron-sided ship. Through my skirts I felt his stumps cling to my hips. Before the war, if any man had come so close to me, someone might have had to take a gun to him.

"Forgive me, Miss Cairnes," he murmured in my ear with hot, dry lips, as if determined to point out the liberties his stumps were taking with my hips. He must have turned his head to get around my pinned-up hair, and it gave me goose bumps. He had sometimes gazed at me with moony eyes as he lay in the bed, more and more as he got well, and I had had enough of it.

"It's nothing, Mr. Bailey," I gasped, and it was true, compared to all I had already done for him. When my brother Richard brought him home with two others wrapped in bloody blankets, we had to hide them in the attic, dress their wounds, and carry chamber pots in our own hands so the servants wouldn't know too much. The first one died the first night here, the second the next day. With no freedmen on the place, I had to help Richard bury them in a back pasture, jumping on the shovel to drive it in the dirt so hard it broke one of my boot soles, mud to the waist before we got them in the ground.

But we had to do it secretly, because you couldn't even feed a Rebel then. The farm was close enough to Gettysburg to hear the guns, but six miles inside Maryland, and under military rule, "Aid and Comfort to the Enemy" could have put us all in jail. Men we knew had ridden out at night to burn railroad bridges and stop Union troop trains passing through, and Lincoln had sent nine hundred Union soldiers to subdue this county alone. He suspended habeas corpus and let them arrest without charge, and when the legislature threatened to secede, he threw them all in jail, not wanting the Confederacy north of Washington.

My father was descended from John Jay, who had signed the Constitution, and he took Lincoln's breaches of it as a personal offense. The worst was in the first months of the war, one hot August day when he heard Lincoln had authorized seizure of Rebel property—including the farm of my father's dead brother, now owned by his son, Sam, who had ridden south to join Lee's cavalry. Outraged, my father galloped to a meeting in the county seat, Bel Air, and died of apoplexy on the way. Which meant my brother Richard could not follow Sam, because the farm was his, and Federals could have taken it the day he went.

But we also had first cousins on the Federal side. Bob Cairnes had once played Joseph in the Christmas pageant, while I was the Virgin Mary, holding a doll, and Bob had his thigh shattered by a Rebel sharpshooter at Gettysburg. Billy Cairnes was epileptic from a fall down a corn shaft, could drop into a fit if we played tug-of-war, and was now dead of dysentery in a Union camp. Closest to us was Henderson Kirkwood, the kind of mild fellow who used to help the youngest tie hooks on their fishing lines when they fished in his parents' pond. Henderson had joined the advance at Chancellorsville and had half his chest blown off, while nearby, Sam (whose hooks he used to tie) was captured from the Rebel ranks. And the night after the truce was signed, Richard had ridden out and not come back. We had no idea where he was or if he had been buried in some pasture miles away.

Now NO ONE was there to stop me. My mother was at church to ready it for Easter services, and my mother's old servant Creolia was churning butter on the kitchen porch. I could hear the steady *thump-thump* of the churn as I lurched down the attic stairs, traversed the hallway on the second floor, down the broad staircase to the front door, across the porch, and down four steps to the lawn, my broken boot sole flapping. The cart was waiting in the lane, a shaggy pony in the shafts, and Mr. Bailey grunted as he grasped the rail to hoist himself inside.

Suddenly the butter churn went still, and around the corner came Creolia, like she could see with her back turned. Thin and brown, she wore a patchwork dress she had made of scraps, blue gingham, pink linen, and green plaid arranged like a quilt, her gray hair tied in a rag. Her wide face seemed playful till you saw the mouth, locked tight with lips so hard they looked scarred, as if from holding back words. Creolia had been a gift to my mother when they were both three, but my mother had freed her and her children years ago, and she now paid Creolia the queenly sum of $10 a month. Creolia had wet-nursed my brothers and me while she raised her son and daughter in the back apartment of the house, and she had been patient with us all. Once I caught her boy riding my hobbyhorse, shoved him off, and broke his nose. She had not punished me but led me to the bed, where he lay sobbing with a bloody rag against his face, so that I could see the damage done.

Now she strode to the pony, took hold of the reins, and examined Mr. Bailey with bright eyes. She knew someone had been ill in the attic, but we told her it might be typhoid and she should not go up there. "What you think you fixing to do this time?"

Mr. Bailey sat up straight on the cart seat and touched the brim of my father's hat. "Miss Cairnes has offered me a ride, to help me on my way back home."

Creolia slowly smiled and went on with an air of geniality, as if to draw him out and find out who he was. "No stopping this one if she set her mind. If she say she gone move the barn, you best make sure you not in the way. Stu-u-u-u-born, yessir, she is."

I ignored her and got into the cart. People said things like that about me, as if I were some kind of mule or bolting horse, "willful," "headlong," and "heedless" being three other words I often heard about myself. In my mother's version, I had scared off all eligible men, my chances shot now as an old maid of twenty-four.

In a family of plump, fair, placid girls, I had somehow grown up skinny, scrappy, and quick, an incurable tomboy. I had dark eyes and hair, and my skin tanned so fast, some said a Cherokee was hidden in the family tree, or a sailor from the Spanish armada wrecked off the coast of Scotland in 1588. At a clan reunion when I was three, to which cousins rode from as far as Ohio, my father had felt the need to hang a sign around my neck reading, 100-PROOF SCOTCH. Even after I'd grown into a woman, long past futility, my mother wanted me to live in hats and lay cucumber strips across my cheeks to bleach the brown, though that never worked.

Creolia's eyes shifted to me and lit up as if at the thought of my mother's frustration.

"Where your hat at, Missy?"

"Never mind." I had on the same old work dress I had worn since dawn to milk and collect eggs, no hoops or bonnet, and that would have to do. Slapping the reins across the pony's back, I drove it down the stony lane, wood wheels chattering our teeth.

"You gone get the cucumbers," Creolia called gleefully.

I did not look back, and soon we rolled between two pastures filled with itchy grass, a smell of wet dirt from last night's rain. The lane was long, rising and dipping almost half a mile, fields on both sides that had once grown hay and wheat, worked by slaves and then freedmen. But no men worked here now, and the fields lay choked with milkweed and berry vines.

I felt Mr. Bailey turn to look at me, so close that I smelled my father's lavender shaving soap. "Miss Cairnes," he began and sighed. "If you only knew how dear—"

"Look! There's a foxhole." I pointed to a bank beside the road, a dark hole just visible under blackberry vines. There had been a fox in there long ago, though if one was there recently, some army would have shot it by this time, and "foxhole" had a different meaning now.

Briskly I went on. "Now, Mr. Bailey, if those legs hurt you, boil some potato peels and soak them in the potato water, hot as you can stand. Is there someone who can do that for you?"

I was so relieved to have avoided him, I did not hear what he said next. I had a feeling underneath my ribs as though I were a paper lantern with a candle lit inside that burned me even as it lifted me into the air. Oh, not for Mr. Bailey, no. I knew who it was for. I slapped the reins again, although the pony was already trotting at top speed, past woods where trees stood bare as skeletons with only a faint haze of yellow green.

It had been a day like this, three years ago, and like now, it had smelled of just-thawed ground, when I had walked with cousins in the woods until we found a deep pool in a creek and an ancient apple orchard next to it, where bluebells tinged the air.

We had sung all the songs we knew and teased each other as we walked, refusing to talk about the war—though my cousins had brought along two brothers, sons of an Abolitionist rumored to have helped slaves escape across the line into the North. I had assumed they would be stiff, unpleasant young men like my second-oldest brother, who was a minister up north in Pennsylvania and a stern Abolitionist. Our parents' oldest had been born a deaf-mute, and our reverend brother maintained it was God's punishment on them for having once owned slaves.

But these young men were not like anyone I knew. All my life I had been surrounded by my family, where half the men were baptized George and therefore called by their middle names, and half the weddings were between first cousins, so we were all related to each other in several ways. Imagine if your mother's sister married your father's brother, and your father's sister married your mother's uncle, whose first wife had been your father's aunt, and each union produced eight children, who set to courting each other at once. All this had been going on for generations, the family tangled in a snarl. Names repeated so often, sometimes a Jane Hope Bay married a John Hope Bay and didn't need to change her name at all.

But I was not related to these brothers, and it was exhilarating just to look at them. The younger of the two, Nicholas McComas, was a handsome fellow with black curly hair and clear gray eyes, lashes drooped across them as if to screen his thoughts. He seemed to carry a repose with him, alert in stillness like a deer pausing to stare at you, hoping to be invisible, but still drawn to you. My cousins had said he lived at home and helped his father feed a family of daughters on a farm that was not large. They said he had read everything ("even the dictionary!") and would keep his nose inside a book through parties, picnics, even church, making clear where he would rather be.

But instead of looking haughty and earnest, he was gently playful, ready to take delight in anything, wildflowers and baby squirrels that clung to a tree trunk. He had a good tenor voice, though he used it modestly, not forcing anyone to hear, and even when we ran out of good songs and had to resort to "Sing a song of sixpence, pocket full of rye" and "Hush-a-bye, baby, in the tree-top," he would lead the descant willingly. I had given him as many chances as a man could need to walk with one of my cousins instead, but he had stayed beside me all that afternoon as if attached by a new kind of gravity, unbroken by trees or rocks or people in the way. We talked of books, *Hamlet*, the Bible, *Paradise Lost*. I had read most everything he mentioned, and he seemed to like that fact.

My cousins cut out photos of the Rebel heroes, mourned "Old Blue Light" Stonewall Jackson and the gallant John Pelham, dead at twenty-three. Among the living they could not decide who was more handsome, fearless Jeb Stuart or boyish Henry Kyd Douglas, hero of Gettysburg, who in his photo had his eyes fixed heavenward, filled with sorrow, murder, hate. But after I met Nick, I cut no pictures from the newspapers.

I had seen him only once since then, one wintry afternoon when his brother married my first cousin in the parlor of her parents' house. I stood beside her and held her flowers when it came time for the ring, and Nick stood by his brother, both in blue uniforms. I knew his brother had enlisted with the Federals, but I liked to think that Nick would not join either side, as I certainly would not have if I were a man. It was true, he had joined not the army but a local militia, formed to keep order in the absence of so many men, though they sided with the Federals. Militias invented their own uniforms, and some wore gaudy braid, gold buttons and gloves, eagle-headed spurs and swords, wide hats with flowing peacock plumes. Nick's at least was subdued, almost Quakerish, the buttons blue, no sword.

But whatever their uniforms were like, we had learned to dread all men in blue. When they stopped by the farm, they might make off with chickens, eggs, cows, pigs, sacks of grain, barrels of beans, bacon, blankets, lumber, buggies, and even horses, including my own chestnut mare, Fancy, and leave us nothing but some worthless paper promises. They eyed me and my mother as if we were fat hens on the chopping block, and they let us know they had the right to take us into custody if we overstepped their martial law—as they had done around the county already, seizing Rebel flags and arresting farmers and their wives if they so much as breathed a word of Southern sympathy. If Nick had become a man like that, I did not want to speak to him.

"Cousin," he said, turning to me when the vows were done. "Kissing cousin?" he asked as if it were a solemn matter, a grave smile extending to his eyes.

My face flushed hot, giving me away, and mortified, I could only murmur a polite few words, pick my skirt up off the floor, and walk away.

"MR. BAILEY," I SAID as we swayed to the *clop-clop* of the pony's hooves, "there are unfriendly militias everywhere. You have to say you were a Federal or that a farming accident took your legs. Can you do that?"

The black pupils in his eyes swelled round, almost crowding out the blue, as if to let me see into his soul. "That would be right hard. The Confederacy will never surrender. We'll dig into the woods like partridges and rabbits and go on till we wear them down."

I wanted to shake him. "The Confederacy has already surrendered, and the army has collapsed. What if you meet Sherman on your way? He hasn't signed the truce."

Sherman's concept of war was to kill anyone with Southern sympathies, down to the children in the yards, burn crops and trees, and salt the land so nothing could be built or grow again. "Every home a nest of vipers," as he liked to say.

"You must promise me you'll tell anyone who asks that you have been visiting a loyal Federalist family who sent five boys with the First Maryland. That much is true at least. You mention Bob and Billy Cairnes and Will and Archie and Henderson Kirkwood.

Most of them are in the ground, but someone might have heard their names."

He sighed. "If I do, it will be only because you ask, Miss Cairnes. And I will always—"

"No! Don't mention that again. Think of your mother down there waiting for you. You go home and take care of her." Though what I meant by that I was not sure—chop wood? Plow fields, with both legs gone?

At last the stand of sassafras appeared where the rougher mill road branched off toward the neighbor's farm. But as I prepared to make the turn, the pony stopped and snapped its head up as a soldier in blue uniform stepped from the woods. He might have been from some detachment of the military government, but something was wrong with how he looked. He was too dark, too dark overall—it was his skin, covered with road dust but not tanned merely from marching in the sun. He was African. But what was he doing in Federal uniform and boots?

"What in the name of . . ." Mr. Bailey murmured.

The soldier fixed his eyes on mine, squinting in the yellow light. "Missy," he said.

I knew the voice. It was Creolia's son, Tim, taller than when I saw him last but with his nose still bent where I had broken it. He had grown up to be good with horses and had trained the ones we rode, including my mare, Fancy.

Scrambling from the cart, I took hold of his scratchy blue wool sleeve, half shaking him. "Where have you been? How were we supposed to manage without you?"

The outrage I felt was out of all proportion—my mother had freed Tim and his sister at the same time as Creolia. But what about loyalty? What about helping the family that had housed and fed

him all his life, with the barn and field hands gone, my father dead,
and Richard usually far from home, doing God knew what?

Tim opened his eyes wide and let me shake him, though he
was now much taller than I was, tall and thin. He seemed not to
notice what I said.

"Missy, Mr. Lincoln been shot dead just yesternight. Some
crazy man shot him in the back of his head and jumped down on
the stage and broke his leg and blood was everywhere. He's gone.
Oh, Lord, he's gone."

I gaped at the wildness of the tale. Hadn't it swept the county
several times before, that someone had shot Lincoln, burned the
White House down? It was never true. It was like the stories
Richard used to make up when we were children, about bands of
Gypsies kidnapping and eating children or runaway slaves killing
for a pound of bacon. He liked to act out stories from the Wild
West in the barn, with Indians who wanted to stake your tongue to
the ground. Tim had to play the Injun every time—or the Gypsy or
the runaway slave—while I pretended to keep house and Richard
saved me from him.

"That's just a wild rumor," I said impatiently.

"Ain't no rumor," Tim said, low and intense, and went almost
pale.

But now he stared past me up the road and took hold of the
harness as the pony started to dance. This was the Tim I knew,
with one long hand on the pony's nose, a soft word in its ear as he
led the cart into the stand of sassafras.

"Mind, missy." He nodded in the direction he had looked, and
I felt a rumble in the ground.

A company of cavalry came at the gallop, flooding the road
with blue, and I stepped out of its way before it passed, thundering, clinking, churning up dust. In between two trees with the pony

cart and Tim, I felt my stomach drop. Could the one on the gray Thoroughbred be Nick?

A moment later he rode back, a heavy holster flapping at his hip, his face gaunt, the skin around his eyes gone cracked. My vision of him shone and wavered in the sun.

He regarded me with his pale eyes, while the dappled gray chewed on its bit with a knocking like glass marbles. "Miss Cairnes, are you in need of aid?"

"Not in the least, Mr. McComas. Please rejoin your company."

He glanced over Tim and Mr. Bailey. "Are you acquainted with these men?"

"All my life," I said defiantly, though it was true only of Tim. To prove it I laid one hand on his scratchy blue sleeve the way I might have done with a white gentleman.

Hackles rose almost visibly on Nick. "Soldier, where's your company?"

Tim straightened tall. "Discharge, sir."

"Do you have papers?"

"He's our Creolia's Tim," I said quickly. "Born on our farm. He doesn't have to show you anything."

Tim undid two buttons of his jacket, withdrew some folded sheets, and handed them to Nick. I felt the urge to demand to see Nick's papers, to hold them in my hand. Did he carry them next to his heart? He was a grown man, at least thirty now. His chest would not be smooth and hairless like young Mr. Bailey's.

With a great creak of leather, Nick swung down and gave the papers back. On the ground he was not so tall as Tim, and he seemed to sag, exhaustion emanating from him like the smell of dust. He regarded me under his drooping lids.

"Forgive me. This is not a day on which it seems possible to trust anyone."

And he proceeded to tell the same story Tim had told me, adding details: the presidential box at Ford's Theatre, a play, the shot, and the assassin's leap onto the stage, the broken leg, and Mr. Lincoln dead. Tim joined in, and they both talked as fast as possible.

"John Wilkes Booth—"

"—he hole up—"

"—swam to Maryland—"

"—some swamp—"

"—we're going farm to farm—"

"—if us ever catch him—"

"—men out everywhere—"

"—hanging be too good—"

My head swarmed. Richard knew a Bel Air man named John Wilkes Booth. They were both members of the Harford Rifles, known for blowing up the railroad bridges, and Booth was now a stage actor in Washington. Could it be true that the president was dead, shot in the back of the head, like a pig, on Good Friday? The war would start again, right here, and go on and on till everyone was dead. Blood left my brain as if a stopper had been pulled, and Nick and Tim both reached to catch my arms.

"Forgive me, Miss Cairnes, for telling you this way—"

"I done told you already—"

The thought of Mrs. Lincoln hit me like smelling salts. Already mad with grief over her little boy, she had brothers fighting for the South, and now her husband had been killed by someone just like them—someone just like my own brother. If she could survive that, no one else should faint. My mind cleared.

"Was Mrs. Lincoln there beside him in the theatre?"

Nick looked at me and only nodded, his eyes shining.

"And are you sure it's true this time?"

"The wires are full of it."

Tears streaked wet and brown down through the dust coating Tim's cheeks.

"Lord," he crooned and rocked back and forth.

My own eyes ached. "And has the war started again?"

Nick looked at me as if surprised I understood so much. "There's new fighting in Virginia, and Washington is bad. There's been some fighting, and a mob has already strung up a few people this morning, though they probably had nothing to do with it. That's why we may still need your man, to help us keep the peace and look for Booth."

I felt the urge to draw him off, like a lark pretending to have broken wings to hide its nest. Not only for Mr. Bailey's sake, but for my brother's, too—because wherever Booth was, Richard might be as well.

"Let Tim go home and see his mother. You can find him at our place if you need him."

Tim tried to control his trembling lips. "I can help now."

Nick looked at him kindly. "It's all right. Go on home for now."

Without another word Tim strode back into the woods, the shortcut to our farm. I climbed in the cart by Mr. Bailey, who stared down where his knees should be, his cheeks dull red. He couldn't have looked more guilty if he'd shot the president himself.

"I suppose we'd better go about our business," I said. "Good day, Mr. McComas."

He put a hand on the pony's harness. "I'll see you to wherever you're going."

"I'm just off to visit a neighbor. Mr. Bailey will accompany me."

Nick didn't glance at him, as if he knew exactly who he was and had granted me the right to help him anyway. "I need to visit all the nearby farms myself. I'll ride along."

It was not a question, and I made no further effort to say no. At least he had not arrested me, not yet. I clucked the pony up as fast as it would go, the gray horse so close beside me, I could see Nick's tall black boots without turning my head.

The neighbor's cherry trees were all in bloom, a froth of pink around the tall white house. The buggy he had managed to preserve from both armies stood by the walk, a horse between the shafts, and the neighbor came out in the yard, excited, red in the face. He was a thin man with sparse white hair, and he wiped his round eyeglasses nervously while Nick repeated the whole story about Mr. Lincoln and Mr. Booth. The neighbor professed his sorrow and alarm perhaps a shade too vehemently, maybe because his own boy had ridden south to Lee.

"A shame," he kept saying and rubbed his spectacles, looking confused and afraid.

"The men responsible may be hereabouts. Have you seen anyone unusual?"

"No, sir. No one unusual, why, not till this moment." He gestured toward the buggy helplessly. "Thought I'd go to Baltimore to spend Easter with my daughter."

"Of course you can," I cried, impatient with his explaining, as if he needed Nick's permission to go anywhere.

Nick nodded. "You'll meet troops on every road."

The neighbor scurried in the house to get his bag. I had tied a bundle of clothes for Mr. Bailey, and I put it in the buggy.

Nick stepped to the cart and offered Mr. Bailey his back. "Into the buggy, sir?"

Mr. Bailey looked startled and tried to sound Yankee. "Why, thank you kindly."

Nick accomplished the shift with surprising grace, speaking to the boy in a low voice.

When the boy was in the buggy, I climbed onto the running board and took his hand.

"Now, write when you get there. And remember, give my love to Aunt Priscilla," I said in light, lilting tones, though no such person existed.

His eyes swam at me. "You haven't heard the last of me. I don't rightly know which place is more my home, my own or yours."

"You'll know when you see your place."

Neither of us mentioned where that was, with the blue uniform in the corner of our eyes.

The neighbor came fluttering out, banging his knee as he climbed in the buggy. Without saying goodbye he slapped the reins and rattled out the lane, and Nick mounted his horse but did not ride away. I climbed into the cart, grateful he had not stopped them from driving off. But why was he still here? Would he follow me home? Interrogate me about Richard's whereabouts?

But he only wheeled his horse and touched his battered hat.

"Cousin, I'll see you soon, I hope," he called and galloped out the lane.

THAT NIGHT I DREAMT that Nick kissed me, and I woke up happy, then guilty. I had been afraid of him the day before, and he might use that gun on Richard if the war went on. Richard was a hothead who would rather shoot a flock of songbirds than read a book, but he was still my brother. I got up and did my chores, and I tried not to think of Nick.

A few days later, Lincoln's body rolled across the county in its special train. Tim went missing for the day, though blacks were not allowed to congregate and had to spread themselves along the tracks. My mother announced that we would take the pony cart to watch it cross the Gunpowder on the reconstructed mile-long bridge once burnt in rage at this same president, and respectfully we dressed in black, arrived in good time, and joined the black-clad crowd, already dense along the riverbanks, and waited two hours in mounting heat.

At last we saw smoke above the trees on the south shore, and the black-draped train chuffed into sight and onto the new bridge, the gray river shimmering below. Mrs. Lincoln was not onboard, having been too prostrate to make the trip, but the little coffin of their son had been dug up and put beside his father's to ride home to Illinois. As the train reached us, you could hear sobs on every side—if not for Lincoln's politics, then for the man, for the war, for all the young men dead. As it reached us, we saw stiff blue soldiers hanging from the cars weep unashamedly.

Within a week, the new president made us even sorrier Lincoln was dead. Johnson seemed to think that Sherman's methods were the best, and anyone with Rebel sympathies could still be rounded up and their land seized, especially those connected to John Wilkes Booth, who was still at large. One day a pack of men in blue rode in to ask where Richard was. I met them in the yard, relieved to see that I knew none of them.

"My brother is very young," I said, as my mother made fainting sounds from the porch. "He's had to run this farm alone since our father died, with no men to help. He hopes to make a living distilling whiskey, and he's gone to look for oak barrels."

Richard did hope to do that, though he hadn't started yet.

The officer in charge rode a big bay, its neck bent in a bow, opening its mouth against the bit while he reined it hard. The man was fair skinned with a stubborn Yankee face, his jaw like a shovel, but he gave off the air of one who thought himself the object of admiring eyes. He gazed around at the fallow fields, still unplowed. "He won't distill much whiskey without grain. We'll be back, and we'll expect to see him then."

When the soldiers left, I found Tim in the barn, mending a harness for our one remaining ox, and together we began to struggle with the plow, ripping out chokecherries and milkweed in the fields along the county road, the ones the Yankees would see first. The ox balked, and Tim had to lead it, speaking softly in its big ears, while I stood on the plow to make it bite into the dirt.

By dark even my bones hurt, and my feather bed felt hard. But the next day at dawn, we were back at work, and in a week we had the front fields turned and manured, wheat, rye, and barley seed scattered, and the first night it was in, a gentle rain pattered to help it set. When the grain was planted, we started on the field beside the house, where we set corn in rows, tomato plants between.

ONE AFTERNOON A MAN in blue rode in the lane, surveying the fields. I saw him, sure it was the shovel-jawed captain, and ducked under the fence from the cornfield to the lawn, hiding my hands in my skirt pockets so he would not see my broken nails rimmed with grime.

But as he rode closer, I saw that it was Nick on his gray Thoroughbred and felt myself flush. Standing still, I waited for him, composing myself.

"I'm afraid you've missed my brother," I said pleasantly. "He has business in town."

Nick put a finger to his lips. "Don't say any more, you'll perjure yourself."

He swung out of the saddle and handed me a dispatch, which announced that Booth had been caught by Federal cavalry in a Virginia barn and killed by a shot to the back of his head, the way he had killed Lincoln. It listed names of men arrested at or near the scene, some of them Harford Rifles, including G. Richard Cairnes of Jarrettsville. The blood that had swarmed to my skin minutes before now sank to my feet and seemed to pour into the ground. Nick took my arm.

"Here, sit a minute." He helped me to a lawn chair and crouched beside it. "Troops may come to possess the farm, but they can't do it till he's been convicted of a crime, and they may not have the evidence to keep him. For now they're only holding him. He hasn't been charged."

My heart raced so fast I had to pant, mouth open, to get air. *They*, he said, not *We*, as if he was not really one of them, as if he did not agree. "Where have they taken him?"

"Washington. Tell your uncle to find a lawyer who can go there."

I knew he meant my uncle Will, my father's oldest brother, who was now father-in-law to Nick's own brother, Alex. Uncle Will owned the big ancestral farm a mile away, and when Nick was gone, I threw the sidesaddle on the pony and rode there through the woods. The big farm was much grander than ours, and after the woods I passed long fields already tilled, a hundred fat cows wandering wide pastures with creeks and oaks. Descending a long slope past chicken houses, hog sheds, smokehouses, icehouses, and corn cricks, all freshly painted jolly shades of red, I reached two blue silos attached to big red barns, one just for cows, built in the latest octagon design.

My uncle was in a far field, sitting on his horse and watching his new cultivator churn the dirt ten times faster than a single-bladed plow. He was a tall, lean man with a straight spine, and he wore a straight-brimmed hat, his long gray hair and beard stirring in the breeze like banners of authority. He was known to be a moderate, a pacifist who had not sent his son to fight on either side, a man who had no quarrel with anyone, except young members of the family who acted rash in any way. When he saw me, he rode over, frowning.

"Martha Jane. Where is your brother? You know you shouldn't ride out alone."

I shook my head impatiently and told him what the dispatch had said.

"The young fool," he growled, at once giving up the lesser project of reforming me.

"Will they take the farm?"

"Not if I can help it. Tell your mother I have gone to Bel Air to get help. You go home and stay with her. She shouldn't be alone there on the place."

I waited until after dinner, the dishes washed and dried, to tell her, and she still fainted away cold. Uncle Will sent his only son, George Andrew, to keep a lookout for the Federals, and he sat up late on the front porch and slept in Richard's room.

In the morning, soldiers in blue had pitched a peaked white tent at the mouth of our lane. But they did not come any closer, and when Uncle Will rode in later to say that he was on his way to Washington, they did not stop him.

A few days later George Andrew brought the cultivator and a team of Percherons, finished the back fields, and churned manure in the garden plot behind the house. Creolia and her daughter Sophie were usually the ones who planted vegetables for all of us, but now they refused to venture out "with all them mens around."

"That's all right, I'll do it," I told my mother and went out.

I could scarcely admit it even to myself, but when Nick took the trouble to ride in and tell me about Richard, something had shifted, and as I knelt in dirt to put in seeds, little sparks lit up around my body at the chance that he might see me from a distance or that I might see him.

Slowly I planted beans, tomatoes, peas, cucumbers, carrots, melons, radishes, lettuce, spinach, and broccoli, arranged to look attractive as they grew. I drew colored labels for each row, with orange carrots, red tomatoes, green peas, and took extra care as I plucked warm eggs from under hens, brought in cows to milk, inspected fields more often than they strictly required.

SUMMER SOON ARRIVED with motionless blue skies and white clouds stalled in heat, cicadas tuning up. My mother had not put down her smelling salts since Richard's arrest, and one scorching afternoon I could not stand the stifling quiet anymore. She was lying down upstairs, shades drawn, when I told her I would walk to visit cousin Isabelle.

"Take your hoe," she said faintly in the gloom. "A lady may go anywhere so long as she takes her hoe. If you meet anyone, say you've gone to scoop up wildflowers for the garden. And for heaven's sake, wear a broad-brimmed hat and don't let anyone see you at Kirkwoods'."

I sighed, annoyed. Isie had grown up on the farm next door, just my age, and she and I had always been best friends. But too much bad had happened in her life since then, her father and one of her brothers killed in accidents, her mother remarried and moved far off. Her one remaining brother, Sam, was our family's only openly enlisted Rebel soldier, and he was still in Union prison camp. Isie herself had been disgraced at seventeen, when she had a healthy baby two months after her wedding day. Half the family no longer spoke to her, and I had no patience for them. So far as I could see, Isie was the one sensible woman in the whole family, the only one who was not afraid of black cats in her path or unlit candlesticks or hats on beds or even spilled salt, and she had always taken the last cookie from the plate, unconvinced that it could make her an old maid. Well, now it certainly could not, as she had borne five children, the oldest only six.

Setting off across a hot cornfield, relieved to reach the woods, I followed a cool brook, crossed Deer Creek on a covered bridge, slipped through a stile, and skirted a herd of black-and-white Holsteins. As I approached the pond where all the boys had fished, frogs leapt, startled, launching in the air, legs akimbo as they *kerplunk*ed in murky green. I laughed and thought of Nick for no reason at all, with a feeling like a private moonbeam in my chest.

Isie was standing in the yard of the small white house her husband had built for her, across the lane from his parents' home. She had a fire going under the laundry pot, a baby on her hip, while the older children crawled and dashed and toddled on the grass, peevish with heat, the grass a welter of popguns and tin horses and dolls with china heads and tiny wood tea sets and whiffs of dirty diaper. Isie's children looked the way she used to, with wavy reddish hair, pale eyes, and perfect skin—all dressed as girls though some were boys, since everyone knew boys were really girls until the age of three or four. Isie teased the boys, called them Edwina and Augusta, while they squealed and pummeled her. Isie herself looked somewhat lumpish in a gray dress, more like a woman of forty-two than twenty-four, a new gap in her teeth, her middle spreading in a way no corset could control, and her hair faded the color of an old bloodstain. Even her teeth had started to erode, and she kept her lips down over them as she thrust the baby in my arms and snatched the four-year-old.

"Stop it, all of you. Eddie, let go of Gus. Molly, take Peggy in the shade and just sit still. Calm down, all of you, or there will be no lemonade. Straighten your pinafores."

The oldest jutted out her lower lip but jerked her sister's dress in place and pulled her to the yews along the pasture fence. Left alone, the two toddling boys yanked grass out of the lawn and offered it to each other to eat. Isie turned her back and rolled her eyes.

"Why does one have so many children? Oh, shaw, almost forgot," she cried and took hold of my arm, gave it a shake as if to wake me up. "Mary Bay was here this morning. And guess what? She was quite green again!"

Mary was my mother's niece, and she had married Isie's young uncle and swelled up like a melon within months—though she had not one shred of humor on the topic and dressed severely in bell-like capes of stiff black taffeta. Mary had just emerged from her third confinement, and Isie giggled, telling what she had seen. "I'm sure of it. Looked like the smell of bacon turned her stomach, and her face had gone all warped. Fourth time in four years!"

I tried to be demure. "Well, I suppose she likes children."

Isie whooped. "I'll tell you what she likes!"

We covered our mouths to keep our laughter from the children's ears. We had once found a pamphlet hidden in an attic trunk, *Your Sacred Duty, or Advice to Married Women*, written by a doctor who railed against women who took pleasure in the marriage bed or used lemon slices or sponges or something called "pulling out" to prevent conception.

"Reproduction is the only purpose of the marriage sacrament!" it had proclaimed, and it said wanton women should have "a simple operation" to relieve them of their urges and make them chaste, or else they risked insanity. This document had the opposite effect on us of that intended, and the sight of a lemon sent us into gales of giggles ever afterward.

But I was puzzled now. "Why doesn't she do something?"

Isie wrinkled her brow as if she had forgotten how ignorant I was, the only virgin older than twenty in the family. "None of it works, that's why."

"Nothing?"

Isie shook her head so hard her hair came half-undone. "Nothing. What do you think, I would have . . . ?" She gestured helplessly in the direction of the children.

The babies turned to catch the nuance floating by—we closed our lips.

Isie grabbed her second-youngest toddling past and sniffed its diaper. "Pew!"

I handed her the baby, took the toddler in the house, cleaned it up, dumped the contents of its diaper in the outhouse, and added the diaper to the bucket on the back porch, which already overflowed, despite Isie's efforts. With the first few babies she still had Black Annie, who was born on Kirkwood place. But one day Annie disappeared without a word, and we heard she had gone to Baltimore, where rumor said that several thousand Negroes lived unsupervised and held a rowdy cakewalk every Saturday. Few freedwomen were left locally to hire, and you couldn't get Irish colleens to deal with diapers or chamber pots, which they called "nigger work."

"We'd better keep the kettle boiling," I said, returning the toddler to the yard.

Isie fanned herself with a bare hand and gasped as if she couldn't breathe. "Don't check any of the others. Let's let the air clear a minute."

"Fine by me. You suppose our mothers did that themselves?"

"Not on your life." Both of us sighed.

Inspired, Gus picked up an old dog bone and threw it at Eddie's head. Eddie shrieked and swung, and Isie swooped to restrain him. The baby gasped, clutched Isie's shoulder, and let out a wail. The three-year-old tottered across the grass and sank her face into her mother's skirt, sobbing.

Like the promise of a cooling rain, a black buggy rocked into view across a long cornfield, riding high with a chestnut gelding in the shafts that clipped along. The buggy belonged to our aunt, sister to both our fathers, who was also Isie's mother-in-law, since (in keeping with family tradition) Isie had married one of our first cousins. Our aunt herself had also married one of *her* first cousins, before producing Henderson Kirkwood and Isie's husband, G. Cairnes Kirkwood.

When their grandmother turned in the lane, the children stopped crying, and the ones who could ran out to her as if they didn't see her every day. The old freedman who drove pulled up at the gate, and the children swarmed in the buggy. Isie tried to put her hair back into pins as she and I walked toward it.

Our aunt gazed at Isie with a sad, excited look. She was still in deep mourning for Henderson, even in the heat, with a black shoulder cape and bonnet, and her eyes shone out from its shade, accusing one moment and softening the next. Her lips writhed as she reached a hand in its black lace glove to Isie.

"Oh, my dear, I just got the mail, and it's in the paper, the list of prisoners released. Your brother will come home, Wednesday, I think, on the train."

Isie forgot her teeth for once and gaped. "Sam's all right?"

Tears welled in our aunt's eyes, and Isie's face went haggard as her eyes filled, too, for reasons neither one of them could change.

I TOLD MY MOTHER I would go to meet the train, and she threatened to faint away.

"How dare you, with your brother's life in danger?" she cried. "You can't have anything to do with Samuel. They'll think we're Rebs! Do you want to lose the farm?"

My mother kept a photo of Stonewall Jackson in her bedroom, draped with a Rebel flag, and she and her closest friends had knit gray socks to send the Southern troops, not very secretly.

"That didn't bother you when we had Mr. Bailey in the attic all that time."

She gave me a beady-eyed look as though she hated me. "He was a badly wounded boy, no threat to anyone, and your brother was not under arrest. Now we can't be too careful. Samuel will be a man by now, a real Southern warrior. A war hero."

I ignored her—of course I would go. I loved Sam—everyone loved Sam. He had been only eighteen when he left, smooth cheeked, fair, and tall, and he had always been the one to win the family footraces, the fastest corn-husker, the best arm-wrestler, the daredevil who rode the meanest horse and swam the Susquehanna in a flood. Sam was like me, a doer, impulsive, efficient, as cheerful as a puppy, and impatient with the slow-moving, cautious members of the family. He was also a joker and a tease.

"Dinner!" he would call and trundle down the lane with a load of manure and such a grin that everyone grinned back, even while we groaned. When we skated on the millponds by Deer Creek, he would fling himself across the ice until he fell a dozen ways—"ice-falling," he said the sport should be called. But when he landed, he would spring back up and start a game of crack the whip, or race at us, crouched like a Russian dancer, blade-first, until we scattered shrieking across the ice.

When he rode south, he had sent pictures of himself in a tri-cornered hat with fingers tucked into his vest Napoleonically. We had heard that in the bankrupt South, Union prisoners were lucky to receive a handful of dry corn of a grade meant to feed horses. Everyone said that prisons in the North had better food, but we would all be relieved when we saw Sam leap off the train. I would drive the buggy to the station, and Sam would drive it back.

Wednesday dawned fair, and before seven o'clock the heat seared like a flatiron pulled out of hot coals. Cicadas whined like overheated saws. After I finished milking, I walked straight through the woods, parting thick vines encroaching on the path. Isie was already in the buggy. The children waved from our aunt's yard as we turned north toward the Susquehanna and the Mason-Dixon Line. Rolling through miles of newly manured fields and blooming woods, we skirted the river past a large camp of peaked white tents, where soldiers in blue cleaned guns or carved pipes, looking bored. I knew Nick lived at home, but still my heart sped up for no reason.

Soon we could smell the sharp tang of salt air and a hint of tainted fish. The train had come from the far north, upstate New

York, and it would travel all the way to Florida, but it had to be loaded on a ferryboat to cross the Susquehanna where it met Chesapeake Bay. When we drove into Havre de Grace, on the Maryland side, soldiers stopped the buggy to examine it. We had brought nothing but a basket of biscuits and lemonade, but a young, red-faced soldier lifted the cloth with the muzzle of his rifle and peered inside before he waved us on.

Around the dock more men in blue stood guard while others stoked the coal engines that would pull the cars off of the boat. Women and old men crowded the landing platform, most of them in black, and Isie and I worked our way through, faces to the wide river rolling in smooth, gray folds. On the far side, nearly a mile away, we could see the ferry called *The Maryland* being loaded down with railroad cars. Already heavy, iron sheets bolted to its sides to repel cannonballs, it soon floated quite low in the water, wallowing, and Isie clutched my arm.

"What if it sinks?" she breathed.

"Sam could swim across and back. He'll save the rest of them."

A crowd of small boys leaned over the rail along the dock, some of them in gray or butternut knickers that might have been constructed out of Rebel uniforms. Two soldiers watched them, looking young and raw, sunburned from guarding railroad lines, and when one of the boys in gray swung under the rail and dashed closer to the water, they shouted "Halt!" and one ducked through the rail and yanked him back. The boy's black-clad mother rushed to him.

"Get back!" one of the soldiers shouted and raised his rifle to his shoulder, aiming at her.

I stood close by, and on impulse I strode to him, stretched out my hand, and nudged the barrel of the gun toward the river.

"Get back! Go on, get back!" the soldier shouted in my face, spraying spit, and I stepped back. But he looked helpless, the whole crowd now facing him.

"For shame! For shame!" several voices called, and more small boys broke free and climbed the rail as high as they could reach.

Across the broad river the ferry huffed a cloud of thick black smoke and began to move. The small boys saw it first and let out a yell that rose up high and stayed high, ululating on the highest note—the outlawed Rebel yell. A hush fell on the crowd—then the sound seemed to swell from all around, so strong and eerie, it made me shiver in the heat.

The Maryland loomed larger, train cars packed together on its broad deck, blue soldiers facing outward, long rifles in their hands. The crowd pressed forward, women's hoops compressed. The soldiers, for the moment, gave up shouting. The crowd cheered as it docked, and when it was secure we all craned to see inside the covered ramp.

An officer in blue strode up first, hand on his holster, ten soldiers after him with rifles cocked. The officer barked something at the soldiers by the rail—they raised their rifles and fired at the sky, a *crack* that hurt the ears. Gunpowder filled the air, and people surged back, soldiers following, elbowing as if with personal grievance. More of them marched up fast and joined in shouting till the crowd had moved against the wall of the station. Black bonnets and hats crowded close together. Isie was smashed into my back, our view blocked.

A long, intolerable moment followed, all of us pressed together in the heat.

"Get them off!" an old man shouted, and several voices shushed him. It was clear by now we would not see our men until the soldiers had been satisfied.

At last a few men started up the ramp, bone-thin in shabby clothes but striding eagerly. The crowd let out a cheer, somewhat more cautious than before with only a few high notes, and here and there a woman broke free to embrace a man. Now others came more slowly, some on crutches, wincing. One man tottered and nearly fell.

"Help him!" someone shouted, and several old men rushed to him.

Now no one was getting off.

"What the devil?" several voices shouted. "Get them off!"

The whole crowd seemed to realize at the same time that men were creeping up the ramp—so thin and bent that a general groan went up. Isie and I began to struggle through the crowd. We pushed by a stern soldier who stepped out of our way as we took hold of the first man's arm. His eyes looked huge and dark in gaunt hollows, his face made up of bones, his arm slack under our hands. His eyes scanned the crowd. A woman who looked far too plump and healthy to be his swooped in with ribbons flying.

"Tommy!" she cried and tried to wrap him in her arms.

The man recoiled and might have fallen if I had not steadied him.

Soldiers began to carry others up the ramp, setting litters down along the platform like baggage waiting to be claimed. The men on the litters had tightly drawn skin with yellow sores that flies crawled over, their clothes greasy and feet bare, giving off a stench like rotting potatoes or eggs stored for too long in root cellars. Where had they been kept? What had been done to them?

I threw my bonnet back onto its strings to see better as Isie passed by, murmuring.

"He isn't here. He can't be here. None of these men are him."

We searched the platform. I felt ashamed of my clean muslin skirt, my white gloves trimmed with lace, my bonnet with a new silk ruche. The men carrying the litters had flesh on their bones and no holes in their uniforms, blue ones like Nick's. Did he know the army he was helping did things like this?

"Sam?" Isie cried and sank beside a long skeleton, curled on its side like a baby bird dropped from a nest and dead on the road. His shirt hung open on a cage of ribs exposed up to the neck. His breath was a tight whistle, his reddish hair dirty and lank. He seemed unaware of us, and when Isie touched him he gave a cough that seemed to start down in his feet, his whole body bent to the baying sound. People close to us stepped back, covering their mouths.

"Hush, dear." Isie fluttered her hands over him, like she did not know where to start.

I looked for water and found a pump inside the station, where I wet my handkerchief. Nearby an old man in a starched white shirt and well-pressed suit cried out to a small crowd.

"Rotted!" he shouted and waved his cane. His lips were flecked with foam. "They rotted them and sent them home to kill us like the Trojan horse!"

"Hush, man, don't speak nonsense," said a liver-spotted man. "They can't hurt anyone."

But the first man would not be quiet. "Don't you know what you're looking at? Consumption. Consumption, man! It's going to kill us, the weakest first!"

The second man cleared his throat and raised his voice higher. "Womanish nonsense. You know consumption is hereditary and confined to the Negro element. Indecent to say otherwise."

The first man grew incensed. "Of course that's what I mean. We've never had consumption here, and now they've sent it home to us."

"Oh," ladies near them murmured and pressed handkerchiefs to lips.

A thin, ethereal young woman swayed and collapsed into her skirts.

Others caught her arms and cried out, "Oh, help, please, she's unwell. Water over here!"

I made my way back with dripping handkerchief and knelt to wash Sam's face and hands. His cough had calmed, and he seemed to come awake. Shuddering, he pointed violently at all the soldiers, his hand lashing like a snake striking. Guttural sounds broke from his throat.

Isie cupped her palms around his cheeks. "Don't try to speak, dear. There'll be time to talk when you're well."

She crouched by him, slid one arm under him, and clutched his frail body to her chest as I grasped his legs. He weighed no more than a small calf, and the crowd parted to let us pass. We maneuvered through the station and out to the buggy on the street.

Isie sat in back with Sam's head on her lap, while I drove hastily away—Sam must see a doctor and be put to bed. The horse caught our excitement, and near the edge of town it bolted and nearly plowed into a company of cavalry, led by the shovel-jawed captain who had ridden on the farm to look for Richard. I felt him stare as we drove on, and I heard a horse trot close behind us, as if he had followed to observe the scene in the buggy.

I gave the horse its head, and it put its ears forward and trotted smartly back toward home.

THE ATTIC ROOM at Isie's smelled of fresh pine, and we put Sam to bed up there.

I took the buggy into Jarrettsville to see if any Drs. Jarrett had come home. Old Dr. Jarrett had served the area for decades, and of his six sons, five had gone away to study medicine. When the Rebellion broke out, one of them had joined the Federals, while the others went to serve as surgeons for the CSA. I did not know what had become of any of them now.

But when I got to the brick house in the crossroads, I found that Martin had come home. He was a wiry, handsome man with large, cool eyes, still young but exhausted, his face brown and cracked from years outside. He was our distant cousin, and when I told him about Sam, he got his bag without a word. At Isie's house he asked for a bowl and towels and unwrapped his knife.

Sam shuddered. "No," he whispered, hoarse. His cough shook him.

Dr. Jarrett waited until Sam subsided, pale and limp with his eyes closed. "The rage is natural, part of the disease. Emotions crest up, and some think they are the cause. Relieving excess blood will make him calm. Hold his shoulders please."

Isie's eyes went red and wet, and I murmured, "Go on downstairs."

Isie shook her head and helped to hold him as the doctor sliced the underside of Sam's forearm, the tender skin where veins were visible. The blood was slow to rise. At last it trickled into the white bowl, bright red. Dr. Jarrett wiped his knife.

"I'll come back and do that every day until he's well. He must have aconite and belladonna, hot cups on the skin, cod liver oil, and plenty of strong broth. Most of all, he needs fresh air. Open all the windows here and put him on the sleeping porch so long as it's warm. He needs sunlight and a mild climate at all costs. If the summer remains fair, he may continue here. But if he isn't well come wintertime, he must be off to Saranac or Florida."

Saranac or Florida meant consumption, a short life. Isie stared at him, afraid.

I braced her shoulders with a steady arm. "Of course he'll be all right. He's always been a big, strong boy. We're all just fine and strong, aren't we? You'll see."

***

Now I HAD A NEW daily routine. After milking cows at dawn, I would look for rugs to beat, curtains to boil, chickens to behead, and beans to hoe, then walk to Isie's and beat rugs, boil curtains, behead chickens, and make poultices for Sam. I spooned broth into his mouth and applied hot glass cups to his back to draw the poison out. On hot afternoons Isie and I would carry him into the yard where any breeze might first be felt, scrub his damp sheets on a washboard, and hang them outside to dry so that when we carried him upstairs again, his bed would be sweet and clean.

When he could speak, he told us that he had been starved, left to eat rats and sleep outside in mud. The camp was in some cold place far up north and staffed by veterans of battles in the South. They wanted every Rebel dead, and many had obliged. He thought the place was called Elmira, but he was not sure.

"Read to me," he said hoarsely when I arrived with newspapers. I read to him of battles doggedly continuing but dwindling down south and of soldiers coming home. The government had lately declared that former Rebels could not vote unless they signed an oath that said they had not even *desired* the success of the Confederacy—while the military constitution still in effect in Maryland implied that blacks were now full citizens, which meant they ought to vote.

"Bloody hell," Sam rasped, pushing himself up. "Let them vote and not us?"

"Apparently some other people think so, too," I said and read an article that told of Night Riders setting fire to barns of Radicals and shooting into their homes. That made me think of Richard, and my voice shot higher, tight.

Sam seemed to catch it right away. "Any news of Richard?"

I shook my head and looked at him. He had never asked why Richard never visited, because Sam had also been a Harford Rifle, and he knew. He watched me awhile.

"You know, everyone thought of doing it," he whispered finally. "Not because we hated the man. Just what he did."

These were the most words he had strung together yet, and he had to fall back on the pillows, gasping.

I ASKED TIM TO HELP ME make a rolling chair, and he devised one from a wicker seatback and a wheelbarrow. When it was done he showed me how it worked, lifting the handles so it bumped along on its wood wheel. He stood back to admire it.

"My, that's fine as 'Lantic City."

I looked at him, startled. None of us had ever been to New Jersey, though I had seen pictures of the boardwalk and the chairs. "Why, have you been there?"

He looked down and spoke slowly. "Yes, miss. I been there, spell back. That ocean *fine*."

I had seen the ocean only once, when my parents took me to the Eastern Shore, and resentment crept into my voice. "I didn't know the Yankees sent their colored soldiers there."

He kept his eyes down. "Just passing through."

I picked up the chair's handles. "Well, thank you. Guess I'll roll it over to Kirkwoods'."

He held out his hands to take the handles back. "I'll roll it there and put the man in, too, give him a fine ride."

Quickly I said, "You know he was a Reb."

Tim nodded. "Yes'm. It don't make no nevermind. The war be over now. I'll carry him."

He set off briskly on the hard dirt road, and I had to race to keep up with him. His sturdy army boots crunched grit, while one of my soles still flapped. I chewed my cheek in irritation. Why should his shoes be better than mine? But it was pleasant to be out, and soon I noticed sheep with lambs, black vultures circling, a white horse in a field.

"Ten points!" I cried and pointed at the horse. It was a game we used to play, awarding points for certain sightings in the world.

Tim laughed as if with sudden delight. "Well, I'll be, you got me there. But I claim twins!" he said slyly and pointed at a doe with two tiny spotted fawns at the woods' edge.

"No fair! It's only for human twins."

"Aw, now, I think it's fair."

I steered us away from the shortcut through the woods and instead took Old Federal Hill Road because a red-haired woman lived there—and a red-haired woman was worth twenty points. Sure enough, she was out pinning up her wash, and by the time we reached Kirkwoods', I had won, though not by much.

Sam was dozing in a hammock, hardly weighting it. His skin looked stretched tight on his frame, and even his bones seemed thinner than they used to be, his collarbone protruding sharp out of the shirt. When he opened his eyes, the change wasn't great. Dull, milky blue, they didn't seem to take much interest in anything.

Tim stood over him and took off his cap.

"We take you for a fine ride, Mr. Sam," he said and slid his arms under him, set him in the chair. "You just say where you want to go, and we be there."

Sam didn't seem to notice anything. But Tim rolled him around the lawn and proclaimed the name of every flower not yet shredded by the children or the dogs.

"My, that a right fine Gabriel trumpet," he said, pointing at a lone white gladiolus. "A whole choir of them Gabriels."

A few calla lilies had come up, and he gestured at one but did not touch.

"This here we call the horn of the Lord, Who done trampled out the vineyard where the bad grapes was." Humming, he pushed Sam along.

ONE HOT MORNING I glanced toward the lane end and saw no blue-coats, even the white tent gone. All morning I watched that way.

Just before noon, as I was setting the table for dinner, I saw Uncle Will's phaeton roll in, a tall, thin young man beside him, his red hair tied back below his hat. Even from a distance he looked like a hooded hawk, and I knew who he was.

"Mother!" I shouted and raced pell-mell down the sloping lawn and jumped onto the running board of the phaeton, laughing, tears on my face.

Richard looked gratified, like this was the sort of welcome he had always deserved. For once he looked his age, twenty-one, his fringed buckskins replaced by a black suit, and more like an itinerant preacher than an arrogant, land-owning boy who thought he could overthrow the government. The flash in his eyes had always been cocksure, but now it seemed mixed with something else—not fear, but possibly confusion, maybe even shame.

Tim unhitched the matched bays from the phaeton while Uncle Will came in to eat.

My mother fell on Richard, sobbing, threatening to faint. I scrambled to find extra ham, biscuits, and hard-boiled eggs and fetched more bottled beans and pickles from the root cellar.

"Don't bother asking for army reparations now," Uncle Will was saying as I brought in the food. "Best to keep your name out of their notice from now on."

For some reason he seemed to point at me especially.

"That means all of you. Just lie low. I called in every favor I had down there, and yesterday it still looked like he might be charged. I tell you, it was a near thing."

He looked at Richard, and his voice went hard.

"You're not to show your face, except in church. If you need something, send word to me and I'll take care of it. If you have to ride somewhere, I will go with you. You're not to be seen in public on your own, and if I hear there's been any Harford Rifles riding in your lane, I'll send you back to Washington, I swear I will."

Richard bowed his head in perfect imitation of our brother the reverend and in every way conveyed the impression that he would not know which side to climb onto a horse.

FOR A WHILE RICHARD DID as he was told, sent me on errands with the pony cart, received no visitors, came out only for church.

The first week in July, four of Booth's conspirators were sentenced to hang, four more to long prison terms. One of the condemned was a woman, and as she sat on the scaffold with a noose around her neck, soldiers held a parasol above her to protect her from the sun. When photos of the hanging appeared in newspapers, all of us went silent for the day, as if the angel of death had passed over the house.

The nation was in mourning all that month, and one Sunday when the air felt like boiled laundry, Richard and I and our mother dressed in stifling black and squeezed into the pony cart to drive on baking roads, wilted by the time we got to our ancestral church. Bethel Presbyterian had a tall spire and stone walls that could store the cool, and as we stepped into the dark interior, I sneezed twice, incautiously and loud, with a high note like a laugh, incurring a sharp glance from my mother.

I could not see a thing at first, except that the pews were full. But as I followed Richard and our mother up the aisle, my eyes adjusted and I saw a neck I knew. The skin was weathered, black curls over it, the head held up at calm alert, surrounded by his sisters' black bonnets. I looked away quickly, but saw enough to notice he was dressed now like the other men, in black linen. Most grew muttonchops and mustaches or beards, but his face was shaved, his cheeks clean.

I felt sudden vertigo. What was he doing here? His family followed the Methodist circuit preachers, known for Radical views. And here I was, walking with Richard, who had nearly gotten himself hung for the murder of the greatest Radical of all.

My mother's pew was near the front, and when we sat down, I opened a hymnal and found the numbers posted by the altar, the bare back of my neck tingling between bonnet and collar, where I could feel eyes turned toward me, two of them maybe Nick's. I could not listen to the prayers and scarcely noticed what I sang. I tried to train my mind to the drone of the sermon.

"The dove of peace has reached the ark, bringing an olive branch, and now the lion will lie down with the lamb. Let there be no thought of vengeance in any heart. We have seen the awful price of vengeance taken into human hands. Rivers of blood have flowed, but now they must run dry, for we are called upon to study peace."

It was the same theme we had heard for months, from the pulpit and in dry, dutiful letters from my reverend brother every week. No one was listening. When the service ended, the congregation stood and roared with chatter, glad to be released.

I shouted at an old, deaf aunt and took her arm to give Nick time to leave. But my aunt picked up a sprightly trot and swept me toward the door. Shrinking as small as possible inside my hoop skirts, I kept my face low as I felt the sunlight strike my bonnet rim.

My head down, I still saw a folded fan slap Nick's lean shoulder, held by one of my fair cousins, the last of Uncle Will's unmarried daughters, a very pretty and flirtatious girl currently swathed in black lace, with cameos that dangled from her ears, a locket on a ribbon round her neck, and bows that fluttered on her mourning dress. The Ladies' Aid Society had said the job of women was to help the men forget, and she seemed more eager than most to do her part.

I ducked around a corner to the cemetery, where limestone angels guarded marble stones carved with weeping willows. Across hot grass I found the graves of my father, my grandparents, great-grandparents, uncles, and aunts. Why didn't I have sensible emotions? Surely all these dead people had controlled themselves. Crouching by my father's stone, I yanked out weeds.

From one side of my eye I could see someone walking down the rows, a man in black, and with sudden odd panic, I leapt up and began to stride toward the cornfields.

"Miss Cairnes," a voice called. It was deep but lilting and playful—a man's voice with the intonation of a boy, and it stopped me like a fishhook in my skin.

"Forgive me for intruding. I thought I'd ask for your opinion of the sermon."

Now I had to turn, as he had the decency to ask what every young man had been taught to say, and I would only have to murmur the expected things—"Reverend in fine form," "a comfort in such trying times."

But his face had an expression of such innocence that something in me pounced.

"Did you know Rebel soldiers have been starved to death in your prisons? Others only half-starved and made deathly ill? Not only in the South, but also in the North."

Instantly mortified at having said so much when he had uttered only a polite, acceptable question, I froze, and my eyes filled. But for some reason he fumbled to take my hands.

"Not my prisons. I never wanted them to do that. Oh, my dear, I've heard about your cousin. I'm so sorry."

Groping as if blind, he pulled me quite close, until my hoops enveloped him. He tried to touch his forehead to mine and bumped my bonnet rim—both of us recoiled, and he turned his cheek and pressed it to my ear instead. Astonished, I breathed him in, a smell of soap and leather, a touch of horse. I could feel the booming of his heart against my chest, while my own felt like a choir of angels bursting into song.

Somehow I must have muttered something, pulled away, because a moment later both of us were flushing red, as we stumbled back to join our families.

A FEW DAYS LATER my mother came back from the dry-goods store with several letters for me. They looked like they were from my cousins, and I took them to my room to read when I was done with chores. Hours later I had one slit open before I noticed it was in a bold and graceful hand I had never seen before.

"Please write and tell me how your cousin is. And send the design of the wheeled chair. Do you think the bleeding helps? I've seen it done but never seen it help. Does he cough less when it's over? Tell me what you've read lately. I only read of sheep, and sheep are even duller when you get to know them well. My father has had the brilliance to buy a large flock, just as the wool market collapsed, with no more army contracts now. God knows what we'll do with them. But the lambs are fun to watch. I'm out with the flock right now, and there are so many little fellows, one is always ready to hop in the air, like popcorn on a fire. Last night just as it was getting dark, a big bird flew over the field. He had a blunt head and wide wings, whitish."

The last page was a drawing of the bird, the flock, and a stone wall by woods, all suggested in a few deft lines and signed with the initials *NMcC*. I stared at them a long while, then found some ink powder and mixed it up, rejected my own bent metal nib, and found a newer one in Richard's desk. With unsteady fingertips I dipped and scratched onto a sheet of good paper.

"What a wonderful drawing, so spare. Was the bird an owl hunting at dusk? I suppose it might take a small lamb. Have you lost any lambs?"

I drew an awkward sketch of the wheeled chair and told him I had read a Dickens and a Brontë that was more to my taste. I didn't like the villains in Dickens, because they seemed worse than real people, too simple, all one way, no good in them. I folded paper for an envelope, addressed it carefully, and on the way to Isie's the next day, I walked it to the Federal Hill post office.

Two days later he wrote back. "I dreamt about an owl because you told me that, but it wasn't a bad owl. I was riding Dick, the pony I had as a boy. It was a wonderful dream."

He sent two drawings, one of a boy on a pony with a shaggy mane and forelock, a big white bird above. The other was of a young black woman resting her chin on folded hands and gazing from the page, done with a minimum of pencil lines. Her skin was lightly shaded, her nose and mouth wide, her hair curled shorter than a man's. Something about it seemed odd. Then I realized—she wasn't working. I'd never seen a servant pictured as if thoughtful and at rest.

"Lovely drawings," I wrote back and described Fancy, who had been a fine-limbed chestnut with a white blaze and expressive ears, one of them often back to one side, as if skeptical of human goings-on. "I wish I could draw her. I miss her, and I miss riding."

I wrote a few bitter lines about the army taking her, tore up the page, and started over. Instead I told him how once Fancy let me stand in the saddle to pluck apples from a tree. One hot day she had cantered straight into a pond and soaked me to the waist.

He sent two more drawings, one of a young woman standing on one leg in a sidesaddle to pluck apples from a branch, and another of her laughing as her horse charged into a pond, the horse's ears pointed different ways and water flying all around. In both the girl's face was startling—straight nose, full lips, eyes large and bold, my own.

He also enclosed an article from a Philadelphia paper:

An incident in Havre de Grace, Maryland, has come to our attention. It occurred a few weeks ago when a trainload of Rebel prisoners was returned to their families at the ferry dock there. The prisoners released that day were the very dregs of the Rebel mob, many of them wasted with fever and neglect by their own officers and saved by intervention of the Union troops. Everything possible had been done for these men, and yet troops standing guard

at the landing dock reported being menaced by ungrate-
ful ruffians in a hostile crowd, some of whom let out the
blood-curdling Rebel yell. Great restraint was shown by
Union forces on this occasion, and no arrests were made,
the unruly mob being allowed to return to their homes.
Peace has been restored in Havre de Grace.

Below the article, Nick had penciled in, "Was this the day
your cousin came home?"

I clutched my pen and dipped it fast, ink clotting in sediment-
ing drops.

"Yes, but it's all lies. Menaced by ruffians! The ruffians were
the ones in uniform."

I described what I had seen, leaving nothing out—soldiers
pointing rifles, the rotted smell of the sick men. Within a day he
sent me back a drawing of a young man on a litter, just a skeleton
with skin, a young woman kneeling next to him surrounded by her
skirts.

A FEW WEEKS LATER Nick wrote to say someone had opened the
back gates to his father's place one night and released the sheep,
and now he had to stand watch every night.

"At least the sky is beautiful, so many stars. Last night I saw
the moon come up. Have you ever noticed how it looks like a great
big bubble of light at first, then shrinks down flat as it goes up the
sky? Why is that?"

Today his ink was green, the writing quick and scrawled as if
he wrote with feeling, and instead of the accepted closing ("Yours,
& co.") he had written "x, Nick"—sealed with a kiss, the way my
cousins signed notes to me, but no man ever had.

That night I stayed up late to see the moonrise, and he was right—it *did* look like a big soap bubble, frail and wobbly, but only for a little while. Excited, I sat at the writing desk beside my narrow bed, below the rose-print wallpaper, and praised his observation like a major piece of scientific discovery. Going to the bookcase in the living room, I pulled out a volume called *One Hundred Favorite Poems* and pawed through it for mentions of the moon and listed them for him.

"Why do poets write so much about the moon?" I asked. "Is it because they never sleep?"

"Goodness, you're good about taking in the mail these days," my mother observed one afternoon. "Actually, I have something for you to take to the big farm, if you're off that way."

"I'm not. I thought I'd go to Isie's and check on Sam."

Undeterred, she handed me an embroidered bed jacket for Nick's sister-in-law, who had just had a baby and was doing her obligatory two-week confinement at her parents' house.

"It's not far out of your way. And don't forget your hoe."

It was a mile out of my way, but even such a distant connection to Nick made me do as she said. The sky hung nearly white with heat, and I was in a sweat before I reached our lane end, crossed the road, and climbed a sloping cornfield, pursued by gnats, to cooler woods, where the sun glowed green through heavy leaves. They broke open to a field where tall gold wheat now stood, with farther fields of hay, barley, and corn. Descending the slope that held outbuildings, I walked through orchards and gardens, a half acre just for raspberries, another for beans and carrots, cucumbers, potatoes, peas, lettuce, and radishes and arrived in the backyard of the big white house, where a cake was baking in the summer kitchen, sugar in the air.

I could feel a paste of sweat and insects on my face and hoped not to see anyone.

But on my way around an enormous boxwood on one side of the house, I stopped still, quivering. A tall gray Thoroughbred stood tied at the hitching post, buckling one leg and switching its long white tail. The saddle was well worn, with a dark outline of Nick's thigh. I felt cracked open like an egg. Didn't he have lambs to tend? How could he be here?

I retreated to the back, afraid he might be out on the front lawn playing croquet with my pretty cousin. I climbed the steps to the back porch and went in the winter kitchen, my eyes dazzled by the light outside, and for a minute I could not see. But I smelled a hint of leather, which meant a man nearby, and lavender, which meant a woman. Setting the package on the table, I turned to flee.

A woman's hoop rustled, and I heard the quiet voice of my aunt, Uncle Will's wife, who set a soft hand on mine. "Hush, dear, don't wake the baby. Hasn't slept a wink all day, and such shrieking you never heard, until Uncle Nick took him. Poor little wight wanted a man."

Now I could see him, by the window with the infant on his shoulder, its small lips slack. His big hands enclosed the tiny swaddled back, and he rocked it back and forth. He looked at me as if amused and crossed the kitchen springily, with rocking gait. Shooting me a lively glance, he carried the baby out the door onto the lawn, as if to avoid all sound. I gestured at the package on the table, whispered to my aunt who it was for, and tiptoed quickly out the door.

I thought I would just slip into the orchard and head home. But when I reached the grass, Nick strode to intercept me, the baby sprawled across his shoulder, given up to him.

"Don't leave me with this infant," he said low. "He seems only to require the absolute attention of three or four adults. But who will entertain *me* if you go?"

Rocking the baby side to side, he led me past the flowerbeds to where a wooden swing hung, wide enough for two, in the shade of a tall maple. I held it steady as he eased into the seat.

"Sit here with me," he murmured.

Awkwardly, I wedged in beside him, my hip pressed to his through my hoopless work skirt.

"That's better," he said. "There's a letter for you in the inside pocket of my jacket. You can save me a trip to the post office if you take it out."

Paper crinkled in my own pocket, but I would not admit it till I saw what he wrote first.

Cautiously I slid my hand behind the baby, inside his linen coat, and felt his hard, warm chest through the thin shirt. He had turned to face me, and entirely without meaning to, my free hand rose and squeezed the hard muscle by his neck, as if it needed to be rubbed.

Astonished at myself, I dropped that hand and slid the letter into my skirt pocket. With one foot in the orchard grass, I rocked the swing, and he lifted his feet to help.

He whispered, "You know letters are my lifeline, don't you? My house is full of people, but there's no one to talk to. I need to hear from you."

"I sent you one a few days ago," I said quietly.

An amazing thing happened to his face—he flushed clear red from his neck up to his brow, exactly the way I often felt my own blood burst into my face when I thought of him.

"And I loved it, what you said about watching for the moon, like you were waiting up for me. If only you could do that some night!"

I flushed, scandalized and thrilled, then horrified—had I said something to that effect?

We were both so absorbed that we did not notice the approach of a huge pink hoopskirt until it flounced right at our feet, and we looked up to see my pretty cousin.

She simpered with a pouting look, "Mother says it's time for him to lie in his own cradle or he never will. Bring him in, Nick, and I'll show you where it is."

Standing, he placed the infant on her chest so fast she had no choice but to take it. He grinned as if it were a game of tag and she was It. "I'm sure he will be happy if you take him."

The baby stirred and quivered, threatening to wail, and without a word she trudged down stiffly through the garden, hoops snapping flower stems.

"There," Nick breathed and stretched his arms. "Now it's time for your constitutional swing. All the best authorities agree that swinging is a requirement for a lady's health."

He took hold of my grubby palm to help me sit and launched the swing with a push that set the rope groaning. As I flew back his way, he caught me round the hips and shoved again, harder and higher till the drop made me gasp. Wind billowing my skirt, I leaned back to watch green leaves rush past till he had cooled me through and through.

While the swing slowed, he went to a rosebush, took out a pocket knife, and cut a white bud. He came back and handed it to me. "Many a rose is born to blush unseen, but this is yours."

And, lifting one hand, he squeezed the muscle by my neck, the same way I had done to him, as if to let me know that he had noticed it.

HE SENT A DRAWING of me leaning back as I flew through the air, my work skirt streaming, my feet bare, though I had not removed my shoes. I kept that drawing close to me and sometimes carried it folded in my pocket, till it was worn to holes. He sent me others, and I wrote back to him. Why was it, then, that all through those steamy months of summer he did not come to call?

August was extremely sultry, the air sweet with crushed hay flowers, and everyone was in demand to harvest and thresh wheat and rye, alfalfa and hay, and see to breeding of dry cows. I had to get up with the first light and milk, make breakfast and wash up, put up gallons of peaches, pears, tomatoes, whatever was ripe. I streamed with sweat in the hot kitchen, often past suppertime. When I could get away, I took a bucket to Isie's and picked blueberries, raspberries, blackberries, gooseberries, anything I found along the way, and canned them all for her and us. When Uncle Will's gray Percherons arrived to pull the whirling blades of the reaper, leaving a flat swath behind, I drove the heavy cart behind it, nudging the ox with a willow switch, so a crowd of hired freedmen following could pile the sheaves of wheat inside. At night I fell asleep the minute dark arrived and slept till dawn, to rise and do it all again.

But one scorching Sunday afternoon, the entire family paused for a picnic on the sprawling lawn of the big farm. The country's mourning for the president had ended, and most ladies dressed today for summer and forgetting, white and pink and blue, hats wide with flowers on the brims. We played croquet or fanned ourselves in wood lawn chairs shaded by a row of elms along the lane, out of the sun but still in heavy heat, our hoopskirts bulging out of the chairs. In the trees cicadas sang like crickets, but higher and faster, whirring to a peak and breaking off. In the brief stillness, calls of peacocks echoed near the barn.

Help! Help! they seemed to say.

"Help! Help!" children's voices shrieked back distantly.

I kept my head low, ducked behind my wide sun hat. My dress was new, of the first cloth to come in since the war, a pale blue lawn like cabbage moths. I had embroidered a flock of them in darker blue across the bodice, with some stragglers on the leg-of-mutton sleeves, and I had imagined wearing it on summer evenings to walk out with Nick. But since he had never come to call, I felt stupid wearing it.

And here he was, invited with his brother as new members of the family, and he had not come to speak to me. Instead he strolled around the lawn with the older men, discussing weighty things. From time to time a snatch of what they said carried across the grass.

"Some provision must be made, of course—"

"No way to let them simply—"

"Damnable business, last time, though—"

I gathered they were speaking of the movement to send Negroes to Africa now that they were free. For years statesmen of every stripe had favored it to stop them from mingling with whites to make "a mongrel race." Some said that very thing had caused the downfall of the South, and before he was killed, Lincoln himself had ordered several thousand freedmen and women shipped to an empty Caribbean island, where most had died within the year.

"Distasteful," Uncle Will declared, and the others gave a murmur of assent. They walked closer, and I tried to be invisible.

But right at that moment, I heard Richard call my name from where most of the younger men were congregated farther down the lawn. They had all seemed tentative at first, but Uncle Will's whiskey had raised their spirits now, and they made shows of friendliness to those who had fought on the other side, laughter and joking perhaps meant to cover silence from the ones who were no longer

there. Richard had taken charge and set a slim vanilla bottle sideways on the pasture fence, and one by one they stood a hundred
yards away and tried to blast it with a rifle. All of them had failed,
and now Richard squinted through the hot sunlight to where I sat,
and raised the rifle high.

"Martha Jane, come try," he called. "Boys, watch this, it's
going to fly!"

"Oh, no, not Martha Jane!" male cousins cried, cowering.
"Incoming! Heads down!"

I bent almost to my lap, extremely annoyed that he had called
attention to me. But here he came with the rifle, exuding whiskey
and tobacco. His blue eyes looked cooked in his red face.

"I've got a dollar says she'll show up everyone," he called
and seemed to inhale the wrong way. His face flushed red as he
coughed and choked.

I stood and took the rifle from his hand, since it hardly seemed
safe to leave it there, the smooth barrel still hot from the last shot.
"Not if there's any betting."

"Debts of honor, then," Richard coughed out. "Some of us
understand debts of honor."

I raised my voice and heard it quaver. "I'm sure we all understand debts of honor. Those are the worst kind. We've had enough
of them and to spare."

The group of older men stopped speaking and turned, alert. I
felt Nick's eyes take me in.

Uncle Will strode toward me, his beard stirring in the breeze
he made. He held out his hands.

"My dear, that is an awfully big gun. Wouldn't you
rather—?"

I whirled. "But I'll try, so long as no one bets. Richard, show
me where to stand."

At the spot where he placed his toe, I shouldered the gun, closed one eye, sited, and snapped the trigger back. *Crack* went the slim brown bottle as it exploded in a cloud of shards.

"Lord, have mercy!" yelped my cousins as they whipped off their hats and slapped their thighs. "Can you beat that? I do believe we've found a secret weapon now!"

"It's just that I'm farsighted," I said for the fifteenth time as I stood behind a table on the grass. Mounding potato salad next to fried chicken, I handed it to a male cousin. "I'm not so good at things up close."

In fact, I could see quite well across the broad expanse of lawn to where Nick stood with my pretty cousin, her dress pink with fantastically large hoops. They swooped around him as she took his arm and pulled him to a picnic cloth.

I forced my eyes back to the cousin I was serving, who had just become a doctor and grown big muttonchops to hide his youth. He fixed his eyes on the horizon and groped around. "Oh, help. My name's Martha Jane. Can't see a thing unless it's half a mile away!"

I smiled weakly and added biscuits to his plate. "Do come back for cherry pie."

I served until everyone was settled with a plate, then visited the children's tables and cut chicken off the bone, mopped up spilt milk. Finally there was nothing left to do but settle back down with the other women in the shade. Most were now mothers, and as I approached, their voices hushed, though they were probably retelling childbirth stories I had heard from Isie about how a cousin had a forceps wound torn in her that had never healed, and how another had an infant stuck inside her upside down for three days, until her womb split open and both of them died.

But they still felt the need to preserve my innocence, and they looked up at me, beaming.

"Ah, Martha dear, have we ever told you about Monsieur d'Estang?" an old aunt said brightly, and others sighed, though all of us had heard of him. Monsieur d'Estang was a riding master who had appeared from France and electrified the countryside thirty years before, when he taught the family horses to lift their hooves high, as though they were climbing stairs. He had won the hearts of several young ladies before he disappeared one rainy night with an Irish serving maid.

"Monsieur d'Estang. Now there was a man!" they all agreed.

I WAS CLEANING UP the food table when my mother came to me, fuming.

"What have you done to your new dress? Look at yourself!"

She swiped at my bodice with a napkin, and I looked down at evidence of all that I had eaten. It was a legend in my family that you could always tell where I had sat by the aureole of food around my plate. They also claimed that I would be the first to tear my clothes, lose hats, blacken white gloves, knock over glasses and lamps, launch small children and house pets from my path. When I brought in the laundry from the line, there was usually a lump of dirt in it that had somehow clung to me.

"It's all right. I'll wash it off at the pump."

I broke away from her and walked up the slope behind the house, glad to have escaped the thicket of family. The air seemed cooler here, easier to breathe, and I worked the stiff pump handle till water poured out cold and sweet, leaping bright in the sun. Suddenly thirsty, I knelt, opened my mouth below the spout, and drank and drank, not caring if it wet my dress.

But when I stopped and looked down, not only were the food stains still there, but the wet fabric was so thin that it had gone almost transparent as well, my corset clearly visible beneath the foolish moths. I could not go anywhere like that, and I had not brought a shawl.

And now I felt someone watching me, someone hidden. I crossed my arms over my bosom and looked around. A young black man sat on the coach house steps, staring. I jumped to my feet, outraged, and glared at him. He was tall and lean with strong bones in his face—almost handsome, you might have said. He stared back, both of us holding the gaze too long.

Abruptly I recognized his face and his jacket, rusty black linen with mismatched tweed patches on the elbows. It had been my father's, and I had sewn the patches on and given it to Tim, who had come today to help split wood for the summer kitchen stoves.

I strode toward him. "Oh, good. Tim, please, quickly, give me your jacket."

He took a step back. "What? No." He exhaled in a rush.

What was wrong with the man?

"Just—just—just until I can get different clothes," I stammered as I began to understand.

Of course that must be what he meant. White people could give clothes to Africans, but they could not take them back and put them on again. I shrugged with impatience. Rules. Why were there so many?

He took the jacket off and held it out in silence, using two fingers, as if squeamish. I slid my arms in and closed the lapels to hide the corset, feeling so awkward that I almost took it off.

But something bulged inside a pocket, a rolled cloth book, and curious, I took it out. It was odd to think of Tim carrying a book. My father had tried to teach him how to read, but he had never seemed especially interested. *The Freedman's Spelling Book*, the cover said, with a picture of a black child writing the word "freedom" on a blackboard.

"Where did you get this?"

He looked amused. "Yankee lady came to town."

"Really?" Before the war you could have gone to jail for bringing Abolition literature into the state, worse for giving it to Africans. It was illegal then even to teach them how to read.

"Where was she from, York?" How grand the woman must have felt, bringing light to the benighted South. York was only thirty miles away but part of Pennsylvania, proud of itself.

He smiled ruefully. "Reckon so. Someplace like that."

I flipped the pages. "Emancipation" had its own lesson, along with "suffrage," "Reconstruction," "forty acres and a mule," explained and used in sentences. In the pictures freedmen tilled their own farms.

"But you know how to read. Why did the lady think you needed lessons from a book?"

"Don't know. But they sure come round 'bout those lessons now."

I pointed to "emancipation." "Like this word here. Bet you know that one."

A look of resignation settled over him as if I were just another lady asking things—when he had known me since birth. When I was two and he was one, I used to lug him round the lawn, and I liked to think that I was the one who taught him how to walk. We spent our childhoods playing in the barn, often alone, daring each other to climb to the top of the silo or jump off the highest stack of hay. Once we let two bull calves out of their pens, and they clattered and bucked across the damp stone floor between the milking stalls, looking much bigger than they had behind bars.

"*Moooo bawwwww*," they had bellowed loud enough to hear in the far corners of the farm, threw their heels up to the ceiling, slid and sprawled across the floor.

In panic we tried to herd them back, but they would not turn. At one end of the dairy, a broad door gaped open for shoveling manure to a wagon parked below, and if a calf fell out, it would break its legs and have to be killed. Tim knew it, too, but neither of us could stop squealing with laughter as we darted after them.

Please, God, I had pleaded in silence. *If you let us put them back, I won't do anything like this again.*

But it went on and on, both of us helpless to fix what we had done.

Tim still looked almost like the boy he had been then, his brown face smooth—though it had some new expressions, hints of scorn. I wondered if he knew of plans to ship him to another continent. He had never been to Africa. His grandparents were born here, maybe others before that—Creolia's mother had been house slave to a judge.

"Why, sure," he said. "I see a *e* there and a *c*."

I smiled encouragement, though my suspicion was confirmed— he knew the alphabet but not how to read words.

"Tell you what. Let's read some, just for an hour every now and then."

A grin spread over him. He seemed to relax for the first time.

"You, missy? You don't mean you can read? Bet you don't know right. Bet they was real careful to teach you some wrong way, so you don't know what they be writing down."

A gust of laughter caught me, and I clapped a hand over my mouth as a bright giggle leapt free into the air.

Suddenly I was aware of Uncle Will bearing down toward me as if coming from the barn, followed by Nick and his brother, all staring hard.

"What do you think you're doing?" Uncle Will boomed out. "Leave that at once!"

HE MARCHED OFF without another word, followed by his son-in-law, and Tim took his book and stepped into the coach house as if on errands he had never meant to quit. What did they think I had been doing? It felt like I was five years old again, the day I had followed a little black girl home and played with her until her mother ran out shrieking, "Get out of here!" and swiped at me with a broom. I had avoided Negro cabins ever since, though I did not know why I should, nor why I could not talk to Tim. And here I had been shamed again in front of Nick.

Silently I turned and started toward the woods, intending to walk home—it hardly mattered, since the situation could not become more awkward than it was.

But after a moment I felt him walking next to me, as close as my skirts would allow. He kept pace no matter how fast I went, and he even caught a bit of skirt between his callused fingertips as if to keep me there, not let me run away. By the time we crossed a field, we seemed to have a silent pact, no need to talk, all understood. Inches away, Nick matched my stride, following me like a dance partner, letting me lead. Efficiently we strode into the woods, along a brook to Deer Creek, and walked along its banks to a deep pool.

"Here," he said softly. "Let me show you something."

He stalked down the bank, and, missing the feel of him close by, I followed. The creek was wide and clear, rocks speckling the bottom, and its surface made a smooth fold. Nick pointed into it, and I looked but saw only stones.

But in a blink a big, speckled fish appeared, as large as a man's forearm, holding still, finning, and I gasped. "Was it there before? How could I have missed it?"

He shook his head. "The whole world's like that if you stare at it." He pointed to a shelf of rock where willows hung. "See that shadow there? There's a trout in there the size of a collie, been there since I was a boy. Too smart to get caught. I tried everything, worms, night crawlers, fancy tied flies. Almost caught it with a peanut-butter sandwich once."

I laughed, and his brow seemed to clear. He touched the sleeve of Tim's jacket. "How did you end up with this? It must be too warm."

"My dress was wet. I needed something to cover up and make me decent." Impulsively I shrugged the jacket off. Underneath the bodice was still damp, but it was a relief to feel the air.

He laughed quietly. "You look quite decent now." He took the jacket from me and examined it. "Not a bad garment, really."

"It's seen better days. It was my father's. I sewed these elbow patches on myself."

He nodded quietly, as if aware of my father's death. He tied the jacket sleeves around his waist to carry it for me. "Here, I'll show you something else."

He led me along a path to a steep rock overhung with vines and parted them to show me marks etched in the rock. Some were circles crosshatched like Chinese embroidery, others like a child's drawing of men, but with blank faces and no eyes. I had been to

Painted Rocks beside the Susquehanna, where people had scrawled their names next to Indian petroglyphs.

But these looked older, lonelier, stranger. The people who had carved them evidently meant to give them no eyes, just blank faces turned up to the sky. I shivered in my damp dress.

"Here, let's get you in the sun again. I had a fort up here, and I've never showed it to anyone. You will be the first."

He gave me a boost to climb the steep side of the rock, and I felt his unexpected wiry strength. When we reached the sunny top, I sat down against the warm rock, reassured.

He took a chink out of a crevice and peered inside. "The boys around here must be fast asleep. There's still some arrowheads I left in here. It must be twenty years ago now."

He handed one to me, cool from the inside of the rock, and sat down next to me.

I felt a giddy rush with him so close and tried to hide it, chattering.

"I had a fort, too, not like this. A tree fort, in a grove of white pines on a hill across the road from us. I used to climb up there to get away from home. My thinking place, I called it when my mother asked me where I went. That's what I did there. Did you think here?"

He laughed quietly. "Small boys don't think. They plot and kill insects. But I suppose I did it here if anywhere. What did you think about?"

I looked down, shy, and tried to hand the arrowhead back to him, but he shook his head and closed my fingers over it to indicate that it was mine. I felt myself flush furiously. My mouth raced to keep up with my pulse.

"Oh, daydreams mostly, about riding black stallions and wearing a ball gown like Cinderella, the kind that would trail behind me when I climbed marble stairs in my palace. But sometimes I just pretended I was making soup. I did that in school, too, sitting at my desk."

He chuckled. "Making soup?"

"Yes. Cutting up potatoes and parsnips and putting them in a pot."

"Show me."

I laughed, too, and felt silly, unable to look at him. But I showed him, making a chopping motion with one hand against a rock, then pushing imaginary vegetables into an invisible pot. It felt magical somehow with him watching me.

After a while, without discussing it, we climbed down the rock and walked along the creek to a meadow, where the grass was deep and flecked with grass pinks, blue forget-me-nots, corn cockles, and yellow bird's–foot like pursed lips.

"Just like when Pocahontas was here," he said and spread his arms, his eyes closed, his face tipped up toward the sun. He kept his back to the far side of the stream, where a farmer's field rose freshly plowed, as if to shut out evidence of our own century. He spread Tim's jacket for me to sit on in the grass and wildflowers, and he sprawled half-prone beside me, propped on one elbow, plucking grass. He asked about the books I liked the most, my friends, my ponies, my little sister who died. His eyes never left me as I talked.

I asked about his sheep, and he told me buying them had put his father deep in debt.

"Poor men should not gamble like that. We may have to marry off my sisters to the highest bidder, but no one comes around for them except old widowers with eight children, and I don't want that for them. You might marry a farm, but it's a person you will talk to every day and sleep next to." Grimacing, he twirled a stalk of grass and threw it away. "Some people have a girl in mind for me, or rather her acreage. As if I could gaze into a bankbook all my days."

I supposed he meant my pretty cousin. Uncle Will had set Nick's brother up on a small farm when he married one of Uncle Will's daughters, and he might do that for Nick if he married another.

I kept my eyes down on the grass while I shredded a blade. "And you, what do you want?"

He let his head drop back so far his hat fell off. "What I want—*what I want.*"

Springing to his feet, he took my hand and pulled me up. "What I want is to stay here with you and see every posy in these woods. Then I want the biggest supper basket ever made, so we never have to leave. I don't think we need a bit of other company. Do we?"

My dress was dry now, and for the past hour it had been so hot out, even the cicadas had stopped singing. But I was still shivering. A lifetime of girl's books had taught me what to do. *How to Be a Lady—Proper Deportment in Every Trying Situation* had said to speak kind words to all and never try to shine, but share in every plan and prospect of your brother's. Strive for nothing but his pleasure and success. Alone with any other gentleman, avoid all sentimental gestures that might lead to an indelicate response. The only amaranthine flower on earth is virtue, and once crushed it never grows again. Most dangerous of all, should you begin to care, you must not let it show. Be pure and cold until the gentleman is driven wild with need, speaks to your family, acquires your hand, your life, your property, and all has been arranged.

He took hold of my chin and tipped it up so he could see into my eyes. "Do we?"

I chuckled nervously but did not look away. "No other company."

Chuckling also, he lifted off my hat and dropped it to the grass, the better to kiss my lips.

HIS LIPS FELT SOFTER than I had ever imagined a man's could be. Was *this* what it was like to kiss? I had tried it once when I was about six and forced Tim to participate, up in the hayloft out of sight. It had been wet and revolting, and we had both squirmed away, wiping our mouths. But this was something else, like sugar in my veins. It made my pulse race like a shaken tambourine.

A clink of metal and a groan of heavy wagon wheels made us stop and turn, as the farmer whose field it was across the stream rode into view on a fat brown horse. Behind him came an ox-drawn wagon and freedmen on foot, who forked manure on the field. The farmer was a cousin of my mother's, and I swept my hat up, put it on, and lowered the brim as we walked quickly to the woods, where Nick kissed me again.

But shadows had started slanting low, and it was time to milk the cows. He walked me as far as our lane end, and as we got close to it, he seemed more sober, as if his light and playful self could come out only in the woods.

He took my elbow. "You know, yesterday I drove my sister to the camps along the river to take the poor fellows some books, and they showed us bullet holes from snipers in their tents. They said horses turn up lame in the morning, when they were fine the night before."

I was not sure who I meant to defend, but I felt a need to make it not be true or deliberate. "Maybe they trip on their tethers in the night. Well, I suppose they would, if someone's shooting near them." I sighed. "Sentiments do still run pretty high around here."

He went silent, his eyes shining as they searched mine. "I wish I could talk to you more often. You understand so much, and almost no one else does."

My heart started to gallop in panic—it sounded like the start of a proposal. "I would like to speak with you more often, too. I will be at home any time you call."

He looked down, his eyes disappearing behind their screen of lashes. "Yes, I would like to do that, but I'm afraid I wouldn't get much welcome there."

I bit my cheek, knowing he was right, when Richard owned the house I lived in and the food I ate. But how could he not call on me, now that we had kissed? "I'd welcome you."

He nodded. "Tell me, cousin, will you study peace with me?"

Warmth flushed up my neck. "Whatever we can do for peace."

FOR SEVERAL DAYS thereafter I was so excited, I could not be trusted with the crockery.

And my spirits rose even higher a few days later, when Uncle Will presented me with a young mare, so I could ride to Isie's place and help with Sam. Her coat was pale yellow, and I named her Butter, dug out my old riding suit and sidesaddle, tacked up, and mounted her.

Her walk was lovely, rhythmical and swinging, and so long as I was in sight of the house, I asked for no more than that, and we moved sedately, ladylike.

But when we reached the county road, in a fit of high spirits I galloped her west toward Jarrettsville, my skirts streaming behind me as I flashed past the sign that said KINDLY WALK YOUR HORSE THROUGH TOWN.

I was onto the King's Road when I heard a shot behind me and slowed, surprised to see the county sheriff standing foursquare and bowlegged in front of the hotel, his pistol pointed to the sky.

His deep voice bellowed, "Young lady! Come right back here!"

I was tempted to gallop off, but I knew he might report me to my uncle, who could rescind the gift—so, meekly, I went back. The sheriff was a heavy man of middle height with pockmarked skin, and I knew him by sight. He wore a holster and a chest strap with bullets slid in slots, a broad-brimmed hat pulled low onto his brow, and wheeled spurs. The Colt's revolver in his hand still smoked, and he blew into the barrel as I approached.

"That you, Miss Cairnes? Martha Jane?" he asked sternly.

"I'm sorry, Mr. Bouldin," I called gaily. "I'm just so glad to have a horse again. Isn't she beautiful? My uncle just gave her to me, and this is our first ride. So you see, I was just excited."

He tried to go on being stern, but his hands betrayed him, twirling his large mustache. "I should have known. Your father told me you had too much spirit by half. 'Joie de vivre,' I think he called it. Said he didn't know if there would ever be a man brave enough to take you on. Now I think he must have been wrong. I bet plenty of fellows want to try, pretty as you look today."

I felt myself flush and tried to simper like one of my flirtatious cousins. "Well, I don't know about that. But I do promise to be more restrained next time I ride this way."

That seemed to satisfy him, and he waved me on as he turned back to the hotel, grinning in a way that meant he was about to tell the tale to all the men in the saloon.

UNCLE WILL TOOK RICHARD off the farm to look for the equipment he would need to make whiskey, and one hot morning he came back from town and handed me an envelope, addressed in handwriting of bold and graceful loops, suitable to sign a declaration of some kind.

"Who is this from?" Richard asked, his voice ominous.

I snatched it, slid it in the pocket of my skirt. "Why, one of my friends."

He watched me closely. "Read it to me."

Pretending not to hear, I went out the kitchen door. I did not plan to let him know that Nick wrote to me. In fact, I would not even open it just yet so I could look forward to it for a while and make it last. Besides, my mother needed me to help her fumigate the chicken house—she was morbidly afraid of fire and would want water now. Houses often burned on farms where slaves once worked, and she kept water by the hearths and rope ladders under beds. Filling a bucket at the big pump in the yard, I scrambled with it up the lane past the barn.

My mother crouched beside the chicken coop, dressed in multiple layers of black—black dress, cape, veil, and gloves—though it was sultry out and close. Tim had moved the chickens to another shed, swept the coop, and sealed it and was now crawling beneath it, using tongs to set hot coals on the bare ground. Smoke began to waft into the heavy air, competing with the smells of cow manure and the rottener scent of chicken dung.

My mother held a black hankie to her mouth and looked up at me. "Really, dear, do stop frowning, it makes lines. Now make yourself useful. There may be sparks." She gestured toward where smoke drifted out. "Take that water over there and keep an eye on what he's doing."

I lugged the bucket to where I could see Tim setting coals beneath the floor. Smoke poured thick and acrid from the crawlspace, but I heard him chuckling.

"That you, missy? Watch out now, think I see a lice on you. Better burn that quick."

Tongs darted out and swiped a hot coal at my boot, and I heard a high, thin laugh.

"I do believe I see some fire," I said and poured cold water on his bony hand.

Snickering, he yanked it back.

When he crawled out, I helped him bank dirt around the crawlspace to keep in the smoke. It was a dirty job and took all morning, what with sealing cracks and watching till the coals burned down to ash. At last we carried water up to douse it and wash the coop.

When we had put new straw in the nests and returned the chickens, it was time to walk into the cornfield and pick ears for dinner. I had to wash and change my clothes before I helped Creolia cut butter into flour for biscuits, fry chicken, boil beans, and slice tomatoes. Creolia retired to her own kitchen in the rear while my mother, Richard, and I ate in the dining room.

When the dishes were all put away, my mother lying down, and Richard back to work, quiet settled on the farm, even the barn cats sleeping in the sun. I dithered for a while on the front porch, altering my old green dress for Sophie, who was fifteen and as tall as me. But she would have no need of hoops, so I took in the skirt and shortened it.

Almost without meaning to, I slid the envelope out of my pocket and studied the forceful way he wrote my name, the nib carving the paper, the writing big and curved. Finally I slit the paper with my sewing scissors, as careful as I would have been to cut a bandage off of skin.

Inside was a single sheet of heavy paper, folded once. It was a drawing of me in a ball gown, with bare shoulders, my long train trailing down a marble staircase. Beneath it was written:

Show me your thinking place

There was neither punctuation nor signature. But a honeysuckle bloom lay folded inside it, still fresh. When I pulled the small green tip, the stamen slid out free and gave up its drop of nectar to my lips.

GRASSHOPPERS PINGED ONTO my sleeves and sprang off as I pushed through corn. The house had a clear view into this field, and I held my skirts in close to keep the stalks from bobbing as I went. Tomatoes had been planted between rows to return minerals to the soil, and when I tripped on a vine, it gave off sweet and spicy scents. Richard and I used to fight in there, pitching overripe tomatoes that splatted on my head and shoulders much more often than on his. Once I enlisted Tim, and we waited hours with a pile of oozing fruit. But Richard was onto us and hid in the house and locked the door, holding his bird rifle, and when I pressed against a window by the door, trying to see in, he put the muzzle to the glass, aiming at my heart. He must have thought it was unloaded when he gazed into my eyes and grinned and snapped the trigger back. *Smash*, *tinkle*, *shatter* went the glass as the ball cut through my dress and skin and pocked a divot in my breastbone.

The cornfield had a cleared edge, scythed short, filled with morning glories and burrs that clutched my hem. Past it, trees rose, cicadas droning like the sound of sleep. A beech protruded from the wood's edge with a bent limb—that was where to turn. Pushing through laurel brush, my feet stirred sharp leaf rot. Webs caught my face. I climbed a dry creek until the brush broke at a clearing spread with red-gold needles and a mound of reddish rocks.

Gray trunks stood solid as the legs of elephants. They were all bigger than before, and I was not sure which one I used to climb, until I saw a branch snapped off for a foothold, limbs spoked like wagon wheels above. The foothold was now higher off the ground, but when I set one foot against the little stump and blindly jumped, I could catch the limb above. The next was an inch closer and sticky with sap, easy to grip. As a child I used to think God made white pines to climb, the way He had made cows to milk and hens to lay and water to freeze starting at the top. The minister who had taught me for a few years said that all other liquids froze from the bottom up, and if water did that, the whole world would turn to ice and never thaw. He said that proved the earth had been created as a paradise for humankind.

Since the war it seemed impossible to think like that, but this afternoon did feel a bit like paradise inside this tree. Yellow sun filtered through green as I pulled myself up branch by branch, each one easier to reach. Soon I had climbed thirty, forty, fifty feet above the ground, where the limbs were thin and springy, close together, soft green needles brushing me on all sides. When the trunk began to feel too limber, like it might bend under me, I stopped and felt it sway in a gentle breeze. The ground was just a patch of red gold smaller than my shoe, an eagle's view, straight down. An army could march through down there and never notice me.

I would wait to see if Nick stepped into the grove and call to him, and let him be the first to climb up here with me. *You are the first*, I would say, the way he said to me.

Braced in a fork, I turned to face the view. Treetops billowed every shade of green, and far off, the red barn stood on its rise behind the white farmhouse, like a toy farm in a train set. In the pasture our five cows stood under an oak and switched their tails. The collie, Rags, shuffled across the lawn and settled in the shade. A wave of sleepiness rolled over me as the cicadas sang.

A twig snapped far below—I held my breath. A limb creaked, and then another closer up.

Needles began to shiver in the next tree over, and a straw hat appeared, a rusty black jacket under it. But it was a jacket I had lately worn myself, and the hand that reached to grasp a limb was long and brown. Tim pulled himself upright, level with me across a cloud of green.

"All quiet on the field, cap'n. My, this be a fine fort. I knowed you was up here, long time ago. But I never knowed you was up here still. Your mama know?" He chuckled to himself.

But I was spluttering, absurdly enraged. "Get down from here. Did you follow me, you spy? Is that what you did in the war, help Yankees spy on people and shoot at them?"

Tim's mouth went slack. "Why, scout we call that, missy. I was a scout and a right good one, too. Shot no man at all. No, sir. Buried some, though. Horses, too. That was a right bad job."

His lips shut firm, and his face grew solemn as he stared over my head. Something about it made my skin prickle—then I knew what. Somehow he looked like Major Henry Kyd Douglas, eyes fixed on heaven, filled with sorrow, murder, hate.

I turned back to the view. But now I heard what he had said. Bury horses! It seemed the first real thing I had heard from any man about the war. Did Fancy end up dead and bloated on a battlefield?

"I'm sorry I spoke to you that way. Oh, Tim, what happened to Fancy?"

His jaw relaxed. "Don't know, missy. It was a awful thing what happened to the ponies, what never hurt a worm." He focused on me, his eyes going red. "When did you get so mean, missy? Everyone so mad now about everything, round this place."

My own eyes ached now, too. "Is that true? I don't want to be."

He closed his eyes and massaged the lids. "You never paid no nevermind, old times."

It was true. I used to let him follow me—I followed him, in fact. "I know. I'm so sorry you saw horses die. I would give anything to make that not be true. You love horses."

My throat closed and I flinched hard, trying not to cry.

A sudden sound made us alert—a clink of metal, like a stirrup or bridle. I froze, and Tim stared back at me. How loud had we been? We might be caught together in the trees, too soon after Nick had seen me laughing with Tim in the big farm's lane. *The impulse of a moment is the start of every error in the world*, some wise minister had said, and it was true—I should have made him climb right down the minute he came up.

His skin went the color of a creek in rain as he shrank against his tree. I was glad I wore an old skirt, its faded stripes once brown and green. Peering down, I scanned the ground, empty as before, and watched for so long that I thought I had been mistaken. No horse was in these woods.

Without a sound, the big gray glided into the grove, Nick's bony body loose in the saddle, his face hidden under a campaign hat. He drew up the horse and, moving light and quick like a man preparing for delight, swung from the saddle and sprang up the rocks. Pulling off his hat, he gazed around with hopeful pale gray eyes—but never tipped his face back far enough. I pressed into the trunk. Could he see my shoes? Could he see Tim's army boots?

Minutes crept by as no one moved. For the second time I had to send up silent promises to whatever unseen power might exist that if this could work out all right, I would make sure it never happened again.

At last he stood, patted the horse's neck, and swung into the saddle with a leather creak. Padded by the deep needles, the horse's hooves made little sound as they went away.

I did not look at Tim. But soon I heard the urgent slipping of his boot soles limb to limb, and in a moment all was quiet in the trees.

SUMMER TURNED TO AUTUMN, with cooler nights and lingering, warm afternoons. We stripped the garden and boiled steaming pots to put up the last peas and beans. Hogs had to be butchered, nuts gathered, hams smoked, sausages stuffed. Richard and Tim put up a whiskey shed, dug a trench, and diverted the pasture creek for cooling purposes. Soon every breath we took felt alcoholic, stinking of sour mash, like oatmeal and molasses going bad.

Each morning my mother marshaled her troops, Creolia, Sophie, and me lined up to listen as she laid out our plan of attack. "The rooster's eating eggs again. Martha, you give him one with mustard in place of the yolk, that'll cure him. And did you finish putting up those pickles yesterday? If not, do it today. Creolia and Sophie, you two clean the hearths and chimneys and start the smokehouse. We'll do bacon later on and sauerkraut as soon as you get those cabbages."

Evenings my mother and I worked for the Southern Relief, knitting sweaters and socks to send south to war-ravaged areas before winter and embroidering clothes and doilies to sell at the church bazaar, the proceeds of which would go to purchase flour, ham, bacon, corn, beans, blankets, and boots to ship south. Anyone who knew a family in a needy area was to contact them, and my mother asked a friend in Virginia to tell her about the Baileys of Horse Pasture.

Her friend sent back a very favorable report. "Fine old family, almost ruined in the war, and their only son tragically injured, as you know. But in a few years they may rise again."

My mother could scarcely think of anyone she would rather help than fine old families, especially those with unmarried heirs, however tragically injured, and she enlisted help from Ladies' Aid Societies in every white church for miles around (excluding Romanist).

ONE AFTERNOON AS THE SUN poured gold light over everything, I picked basketfuls of beans and peas, and after a while Tim brought out a hoe to dig potatoes, both of us working silently. I had not spoken to him since the day I ordered him out of my tree, and as for the idea of reading together, we had let that drop. But I knew it was my fault. I had let my feelings for Nick make me reckless of others, and guiltily I fumbled for a way to break the silence.

"So," I said, voice quavering, "have those good ladies from York come around lately?"

He kept his eyes down on his work. "Once in a while, reckon."

Relieved that he had answered me, I went on. "Where do you see them, anyway? Do they come to your church?" I had never seen them on the farm, but I knew Creolia went every Sunday to the Colored Church, a humble building on a side road.

"Yesssss," he said, and drew it out as if unwilling to say more.

"And do they still bring books round?"

"Oh, I seed all the books they got."

"And do you like their books?"

He sighed and resettled his hat on his head. "Well, like I say, I seed them now."

"Guess you need some better ones, with some sort of story to them."

He hoed in silence. But he did not say no, and when I took in a bushel of tomatoes, I looked at books on Richard's shelves. Most were adventure tales with pictures, and they seemed wrong for a man who had buried horses in a war.

But I took one out to Tim, ashamed. "There might be something in here. I don't know."

He leaned his hoe against a tree and walked over to the barn steps, where the sun was warm, and started to thumb through pictures. I walked closer to see what he was looking at, a picture of a prancing horse decked out in gold-edged silk with tassels hanging down.

"They put right fine raiment on them," he said. "My, my. Fine raiment."

He looked pleased with the word—I supposed he knew it from the Bible. My father used to read it to us all, including servants, on Sundays, and the white ministers who took turns preaching at the Colored Church probably read it out loud, too. But I was pretty sure he would need help to read a text like this, though I was afraid I might insult him if I suggested it.

At last he chuckled. "Reckon you need someone to read out this here storybook to you, since you don't read right."

I laughed and sat down next to him on the warm steps. It was slow going, but for every word he puzzled out, he threw in a paragraph or two of his own.

"It was a fine castle Mr. Ivanhoe lived in, with glass windows and them goose pillows, you know, and every kind of *jam*. He got hisself some pigs and chickens and a mule and whacked up a old tree for a plow, and fore you know it he got greens and 'tatoes and ham he done smoked hisself, so much he haul some into town on this here horse, and folks give him cash money for every bit of it. After a while he went round to talk to all the fine gentlemans, and they had a lection and said he the *knight*."

I felt drowsy, like a child hearing a story. He sat easy on the steps now, in loose trousers and an old blue shirt with rolled-up sleeves, holding the book in front of him. His bare forearms were long, lean, and muscled—beautiful, in fact. That thought startled me awake—did it mean anything that I could think a thing like that? Thank God no one could read my mind!

A hundred yards away the screen door to the kitchen creaked open, and Creolia's voice called out, "What you doing there, boy? I asked you to hoe up them 'tatoes."

Tim clapped the book together, handed it to me, and returned to work.

But I left it lying on the steps, and later, when I looked again, the book was gone.

WITH SO MUCH WORK TO DO, Nick and I wrote less often, though he did send me a fine drawing of the wool cleaning and carding that absorbed them on his place.

But one cool night past dark, as I was finishing inside the dairy room, straining whey to set in cheese moulds, my lamp went out as if the wick had burned up, though it was still new. A moment later I felt a warm hand on my arm and caught the scent of leather, horse, and sheep.

"Don't be afraid, it's only me," Nick's voice said warmly in my ear. "I couldn't stand not seeing you, and here you are, so hard at work, such a good girl."

I gave a startled cry, half laughed, and turned into his arms.

"How did you ever manage to get here? Richard will shoot you if he finds out."

"I'm sure Richard has never actually shot anything," he said drily. "At least not anything he was aiming at. Let's hope he doesn't do himself an injury. But come on, let's find someplace safer than this."

In the seamless blackness of the unlit barn, I felt my way through the familiar milking stalls, past calf pens, up the simple wooden stairs to the loft and the hand-hewn, uneven rungs of the loft ladder to the top, where the new-hay smell was intense, so green that it had a tang like licorice, sticky to the touch. He caught me and surrounded me, tugged me down till we lay side by side. He kissed me thoroughly awhile, and through my clothes I felt all of him stretched against me. I don't know what possessed me, but I slid one finger between the buttons of his muslin shirt and found his skin, a silky shock after the roughness of his cheeks. How long we lay like that I could not say. It seemed to be a dream, over in a moment, lasting for all time.

A screen door banged in the distance, and lantern light began to wobble in the high window of the loft. That would be Richard coming to secure the barn for the night, or my mother wondering why I was so long with the cheese and my lantern gone dark. We lay still and listened to the footsteps in the milking room, as light leaked through gaps between the old rough planks of the loft floor and threw shadows on the walls.

My mother would call my name, and since no one called, I knew it was Richard. The wood steps groaned as he climbed into the loft, and I put my hand over Nick's mouth, held my own breath. Richard walked into his tack room, where he kept rifles oiled and ready on the walls. We heard the *clack* as he shot the chamber back on one, clicked in more balls. The heavy loft door rumbled back and forth, and his lamplight receded toward the outbuildings.

"You had better go," I whispered to Nick.

Playfully he slid his hands down to my skirt and pulled me against him. "Why? I'm not afraid of that puppy."

"Maybe not, but I have to live with him. Is your horse out there where he can find it?"

"No, at Smithson's," he said, naming a tavern on a neighbor's farm. He paused for a bit as if considering something. "If I come again tomorrow night, will you be here?"

This made me happy, and I laughed quietly. "What if I said no?"

"What, you'd rather stay in the house and write letters? It's going to be a long, cold winter, and there will be times when we can only write. I need your letters, but they won't keep me warm. That's *your* job, in person," he said, chuckling, and pressed me close again.

I forgot everything and kissed him for a long while, filled with a new bodily pleasure I did not know was possible—though this was hardly what I meant when I said he should come to call, and I knew enough to try to put him off.

"I'll come back," I said finally. "But not tomorrow night. Let's see, is tonight Wednesday? I'll come out again next Wednesday night, as soon as I can get here, after dark."

He sighed. "All right, I'll live for Wednesday then."

Meekly he followed me out through the dairy, where the door did not rumble, and once outside we went our separate ways. A

few strands of hay had stuck in my hair, and I plucked them out
and smoothed it down. Now it seemed safe to let my spirits rise,
because he had come all that way on foot to see me, and I walked
with light steps to the house.

AT THE FRONT DOOR, I greeted the collie noisily, like it was any
other night. Richard was not in evidence, all dark upstairs, but
candles burned in the kitchen and I heard voices there, my mother
and Creolia arguing as they put away the clean supper dishes. My
mother murmured fiercely, half-covered by the *clank* of crockery,
and I moved closer to hear.

"How can you let her run wild, right here in front of me? It's
disgusting. Who is the man? I demand to know!"

Amazement made me dizzy—had Richard told her I was in the
loft with Nick? He had not let on that he had noticed us. But how
else could Mother know?

Creolia laughed. "My baby girl's not wild. But you best watch
your own."

Wait—could they be talking about Sophie and not me? The
relief was so intense I almost missed my mother's reply.

"She most certainly is. I saw the man myself, or nearly, as he
was running off. It was dark, but I saw his skin. Couldn't miss it,
he was stark naked! It's too disgusting to say, but I will. He was
white. White! A decent man! And there she was, with her dress
all undone, the hussy! You have raised a Jezebel, and she has corrupted some poor weak man!"

There was a sharp *crack*, and my mother gasped. Could
Creolia have slapped her? Or just smacked a wood spoon on the
iron stove? I had seen her do that, though there was nothing usual

about the rest of this. Sophie was born past Creolia's middle age, when I was old enough to wonder how she got a baby with no husband. That time my mother had only shrugged.

"It doesn't do to look too closely into the relations of servants," she had said calmly, "so long as they're good in other ways. They bring forth like the Virgin Birth. And besides, we can always use the extra hands."

But this time she seemed unable to take her own advice.

"Hush," she hissed and called out, "That you, Martha dear? Where have you been?"

I stepped into the doorway, and they both faced me with closed lips, Creolia's head wrapped in a tablecloth she had appliquéd with purple flowers to hide a mulberry-wine stain.

"Oh, just stargazing," I said. "It's a fine night."

"Well, I'm sure it's time for bed. We have another day tomorrow. Creolia, come upstairs with me. I have more to say to you."

Creolia leveled a flat glance at her but left the kitchen with her head held high.

When they were out of sight, I heard my mother hiss, "Have you no shred of decency?"

Creolia spoke clearly, a note of triumph in her voice.

"You all be happy I took pity and stayed round here long enough to work this sorry farm, else you be starve."

THE ARGUMENT RESUMED next morning, my mother oblivious to all else.

My mind was full of Nick, until I saw Sophie kneeling at the washboard in the backyard, her slender arms exposed. She was pretty, lighter skinned than her mother, and with long hair that was almost straight—Creolia was proud of it and did it up in many tiny braids.

But she looked more child than woman. Had some man really lain with her? The thought made me flush, and another feeling vied with my disgust—could it be jealousy? So young and already she knew so much. But she was *ruined*, or would have been if she were white. Maybe she was ruined in the black church, too. Either way, how could I envy her?

Now a thought struck me so hard, I could not move. Because who could the man have been? Only one white man lived on this farm, and I could not imagine Richard doing such a thing. Hothead he might be, but only when it came to guns and foolish causes. If he had ever shown an interest in a girl, I did not hear of it.

Now my heart ratcheted up a notch—because, yes, one other white man had been here last night, and did I know him well enough to say that he could not do that? Men had impulses, and he was over thirty, with no wife. It was a crime for a white woman to lie with a black man, but not for the reverse. A white man could lie with a black woman, risk free—though under slavery, if he did so with another man's slave, the owner had the right to horsewhip him.

A few days later, Tim, Creolia, and Sophie all failed to appear for work, and when my mother went around back to their door, she found the apartment empty, all their clothes and bits of crockery removed. Richard rode to several Negro cabins in the neighborhood and came back with no word of them. He got back on his horse and thundered out the lane again.

My mother was struck dumb and seemed unable to get dressed. She sat at the kitchen table in her flannel robe and stared out the window as if her eyelids had been pinned up to her brows. The nightgown she wore had been embroidered by Creolia, just the way she liked, white edelweiss on clean white lawn, and how long had it been since anyone besides Creolia laid the fire in the cookstove?

I had to split logs with a maul, carry pieces in, and get them lit, fry eggs my mother did not eat, and carry water for the washing up. Cream waited to be churned, but Creolia was the only one who did it well. It needed to be chilled but not too cold, so it would turn to butter and not hard as candle wax—but how did she know when it was right? She had never told anyone. The day was hot and the sky clouded over, threatening a thunderstorm, as I thumped the heavy wooden churn on the back porch. I kept on till my arms burned, but the cream refused to turn.

My mother brooded at the kitchen table, and she made no move to dress or start dinner. I saved the wasted cream for making cheese, caught a hen and wrung its neck, chopped off its head, hung it to drain, pulled all its feathers out, removed its guts, and washed it well before I cut it up, rolled each piece in flour, built up the fire, melted lard, and fried them brown by dinnertime. Today there'd be no biscuits, and last week's butter was half-rancid.

But I walked into the field and plucked ears of corn and husked them, carried water for the pot and more logs for the stove, picked beans, and sliced tomatoes for each plate.

I had so much to do I almost didn't notice hoofbeats thudding slowly to the kitchen door, but when my mother stood up suddenly, I turned and saw Tim outside, bareback on a strange mule. He slid to the ground and took off his hat, standing at the bottom of the steps, his shirt buttoned wrong as if he had been too excited to dress right. My mother opened the screen door, not seeming to care that he could see the hem of her nightgown and her long, unbound gray hair.

The porch was high, and he looked up at her with large kind eyes. "I'm sorry, Miz Cairnes. Now, we gone help you till you find yourself someone. But my army pay done come, and I found us a farm, not a big place but right pretty, not too far neither. Mama can come help you ever now and then."

My mother's face was pale gray, her voice a quaver. "Will Creolia have a house?"

"Yes, ma'am, right fine. No stove or nothing, but she's got a garden and a spring. I spect she's out there this minute, scrabbling in the dirt. Told her it was too late to plant 'tatoes, but she don't hear good." His smile flickered.

I took my mother's arm, and she leaned heavily on me while my own head swirled. Was it because of Sophie that he was taking them away?

"Wait here," I said to Tim, and helped my mother to the parlor sofa to lie down. Of course he had come for their wages, and I found my mother's coin purse.

"When did she pay you last?" I asked, embarrassed, as I stood on the porch.

"Last Saturday, reckon."

I was pretty sure my mother did not pay Sophie, at least nothing much. But to be sure I counted out a whole week's pay for each of them. It seemed a great deal of money—more than $6—but I put it in his hand. He thanked me and swung up onto the mule's back, as easily as if he had a saddle and stirrups.

Something in his cheerful look made a metallic taste pour in my mouth. The nerve of him, thinking he could just go—while I was rooted here with no more freedom than a tree. He had been born a slave. Wasn't I ahead of him? Didn't I deserve that much?

"Very fine for you," I called. "And will you never come to help us anymore yourself?"

His smile faded, and he looked down from his perch up on the mule. "You need something, missy, I help you sometime. But just now I got to plow."

"Plow?" I cried with scorn I didn't know I felt. "Where did you get a plow?"

His eyes went on being kind. But he lifted a hand to wave, turned the rope on the mule's neck, and tapped his heels into its flanks. The mule pointed its long ears forward and began to lumber across the lawn. I dashed after them and caught the halter.

"What will you eat this winter? It's too late to plant. Can't you wait till spring? It's dangerous out there on your own. It's too soon after the war. Please stay."

I had just read an article about a former slave-owner who used a bullwhip on a freedman in the street, a man he did not even know.

Tim sighed. "I know, missy. But we be all right. Don't make no nevermind."

I bit my cheek. "Wait here a minute, I'll be right back."

Running into the house, I grabbed a sack of cornmeal and a slab of bacon—he would see he couldn't just wash his hands of us. I would help him whether he liked it or not. Piling potatoes into an old pot, I bundled it all in a burlap sack and took it out and lifted it to him.

He wrapped his free arm around it. "Why, thank you, missy. You most kind."

"I'm not kind," I cried, exasperated, barely making sense. What I meant was, he was *family*—all of them were. They were *ours*. They could not just walk away.

He looked shy and stubborn both. "We be all right. Now don't you nevermind."

And the mule trotted smartly out the lane.

"You've got to get the law to bring them back," one of our neighbors said in the parlor. He had ridden over as soon as he heard, and now he was closeted with Richard and four other neighbors behind a closed door, since this was men's business and might lead to unpleasantness.

But I could hear them quite well from the hall, and though I held a tray of glasses, whiskey, and cigars, I put off going in there for a while.

"It's illegal what they did," an authoritative voice agreed. "They can't leave jobs without permission, and the Orphan's Court can indenture them to you, make sure they're taken care of properly. Children especially, and I believe there was a half-grown girl with them?"

"If there was, you can get her bound to you tomorrow, and probably her family, too. They were once yours, or your father's anyway, and that means you can keep them if you want to. Isn't your mother's brother a judge in Orphan's Court? Just ask him. Course, the law says you have to feed and clothe them and maybe teach them how to read. But otherwise you own them, same as before, and their offspring, too. Right of chastisement and everything."

I knew that meant the right to whip their naked backs, and impulsively I burst into the room, rattling the tray, trying to exert a moral influence.

At once they all went genial, smiling. "Nice fall weather, isn't it, Miss Cairnes?"

"Caterpillars had a lot of wool this year. We could see some snow."

Ignoring this, I said with special emphasis, "Winter doesn't worry me, so long as we have peace, and I do mean peace with *all* of our neighbors."

The men fell silent, and some glanced Richard's way, as if in pity or reproach at his inability to curb his sister's tongue.

But when I left, they resumed seamlessly, drowned out slightly by the clink of glassware, the striking of lucifers to light cigars.

"You have to bind them," the first man's voice repeated. "It's the only decent thing. They don't have the first idea of what's good for them."

A coarser voice broke in, probably the fat farmer who had lately bought a stretch of bottomland, having emigrated here from deeper south. "That's damn right. Can't just let 'em go. First bunch of niggers gets away with it, ever last nigger will go."

Silence greeted this, maybe because hereabouts the polite terms were "Negro," "African," "colored," "freedman," and "black."

When the air had cleared for a few beats, a calmer voice re-set the tone. "I suppose we really ought to worry for their safety. Left to their own devices, some of them will do nothing but drink moonshine and lie about, while their children sicken and die. It's such a waste."

Richard's reedy young voice quavered for the first time, sing-song. "I know, I know."

Another man agreed. "Seriously, young friend, you ought to get the sheriff. You know you got to bring them back. How you going to get your hogpen cleaned out now? And if you don't mind me asking, what about your privy? Got to shovel that out, too, you know, from time to time. Can't get no Irishmen to do that kind of work. Half the Negroes won't now neither. Damn stupid thing to let them join the army. Army needed privies cleaned out, too, I guess, but they didn't need to put them in those damn blue uniforms. Gives them damn airs."

"I know, I know," Richard almost moaned again, like that was all he knew to say.

Older voices rumbled over him, about how a Colored Church had started up with no white minister to sanction it. It even had a Sunday School, as if black men could teach the Word of God to black children. They seethed at the changes brought in by the military constitution.

"We've got to get the Black Code back, by God. Negroes roaming around free, reeling drunk, menacing decent women? We can't have that here!"

"And the women are worse than the fellows. They're degenerates, full of disease, corrupting our youth. Even the little girls, I swear."

"That's right, Negro girls can't help themselves. They're over-heated by nature, worse than the fellows, I swear."

A more refined voice said gently, "Some are not so bad. That one you had, Cairnes, what was her name? I suppose she ran off, too. Pity. She was a pretty little thing."

"Taste for chocolate, have we?" a deep voice asked, and a few men laughed.

The authoritative neighbor's voice broke in. "It's not a laughing matter, gentlemen. There's too much of that around already, mongrels everywhere you look. That girl just mentioned, she's a mongrel herself, isn't she? I'd say she's too light by half."

The refined voice broke in with a chuckle. "Did you hear what Winter Davis said? All those afraid they might marry a Negro should petition the courts to punish them before they succumb."

A deep rumble of laughter followed, and the bottle clinked against glasses.

"Well, it isn't marrying we're speaking of, now, are we," a man said flatly.

"All the more reason to keep them here," the deepest voice put in. "Especially the comely ones. It isn't only that they work for cheap. Takes the burden off of decent wives."

Voices murmured in alarm. "But is it safe to let them so close to white women, degraded as they are and all? Might pass it on to wives and daughters. Think of that."

A rumble of assent was followed by another voice. "Speaking of that, you know what Martin Jarrett said to me last week? Those foot-pedal sewing machines—have you seen them?"

"I just got one for my wife. She swears by it—"

"Well, you'd better watch her, man, I'll tell you straight. He says we shouldn't have them in the house. It's the motion of the thing, you see. Don't mean to be indelicate, but it works them up, and you know a real lady isn't built for that, leads straight to insanity. It's all right to let the black ones work it, when they're like that already. But for God's sake, keep your daughters off of it, and if your lady takes a little too much interest in, you know, the marriage bed, get the doctor right away. There's things he can do. Nip it in the bud, so to speak. You'll be glad you did."

I listened, appalled. To think that men could talk like that, the way they spoke of cows ready to breed or stallions standing stud. They were all big white men with beards, waistcoats, and watch fobs—landowners, elders of the church, men who were always right.

Quickly I walked to the dining room, opened a window, and fanned my cheeks, though the day was cool. My mother had a foot-pedal machine, and I had used it to make my blue-moth dress. Worse, I often thought of how Nick kissed me in the loft and pressed into my skirts. And there were other things I could not even think about—things that happened in the dead of night, in my bed, in the dark, alone. Did that mean I was wanton, not a "real lady," headed for insanity?

When the parlor finally opened and the men came rumbling out, I handed each his coat and hat, not meeting any eyes, as if cool spring water flowed in my veins.

"I WON'T HAVE THEM bound to us," my mother announced at supper that evening. She had washed and dressed and seemed calmer, though her chin shook as she spoke. "Creolia will have to come back on her own. I won't have her forced. We'll let them be."

Richard looked relieved, buttering his rolls, lank hair falling in his eyes. "That would serve them right, when they see how hard it is. They'll soon appreciate what they had here."

He and my mother exchanged a long look, which seemed to soothe them both. Chewing, they looked almost identical, noses turned up alike and heavy lids like hoods over their dark blue eyes. They seemed to lean together, murmuring as easily as breath.

"That is the last time I will say her name," she said.

"Same here," he agreed.

"We're through with her."

"We're through with all of them."

"And if any of the neighbors ask you, tell them not to be concerned."

"Certainly it's no concern of theirs," Richard agreed.

She turned to me with tight lips, as if she knew I had overheard too much in recent days.

"And Martha Jane will recall that chastity begins in the mind. Never let yourself dwell on the sins of others. That's a base unchastity."

"A *base* unchastity," Richard said, with a triumphant look.

For good measure he went to get the Bible and read it to us as he stood before the fire.

"But if this thing be true," he read, "and the tokens of virginity be not found for the damsel: Then they shall bring out the damsel to the door of her father's house, and the men of her city shall stone her with stones until she die; because she hath wrought folly in Israel, to play the whore in her father's house: So shalt thou put evil away from among you."

THAT NIGHT I DREAMED I was stark-naked and shackled in the stocks, my legs spread, on public view in front of our church, and I woke in terror. Getting out of bed, I lit a lamp and wrote to Nick, prudent enough for once not to say much, since letters can fall into the wrong hands.

"That plan we made won't work. We need to meet in daylight, in public. Sometimes we can be alone, but not at night, not yet. We need to talk and get to know each other well."

Next morning, before I changed my mind, I walked it to the Forest Hills post office, got it franked and sent. Too restless to attend to anything after that, I walked on to Isie's place.

Sam was on the porch, and he seemed cheered, the crisper fall air easier for him to breathe. When I suggested an excursion in the wheeled chair, he stood up and walked to it alone.

I tucked a blanket around him.

"I feel as tight-packed as a cigar," he protested.

"A fine Cuban, I hope," I said and pushed him out the lane. "But *oooff!* You don't feel like one. How many cigars would it take to be this heavy, I wonder? Next year when you're well, I'll make you push me all the way to Baltimore."

"Don't press your luck." But even chuckling didn't seem to make him cough.

The lane slanted up, but we soon reached the flatter road. Nick's father's place lay less than a mile west, in Black Horse, and it seemed harmless to head that way. Fall rains had settled the dust, and we passed woods with red and yellow maples, purple sassafras, and red sumac. At the crossroads in Shawsville, a black-and-white border collie came wagging from a house.

Sam freed a hand from the blanket to stroke its ears. "Good boy. Fine fellow."

It was the most interest he had shown in anything for months, and, feeling cheered and optimistic, I turned us south toward Black Horse, the collie trailing along.

In the distance we could see two men riding north toward us. One was a tall, skinny man in black, on a big black horse. He might have been a brimstone preacher, bony and straight-backed and pale, with long white hair under his straight-brimmed hat, but he held a rifle on his lap. As he came near, I saw his eyes—clear and gray like Nick's, unmistakable, but colder in his face, with the stern and righteous look of an Abolitionist. Could he be Nick's father?

But I was distracted by the sight of the other man—a black man on a mule, legs flapping to the trot, also holding a rifle. Negroes cleaned guns but had never been allowed to carry them. With a shock I saw his jacket, rusty black linen with mismatched tweed patches.

"What in tarnation?" Sam said from the chair.

Both of us gaped up as they trotted past.

What was Tim doing out riding with Nick's father and a gun?

III.

Nicholas McComas

1865—1869

I WAS NOT A LEARNED MAN. Rumors of knowledge, that's what I had. I read what I could get my hands on, asked other men to tell me what they knew, and listened to the preachers, who at least read Latin and Greek. I once heard a preacher say that the word "Secession" came from the Latin term for cutting your own throat—separating head from body, as it were. I did not know if it was true, but the one time I tried to call on Martha Jane, I ended up telling it to her mother, who was not amused. She met me on the lawn and turned me away as deftly as a collie turning sheep. Mrs. Cairnes was a fine figure of a woman, taller than her daughter and all in black mourning.

"We are not at home today, Mr. McComas," she said in a voice so quiet I had to lean in to catch it, and it felt like something she did on purpose, to show that she could control me. She looked me up and down as if noting my frayed cuffs, only partly disguised by my mother's perfect ironing. "We are quite occupied, working for the Southern Relief. You know very well the poor South has lost everything, when it never asked for it, and it's distressing to see how *some people* prosper when they don't deserve to. Good day."

I don't know what came over me, but when I gave her the preacher's Latin lesson, she pulled herself up haughtily. "You have no right to refer in any way to the Confederacy, and I'll thank you not to do so again. It is no fit subject for levity."

With that she walked away, left me there, and firmly closed her big front door.

So I did not see Martha Jane that day and could only think of her wistfully. Unlike her mother, Martha Jane had more sense of humor than most women combined. She could laugh like a lunatic or like music, and when she let me hear it, it was as good as all the money I had in the world, though that wasn't saying much. She never shrank from anything or stepped back modestly to let others speak. She was vivacious as a colt and just as gawky, and she was always as free and natural as any man, things women were not supposed to be. Though if my father was to be believed, we were all just higher monkeys, women as well as men, and if monkeys were not natural and free, hanging from trees and swinging limb to limb, I did not know what was.

That's what I mean about rumors of knowledge.

But it changed you just to hear that you were closer to animals, closer to bears and wolves and eagles than to angels in the sky, though what had happened in our country the last few years should have convinced anyone. Once I rode onto a farm to check the family of a man off fighting under Grant and found his wife and children killed, the wife bayoneted in the belly to make sure the baby there was dead. Apparently some Rebel outfit had required their miserable porridge and their laying hens, but they could have taken them for less than that. Two days later, the chickens would have been consumed, but that man's family was still all dead. For all I knew, he might have been off killing other people's wives and babies in the South. It was what some men did.

"AND YOU, HAVE YOU killed anyone?" Martha had asked me on that sweet night when she let me capture her inside her brother's barn. We were lying in the hayloft, and it was so black we could not see each other's faces from an inch away. But every cell in our bodies reached to touch the other through our clothes.

"Not that I know of," I said and tried to draw her back into a kiss.

She felt small and light in my arms, but she went stiff to hold me off. She could be persistent as a terrier when she wanted to know something.

"But you would know, wouldn't you?" she said low but urgently. "You haven't been in any battles, have you, or served on any firing squads? So you should know."

I sighed. "I have arrested men and never learned what happened to them. They were sent to prison camps, and you've seen what happens in some of them."

It was one of the things that made me wake up in a sweat at 4:00 AM, along with that farmer's murdered family. I tried to imagine the real scale of the war, how many innocents had been slaughtered casually. And me, could I hate any stranger that much? I could.

"There are some I wish I could have killed, like John Wilkes Booth, when he was still at home in Bel Air. If I had only known what he would do someday!"

She seemed not to blame me for that and soon nuzzled her face into my neck. I tried to clear my head by exploring her hair with my nose. It did not smell like perfume or flowers, more like fresh-baked bread. That scent was especially intense on either side of her nose, and it made me wonder if there was a sort of musk gland there, something I had heard deer possess, along with all felines, from house cats to tigers. When my nose insisted it should be allowed to root there for a while, she surprised me with a long, passionate kiss.

This pleasant development was interrupted by the arrival of her brother, the obnoxious pup, settling his holdings for the night, and in no time she had ushered me outside and disappeared down toward the house, leaving me alone and cold, bereft, with nothing to look forward to except a pint at Smithson's before riding home.

The moon was dark that night, with clouds over the stars, and I had to find my way out to the road mainly by feel. Before I got there, a horse came galloping behind me and a potshot cracked in my direction. I had to slide down the nearest muddy bank and lie still by a creek while he galloped back and forth across the fields, blindly firing in the dark. Flashes of gunpowder marked his movements, erratic as a giant firefly. Young fool probably thought I wanted his whiskey still. I was lucky his horse didn't trample me.

When he finally gave up and rode back to his barn, I scrambled through the woods to get my horse and pint. I was glad to get inside the warm interior of Smithson's pub, filled with tobacco smoke and candlelight. Gabriel Smithson was a jolly man, portly and fair, and we were old friends, having gone to school to the same minister and engaged in various violent boyhood activities on the way home. He was long since married with a pack of children, and was taking on the look of middle age, which I did not see yet on myself, though it had settled soon after matrimony onto every man I knew. Tonight he whistled at the sight of me.

"Hope she was worth it, man," he said, twinkling, and stood me the pint to celebrate the mud all over me, though he was only guessing where I had gotten it.

I THOUGHT NO MORE about G. Richard Cairnes of Jarrettsville until a few days later, when I got Martha's letter, saying we could not meet like that again, and it put me into a foul mood. She alone of all the women I knew seemed like a person who could be not just a lover but also a friend. Or maybe she only pretended to be to please me. You never knew with women, never knew their hearts. And what was wrong with a few kisses in the dark? I was more disappointed than I would have thought and did not write back to her.

So instead of more pleasant activities that Wednesday night, I went with my father to a meeting in Bel Air, both of us taking guns. The place was packed, men of all stripes shouting, spit flying, plenty of them Harford Rifles or Harford Light Dragoons, both insurrectionist militias that included a few full-grown curs, more dangerous than any pup. Rumor was the new legislature would repeal the law that prevented blacks from testifying against whites.

"They think we'll make an insurrection, and they want to turn our Negroes into spies," one man shouted at the podium. "What's after that, the vote?"

"That will never happen here!" men yelled back.

"They'll get their insurrection if they don't watch out!"

None of that deterred my father, who stood up and walked to the podium.

"I would rather give the vote to Africans than to any known Rebel," he said in a deep, sonorous voice that probably carried past the walls.

It was hardly a new thing to say—Lincoln himself had said it, and three days later he was dead. Even some in his own party wanted to shoot him, probably.

But the howl that ensued that night in the Bel Air hall became a brawl, shots fired into the ceiling and broken chairs, a few broken heads.

We got out of there all right. But the day after, my father received an unsigned letter, reading, "You are a black-hearted, nigger-loving son of a bitch not worthy even to be killed, because your blood would pollute the earth. God Himself will strike you down." The closing salutation was "GOD DAMN YOU," underlined three times.

A few days later, I woke at first light, having dozed off in the raised blind above the sheepfold, where I was supposed to keep watch. I could not see the ram in his pen. Swinging down, I found him behind the back gate, lying on his side in a pool of blood, his throat slit.

I could hear my father splitting wood behind the house, and quaking inwardly, I went to confess my latest failure. He was a sort of demigod to us, a tower of righteousness, while my brothers and I were mere mortals, not one of us even literally as tall as he.

I stood up as high as possible and tried to meet his eyes as I told him.

"It's my fault. I don't know what I can do to make it up."

"No, it isn't," he said calmly and wiped his hands on a rag. "And I'm glad that it was not your throat. It's dangerous to do the Lord's work. Come on, let's butcher it."

Neither of us had a taste for mutton anymore, now that we tended sheep, watched them frisk around as lambs, grow up to be gentle and curious, come to search my pockets as I lay reading on the meadow grass. It was a secret I knew about myself, that I felt closer to animals than to people, animals I knew especially. My horse, Captain Jack? When I looked at him, it felt as if I was looking in a mirror. I knew how horses thought, why they fled first and asked questions later, and if one horse bolted off, so would all the others within sight or sound. Any two horses are a herd, and a herd acts like a single animal, using its numbers to lower the chances that its members can be singled out and caught.

Sheep are something like that, too, at least when it comes to moving as a group, though they are not so easy to spook, rather sleepy and dull compared to any horse.

But the ram had been a character, full of himself. He would strut around the ewes, high-stepping like a fancy horse, and he was uncowed by the dogs. He would lower his curled horns and butt at them, and when they scampered away whimpering, he'd prance around, a spark of triumph in his eyes. He liked to try to knock me over, too, put me in my place, though I did not fall so easily.

Now we had to shear him, skin him, cut him up. We were in no position to waste anything. We would sell the wool, cure the skin for saddle pads, and give the meat to my brothers. My father's strategy for dealing with his debts was to borrow even more, shoot for larger wool volume, and hope the market would bounce back, and he had hired a black veteran to help us expand the flock. The veteran's name was Tim, and he looked familiar, though I could not place him. My father, brothers, and I felled trees for a clearing in our woods, stripped logs, and hoisted them to make thick walls for his cabin, mortar in the chinks.

Soon the cabin was done and the man installed, with his mother and sister. He was good with horses and quick to learn about the sheep, worth two of most hired men. My mother grumbled that she had no work for his womenfolk, since she had three daughters still at home, and why had we taken them on anyway? But she went herself to neighbors and found jobs for them, close enough to walk to from the cabin.

When Tim had learned enough to mind the sheep alone for a few days, my father and I rode north across the Susquehanna to the market in Lancaster, Pennsylvania, where we borrowed more money to acquire a prize English ram, along with a wagon to haul him home in luxury, since it was bitter cold and it seemed too far to make him walk through ice and snow.

FOR A WEEK AFTER we brought the new ram home, my father stood watch himself, since he could hardly trust me now with such an important charge. Found wanting as usual, I slept in my own bed and dreamt of losing lambs and never finding them, or feeding them the wrong food so they swelled up and died, or breaking the leg of my father's horse.

One night spent in those pursuits, I woke to candlelight, my mother shaking me.

"I heard something," she said, looking afraid.

I was inclined to tell her to go back to bed, that it was nothing. She was a short, round, timid being, who in every way seemed an odd match for my father, or perhaps the relations of one's parents were always a mystery. I rubbed a hand over my face. "What did it sound like?"

Her eyes were huge, showing the whites, like a scared horse. "It was a cry like that barn owl. But it sounded like a man, and I heard hoofbeats, too."

That got me up. Back in pants, boots, jacket, hat, I tramped out into the snow, carrying a lantern that wavered in gusts of icy wind. I had to hold it high over my head to inspect the sheepfold and count its inhabitants: forty-eight ewes huddled together, most of them in lamb, the ram alone in his own pen. All were accounted for except my father, who was not in the raised blind. I climbed the ladder, held the lantern up, but its feeble light showed nothing odd in the dark fields and woods beyond.

I went to the barn, rumbled the loft door back, and found my horse in its stall but my father's gone. He must have had some errand off the farm, and now I should watch the sheep. An army blanket lay in the blind, not folded neatly as he usually left it, but in a heap—but that was all that seemed off. Wrapping it around myself, I hunched in the blind and must have dozed, for when my stiff limbs woke me, it was gray dawn light, snow falling fast.

But right away I was alarmed. My father's horse was a big, black warm blood, Dutch, easy to see through falling snow, and he stood snorting in the barnyard, our three cows huddled cautiously away from him. His saddle was still on his back, and his reins were snapped. I climbed down and crossed the barnyard, moving as slow as water so as not to startle him, and patted his neck, but he quivered and withdrew.

My father called him Honest Abe. "Easy, Abe," I said. "It's all right, boy. Easy."

I knew this meant the worst, but I stroked him till he was calm, retrieved his broken reins and led him to his stall, took off his tack, dried his wet coat, and threw a blanket over him.

In dread, I walked to the house, where my mother's face told me my father had not returned. My feet were frozen, and it was hard to walk, but I took a rifle and set out, past the fold to the back gate. It was already blocked with drifts, and I swung over it, into deep, cold snow.

"Father?" I shouted. "James McComas? Are you there?"

Nothing but wind answered, and new snow had covered any tracks I might have seen. I searched the woods, the blank, white fields, nothing showing but the boulder in the east meadow, big as a ship's prow. I went on to the new clearing and enlisted help from Tim. Fanning out, we shuffled through the frigid snow, parallel to each other, calling my father's name.

We found him in the woods, his body nearly hidden under drifted snow. Already half-frozen, he lay on a large, flat rock, the back of his head crushed, as if he had fallen by himself. But he was too good a rider for that, and Abe was gentle and well trained. His hat lay a few yards away, but his rifle was gone, and he always had it at night.

It took both of us to lift him and carry him back to the house, my mother standing at the back door, watching as we came, seeming to grow thinner, crags in her face, as her fearful view of life came true.

We laid him on a bed, opened his shirt, and found a deep purple bruise in the center of his pale chest in the shape of a horse's hoof. Honest Abe would not have stepped on him, even in the dark, or at least not in the center of his chest. I knew someone had made a horse do that deliberately, to let us know it was no accident.

THE DAY OF THE FUNERAL was cold and bright, buggies and wagons gathered outside Bethel Church, where the cemetery yard was large enough to serve all local Protestants, and a few spare graves had been dug in the fall before the ground was hard. I did my father honor in my militia uniform, my brother Alex in Union blue, the rest of my militia turned out in uniform as well to stand along the aisles and ensure that order would prevail. The crowd was small, but our family alone filled the first three pews, the women all in stiff black taffeta and veils.

Two Methodist circuit preachers had come to praise his Abolition work, and other eulogies extolled his compassion and unwavering rectitude. When they were done, my brothers and I stepped up to the coffin and took the handles in the order of our births, Jackson and Alex in the front and me alone in back with no one to balance me, so I took the handle on the end.

As we shuffled toward the door, I noticed Tim alone at the rear wall. I held his gaze and used my head to beckon him to join us. He lifted his long, pale palms, trying to refuse. But my brothers must have reassured him with their looks, because he stepped to us quickly and took a handle on the near side, while I shifted to the one across from him. Better balanced now, we carried the box outside and set it on the ropes held by militiamen across an open grave.

Taking the ropes from them, we held up the coffin while the small crowd in black assembled around us and sang a hymn. The benediction read, my mother laid her wedding ring on top of the box, and we gently lowered it till it came to rest on hard clay.

My mother returned to the cold church nave before they shoveled in the dirt, and I went with her, held her arm, and listened to murmurs of condolence from the line of women rustling toward her. One of them was Martha Jane, in mourning dress and black bonnet, her eyes downcast, not looking at me. She offered her gloved hand to my mother.

"I am so sorry for your loss," she said. "He was truly a good man."

My mother took her hand and nodded but said nothing from behind her veil.

Martha had nearly walked away, when I was overwhelmed with a need to keep her there. My hand shot out and grabbed her arm. "Stand here with me."

She did, and I pulled her against my side and held on like a man about to faint, blinking rapidly. Was I going to cry? I curled my arm, and when she turned into me, I buried my face in her neck and felt tears I did not know I had rise to my eyes. My father had held up the sky for me. He was the man who had known everything, who was always in charge. How could he be killed so easily? He had fed and clothed the family and kept the sheep alive. How could all of that be up to me? How would I ever manage it?

Martha clung to me.

"I'm so sorry your father died. I'm so sorry I wrote that to you."

"What? No."

I felt a sob quiver through her chest, and I rocked her, both of us oblivious to anyone who might have watched. It felt natural and right that I should hold her in a church, and it struck me with lucidity that I could marry her. I would not have to do it all alone. Martha would be there. She would hold up the sky. It should happen now, today, tomorrow, as soon as possible. The farm would be mine, the sheep, the land—the debts—but wasn't there a way to make it work?

"You have to marry me," I said into her ear.

It only made her cry harder, but I could see it all. My father's house was small and occupied already by my mother, three sisters, one aunt. But it had an attic, where my brothers had slept when they were old enough to need the privacy, and it might work for us. We would float high above the five women downstairs, alone in peace and rest.

STRANGELY SERENE, I went the next day to speak to her uncle Will, who was now father-in-law to my brother Alex, and he agreed to let another McComas into his family. I wrote to Martha Jane that we would come to speak to her mother and brother next Sunday afternoon.

When the day arrived, it could not have looked less promising, snow flurries blowing horizontal across barren fields, ground frozen hard under our hooves. But my brothers and I rode to Will's farm, and he came out with a beautiful wild turkey, so freshly killed that it was still warm and perfectly intact, as if he had wrung its long neck. He handed it up to me as I sat in the saddle.

"Peace offering for my nephew," he said solemnly but with wry eyes and got onto his horse. His son, George Andrew, also mounted up and came with us. I held the turkey by its big, warm claws, which cooled as the five of us rode to the farm of G. Richard Cairnes.

When we rode in the lane, no one appeared on the porch to welcome us. In the silence of the harsh cold air, the horses chewed their clinking bits and a rift of light snow swirled and tumbled like a ribbon on the porch.

From inside the house I heard a clock strike twice, the time I had told Martha we would arrive. Sure enough, soon the front door opened and she came out looking radiant in a white wool dress with a red shawl, her eyes fixed on me and no one else. I smiled, took off my hat, let snow sprinkle my head.

Behind her came Mrs. Cairnes, taffetas rustling, and Richard, who had evidently not been warned and looked as if he had still been at dinner, a blue napkin tucked into his collar. He yanked it out, looking young and belligerent, and it was his mother who spoke up.

"Why, Will. To what do we owe the pleasure?"

Will kept his hat on and one hand on the rifle in his lap. "Afternoon, Mary Ann. We thought to bring you something. You know Nick McComas, I think, poor James's boy. Young Nick has asked for the hand of my niece, Martha Jane, and I have said yes. I'm glad you're all here today to hear me say it plain." He paused and fixed his eyes on Richard for a while. "We're not at war in this county. All that is finished. I have approved this marriage, for the sake of all of us and peace. That is"—he looked at Martha and smiled—"if the girl agrees."

Her face went sweetly pink, and she looked younger than I had ever seen her, closer to fourteen than twenty-four. But when she spoke, her voice was strong and lilting, with no quaver. "I do."

Mrs. Cairnes gave a small cry and pressed a handkerchief against her mouth. "If only my husband were alive!"

Will waved an impatient hand. "If my brother were alive, he would agree, and so shall you. It's for the best. Now, Nick has brought you a wild turkey, haven't you, young man?"

I was grinning like an idiot at Martha and couldn't stop, and she grinned back. I held the big bird out by its warm neck, its green and rust feathers arranged in fine display, without one drop of blood.

MARTHA WANTED TO ELOPE, gallop off a cliff holding my hand, and I loved her for that.

But by now I knew she had a reckless side, and my role would be to steady her, channel her bravery toward more constructive ends—though I had no plans to tame her or teach her to obey. I knew a hundred spineless girls, and if I had wanted, I could probably have cornered one. But I preferred the challenge of Martha, the way she took nothing lying down. Well, some things of course I wanted her to take that way. And I had reason to hope she would.

"My mother wants us to wait a while," I told her with real regret.

My mother had not asked me that, but I knew she was devastated by my father's death, and she should not have to make further adjustments yet.

It was adorable the way Martha tried not to pout, and as a reward I gave her a ring that had been my grandmother's, an opal with pearls on either side. Some people thought opals unlucky, but she told me she wore it every minute of the day, often on a ribbon round her neck, since her hands had to pull cows' teats and plunge into hot water to scrub clothes. I liked to think of it resting between her breasts, against her silky skin. Would that spot smell like rose water or like the fresh-baked bread I liked to sniff beside her nose?

Now at least I had more chances to find out. We met in Alex's home, only a half mile from Richard's, though it might have been another planet, for its happier feel. The more time I spent with her, the more peaceful I felt, my terrors calmed. Alex's wife was Martha's close friend and cousin, Hannah, a lively girl who loved plays, especially Shakespeare, and on long, snowy evenings, the four of us would choose parts and read those grand speeches out loud to each other. When we felt ambitious, we would also act and posture, me posing as the gloomy Dane, a role I could see too well, with my own father murdered, unavenged. But another evening I was Romeo, much more to my taste, though he also ends up dead.

And I could see now that Martha was right when she had written that we ought to meet in company awhile and get to know each other in the light and not just in the dark. I got to see how she would react to situations, things that I was glad to know before it was too late. For instance, one night Hannah went to all the trouble to behead and pluck and roast a chicken for us. My brother loved the skin, considered it a treat, and Martha admitted that she did, too.

But when Hannah brought some out in a cup and Alex insisted Martha take some first, she only gaped at it awkwardly, not saying why she seemed unable to take any, though Alex teased her for long minutes.

"Martha? Come on now, have some skin. Come on."

I could not blame her when I glanced into the cup and saw a flabby, yellow mass.

But she could not find a way to extricate herself, and in the end she mutely thrust the cup at Alex and left him puzzling.

Later she explained to me: She did love the skin, but only when it was crisp and brown.

"Well, you could have said something," I pointed out.

"Said what? I didn't want to hurt her feelings, and I don't know how to lie."

This made me laugh. "Really? You can't lie, not about anything?"

She looked stricken and adorable, her cheeks coloring pink.

"No. Not if someone asks me something. It's as if they've woken me up in the middle of the night and shined a bright light in my face. I can only tell the truth."

I laughed and felt lucky. In a flash I understood that, having grown up with few servants, she had learned to cook delicious chicken, make piecrust and bread, put up produce for the winter, smoke hams, stuff sausages—all skills that Hannah lacked, having been born on the big farm, daughter of a first son and heir.

"And now you and Hannah have to cook for us poor brothers," I said with real remorse. "But I'm sure glad to know which one of you will cook for me!"

Other evenings were not so pleasant, when we read the gloomy newspapers. That winter Johnson closed the Freedmen's Bureau and vetoed the Civil Rights Act. Congress overrode him, but the governor proclaimed it void in Maryland, where "it would cause Race War." He was a Republican, of Lincoln's party, yet he thought Negro suffrage would mean "Black rule of the White race"—because on the cotton-growing Eastern Shore, blacks did far outnumber whites. To stop it, he decided to let Rebels vote, even those who had not signed the Ironclad Oath.

If Lincoln could have seen what happened to his party then! The Republicans began an unseemly scramble to court Rebel votes, transforming themselves overnight into the party of the White

Man's Government, though that honor had always belonged to
the Democrats.

Other horrors also crawled out of their holes. Some editors
proposed that we "do the Will of the Creator and return to slavery." Others revived the movement to send Negroes to a reserva-
tion in the West or Africa. My personal favorite was the visionary
who suggested they could be removed more expeditiously.

"The Negro has no rights, no rights at all," he wrote. "Fewer
than a mule, since a mule is a valuable possession and the Negro no
longer is. He is a noxious infestation, and he should know that he
is liable to be murdered, as some recent juries have acquitted those
who have seen fit to eliminate some particularly egregious example
of African degradation."

Reading such stuff could throw me into helpless rage and grief
for my father, and only holding Martha on my lap could keep it
off. She would hold my head and whisper in my ear, warm me so
much that I did not feel the cold, not even when my brother and I
took the sleigh to deliver her back home.

FINALLY, SPRING BEGAN TO inch our way, and one day in March,
when I could smell the dirt, its top layers thawed enough to let
crocuses break through the lawns, I rode toward Shawsville, past
the Colored Church where my father had helped a black teacher
to start a school. It was a low brown building set back from the
road, its almost unmarked cemetery plot buried in weeds. The last
time I had ridden by, its doors were open, children inside reciting
math.

This time I smelled char from five hundred yards. The building
almost looked intact, just sagged slightly toward the ground. But

when I got there I could see fire had gutted it, the roof fallen in, only the front wall left standing.

It was Tim's day off, but I rode out to the clearing to make sure he was all right, thinking I might suggest he move into the little house across the lane from us. It was rented to a German family who spoke very little English, and God knows we needed the cash. But I wanted to at least offer it to him, for safety's sake.

When I got to the clearing, he had his mule hitched to the plow and was churning every square inch of ground, though it was still frozen underneath. When he saw me, he grinned shyly, stopped, and lifted his hat. I waved at him to carry on.

"Good-looking garden," I called. "What are you going to plant?"

He shrugged and rubbed his head. "Why, everything, reckon. Cabbage, corn, greens, 'tatoes, 'matoes. Man's got to eat."

"You should bring out some of that horse manure from the heap beside the barn. It's been there long enough, I think. If it's aged right, it's the best for vegetables. I don't know about sheep dung. Not sure I'd use that."

"No," he agreed and looked at me like he was expecting some sort of order.

I looked around elaborately to let him know this was a social call. I admired the rabbit hutch, already full of bunnies, and the chickens scratching on the ground. He had a good spring, at the bottom of a hill, and he had built a stone cistern over it. Of course he would not want to move.

I told him about the Colored Church, and he nodded like he already knew.

"Listen. If you ever feel in danger out here, bring your family to the house. All right?"

He nodded somewhat warily. "We be all right."

I nodded, too. "Just in case."

A young woman came out of the house and walked to the cistern with a wooden pail. She looked very young and pretty, dressed like a white woman, with a full skirt. She was clearly with child, and when she smiled at me, I smiled back and felt the urge to compliment Tim again.

"I didn't know you had a wife," I said in admiring tones. "And such a pretty one."

He seemed to go stiff all over and hauled himself up tall. "Not wife. Sister."

He put his hat back on, chucked up the mule, and plowed fast away from me, and I knew I had committed an error, though I wasn't sure exactly what it was.

"Well, good," I called. "Is her husband here? Bring him along. I'll find work for him."

He did not turn around, and as I left, I could only wave to his retreating back.

APRIL STAYED GLOOMY, though so many apple, pear, and cherry trees burst into bloom at once that pink and white petals blew on the breeze, fluttered in windows, littered floors. Pink magnolias and dogwoods flowered, too, while finches, robins, thrushes, and cardinals filled every hollow of the woods with yearning song. Martha was having wedding clothes made up, and she was as cheerful as a bird with bright new feathers, preparing to take flight in spring.

On the first anniversary of Appomattox, Federal veterans and militias put on a parade at Jarrettsville, with an exhibition of cavalry maneuvers in a field. Most of the neighborhood stayed home, pretending to be utterly absorbed in planting fields and garden beds.

But Martha came on her mare, looking splendid in a blue velvet riding suit that had been made for her trousseau, with a small matching hat. After the parade and our silly maneuvers, my big gray and I chased her and the mare into the woods. When we caught them, I plucked Martha down and took her in my arms while Captain Jack cautiously approached the mare and scratched along her mane with his big teeth until she scratched him back.

The next day, at my urging, Martha rode out to the pasture where I had the flock. I was lounging on the sun-warmed boulder, trying not to feel anxious, and when I saw her, I jumped up, scrambled off the rock, and lifted her out of the saddle, feeling like I could breathe again.

"There you are," I said. "There you are."

I untied her bonnet, plucked the pins out of her hair, and tucked them in the pocket of my shirt. Fingers trembling, I combed them through the long waves down her back, my eyes lavishing delight. In the sun her hair was every shade of brown and gold, shining like silk, and her eyes crinkled as she tried not to smile.

We kissed and walked around the edges of the flock and kissed again. We sat in the warm grass by the rock, and I showed her sketches in my pad. From time to time one of the sheepdogs scudded up and gave me an alert look, as if reporting in, then slunk back fast to turn a sheep that had strayed half a foot. The sheep watched us with their black faces and turned at the dogs' commands. A smell of mutton and crushed grass rolled back to us.

We drowsed against the sun-warmed rock and talked of everything we thought about, my arms around her as she leaned against my chest.

"You know," she said dreamily, "Isie was lovely before she got married, but then she changed. It isn't fair what those babies did to her. It makes a girl afraid to be married."

She kept her voice light, but I could hear the serious note under it.

I pulled away and looked at her with a mock frown. "I can see I'll have to keep you far away from Isie's ruffians. They've given matrimony a bad name. But you know we won't have half so many and we won't have any with red hair. I wouldn't let them in the house."

She pulled me back to her and cradled her cheek against my chest, as if to hear the thudding of my heart.

"Isie says there isn't any choice in it. They just keep coming, willy-nilly."

I patted her, wondering how much I should say. I had been initiated at fourteen by a freedwoman, and my education had been furthered by a young white woman whose husband was old and frail. She had seemed to take comfort from me, though we were not in love, or at least I wasn't. She claimed I broke her heart and that I had given her a child, though I didn't think that could be true. She might have been the one who told her husband. In any case, he challenged me to a duel, though I declined to participate. Recently I had heard of his death, but that did not make me want to seek her out. In fact, I lived in fear of running into her at the dry-goods store.

"It doesn't have to be that way," I said cautiously. "There are things we can do."

"Isie says none of it works. What do you mean, there are things we can do?"

I smoothed her hair. "Young Cairnes was still a whelp when they were wed. Believe me, there are things that work. Your condition won't be delicate until that's what you want."

Breaking my grip, she sat up with huge shocked eyes. "How did you learn such things?"

"Ah, well."

I shifted away from the rock wall to lie on the warm grass and closed my eyes.

I tried to pull her down to me, and she resisted, placing an accusing palm against my chest. I suppose it was a test—engagements had been broken for less, once a man's "impurity" was uncovered. It could be grounds for breach of promise and complete release.

But if she really was the wife for me, she would not see it that way.

"It's ridiculous to expect a man my age to know nothing of sex. Or to call something that natural impure. If I had any money, I would wager most men lie about it anyway. There's not a man past puberty who can truthfully claim that sort of ignorance."

She was breathless with self-righteousness, though I also detected a thrill in her voice. "What woman have you known? Tell me at once!"

Her hand rose and gave my breastbone a small slap, and then another one.

I caught her hand. "No lady, I assure you. No one of the slightest importance."

She tried to free her hand, but I kept hold, squinting in the light to make her look at me.

"No one, ever, half so beautiful as you."

She twisted away and seemed torn between desires to kiss me and to hit me more. "Tell me her name. I have to know. Or was there more than one, you wretch? More than one!"

I laughed. "You shouldn't want a man so ungallant as to say. Their secrets are safe, and so are yours."

"There *was* more than one!" she cried and buried her eyes against my chest, as if determined not to look at me ever again.

I kissed her head and ears until she half shoved me away and kissed me violently, kisses meant to lash and put me in my place.

But I met her force with surrender, opening my lips, and she seemed surprised to feel her tongue slide in my mouth and meet the soft tip of mine, which teased and beckoned till she followed it, then pushed back.

We went on like that for quite some time, and she seemed sorry when I stopped. Leaning on one elbow, I lifted strands of hair out of her eyes and said half-teasingly, "Where did you learn to kiss that way? Some lucky fellow, I'm sure."

She gasped and tried to pull away. "What a horrible thing to ask. You're the first man I ever kissed in my whole life."

"On your honor, never before me? You can't lie to your future husband, remember. Troth means truth, so now confess. We've pledged our truth."

"I told you I can't lie. That is the truth. Unless you count what children do. All right, I'll tell you. I kissed a little Negro boy when I was five or six, in the hayloft. There, now I've told you everything. And will you do the same?"

My mouth fell open in mock shock. "You didn't." Laughing, I took hold of her and gave her backside a quick swat. "Bad girl!" I swatted her again, and we rolled laughing on the grass until she lay exhausted on my chest.

She looked up at me musingly. "But that was it. No *man* ever, except you."

I meditated on that. "Well, I know how fortunate I am. I've never known a white woman so fond of spooning with a man."

She made a disgusted noise and almost leapt out of my arms, but I held her firm.

"You know, don't you, that you have to forgive a man some things? That is, a man who's not a milk-fed pup and who took as long as I have to find the woman he could call his wife. Because, you see, I wouldn't settle for anyone else. I waited all these years for you, and I want us to tell the truth and feel free to say anything. Can you do that?"

She closed her eyes, like she was not sure she should forgive me anything. Finally she looked at me boldly. "You wretch."

But she was smiling, and I pulled her down and kissed her till she relaxed. To seal the pact, I gently ran my hand up the whalebone corset caging her bosom, reached the top, and slid one finger between the buttons of her blouse to touch a tiny square of her bare skin, smooth as a crocus petal and warmer than the sun, her heart shuddering beneath.

IT WAS TIME TO SHEAR the sheep, a filthy, sweaty job that kept both me and Tim occupied, along with two hired Irishmen. Every move I made reminded me of my father, and sometimes as I worked, tears mixed with the sweat, to think how easily he had been reduced to the sack of inert flesh and broken head I had found in the snow. He was not a demigod, just a strong man, morally and physically, and human strength is an illusion, fragile underneath. Every animal has an Achilles heel. For a horse, it is slender legs that have to carry so much weight, propelled by so much muscle strength. For a man, it is an eggshell skull around a heavy brain, easy to crack and kill the finest mind.

But not even my father's muscles had been passed along to me. He could hoist a sheep by its rear legs and peel away great swathes of wool like corn off of a cob, until the sheep was bare, skinny, and unhurt in a few minutes' time. It took me ten or fifteen minutes to do one, and if I went faster, I nicked their skins. It took days to do them all, and every night I was caked with tufts of wool, sheep blood, manure, and a heavy mutton smell, and I had to stoke the stove with wood, heat gallons of water to pour into the copper tub, and scrub it off.

But I was glad I had taken that precaution, because the day after we were done, Martha rode to where I was in the sheep meadow. We talked easily awhile and laughed, and she seemed to have forgiven me my lack of ignorance. Before the afternoon was over, I led her into the woods and kissed her against a tree, and she slid her hands inside my shirt to feel my skin and even let me press one leg between her skirted knees. She seemed breathless and amazed at the feeling that gave her, and I was pretty stupefied myself. Maybe it was being finally in love. I never knew that it could make even kissing that much more intense.

After that she met me in the meadow any afternoon she could, and as the summer grew hotter, the days long, we lost ourselves more and more. Sometimes we dispensed with the preliminaries and went straight into the woods, rolling and panting on soft moss, though still in our clothes. This could not go on forever, but it was so sweet, I didn't want to rush. And anyway, how much longer would we have to wait, only a few months?

The first week of July, I received a letter from my father's bank in Lancaster, informing me of several mortgages I did not know he had, plus penalties for my not paying them down. They threatened to liquidate the flock and repossess the farm, the woods, the land.

I broke the news to Martha one day as we sat on the big rock in the sheep meadow. "I have to sell a little piece of land or try to get better prices for the wool. I suppose I may have to sell some sheep. And that's *before* I can think of taking on bigger responsibilities. I'll need to do that just to break even. I'm sorry, but we'll have to put the wedding off."

She gazed at me calmly before saying anything. "What can I do to help?"

"I don't deserve you," I said, meaning it. "You should have picked a richer man."

She shrugged this off. "I knew you weren't rich, and it's still you I want. But I think we should get married and face it together. Why shouldn't we? I would sleep in a barn with you, and maybe there are ways that I can make things easier."

"You already do."

I closed my eyes and pressed them into her shoulder. Why did I feel reluctant? I had thought of moving us into the attic. But women were expensive to maintain, and I had five already. The attic had a low ceiling and only a small window at each end, so it was scorching in summer.

And now I saw a vision of her in the kitchen with the five women whose territory it already was. My sisters squabbled constantly over the chores, and my mother shouted over them and argued with my aunt, whom she could not stand, though they had to share a bed. The house had only three bedrooms, and all three of my sisters slept in the second one. True, the third was mine, but it was too close to the others for privacy, or for the kind I planned to need when I finally got Martha in my bed. Like all young men, I had feverish dreams to bring to life, and I wanted us to feel as free as leaping off the barn roof and knowing how to fly.

I knew she was growing more willing to just act naturally. But I was careful not to press her, wanting her to come to me freely. Instead I took cold baths at home, standing at the pump naked, preferably in a chilling breeze.

And I concentrated on the mortgages, which seemed to have a similarly anti-aphrodisiac effect. In any case, we made it through the summer, her virtue still mostly intact.

THAT FALL, ON A LOVELY autumn afternoon when we had planned to meet, she did not appear. I rode along the trail she took to Isie's, got all the way to Kirkwood place, and skirted it discreetly, hoping to see Butter tied in front, but she was not there.

Disappointed, I turned out to the road and had not gone far when I met Martin Jarrett, who told me Martha's cousin Sam was dead. He shook his head sadly.

"They took him off treatment a month ago. Martha Cairnes did. She told me they didn't want me letting out the excess blood, though I told her it could kill him. What they should have done was send him north," he said with evident distress. "Consumption just festers here."

I resented his implying that it was Martha's fault and not his own, when he had drained out half the poor man's blood. When he drove on, I turned back toward Isie's, feeling bad for Martha but sure I should not intrude on the family's grief. I hardly knew Sam, though I had gotten glimpses of him before he went south, when he was the sort of cocky, good-looking boy that mostly got his way with everyone.

It had occurred to me to wonder what exactly Martha felt for him, and I had observed her closely the one time I saw them together. It was a day like this, a year ago, and I had met her pushing him in the wheeled chair, not far from where I now sat on my horse. I had dismounted and walked with them a ways, and I deliberately told them some news I had read. My father had subscribed to several northern newspapers, and they still came in the mail.

"It seems three men jumped a Negro near Annapolis and beat him up, just for driving a wagon on his own. And right here, someone apparently burned down a colored cabin over by Shawsville and almost killed the tenant."

I said this not to bait Sam but to see which side Martha would defend. I needed to know if I could separate her from the traitors in her family.

"Why don't the Bel Air papers tell us things like that?" I mused out loud.

Sam was pale and thin, lying back in the chair, wrapped in a heavy blanket, his eyes closed, and I thought he was asleep. But he raised his head and twisted around to glare at me.

"Because it's a damn lie, that's why!" he rasped out, hoarse. The effort sent him into a coughing fit, and he continued to glare as he coughed, face red, then gray.

We walked in silence a few steps, and I glanced at Martha, her cheeks slightly flushed. She looked at me apologetically. "Yes, it could be. But some of our neighbors say the same things. I have wondered that, too, about the local papers."

Sam's jaw set at that, and he glared straight ahead, maybe feeling outnumbered.

I thought she had given me my answer, and, exhilarated, I went on.

"The reporter blamed the Irish, because they supposedly hate blacks for working cheap. The Irish show up dirt-poor here, and I guess they're afraid of never getting a toehold. I did hear of a few who helped to run off some poor black fellow because he went to work canning oysters for three bucks a week. But I don't think it's just the Irish. As far as I can tell, it's veterans, and not just from the South. From *both* sides, guys who might have killed each other two years ago. Even Union men, who were supposed to fight to set the Negroes free, they all hate them."

Sam grew incensed. "Nobody fought for that!" he shouted and started to bay again.

Martha waited till his cough had calmed. "What did the Federals fight for, then?"

She gave me a quick glance, and I knew she had come over to my side.

Sam inhaled deeply, and his voice came clear and strong, as if cured by rage. "To steal our land and make us into nobodies, nobodies like them, like all their mongrel hordes! Steal our woods and fields and put up factories instead. Destroy our way of life— *for money!* Damn you if you can't see that!"

"My father thought that, too," Martha said evenly. "He didn't think most people in the North really cared about the slaves. He said they only wanted to bring Southerners down a peg, like the immigrants up north, destroy their way of life, because they had it too good."

I liked this less, but at least she did not say "we" in reference to the South. "I suppose those were some people's motives, same as the South wanting to keep its money and its property. I like to think it was all high motives, but of course it never is."

Sam tried to speak and could only cough. Martha touched his shoulder, but he shrugged her off. For a minute I could see the cocksure boy he used to be, his spirit still the same, though he looked like he had been replaced by his own skeleton.

NOW I WAS SORRY he was dead, not just for Martha's sake. I would rather he had lived and let me convince him. I wrote my sympathy to her and asked if there was anything I could do.

She wrote back a long, rambling letter, tear-stained, about how horrible it was that he had died like that, from a massive hemorrhage while she was there, cupping his back. "What kind of world is it where men shoot each other and cage up boys of nineteen to starve and die of disease? It's never going to end. Isie's coughing now! And she's just had another babe. If it's consumption, both of them will die, all from a damn Yankee prison camp! If there was a God, He would not let men do things like that to each other. So I know there isn't one. It's all a myth. Like you said, we're just vultures tearing out each other's eyes."

I was not sure I had said that, and the way she sounded worried me. No one at the funeral would exactly welcome me, but I decided I would go, pay my respects, and try to steady her.

When the day arrived, it was a golden morning, autumn sun on red and yellow leaves, full blown on every tree, a day to think of harvest and full granaries and not of death.

But Bethel Church was jammed with mourners, filling the aisles and nave, the rustle of black taffeta and crinolines almost drowning out the bitter eulogies. The county's best-known orators all had Rebel sympathies, and today they had come out to speak of this new casualty and the tragic end of that most beautiful of empires, the Confederate States of America.

"He was the flower of our youth, cut down by a heartless and immoral foe who does not fear the laws of God or man," intoned Henry Farnandis, a tall, white-haired man with a rich, deep voice, who had served as a Secessionist state senator and fled the country when he was indicted for burning railroad bridges early in the war.

"He was a loving son and brother, gentle friend to man and beast, kept in chains and starved until he broke. Words alone cannot describe the perfidy of this injustice nor repay for it. But we can rest assured, legend will not neglect him, and through the ages, when deeds of valor are recounted, his name will resound. He is in our hearts from now until eternity."

His younger colleagues spoke in the same vein, but less well, and it needled me that I could not see Martha, who must be in the front row. I was sorry I had not already married her and removed her from their reach. When the orators finished, I maneuvered to a position where I hoped to snag her as the family followed the coffin out.

Tears streaked the faces of the pallbearers as they bent to take it up, Richard in front, with Isie's husband on the other side. Behind Richard came George Andrew Cairnes, and across from him was Archer Jarrett, founder of the Harford Light Dragoons. Federal troops had imprisoned him for months when he refused to tell them where the militia hid its guns.

Last, lifting the coffin's end, was Herman Stump, organizer of the Harford Rifles, a tall, dashing blond cur who liked to affect the name of Colonel Stump, a rank achieved by treason in a Rebel militia. He had boasted of burning railroad bridges and leading raids against *The Maryland* when it carried Union troops, and the military government had placed a bounty on his head. But he had evaded capture, danced at balls, and written taunting letters to the newspapers. He had divested himself of the titles to his Harford County property, knowing the Federals would just as soon seize it as capture him. Some said the governor had supplied his unit with an armory of guns, paid for with state funds. A Bel Air paper had printed a treasonous letter from the governor, in which he asked of Stump and his militia, "Will they be good men to send out to kill Lincoln and his men?"—a desire the governor had needed to retract when Lincoln sent troops to keep Maryland in line, and Stump had exiled himself to Canada until the war was done.

Sam had weighed so little at the end that when five strong men lifted the coffin, it seemed to fly up from their hands. They rested it on their shoulders and swayed up the aisle, hands folded in white gloves and eyes cast down. The dark, polished coffin had been draped with the crossed Stars and Bars of the Confederacy, and the crowd jostled to touch it with reverence, women in black pressing in as close as their skirts would allow.

Now the family came slowly after it, Isie first, draped in a black veil and sitting in Sam's wheeled chair, pushed by one of their uncles, two babies on her lap. Three older children grasped some portion of the chair, and Martha followed, also veiled and carrying a small, red-haired child who must have been another of Isie's, its head against her shoulder, mouth slack.

Too many members of Martha's family had crowded in between us, and I could not reach her without causing a scene. She didn't even seem to see me as she passed. I wedged in the first phalanx of mourners behind the family and inched out to the cemetery yard.

Not even the glorious fall day could disguise the hole dug deep beside the graves of Sam's father and brother, not far from those of my father and Martha's, and it exhaled a smell of cold, wet clay. Martha stood at its edge and seemed to waver unsteadily. But I could not get to her, and her arm was taken by one of the Harford Light Dragoons.

In the dense crowd it was impossible not to step on someone's grave. My father's was only a few yards away, covered with new sod, and I watched helplessly as boots trod on it. The minister intoned a prayer, and the pallbearers began to let the coffin down on ropes.

Suddenly Martha burst away from the Dragoon and rushed to the front end of the coffin.

"Is this his head?" she cried and placed a hand on the wooden lid, looking horrified.

The cemetery yard sloped down, and I knew at once she wanted to make sure he would not lie head-down for eternity.

But Richard only stared at her as he held a rope. His face was haggard, and his overlong red hair hung limp, swinging as he jerked to stare at the coffin, half-inside the hole.

"Stop!" he cried. "Stop! Stop!" He tried to haul his rope back up.

Martin Jarrett elbowed from the crowd and took the rope from him. "It's all right. His head is on this end, uphill. I put him in the box myself. He'll be all right."

But this was so far from the truth that even my eyes ached, and around me people sobbed.

I COULD NOT EXTRICATE her from her family that day, and she left in a closed carriage with Isie and the children. I did have the chance to comfort her a few days later, and every few days after that. But the approach of winter meant major chores for both of us, Martha canning, smoking, pickling, me carding wool to sell, and we could not meet as often as we liked. With the proceeds from the wool, I leased a neighbor's pasture to expand our grazing space, and Tim and I started a new fence, continuous from our meadow and enclosing the new land. I wanted stone, the kind we had in front, and we quarried shale down by Deer Creek and dragged it home.

One cold afternoon as we stacked the stones, trying to be artful in the old way, Tim's sister walked across the pasture, probably returning from work in a neighbor's house. As she got closer, I saw that she was no longer pregnant, and she had the baby slung across her back, wrapped in a shawl. It appeared to be several months old, well grown enough to hold up its own head, and it had rosy skin and a dusting of red hair. I supposed it had to be her own child, the one she had been carrying before, and it looked lighter than she did. Its skin was almost white.

When they were gone, I turned to Tim, feeling foolish not to have asked before. "Where did your mother and sister live while you were away with the army?"

Tim was wrestling the shale into tight formations, and he didn't answer right away. When he spoke, it was in better English than I had heard him use before, carefully pronounced.

"My mother was a slave to Mrs. Cairnes, but she got freed a ways back, before Emancipation time. That's where we lived till we come here."

I was not sure I wanted to know which Mrs. Cairnes he meant. "Mrs. Will Cairnes?"

He did not seem in any more of a hurry to answer than I was to be corrected, and I had stopped expecting it when he spoke.

"No, sir," he said, drawing it out. "Mrs. George Cairnes. Mr. George Cairnes died, and now she live alone with Mr. Richard and Miss Martha Jane. She's their maw. Believe you know Miss Martha."

I was not sure why this was such bad news, though I knew it was. I pressed on. "And when you left there and came here, why was that? Why did you move?"

His face clouded over, and he shrugged. It was clear he did not want to say.

I didn't blame him, and I didn't ask again, just worked beside him until dark. It was still against the law in Maryland for blacks to speak out against whites, and he might also be ashamed. If some white man had taken advantage of his sister, he might have wanted to remove her from his proximity. I wondered if my father knew that when he took Tim in, and how much else I could not see when it was right in front of me.

As for who exactly that white man might have been, I did not like to think. I already knew a great deal more than I wanted to about G. Richard Cairnes.

I KEPT THIS NEWS from Martha all that winter, and we had many happy evenings at my brother's, in company, but with kisses stolen in the pantry or the hall, during games of hide-and-seek that amused us all. We staged Shakespeare readings, but only comedies this year, me as Malvolio in crossed garters or as poor Bottom wooing in a donkey's head improvised from a brown sweater and a wool cap with socks attached for ears.

At last it was the first sweet day in spring, and she rode over to meet me at the rock. After a hungry hour of kisses, she seemed to read my mind.

"Tell me," she asked, "do you know a freedman named Tim? I saw him riding with your father once. At least I think it was your father. He was a tall, stern-looking man with your eyes, skinny, like Ichabod Crane. He had a rifle with him, and so did Tim."

I had to confess. "My father took them in, and I never thought to ask him where they came from. He helped a lot of Negroes, most of them from farther south. But Tim told me lately that they used to live with you."

She stared at me. "You really didn't know they were ours? I grew up with Tim. His mother was wet nurse to all of us when we were babies. They're like members of my family."

I nodded, wondering if she knew how true that might be. "Did his sister live with you as well? She has a little baby now."

She gasped and sat up, alert. "A baby? No. That can't be." She held stock-still a moment. "Have you seen it? What does it look like?"

Something about this question worried me. "Oh, well, you know, all babies look alike."

"Did it have light skin?" she asked impatiently. "Lighter than Sophie's?"

"Is that his sister's name? I couldn't say. It's just a little mite. I didn't get a good look."

"Tell me what you saw. A general impression is enough. Call the baby up to mind and tell me if its skin looked brown, or beige, or more on the rosy side?"

She seemed to have a theory, and I wondered if it was too late to keep her innocence.

"Well, I could be wrong, but it did look somewhat rosy."

She was excited now. "I knew it! It's so strange. You know Creolia, Tim's mother? I saw *her* mother once, and she was really black. But Creolia is only brown, and Tim and Sophie are just tan, and now it sounds like this baby is lighter still. What do you think, could it be evolution, from living here, in a colder climate? I mean, northern Europeans are the lightest skinned, and Spaniards and Italians are darker, with the darkest people farther south, in Africa."

I was trying not to laugh at her, something I never wanted to do.

But she smacked my shoulder anyway. "What? What are you laughing at?"

"I'm not laughing. You're adorable." I pressed her chin between my thumb and forefinger. "I want you to stay the way you are. The world could use more innocence."

I had another reason for not telling her—I didn't want her stirring up a hornet's nest at home. And if anyone was likely to do that, it was my fearless Martha Jane.

Now she was offended and pulled away from me, sitting by herself. "What is so innocent? I bet you can see it, too, in other Negro families. They start to look more like us over time."

I tried tickling her, holding her down, and tonguing her ear, which made her laugh and squirm, but she would not give up. When I put my tongue in her mouth, she bit it.

"Ouch!" I said and pulled back. "That's a nightmare, that is. If that shows up in my dreams, it will be your fault."

"Serves you right for making fun of me."

I stuck my tongue out and tried to look at it. "Is it bleeding?"

"Not yet," she said and bared her teeth in a growl.

I leaned back against the rock. "Come back here and behave yourself."

"Not until you tell me."

I sighed. "All right, but don't blame me if you don't like it. If your idea was right, people who changed continents would also change color over time. But that only happens from one generation to the next, and it works because children inherit traits from both parents. If each generation gets lighter, it's because of white blood mixing in. White fathers, in this case. There, are you happy to know that?"

"What a disgusting idea!" she cried, leaping to her feet. "How can you think that?"

She walked away across the grass and stood with her arms crossed, glowering. I knew she would have to huff awhile, to save herself from understanding that Creolia's children might be half siblings to her and Richard, the new baby nearer still. I let her take her time.

After a while she came back but would not sit. She asked where Tim and his family lived, and I pointed to the woods. Then she left, not kissing me goodbye.

SHE SOON FORGAVE ME, and we met as often as before, in the sheep meadow or woods every chance we got. As the spring heat beat up, I felt her resolve slip and recklessness move in to take its place, and though I liked to think that I would let her plunge all by herself, I was not in charge of everything I did. Something in me knew it was not wrong for us to be together naturally, and it would be soon.

One Sunday morning when no circuit preachers were scheduled close to us, I drove my mother and sisters to Bethel Church, all of us still dressed in starkest black mourning, though I was happy at the thought of seeing Martha there. I found a spot beside the graveyard for the wagon, hitched the horse to a post, and was just helping my mother down when a big, open landau pulled up out front, filled with ladies in gay frocks and wide, almost translucent hats, all in shades of the palest yellow and cream. A black groom in dove-gray livery drove a pair of beautifully matched chestnuts with braided manes, and a second black groom in the same attire clung to the landau's running board in back.

It was the sort of picture no one in these parts had seen since before the war, and I gazed at them awhile before I noticed Richard Cairnes beside the carriage on his horse. My eyes flew to the ladies then—yes, amazingly, one of them was Martha Jane, in a spring dress I had not seen before. Beside her was a young, fair-haired man in a gray coat—Rebel gray, it looked to me. She appeared to be laughing at something he had said, and I took exception to that fact.

My mother touched my arm. "We'll leave you to this, dear. Don't be long. It's time."

My sisters took her arms to escort her inside, and I stood in plain sight of the carriage, determined to remain till my intended noticed me. The groom who had been riding on the back opened the carriage door and bodily lifted the young man down. Now I could see that his legs were gone, his trousers sewn closed, and it came back to me: the boy she had been taking to a neighbor's in her pony cart the day that Lincoln died. He would be two years older now but still a boy. And yet somehow he gave off an air of command despite his youth and lack of legs, lost no doubt when he was also wearing gray or butternut. The servant held him unobtrusively and seemed trained to turn him so that he faced wherever his eyes looked, and it was Martha he was looking at, gazing up to where she still sat as Richard helped the other ladies down. Why had I not grilled her more about that day she drove him in the cart? There clearly was a story there, and it was not entirely in the past.

The three other ladies rushed to where the legless boy hung suspended aboveground, brushed him off, and arranged his yellow hair behind his ears. He seemed to suffer them in a good-natured way, his eyes on Martha all the while.

"Darling girl!" he called in a soft drawl, every syllable prolonged. "Won't you come rescue me from all these fussing women?"

Martha flushed rosy pink, her big eyes shining as she shrugged off Richard's hand and stepped down by herself. But as soon as her foot touched ground, she noticed me, flushed darker red, and froze. Abruptly she started toward me, but her mother caught her arm.

"Why, where are your manners, honey?" Mrs. Cairnes said in an accent worthy of Louisiana, though I had not heard her speak that way before. "You don't want to leave poor Mr. Bailey by himself, now, do you, dear? Here, take his arm. We're late enough, I'm sure."

She took Martha's hand and planted it on the boy's sleeve. Richard took up a place behind as if to shoo her into the church, casting me one slow, scornful glance, and in a moment they had all swept past, her mother's eyes proud, victorious. Martha looked at me helplessly, her eyes red, and shook her head as if to say that nothing was as it seemed. I nodded with my eyes before she disappeared, trying to look calmer than I felt.

We had no chance to speak after the service, both of us embedded in our families. But that afternoon after dinner, I dismissed Tim and watched the flock alone, reading the same paragraph of Fenimore Cooper over and over, my mind refusing to take it in.

After a while hooves thudded so hard on the woods trail, I heard them well before a yellow horse came at the gallop, its rider sitting sidesaddle in bright blue. The gate into the sheep meadow was shut, but she did not get down to open it, just stared at it as if willing it to open by itself, her mare prancing impatiently. Throwing an exasperated look my way, she circled her horse to pick up speed and galloped toward the gate. The mare looked startled but jumped well and cleared it easily, and they galloped all the way to me, both sheepdogs charging up as if to herd them back out toward the gate.

"Well," I said, laughing. They had arrived so fast, I still lay reclined along the grass over the book. From this angle the mare looked several stories tall.

Martha leapt to the ground, already talking at a frantic pace.

"It was a plot by our unspeakable mothers. It's as if they don't believe I am betrothed. My mother invited Mr. Bailey and his mother and sisters to come visit, and they drove up all the way from Virginia so that he could propose to me. It seems he has land down there and a sawmill and I don't know what all. I tell him every day I am not free, and he just looks patient and goes on about how prosperous he is. He's rebuilding the big house and says he will do it exactly as I choose. My mother says I am a fool."

This started a slow burn around my heart, but I reached for her hand and pulled her down. "Perhaps you should accept. Far be it from me to stand between you and your own sawmill."

She gave a disgusted gasp and sat aloof from me. "Don't you start, too! What do you mean, saying that? Here I've told Mr. Bailey I can't give him hope. I told him I'm as good as married already, and you should have seen the shade of white he turned, as if he thought you had ruined me. He got that look, you know, like Henry Kyd Douglas, transfixed with hate? Ready to murder every Federal and desecrate his body afterwards. He said I was practically his sister, and if you had dishonored me, it dishonored him as well. He got all puffed up and said, 'This has to be addressed.'"

She dropped her voice to imitate him, though I doubted his voice was very deep. Then she stopped and stared at me as if afraid to go on.

"I haven't told you this, but I nursed him back to health. Richard brought him home and we hid him in the attic for months. Him and two others, but the others died and we buried them in a back pasture. There, now, go ahead, arrest me for aid and comfort to the enemy."

I pressed one finger to her lips to make her stop. "Hush. Of course you nursed him. I might have, too, if he had shown up half-dead in my home. And no wonder he loves you. You saved his life."

She gave me a look of wonder and started to cry. "All this time I thought you might not marry me if you knew."

I sat up to put my eyes level with hers and tucked stray hairs behind her ears. "What else have you not told me?"

She flushed and blinked hard to clear her eyes so that she could stare at me earnestly. "Absolutely nothing else. That was my one secret."

"Then the sooner you send Mr. Bailey packing, the better. That is, if you are sure you want to live in a small house with five other women and no servants at all. Or maybe I could get myself a suit of livery."

At that she flashed a watery grin, pushed me back down to the grass, and kissed me so hard it almost knocked me out, right there in the open meadow where anyone might see.

In June my mother, aunt, and sisters wanted to attend a three-day Methodist camp meeting twenty-five miles away. It would be held where the Gunpowder and Bush rivers converged at the Chesapeake, and I would have to go to protect them. Methodists let Negroes worship alongside whites, and every Segregationist group in the nearest five counties was expressing hostility to the idea of an overnight meeting, both races in one camp. I groaned at the thought of going, having spent interminable hours at tent revivals in my youth.

"Nothing but hymns warbled," I told Martha in the meadow. "And then there are the ones who have to shout in tongues, and other forms of mild insanity. I may die of stupefaction."

"Then maybe I'll go, too," she said, lilting and light, as if she knew the thrill that would shoot into my veins. "I could use a change of scene."

The way she said it made it sound like code for something far more sensual—three days, three nights!—and I cheered up at once. "That would certainly put a different face on the experience. But will your mother let you go?"

She grinned. "I'll say I feel the need to renew my faith. I have a Methodist aunt who is very devout. She's probably going. I'll see if I can go with her."

A few days later it was arranged that she would ride with her aunt and stay in her aunt's tent, and now I could hardly wait. As the women in my household washed, ironed, and packed their summer clothes, I pitched in with rare zeal, loaded the tents, cots, parasols, foodstuffs, dishes, and pots into my one wagon. My brothers would drive the women in their buggies, and I would follow like the humble supply wagon at the end of a brigade.

The day was hot when we set off and hotter still when we reached the high road of the long, narrow peninsula, where green meadows sloped down to broad rivers on either side, a white farmhouse each few miles. We joined a throng of buggies and wagons inching toward the encampment, which had been spread on the last slope, facing the Chesapeake, a wide meadow flanked by woods, white sails on the water gliding calm beyond. Many had arrived before us, and hundreds of tents with peaked roofs gleamed white in the sun, exactly like an army camp, except for the ladies in hoopskirts meeting and embracing here and there as tent walls rippled around them in the light salt breeze.

I did not find Martha and her aunt till evening, inside the main worship tent, two hundred people singing hymns while a foot-pedal organ pumped the melody. In front knelt an ecstatic throng, white as well as black, blond heads bending next to brown. Martha and her aunt sat on a rug some ways back in the crowd, and they slid over for me. Close to Martha, I sat and secretly stroked the fine skin inside one of her wrists. The sun began to set, turning the air gold, then pink, then blue. The wheezy organ launched into the melody for "Abide with me, fast falls the eventide."

In the silence of the benediction, I leaned near Martha's ear and whispered, "Abide with me tonight when the others are asleep. I'll wait for you at the pine grove above the tents."

She looked at me and nodded with shining eyes, her cheeks pink, and with electric limbs I helped to set up tables for the picnic supper, carried plates of cold ham and biscuits, cheese and pickles, then scurried off to wash the dishes in the creek. Twenty ministers were present, and one of them stood on a chair to offer up a meditation on the parable of the loaves and fishes. In the deep dark, children dashed around the grass catching fireflies in jars.

Soon the children were put to bed in tents, the benedictions said by candlelight, and the campfires banked. I went to the creek to splash myself with cold water, not for the usual reason, but to make myself presentable in nothing but my skin. Dressed in a loose shirt and clean breeches, I walked up the hill. The line of pines stood halfway up, and I found them by smell.

After a while all light had been extinguished, no sound but the soughing of the pines and frog song from the creek. The air was warm, a veil of mist across the stars, but I could see and hear acutely, even as my heart raced at twice its normal speed.

I saw her before she saw me, the glimmer of her pale wrists and face as she climbed blindly, almost passing me. Her head snapped up, aware of me, and she stepped to my side.

"I couldn't find you in the dark," she cried breathlessly.

"You weren't seeing much. I could have had your scalp." I reached for her and felt rich silk all over her, a sort of robe. "Good God, what is this marvelous garment?"

"Do you like it? It's my best treasure, a kimono from Japan. My aunt in Baltimore gave it to me. She had it from a sea captain."

I felt silk threads lavishly embroidered on the back and the wide sleeves that hung down. "What's embroidered on it? I wish I could see!"

"I'm sure you will someday. It's dark blue, with white cranes flying across the back and red chrysanthemums on the sleeves. And feel this, it has frog closures."

I set to work industriously to undo one. But I felt a cool stab of misgiving and paused.

"You do know, don't you, that I'm a miserable wretch? I'm poor and my house is overrun with women who will probably never leave, and they may not be nice to you. I am no bargain. You should turn around and go back to your aunt's tent." A giddy impulse to laugh took hold of me. "Your aunt's unsullied tent. Her immaculate tent. Her *pristine*—"

She gently put a hand over my mouth. "Don't talk of misery on a night like this. My aunt's amaranthine tent can wait. She's in there snoring. She won't miss me."

Subtle as an eel she slipped away and ran lightly uphill on the rough grass. I gave chase, both of us laughing, out of breath. In a minute we had reached the top, and below us the two rivers met the bay, glimmering in the black. The air moved big and sweet with hints of grassland meeting salt, seaweed brushing trout.

"You. How can you drive me mad, when you know you should throw me over for a fellow in a better condition? Be careful, I may kiss you half to death."

For answer she pressed against me, unbuttoned my shirt, and stroked my chest hair. "Is this gray? I bet you were a smoother fellow when we started. We've had to wait too long."

She kissed me hard as if to make sure I agreed, and soon we lay on the cool grass. Parts of me wanted to stampede at her immediately. It hurt physically to pull back onto my knees.

"Wait. Surely there are things I need to say. I don't know when we'll be able to marry. And you may never have a house of your own. I wanted to build you one, but it's impossible, even if I use my own wood. There's brick and pipe and sinks and furniture. Ah, I'm so miserable. You may be very sorry if you give yourself to me."

She got up onto her knees, too, and I saw her brave chin lift, pale against the black.

"It seems to me we're already married. I couldn't give myself to anyone but you."

My arms went around her tight. "Do you know it burns me every night you aren't with me? And every time I see you, trying to keep my hands off you."

We knelt like that for long seconds, holding off what would come next.

With a foolish sort of hope, I had brought my grandmother's wedding ring, and now I reached into the pocket of my pants and felt the thin gold loop, worn finer on one side.

"I thought to give you this sometime. It was my grandmother's, like the opal. It's gold with an old floral design. I wish I could give you so much more. But will you have it for a wedding ring?"

She slid the opal off her ring finger. "Put it on me."

It slipped on easily, too big, threatening to fly off. But she put the opal back on to guard it and closed her fist to keep both of them on.

"Then I am satisfied," she said and opened up her arms.

I TRIED TO INTRODUCE HER gently to the mysteries, though she insisted on the full experience, not once but several times, claiming the pain diminished as the night went on. We did not sleep, or if we did, I did not notice it.

But the night could not go on forever, and when black sky began to fray along the eastern shore, replaced with faint rose, I helped her close the silken robe.

"You'd better get down there and mess up your cot," I said and chuckled in her ear. "I want to see you scrubbed and shining in the preaching tent."

"And you as well." She stretched leisurely as a cat. "Is this how married women always feel? I'm so limber, I feel like a newborn infant. It feels like my bones can bend. Let's never go home. Houses are just cages. Let's never go inside again."

I kissed her for that but was afraid to linger. The landscape was becoming visible, all of it still in shades of gray. "I'll go down first, and you come by and by, another way. If anyone asks, say you went for a walk. It's true enough."

We grinned at each other and kept our hands joined till the pine grove, where I set off fast downhill through dewy grass, glancing back once to make sure she could not be seen. I strolled down a ravine of laurels, paused to wash myself in the creek.

Still bare-chested, in bare feet, letting myself dry in the air, I climbed the creek bank to where I could see the rope fence with fifty horses penned together, starting to play and joust with each other, and below them a flock of tents. A young black woman stepped out of one in a dark dress and neckerchief and lifted her face to watch the dawn.

I felt a rumble in the ground and, startled, turned in dread. A horse and rider raced full tilt downhill, a bandana over the man's face, past the horse pen, toward the tents. Twenty others followed, hooves thundering as they keened the Rebel yell.

"*Hoooooooooooah-hooooooooooooool!*"

They plowed into the tents, lashing with whips, trampling and crushing all they could, and people burst out of them and sprinted for the woods along both sides. A young minister was on his knees praying outside the preaching tent—gunshots cracked the air, and he slumped on his side. The girl in the dark dress ran stumbling, pursued by a man on horseback who lashed her with a bullwhip, tearing away her neckerchief on the first strike.

I chased the man barefoot and grabbed his bullwhip. He had the advantage on his horse and flicked it away from me, but I grabbed his leg and tried to pull him off.

The light came up a notch, and colors returned all at once, grass green, the man's bandana butternut and slipping off his face. He was no one I knew, and when he lifted the whip to lash me, I dropped to the ground and rolled fast to get away.

Within a minute the whole posse thundered back uphill and vanished. A few men scrambled bareback onto horses to pursue them, while others knelt beside the fallen minister, who did not move. Someone went to fetch a doctor, though it was fairly clear he would not come in time. Others wandered dazed around the camp, weeping, looking for their families, or rushed exclaiming into the big tent, where women set anxiously to work tending wounds.

When the young minister was pronounced dead, the remaining clergymen conferred.

"God is with us. We will meet again," a gray-haired minister announced. "But on this sad day we must take our women and our children home for safety's sake."

I managed to find Martha packing her aunt's things. She was in tears over the minister but said she was all right, and I told her I was, too.

Quietly I asked, "You know that old orchard where you and I first walked, years ago, with your cousins, in the woods? See if you can meet me there, Wednesday at three o'clock."

She looked relieved to know a time when we would meet again.

"All right," she said in a whisper that made my hair stand up.

How could I want her again so soon, after a night like that and so much violence in the morning? But I did. I could hardly think of anything else. I felt like a danger to myself, and as if I could bring a block of wood to life if I put my hands on it. But I set to work to help my mother pack and take her home.

The raid on the camp meeting was condemned by editors and senators, especially those who once had Rebel sympathies, wanting now to seem upright, law-abiding, never implicated in such violent activities. The governor attended the funeral of the young minister and vowed to bring the guilty to justice, though no arrests were made.

All that summer Martha rode to meet me in the orchard, our happiness far better than I thought was possible. Old stone walls of what had been a house still stood there, floors and roof long gone, and we lay in a grassy corner, out of sight if anyone came by. It took some doing, but I convinced her to be unafraid and naked on my army blanket, watched by the blue sky. I explained the ways we could prevent a child, some of which she had heard of but did not understand. She liked to run her tongue tip down my side, along the inside of my arm, any hairless skin that she could find, giving me chills, until I shuddered and recaptured her tongue.

Far too soon the apple blossoms that had showered down on us gave way to hard, green nubs of fruit that swelled day by day and tinged slowly red. Full, sweet, and ripe, bored into by worms, they began to fall. Sunlight glowed with a declining slant that only made it look richer, and we lay together in a winey smell of rotting apples, swarmed over by dying bees.

On one of the last afternoons when it was warm enough to graze the sheep outside, Tim took them to the meadow while I groomed Honest Abe, who still looked for my father every time the barn door opened, crestfallen when it was only me. I put a saddle on him and took him out for a good gallop on the roads, then brought him back and groomed him again. When I had done the same with Captain Jack, I gave them each a bucket of oats with molasses for a treat.

After dinner in the house, the afternoon promised cold sun for a few hours, no smell of snow as yet, and I walked out to the sheep meadow to take over and send Tim home. Cutting through the woods, I heard the pleasant sound of him signaling the dogs to turn the flock back toward the rock, his whistle sharp and true as a train's but far more musical.

As I left the trees, I was surprised to see that he was not alone but sitting with a woman on top of the big rock, both of them so engrossed in whatever they were saying, they did not notice me. Not far from the flock, the yellow mare grazed by herself, and when I saw that, something hot flashed in my chest. We had made no plans to meet today, but here she was. Was it Tim she came to see?

I almost turned and left them alone, when I saw him swing down the steep side of the rock, drop to the ground, and give me a salute before he set off toward the cabin, not waiting to greet me or see what I would say, and I wondered what that meant.

Now Martha was coming down, and I watched as she hastily grabbed fingerholds in the rock wall and set herself down on the grass with ease, as if she had practiced that far more often than I knew. Briskly she walked toward me.

"I—I came to look for you," she called, stammering. "And he was wearing your old hat. From a distance I thought it was you."

I wondered why she felt the need to explain so much. Only a few feet away from me, she looked very pretty, cheeks pink (flushed from what?), eyes wet (moved by what?). Her hair shone clean, and I wanted to believe her, that it was for me she had prepared herself.

She stepped close and kissed my face. "You're so quiet, dear. Are you all right?"

My hands moved by themselves, one to her head, one to her waist, to cradle her and rock her gently back and forth. With great clarity I realized that this person was precious to me. Her independence and her bravery were things I loved, and did I want to clip her wings? My grandfather would have. He forbade my grandmother to speak unless she was spoken to, and she seldom left the house except for church, accompanied by him.

Of course I didn't want that. But for the first time I felt a shadow underneath my happiness, producing a chill. We stayed that way a long while, listening to the last songs of crickets in the woods.

FOR THE FALL ELECTION Rebels were allowed to vote, but not Negroes, and when the votes were tallied, you could almost hear the damn Rebel yell reverberating through the countryside. Newspaper headlines broke the happy news:

Counter-Revolution! Victory for Law and Right!

Former Rebels had been put in office all over Maryland, and a new state constitution that included the return of the Black Codes had been approved by a vote of two to one. In the early, heady days, some pundits called on Negroes to choose masters and return to slavery, and "State Rights" flyers were tacked to fence posts and the sides of dry-goods stores. Our local paper, the *Aegis*, published in the county seat, Bel Air, adopted a "States Rights" header with a drawing of Justice as a buxom woman in a blindfold holding up the scales.

I started to carry a pistol everywhere I went, and I tried to give Tim one, too, one day when he was out watching the flock. He was holding a black border collie puppy I had given him from a litter produced by my sheepdogs, the pup chewing on his knuckles happily. Under the Black Codes, Negroes were not allowed to own guns or keep dogs, on the assumption they would use them to poach on someone's land, and that was reason enough for me to give him both. I knew he had used my father's rifles but did not have one of his own.

But when I held the gun, butt out, toward him, he did not take it. His eyes on the sheep, he said, "Trouble with guns? If you got one, you might could have to shoot someone."

"Better that than what someone might do to you."

He looked off, petting the pup. "Reckon they gone do that more, if I got a gun."

He might have been right, and I let the subject drop. But I took to riding by his cabin several times a day, to make sure all was well.

A few weeks later, after the first snow, sheep growing curly coats of wool, he did not report for work, and I rode out to the cabin to see what was up. When I reached it, I saw horse tracks in the snow, coming from the other direction, from the hilltop down into the glade, and they worried me.

His mother opened the door and glared, not answering when I asked for him. I took a step closer and tried to peer in, but it was too dark inside.

"Is everything all right? Is Tim all right?"

Without the smallest sign of invitation, Creolia walked into the house, and I followed her. The main room was windowless and smoky from the hearth, but at the cabin's back we had built a room with a large, unglazed window, and the shutter was thrown open now, despite the cold. Tim lay on a low bed under it, looking gaunt, a bandage on his head that was black with dried blood. His lips were cut and bruised, one eye swollen shut, his arched nose smashed.

I walked quickly to his bedside. "Good Lord. What happened to you?"

His one good eye threw me a fearful glance, and his mother answered with scorn.

"You don't know beating when you see it? Like this, with a damn fence post." She swung her hands in the air over him to demonstrate.

Tim moved his lips and winced—they were too hurt to use.

"Who was it?" I demanded.

But not even Creolia would answer me this time, not trusting me to keep it to myself, when saying who it was might only earn him worse.

I glanced around. The window shutter looked too flimsy to keep out anyone who wanted to get in. On the bed beside him lay a book, open to an illustration of a knight in armor on a horse. But there was little else of cheer around the place. In the kitchen I saw nothing but an empty cornmeal sack carefully washed and folded on a rack to be a towel.

"I'll be back in a while," I said. "I'll get the doctor and a clean bandage."

"Don't need no doctor," Tim struggled to say.

"Don't need nothing," Creolia said quite clearly.

I rode straight to Jarrettsville and talked to Martin Jarrett, who was not the doctor I could have wished for, but he was the closest. He said he would try to find the place, though his face told me he would not.

The next day, when I took out all the food my mother could spare, a little ham and cornmeal, and a roll of bandages, I asked Tim if Jarrett had been there, and he said, "No, sir."

Yet his head was clean and bandaged with a long strip of pale blue cloth I thought I had seen before, embroidered with dark blue moths. And on the hearth a pot of stew was steaming, smelling of beef and potatoes, though nothing of that sort had been there the day before.

I TOLD TIM TO REST till he was well, and I did not ask Martha if she had been to the cabin, hoping she would tell me so herself. We had fewer chores in winter, and I could do them all myself, now that wind rattled the windows and the ground was frozen hard, too cold to lie on even with a blanket underneath. Martha and I sometimes met at my brother's place for supper and charades and longing looks, a few furtive squeezes in the hall when no one was watching us. But she said nothing about helping Tim, and I was puzzled, not sure what I should think.

So my afternoons were free to fix things that had needed it for months. I liked working by myself, alone with my thoughts. My father had rigged a suction pump to send springwater through a pipe into the kitchen, and the pump got clogged with pebbles and dirt and needed to be cleaned out every few months. I took it apart, honed the pieces that had been worn down, oiled it, and hooked it back up, then packed around the pipes with straw to insulate them from the cold.

One day when I was in the barn, mending tack, a man rode up my lane through the snow. He was all in black with a black hat, his face hidden in a gray scarf that flapped behind him in the wind, and his horse was a large dark bay, not one I had seen before. I watched him through the window of the barn, then pulled my gloves back on and walked out to where he sat on the horse, as if expecting a footman to come help him down.

I looked up at him inquiringly. "Are you lost, sir?"

He unwrapped the scarf from around his face. He was no one I knew, but I had seen him somewhere, a big man in middle age, with sandy hair showing under his hat brim. He regarded me a while as if taking my measure before he spoke.

"Mr. McComas, Nick McComas, am I right? And you are betrothed to a lady by the name of Martha Jane Cairnes, am I correct?"

I told him that he was, and his mouth closed in a straight line.

"Then I hate to be the bearer of bad news, but you have the right to know. There's a Negro with a cabin near here, works for you, I think? Yes. Well, your lady has been seen riding there more than once, when he was alone, his mother and sister away from the place, and she stays a good while. Yesterday I saw her go in, and I waited for her an hour, and then followed her to make sure I had the right woman. She stopped to speak to me and uncovered her face. It was her all right."

I felt the blood drain from my lips. "Who are you, sir? I demand to know your name and what business you think that is of yours."

He waved that away. "Consider me a friend, looking out for your interests."

"I'll thank you not to do that in the future. If you must know, that man was a member of Miss Cairnes's household, and someone beat him savagely about two weeks ago. I imagine she was there to help him. Tell me, have you beaten any Negroes with a fence post lately?"

For answer he smiled grimly, wrapped the scarf around his face, and wheeled his horse.

"Never set foot on my land again!" I shouted, running after him with all the menace of a chipmunk chattering to chase away a wolf.

I LOATHED THE MAN who had told me that, and I knew I should shake it off, but I could not. It began to eat at me. I knew it was a mistake to test her, but I could not stop myself. Every time we met, at my brother's house or at church or on a few happy evenings in a frozen barn, I brought up Tim, giving her an opportunity to tell me easily. But she did not.

Snow fell hard that winter, and I used it as an excuse to meet less often than before, while I tried to decide what her silence meant. She knew something was wrong but not what it was, and sometimes she looked at me fearfully, her face winter pale. In the harsh glare of snow-reflected light, I could see that she had begun to age, fine lines beneath her eyes.

Out of petulance, wanting to punish her, I said no more about the wedding date. At night sometimes I would wake up in a sweat and wonder if I knew anything about her. Had she really been a virgin that night on the hill above church camp? She had been eager, not reticent, and gave little evidence of pain. What if she had lain with Tim when they were growing up, out in her barn? She had admitted once to kissing him, and I knew it was rare for anyone to tell the whole truth to a new lover. I certainly had not told her everything, and she would have had more reason to keep it to herself if she were unchaste. Most people overlooked a man who fell from grace, and they might even chuckle at it. But disgrace fell on ladies for much less, and for that reason I could not trust what she was willing to say.

One gloomy night, trying to shake off thoughts like that, I stopped in at Smithson's place to drink a pint, and he looked at me in a puzzled way as he set a glass of ale in front of me.

"What?" I said and scrutinized him back.

He wiped his hands on a towel and regarded me with his brows pulled down. "You're a famous man these days. Did you know that?"

I took a drink and smiled in anticipation of the joke. "That can't be good news. Fools' names and fools' faces, often seen in public places, as my mother likes to say."

But he did not smile back. "It's worse than that, man. I'm serious. You haven't heard the word about yourself? What Richard Cairnes is saying about you?"

Ordinarily I would have laughed, and it was galling that I had to care now what sort of impudence might be produced by my future brother-in-law. "I don't think I want to know."

He nodded. "You don't. But you better, for your own sake. Tell me first, is there anything you may have done, say, in regard to the Negroes living on your place?"

I thought he was implying that I was the one who beat Tim, and it made me angry. "Nothing but good, I'll tell you that. But go ahead and tell me if you think you must."

My voice was too loud, and he glanced toward the other men around the bar. Richard was not there, but his farm was right next door, and some of them were no doubt his associates.

Smithson wiped the bar and leaned toward me, speaking low, for my ears alone. "He says you've got a child by the little girl, the one that was his slave. He says that's why you moved them there, so you could have your way with her."

A white flash blinded me, and I set the pint down so hard half of it sloshed out. "That's a damn lie. I'll tell you who the father is. It's him. She was already with child when they came to us. What is she, fifteen? Any man who did that is despicable."

Smithson's face went bland and neutral, his voice even lower, as if to set an example and make me lower mine. "I wouldn't know, never seen her. But it does look bad. The child was born on your property, and that makes people think you're responsible. There you are, still young enough and no wife. Why wouldn't they think that? I've heard it said every night this week, by all sorts of men. Some say the Rifles and Dragoons may take it up officially."

I had to laugh. "Officially? What sort of office do they have? Don't let them get to you, man. You're talking about a gang of ruffians and traitors. I'm not afraid of them."

His face closed, and he took another swift glance at the other men. His voice got very low. "I've told you what I heard. You know they're full of beans again, like the old days. They come in and howl about the Honor Code, like they think they won the goddamn war. And as far as I can tell, they did, at least around here. So, word to the wise. The girl was Richard's slave. So it doesn't matter what the truth is. You better look out for yourself, that's all."

I ignored what Smithson said and moved around as freely as before, though I stewed more than seemed sensible. Something had curdled in me, and I made excuses not to meet Martha. Was it

possible for a woman to be truly different from her brother? He
had found a way to get at me, with his foul tongue. Martha had a
tongue on her, too, and you never knew who someone was until
you lived with them. If she had even a particle of Richard in her,
that would be too much. Surely she could not be entirely free of his
views. They had the same parents, the same upbringing, the same
influences, and she still lived in his house, under his puny sway, sat
at his dinner table, washed his clothes. What if she turned into him,
like a cuckoo in my nest, crowding out my rightful family? Could
I take the chance that my children would resemble him? She might
be hiding who she was, to capture me.

But why would she do that? She knew that I was poor and
not approved of by her family. She had no motive to fool me, except love, and love was what I wanted. Should I have married her
straight off, when I first wanted to? Should I marry her now and
put an end to the talk? I knew that she loved me, and I could not
give her up. My senses required her now, if nothing else.

But all through Christmas and into the New Year, I stewed,
unable to act.

ONE FRIGID NIGHT in deep winter, I dreamt that the barn was on
fire, and I could not run to save Abe and Jack while they screamed
in pain and terror. I woke up horrified and pulled on my boots and
ran up in the snow to make sure it wasn't true.

The barn stood intact, and when I went inside and held the
lantern up, both horses lay sleeping in their straw, curled up like
cats for warmth. I gave them each a pat, stepped outside again, and
caught a whiff of char, most likely from a neighbor's hearth. For

good measure, I checked the hearths in our house, both properly banked down, giving only a small glow, and I went back to bed.

But in the morning, outside in the snow, the smell was stronger, and I followed it in dread. At the sheepfold, all seemed well, and I could see nothing out of place across snow-covered fields into the woods. But I saddled Jack and rode him out to look for the source.

At the far end of the sheep meadow, the gate should have been closed, but it was open, horse tracks trampling snow. To get to Tim's clearing quickly, I cut through the woods, where the smell was overpowering, with a menacing, low scent of death beneath the char.

I almost didn't notice something hanging from a tree—two trees. Startled, I stopped to stare. A white chicken had been strung up by its yellow claws, its belly slit and bloody entrails tied around its feathered neck. A headless rabbit dripped gore, its head stuck on a stick plunged in the ground. And there were more, all through the woods—chickens and rabbits quivering on sticks or twisting on strings. The last one I refused to see. It could not be a black puppy with soft ears and a long tail.

"Go on, go on," I said to Jack, digging in my heels.

But he had seen them, too, and bolted from the woods into the clearing, where piles of charred logs smoldered. Tim stood where his porch had been, picking through black rubble. He looked thin and hunched, far older than he was, his body no more than bones inside his patched jacket. His face had healed flatter on one side and scarred from the fence-post beating, his nose smashed, lips permanently split, and one eye half-closed. He did not look at me as I rode close.

"Tim, dear God. Who did this?"

He seemed deaf, like a man in whose field of vision you had to stand before he knew you were there. His mouth slack, he pulled a burnt beam from the pile and dropped it back again. He shoved another with his foot.

I didn't see her coming, but Creolia rushed at me from somewhere, her face swollen and a tin ladle raised in one hand. "Go on!" she shouted as if to scare a snake. "Go on! Go on!"

Lashing the ladle, she whacked my knee.

With sudden energy Tim strode to her, twisted the spoon away, and glared at me. "You heard her now. Don't none of us need messing round here. Y'all go on."

For a moment I thought it must be a mistake. They must not have recognized me. They must have thought I was one of the men who did it, come back for more.

"Tim, it's me, Nick. Are you all right?" I realized that I had not seen Sophie. "Where's your sister and her baby? Are they all right?"

Tim seethed up at me, split lips peeled back to show his teeth, and did not speak.

I tried again. "Listen. You're not safe here. Bring your family and come to the house, I beg you to. Come today. We'll make room for you."

He glared at me and his voice shook. "Not no white man's house, no sir. Not ever again."

Creolia dashed at me and struck Jack with her bare hands. The horse whirled in fear, and I went with him as he galloped away.

THAT EVENING WHEN I went out to try to bring them to the house again, they were gone.

I took it harder than I would have thought, blind, ferocious rage making me shake. I wanted to kill the men who beat Tim and burned his house. For what, because he had a dog? Because he read a book? Because some villain said my Martha lay with him? I wanted to kill every man who thought such a thing.

Of course I would not kill anyone. I was my father's son, and I had to honor him. But at what point did you stop turning the other cheek? Even Jesus said, "I came not to bring peace but a sword." I had to do something. I didn't care if it was dangerous. No, dangerous was better. Dangerous was what I meant to be.

A few days later the papers announced a meeting in Bel Air to discuss the next move of the state's Republicans, how to counter the results of the new Rebel government. I knew the Rebels would turn up, too, so many that I would be badly outnumbered, and that was fine. It was the kind of frigid winter night when nothing seemed to move, no moon to light the snow, when I rode there in the dark and waited for my turn onstage.

The others did not address the stated question for long. Instead they stood up to accuse their fellow Republicans of "unnumbered crimes." They pointed fingers at each other for the shambles the party had become, Radicals blaming Conservatives and vice versa, each side shouting that the other had thrown away the victories in battle, Radicals by asking for too much, Conservatives for refusing to take what had been won—both sides drowned under the jeers and catcalls of the Democrats, who had come out in force to gloat.

I had no desire to speak in public, and when it was my turn, I stood at the podium, trying to imagine that I was my father, that I stood that tall. The hall was dimly lit by torches, but I could feel a hundred eyes boring into me, most of them with hate, voices already shouting over me.

"My fellow Republicans," I said with irony, wondering how many were still there.

"They've all gone home! Sit down! Give up!" voices howled with glee.

Rage fired my voice. "Why are we so busy calling each other scoundrels? Haven't you noticed we have lost the state? Let's get together to defeat the Democrats next time!"

Shouts of laughter from the hall.

"You know they did it illegally. They stuffed ballot boxes in Baltimore. If you don't believe me, read the *Philadelphia Enquirer*! Read the *New York Times*! The guys who did it bragged about it, and some people who tried to protest got chairs broken over their heads. No one was even arrested. That's what we can look forward to with Swann in Congress and Hamilton in the Senate and Bowie for a governor. I never thought to see the day a man so ignorant would get hold of the state."

The howls of laughter now turned to outrage, rolling toward me like a wave. But I kept on shouting, mad as a rabid squirrel. "Right here in our own neighborhood, hoodlums have burnt cabins of law-abiding freedmen and beaten them almost to death. They have impregnated little black girls and blamed innocent men for it. I can tell you who did that!"

Someone fired a round into the ceiling, and two men actually leapt onstage and took my arms. In short order I was railroaded out a side door into the black night, a crowd sweeping me forward so hard I fell face-first into the snow.

I was astonished at their nerve, and as they yanked me up again, I tried to see their faces, but in the dark they all looked alike, white men, faces blurred. Two men lifted my legs, two took my shoulders, and they all broke into a run, headed for the stables behind the hall. Jack was in there, and if I could break free, I might get away.

But the swarm of men around me was too dense, and a loft door rumbled back. They carried me inside, where it smelled of green hay and warm horse manure, smells I usually found comforting. Someone lit a lantern, making shadows leap up bales stacked on all sides and lighting each face eerily from below. Some of them I recognized from pictures in the newspapers and from Sam Cairnes's funeral, prominent Secessionists involved in every plot to help the CSA.

And now Richard Cairnes stepped from their midst, looking frail and pale surrounded by the sun-cracked faces of the older men. The code had specified a horsewhip, but someone handed him a thick black coil of bullwhip, capable of doing real damage. Hands behind me yanked my shirt and jacket open, popping buttons, peeled them down to expose my back, and held me flat over a bale, a man on each limb, straw stalks poking into my bare skin like a bed of nails.

A sonorous voice pronounced over me, and it sounded like Henry Farnandis.

"For crimes against the Honor Code, you will be punished by the man most aggrieved. Richard Cairnes accuses you of lying with a woman of his household and moving her to your domain, the better to enjoy her illicitly. We have all sat in judgment of this crime and found you guilty. Prepare to take your punishment."

Richard did not have the decency to say a word. But at least his first crack of the whip was tentative and hardly hurt.

"Bring your arm back farther, son," a deep voice said.

"Put your back into it," a gruff one put in. "That's it. Harder, man!"

The baby asp can be more venomous than the adult, I had read, and now the baby asp that held the whip gave it his all, lashing harder with each stroke as if to prove something, his breath a savage pant. When the whip cracked, I could not stop my body from trying to squirm away. After nine or ten such hits, my back was all stripes, and each stroke gored already broken skin. But after twenty hits I could not feel the cuts, only hear the whip. My cheek pressed to prickling straw, I sank until I felt nothing.

I HAVE NO MEMORY of the remainder of that night, though I'm told my brothers came to look for me, took me home, and did the chores around the place. I remember waking up to searing pain and wishing I could sleep again. The ointment my mother made burned deep into the cuts but kept them clean. They did not fester.

But I lay in bed far longer than was necessary, seeing no reason to rise. In a month the scars had healed to broad purple cicatrices, like fat worms across my back.

When I finally got up, I had lost flesh, my clothes hanging on my frame. I had lost more than flesh, but I was not reckoning it up. I was a different man, I knew that much—if I was still a man at all. Where there had been heat and motion in my chest, there was now an icy stone.

I had heard of such things happening to slaves. Maybe Tim had felt this way when he was beaten with a fence post. He had been born in slavery, but later he was free, and the army even let him use a gun, before someone tried to beat him back to slavery. The first slaves would have felt it worse, proud men of Africa chained and beaten until they forgot who they had been. Those men were my brothers now. I understood why some of them preferred to go on in defiance until they were killed or pretended to be broken as they waited for the chance to kill instead.

I was well enough for light work, monitoring ewes at night out in the lambing shelter, waiting for the births, so long as I did not lift anything or make a move that might open the seams in my skin. The litter of border collie pups—all but the one I gave to Tim—were old enough to train, and I would have to teach them if they were to work for me, to respond to whistled signals telling them which way to turn the sheep, to divide the flock, to sort ewes from lambs, or to bunch them up. But I had no energy, and I felt sick to look at them, with the memory of their brother hanging from a tree.

I saw no one outside my family and did not leave the place. I seemed to have become a very old man, prematurely aged. My mother went sometimes to pick up the post and would leave it on my desk, and I saw the envelopes Martha had folded carefully and addressed in her clear hand. They came every day at first, then tapered off. I did not open them. I didn't even pick them up. They stayed where my mother had put them. They seemed not to have anything to do with me, and I was relieved when I realized they were no longer there. My mother must have taken them away.

In my more lucid moments, I expected Martha Jane to sue for breach of promise, and I watched for a summons, though it did not come. I wondered if she knew what her brother had done to me, and if she understood. Sometimes the thought made my back clench and revived a stinging pain. Other times I felt great tenderness for her and wished I could explain.

But it was clear to me that I would have nothing further to do with the kin of G. Richard Cairnes. As frozen, snowy days gave way to weeks and months, I ceased even to be curious about what was happening to her.

MY SISTERS WERE TOO FRAIL to help with lambing, so I got it done myself, sleeping in the shelter, waking at the first bleat, and I lost no ewes or lambs. In exchange for teaching a neighbor the rudiments of working with sheepdogs, I arranged to use his high-sided wagon and draft horse, and one late winter morning I loaded a small flock of lambs inside and set off north toward Lancaster.

The wide Susquehanna had been frozen hard but was now beginning to break up, a rivulet of shining blue-green at its middle, catching in smooth folds on the pilings of the long red covered bridge. A farmer in a black buggy was following a herd of brown Jersey cows as they clambered onto it, moos of protest echoing under the roof, and I waited for them to cross, not wanting to overtax the bridge. When the cows had lumbered off, I let the horse trot across, hoofbeats ringing on the boards.

The air seemed clearer on the Pennsylvania side, the farms more bare of trees, the houses older, built of brick and stone instead of wood. The way to Lancaster was straight and wide with long, slow hills, wagons and buggies thick on it as I drew close, and farms gave way to stone mills and blacksmith shops, tall houses on tree-lined streets. The road led to a square with markets for animals and dry-goods stores, where ox-drawn wagons, manure caked on their wood wheels, rumbled over brick right next to buggies taking home ladies in hoops and hats and gloves.

At the market I sold lambs to several Amish men and marveled at their peaceful demeanors, so different from my neighbors' forty miles south. I wondered if my father had been tempted to move there, though I knew his mission was to stay below the Mason-Dixon Line and be a final outpost for escaping slaves. That work was over now, and before driving back across the Susquehanna, I made inquiries about farms for rent near Lancaster.

I thought of selling off my father's farm to clear his debts. But when I got home and told my brothers of that plan, they said they would assume the debts and keep the place for our mother so she would not have to leave her home. They planned to stock the farm with cows and give our sisters work in the dairy, milking and making cheese for delivery down to Baltimore.

That meant I could take the sheep, and I found a small farm that was right for them, with rocky hillside pastures and a natural spring. I doubted anyone would want to slit rams' throats up there, the neighbors Amish folk who barely spoke English. It seemed easier to breathe up there, and I knew I would not mind living alone in the stone cottage. I would be close to markets for the animals and mills to buy the wool.

Two of my sisters offered to come and keep house for me, hoping to take their searches for husbands to new ground. But I had lived too long surrounded by my female relatives, and I was eager for a change. I found an Irishwoman to clean and cook for only a few days a week and leave me alone to read in peace. In March the snow melted to mud, and my brothers helped me herd the flock to its new home, across the Susquehanna on the covered bridge, escorted by the excited dogs.

Crocuses on my new lawn soon asserted tender petals, but two weeks after I got there, they were smothered in the deepest blizzard of the year. Huge, wet snowflakes flopped from clouds, so thick that they crowded out the air, obscuring sound. Cattle froze in fields, and even churches had to close. I had no proper sheepfold yet, but the dogs helped me to pack the flock into the barn, and we all slept together in there, pooling body warmth. Life seemed to pause, muffled, motionless, and white.

Two days later the sky cleared, and warm sun reflected off the snow. Rivulets trickled sparkling from snowpacks on roofs, and water gurgled under every drift. In the woods the trees stood bare like markers on a thousand graves, but cold sweet air scoured the lungs, and here and there a cardinal sent out its yearning song. I could not help it, the approach of spring made something stir in me that I had not felt in a long while, a rushing in my legs, a desire to leap and run. I felt like a dead tree in which sap starts to flow again.

My brothers wanted to consult with me about the debts, and I told myself that was all I meant to do as I slogged to the barn, my cuffs soaked with melting snow. Saddling Jack, I retraced our route south, across the covered bridge, through snow as sticky as flour paste. Jack could only plod, and yet he seemed exhilarated, too. Sun flashed hot off snow, and soon it felt like June. I had to strip off gloves and jacket and roll up my sleeves to feel the air against my skin.

I did not ride directly to either of my brothers' homes. Not admitting what it meant, I took the route through Forest Hill and along the county road where Martha lived. Did I want to see her, or just to run that risk?

I passed her farm on tenterhooks, but no one appeared. Mildly disappointed, I went on to Smithson's place. He seemed glad to see me, poured me shots of whiskey, and would not let me pay. He asked about the new farm and why I left, and I wondered if he knew about the bullwhipping. Men talked in his pub, and he must have heard something. But he did not let on.

"Needed a change of scene," I said and drank his whiskey, letting it burn my chest. It fed the new sap moving there. Had I been dead all winter? Possibly. Why had I let them beat me down so far? Why had I let *Richard Cairnes* do that to me?

Smithson filled my glass and gazed at me with solemn eyes. "They say you've jilted her." As if I would not know who he could mean, he added, "Jilted Miss Cairnes."

It hurt to hear the phrase. Hell, Smithson was a friend. I ought to tell him that much. "My quarrel is with her brother, not with her. I never loved another woman half so well."

Quarrel, what a limp word! My quarrel was with my hands, because they had not murdered him. My quarrel was with my father, who even from the grave could stop me doing it.

"But not anymore? You don't love her now?"

"No, that's not what I mean." I had not seen her for months, but it struck me that, of course, I did love her.

He looked relieved. "I'm glad. She's a good woman, and I understand she has felt very low about your leaving that way. I hope that's why you're here."

I felt lightness in my heart—was that why I was here? Smithson did resemble Cupid, fair and round, though somewhat oversized. I chuckled at the thought and tossed back several more shots, feeling more alive each time. When I finally went out, blue shadows were already lengthening across the snow in the bare woods.

I let Jack walk back toward her place, savoring the possibility of seeing her. I would never ride onto her brother's farm, and if I met him on the road I might kill him. I was not sure which possibility I favored most, seeing her or killing him. I kept close watch on every side.

But I was still startled when a blue sleigh dashed around a bend toward me, too fast for safety on the melting snow, bells tingling. Its sole occupant wore a tailored riding suit of bright blue velvet, a yellow horse all in a lather between the shafts. In sudden panic, I turned Jack into the woods and trotted between trees too close together for a sleigh.

The shush of runners paused behind me, and I heard a cry. "Nick? Nick!"

I fled farther, to a stand of blue spruce, and hid behind thick needles.

Glancing back, I saw her try to follow in the sleigh, grim and silent, slapping the reins. She almost reached the spruce grove, when with a *thunk* she ran into a tree.

"How dare you?" she shouted with a sort of sob. "How dare you!"

I had reckoned without the way she made me feel just to look at her, even with her face bright red with rage and tears. She looked as helpless and as beautiful as I had ever seen, frailer, as if wasting away, and seeing that gave me a rush of tenderness and shame.

I could not move for long minutes. But Jack became impatient and started from the grove, right toward the mare, until his nose touched hers, and they greeted each other with *harrumphs*. Hampered by the bit, he tried to scratch the mare's neck with his big teeth along her mane, and she lowered her head to make it easier and leaned into it.

With colossal effort I lifted my eyes beyond the horses, to where Martha sat in the sleigh, dumbstruck, staring up at me. With a sinking in my chest like I might faint, I knew it was an error to ride this way.

But I supposed I owed that much to her, and slowly I got down, left the reins on Jack's neck, and walked to the sleigh, parts of me shrinking back with every step.

She reached out both hands—to block me, I thought. But no. She pulled me in the sleigh until I sat beside her on the seat, wrapped her arms around me, and sank her face into my neck. I could not help but smell her hair, her fresh-bread scent, and the whiskey in my blood sprang up. Would it be wrong to gather her up greedily, the way I used to do? She smelled so sweet.

"Sweet," I said, as if I had lost the power of more words, and a sob rose in my chest.

She held me, rocked me, and I felt tears on her cheeks, though they may have been mine. She undid two buttons of my shirt and slid her hand inside and around toward my back, trying to touch the broad, flat scars—I stiffened and pulled away. So she had heard. Well, she could not have that. No one could have that.

"Oh, Nick, where did you go?" she groaned. Her throat caught, and she took hold of my shoulders and shook me, hard, as her voice rose high and tight. "Why didn't you take me with you? Why did you leave me here?"

She did not wait for an answer. Something ferocious seemed to possess her, and she took my mouth in hers, her jaws moving as if to masticate me, as if every minute we had spent apart poured over her in a white avalanche. I sprang up hard at once—deep, painful lust seemed to flame forward from the bottom of my spine. But I did not have to do a thing. She undid my pants, pulled off her drawers, and straddled me, knees on the seat, so I was pinned beneath her with no choice, her body in a fury of its own. Down she thrust on me, down, down, driving me up into her so far I felt her pounding heart. She was already crying out, and the sound brought me too close, though I struggled valiantly to pull away in time. But she only pounded down harder, faster, shuddering, till I lost the battle and exploded while she uttered hoarse cries like shrieks of rage.

We were silent for a while, her body giving final jerks as the spasm ebbed. I was embarrassed for us both. She had pinned me with my back to the road, and I could not turn my head, but I knew we could be seen if someone were to pass, and the sounds she had been making would have carried half a mile across the silent snow.

She finally went still, her body like heavy clay fastened intimately onto mine, and I wanted her off. I had not asked for such a violent display—she had stolen that from me, assumed she could just take it without bothering to ask. She seemed so strange, so little like herself, that cold thoughts crept up my spine. Could a chaste woman have accomplished this? She had been driven to this frenzy after only a few months without a man—and who knew if that was even true? There might have been others besides me and Tim.

At that thought I took firm hold of her hips and lifted her off of me. I could not look at her and busied myself adjusting my pants, finding her undergarments, and helping her back into them. She did not help me, but sat abandoned, limp, and weeping, as passive as a child.

When I stepped out of the sleigh into the snow, she lifted her head and stared at me like the Medusa, her hair having sprung free and wild as a halo of snakes. "That's all? You're not even going to speak to me?"

Unwillingly I looked at her. "Speak to you? That didn't seem to be any part of what you wanted. You didn't even care if I wanted that. I know I have hurt you, but you can't blame me for what happened here. I never thought a man could be taken by force, but I wonder now."

She gave a yelp, gritted her teeth, and swung her arm back, trying to hit me, but I caught her fist. No one was allowed to hit me now. No one.

"So you are your brother's sister after all. I'm sorry you never showed me that before. It could have saved us both a lot of trouble and heartache."

Now she sobbed, fat tears rolling down her cheeks, and I felt a moment of misgiving. I did not love her now, no, not after this. But I had loved her, and I knew she loved me. I held out a hand

and touched her cheek, half-afraid she might bite it. But she only closed her eyes.

"Come on," I said quietly. "I'll help you get the sleigh back on the road."

WITH GREAT RELIEF I went back to my rocks and sheep, the frisking lambs. Moving north felt like the best thing I had ever done, homecoming to the place where I had always belonged. I would have joined the Amish if they would have had me. But members of the Quaker meetinghouse nearby had also helped escaping slaves, and they welcomed me warmly as my father's son. Each Sunday I spent with them, I felt more peaceful, calm, and sure. These were the people I had always wished to know, peace-loving, reasonable, thoughtful, quiet.

Under their influence, I did not ride to Jarrettsville for Appomattox Day that year. I told my family that they were always welcome on my place, but I had much to do now, tending sheep alone, so I would not come home for a while. When spring arrived for real, my orchard turned pink and white, petals flying on the wind. I repaired the old stone fence around my steep meadows and took a pallet up there to sleep with the flock, the dogs happy to be out all night, me not in want of any other company.

As the earth tipped closer to the sun, bringing warm summer drowse, I took on the job of shearing the whole flock alone. I thought of only one sheep at a time, working carefully and doggedly, and it took me a whole month. But I got the job done.

One hot afternoon in July, my brother Alex drove some steers to market, then came by my place and found me in the hayloft, cleaning the enormous heap of wool I had produced. I had made a crude table, an old door on two sawhorses, and on it I would spread handfuls of wool and pick out burrs, dead ticks, and clots of mud and blood.

I was glad to see my brother, though he was nothing like me or our father, as far as I could see. Like all the married men I knew, he had grown a big beard and a portly belly that he dressed up in waistcoats and watch fobs. Any space he entered, he occupied with authority, standing proud and foursquare, as if assuming command. I had no idea what moved him really, if anything. All he seemed to care about was making money and keeping a good reputation in the world, and he was more than ever like that now that he had a family.

It had been a long time since I talked to anyone outside of Sunday meeting (and not much there, as most of the Quakers were as quiet as I was). I felt rusty at it, but I did not have to say much, since Alex liked the sound of his own voice.

"Well, the dairy is already turning a profit, don't you know. I'm pretty pleased with the delivery service down to Baltimore, and it seems like city folk are happy to get fresh milk and eggs delivered to their doorsteps. We added chickens, did we tell you that? Yes, eggs, milk, cheese, and butter, the whole package, they can get it all from us, straight from the farm. And they pay a pretty penny for it, too."

When he paused for breath, I asked him for the details of dairy farming, hoping to learn something while I worked, and he gave me an earful for at least an hour. At the end of that, he shifted smoothly into family news and told me Hannah was expecting their third child.

My mind must have wandered, because I noticed he had stopped speaking and was giving me a quizzical look. "Do you hear anything from Martha Cairnes?" he asked, watching me.

I tried not to show that he had startled me. "Is she all right?"

"Well enough, I think. But Hannah says she is with child."

So that was why he had come here. A wave of pity for her made my knees buckle, and I sat down on a hay bale, my mouth almost too dry to speak. It felt like I might vomit.

"Who is the man?" I croaked.

He looked at me, startled. "What do you mean? You're still betrothed, aren't you?"

Bitterly I thought of the day her uncle gave me a turkey to secure her hand.

"No one's sued me yet, if that's what you mean. But I have had no contact with her for quite some time, half a year or more, I guess. So I doubt she'd hold me to that promise. Did someone ask you to come here and tell me this?"

"No, no," he said quickly. "Nothing like that." His brow furrowed, and he stared at me, his eyes horrified. "Why do you ask who the man is? Have you really not seen her for so long?"

Something scurried in my chest, a squirrel in a wheel. Half a year was true if you left out that day in the sleigh. But that had been her doing, not mine, and how did I know she was not already pregnant then? That would explain why she had seized me like a succubus and would not let me pull away, to make me think that it was mine. If the child was Tim's, she would go to jail—unless perhaps she had a husband who might claim it. I felt so sorry for her I wanted to cry. But it still made me sick.

My brother removed his hat and stood rubbing both hands back and forth across his thinning pate as though his head hurt. He resettled the hat and looked at me as if from a great distance.

"What I don't understand," he said carefully in his deep voice, "is why you never married her. What happened between you two? Hannah says she doesn't know either. You seemed happy enough. And I never saw a girl more in love. Hannah says Martha still loves you. Oh, we've heard the rumors, everyone has. People have to say things when a betrothal breaks, and it's pretty clear yours did, the way you went away. *Was* there another man?"

I could not look at him now. We never spoke about the night he found me at the stable in Bel Air, flayed and broken like a slave, and I had been too proud to tell him who had held the whip. Everyone assumed that I was beaten for my views, for what I said in the meeting, and that it was a posse of Harford Rifles or Dragoons. That was true, as far as it went. Dragoons and Rifles had been there, and I *had* been beaten for my views, and maybe for my interest in the wrong man's sister. But that was not the excuse for the beating, and the excuse was too despicable to say. I stood up and fetched more wool to clean.

But something pricked at me, pride or a stubborn kernel of truth.

Reluctantly I said, "I don't know about that. I suspected her, but I don't know for sure. Sometimes things just break between people. Really, the break was not between me and her."

He looked more hopeful at that. "What was it then? What broke?"

His eyes were lively, and I could see there that he had an inkling of the truth. When I did not answer, he spoke low.

"Those men that beat you—that was it, wasn't it? Why would you never tell us who it was? That day we found you—well, you were in sad shape, your back in bloody ribbons, but you would not even speak. Don't you know it may have been the men who killed our father and trampled on him with a horse? Are you *protecting* them by not saying?"

I shook my head and let my eyelids screen me almost out of sight.

Exasperated, he snorted. "You are certainly our father's son, more than Jackson or me by a long mile. You're as stubborn as he was." His eyes probed me hard. "Do you know what they're saying of her now at home? That she lay with a black man. That she's having a black bastard and that's why you went away. Hannah has denounced the rumor as impossible. But I don't know—where there's that much smoke, there's usually a fire."

I gave a cry like he had punched me in the gut. "Is that why you came all this way, to slander the best woman I ever loved? If that's it, I'll ask you to leave me be."

Alex held up his hands and backed a few steps. "Whoa, brother. All right. But what is it then? Can't I have an answer of some kind for why you have disgraced the girl and left her so alone? Because you clearly had your way with her, or someone did. Someone did."

I sighed and hung my head. But he was so hungry for a way to understand, I had to give an inch. "Let's just say I realized I could not be a brother to Richard Cairnes. I would sooner murder him, and I don't even like to think that. Did I tell you I have turned Quaker? Yes. I have. I think it's really what Father was, and it feels right to me. That's all. I'm finished with the violence that seems to breed down there."

He nodded and set his jaw. "I suppose you're right. But it's a shame, a girl like that brought low, a girl of such good family. If there is any way you can see your way to help her, clear her name, I hope you'll think on it. Please consider it."

I told him I would. But when he drove away, his brow was still in knots, probably in fear of what he had to tell his wife, and that night I was grateful for the hundredth time to eat my supper in my house alone, no one in need of having anything explained.

THAT FALL, I DISCOVERED that my orchard included apples and pears that needed to be picked, and the Irishwoman canned them for me and made applesauce and chutney and cider, dug up the potatoes and turnips she had thoughtfully planted, picked all the green tomatoes, and set them along a windowsill to become slowly ripe. She helped me with the final cleaning and baling of the wool, and we talked a little as we worked, her thick, red arms so competent that she could bale faster than me.

With the autumn ripeness all around, my mind could not help going back to the old orchard where Martha and I had lain so happily the year before, buzzed over by drunk bees, and I felt a hard pang, missing her and that. My mind would torture me with pictures, her face above me or below me, pink and abandoned, her sweet, round breasts. I had always been sad to see her start to dress. I would do the hooks in back for her, kissing each bare vertebra.

But I knew it was only autumn rut, the same that rams and stags and stallions feel, and I set myself to get the wool to market, cleaned and bailed and hauled, as I ignored the thing ballooning in my loins and threatening to burst.

When the wool was finally all sold, it was a hot September afternoon, leaves not yet turning red, and I went to drown my impulses in whiskey at the Dutchman's Arms in Lancaster. Other sheep men were in town to sell their wool as well, and all had money in their pockets now. We took turns standing rounds.

Soon my senses were quite numb, and the crowd inside the bar was loud, the air thick with smoke and jests and tales of derring-do, when I glanced out the open top of the Dutch door and saw a woman awkwardly dismounting from a horse. She looked oddly rounded, in a long, loose black garment that had been fancifully embroidered with cerulean and crimson birds, and as she slid down to the ground, I realized that she was big with child. The hitching posts were occupied, and she tried to tie her horse up to the low limb of a maple tree, but her fingers looked as big as sausages, so swollen she could hardly make them work. I was thinking that some gallant man should go and help the poor matron, whoever she was, when she turned with a grim frown and studied the horses tied outside.

With a jolt that almost stopped my heart, I recognized her, though her face was dead white from the heat and bloated like a gibbous moon, streaming with sweat and dust from the ride. Her expression bore no resemblance to the laughing girl I knew—she looked like a harpy come to tear my liver out. And she seemed to have spotted my horse, because she charged straight up the stairs, headed not for the ladies' parlor but the gentlemen's saloon.

If we had met more privately, I might have acted more mature, but now I did not stop to think. I dove through the crowd, around a corner to the hot kitchen, and a clap of laughter followed me, as if the drinking men knew right off what was up.

Near where I crouched, a red-faced woman with bare arms was kneading dough, a few strands of brown hair straying from under her white cap. She gave me a quick grin, and I put a finger to my lips and pleaded with my eyes. There was a service window leading to the bar, and with exaggerated caution, on tiptoes, she stepped to it to watch.

I heard the bottom of the Dutch door slam against the wall, and all laughter stopped. The floor creaked underneath a man's tread, possibly the innkeeper's.

"Now, madam," said a grave male voice. "You know you can't come in. This is the gentlemen's. If you would care to step next door into the ladies', I am sure my wife will bring you some nice sassafras tea."

Silently I prayed I was mistaken and that it was some other pregnant lady invading the gentlemen's saloon. But the next instant I heard her voice and knew I would not get my wish.

"Help me quickly, sir. I must speak to Mr. McComas, and his horse is here."

He tipped his head to one side. "McComas? You mean James McComas, the sheep man? I am afraid he's gone to his reward, and his boy Alex isn't up to town today at all, so far as I'm aware. You boys seen Alex anywhere?"

"Not Alex, Nick! I know his horse. It's that gray Thoroughbred outside. My mare knows it and greeted it. Now stop pretending you don't know he's here!"

A few men started to laugh low among themselves. "So his horse has been consorting with her mare, and now the mare's in foal! She's come to call it to account!"

The innkeeper tried to keep order with a soothing voice. "Why, there are plenty of grays around. Which one of you boys owns the gray Thoroughbred?"

Gusts of laughter greeted this, and some guffawed. "What, with a mare on rampage?"

"You think anyone will own up to that big gray now?"

I heard a small exasperated cry, and in a moment she retreated, slamming the Dutch door.

In the bar, men seemed to exhale all together, laughing with relief.

"Where is that rotter, anyway?"

"Halfway to Philadelphia by now!"

"He's dipped his wick, I swear!"

"Not bad looking, for a little ball of wax!"

"She's come to fetch him on the carpet now!"

"Now, gents," one man said gravely. "It's a sad story. My wife has kin in Jarrettsville, and she heard something of it. Says the baby isn't his."

All laughter stopped. "Whose is it then?" asked several men at once.

The grave-voiced man spoke quietly, but it carried all the more. "Some Negro of hers. They say McComas took him in to get him off her. Wasn't any other way."

A disgusted silence followed, and I glanced around for a door to the outside. What would be worse, to meet Martha waiting out there, or to stay in here and bear this shame? I could not even face the cook, but I could feel her looking sympathetically my way. Wiping her hands, she lifted the hinged counter to the empty ladies' parlor and led me to a discreet way out back, toward the privy. Opening the door for me, she gave my shoulder one quick pat.

"You'll see, it'll all come right," she whispered, as if she knew. "Handsome fellow as you are? You come on around here anytime you like."

MARTHA WAS NO LONGER outside, and I went home unimpeded, feeling like some creature crawling back under its rock. In honesty to how I felt, I could do nothing else. I could not even write to her for fear that she would track me down, and I had no desire to read what she would write. Something would have to break the logjam in my heart. I could no longer deny she was with child, having seen it with my eyes. But I still could not fully believe I was its source.

For the remainder of that fall I tried to be industrious, felled trees for firewood I would need that winter, whacked off their limbs, and dragged the trunks back to my yard, where I split each one with a maul and stacked the logs in a dry shed. I mortared the holes in the cottage's stone walls, mended tack, and sharpened knives.

The Irishwoman was making soap and candles for the dark ahead, and I asked her to teach me how, though she was clearly reluctant to do so, since it implied I might one day need her less. She was still young, and sometimes I caught her watching me with a look I recognized, as if the job of wife might suit her more. I might want a woman of my own again someday, but it would not be she, and I resolved to become more independent so that I could let her go.

But now I had nothing left to do but read and watch the sheep, and I felt restless with inactivity, dreading the long, cold winter solitude. When Gabriel Smithson sent an invitation to a corn husking at his place, I jumped at it, hired a neighbor's boy to feed the dogs and sheep, and happily rode south on bone-dry early snow in time for supper with my mother and sisters and my aunt. They all fussed over me, and by the time it was cold dark, I was in a good mood, ready for some whiskey and some easy time with other men.

Out back behind Smithson's pub a bonfire already roared, its warm light dancing red-gold on the faces of happy, joking men and barmaids bringing pints of ale and hard cider. We all competed at husking fastest, at amassing the biggest pile of hard seed corn, at throwing the most husks onto the blaze, and the man who lost each round had to chug another pint, to general jokes and merriment.

I lost a round or two and was into my third pint, plus pulls from the whiskey going round, my hands quite raw, when one of Smithson's boys came up to call him to the house. Smithson soon returned, walking through the early snow, straight to me. He had imbibed a fair bit, too, his face red, his expression loose and relaxed, though his eyes tried to be grave.

He took hold of my arm. "Hey, man. You need to come with me."

No good ever came from such a summons, especially not so close to Jarrettsville and Bel Air. With a reflex to flee, I glanced toward the dark stable, where Jack stood resting in a stall.

"No, you can't leave yet," Smithson said and tightened his grip. "Come on, no one's going to hurt you. There's just someone who needs to speak with you, and I think she has the right. I think you owe her that at least."

A fizzy feeling came over me, a mixture of doom and thrill, as though I had a noose around my neck but could already see the angels flying down to take me up. "Did you tell her I was here?"

He looked away evasively. "It's for the best. Come on."

I felt pulled both forward and back. But I followed him down to the house, where most of the rooms were as black as the night, the bonfire flickering on the white walls, a smell of wood smoke and green cornhusks in the frozen air.

A fire was leaping in the parlor grate, and through the window with a shock I saw the even more swollen outline of Martha, as she tried to bend to stir the coals but couldn't reach. Her mother took the poker and stooped herself in her black taffetas.

Smithson's big hand had hold of my bicep and propelled me up onto the porch and through the door. He removed my hat and deposited me in the living room.

Mrs. Cairnes's skirts rustled as she rose to confront me.

"Take off your cloak," she hissed to Martha.

I couldn't bear to look at them, but from the corner of my eye I saw Martha obey. But she turned her belly toward the fire as if ashamed, while she stared up with feigned interest at a framed embroidery of the Smithson family tree. For a long time, no one spoke.

Smithson's deep voice called out, jovial and hearty, as if nothing were amiss.

"I see I'm not wanted here." With obvious relief, he tramped out the door, leaving us alone.

Slowly Martha turned and seemed to flinch, as if the sight of me could knock her down. She looked far better than when I had glimpsed her last, her creamy cheeks now ruddy with cold. Her heavy hair appeared fairer, coiled on her slender neck in back, and she gave off the glow that young mothers were often said to have. My eyes skittered to her belly and shied away.

Her mother stepped between us, staring at me coldly. "We've come to demand that you do what's right. It's an easy thing to do. You need only stand beside her for a few minutes and sign the document, and then you'll be free to go. I'll keep her and the babe if you give it a name. You needn't trouble yourself about them again. But you have to do that much."

For a few seconds I wanted to rend my clothing, fall on the floor, and beg Martha to forgive me. I cast about to think if I could stand to do what her mother had asked.

"You won't—" I ventured, but my voice broke, my throat suddenly parched. I had to swallow hard and try again. "You won't think the less of Martha Jane?"

Mrs. Cairnes's face closed like a tombstone dropping on a grave. "I won't throw her out of doors if you will marry her."

Blood branched deeper into Martha's cheeks, and her mother turned to gaze at her.

"I'll go see about another log," Mrs. Cairnes said, clipping each word. She left the room.

When we were alone, some hopeful worm in me lifted its head, gave her a lively look, lips parted. We had always been so playful together, teasing, kissing, falling into passion from a laugh. I missed that desperately, I realized, and I did not know how else to speak to her.

But there was no play in her face tonight, and I sighed. My eyes ached, and water stood in them. I hated myself for this display, as if it were me who needed sympathy.

"I'm sorry," I whispered and tried to take her hand. By accident my fingers brushed her belly, and she slapped my hand away.

Her voice sounded remarkably like her mother's hiss. "You have ruined me, and now there's only one thing you can do for me. You'll marry me, or I will shoot you dead."

This time I did catch her hand roughly, overpowered it, and held it hard as I searched her clear blue eyes, so deceptive, full of lies. "Fierce to the end, I should have known. I've always loved that in you."

A wave of desire shocked me, and I pulled her closer till her belly rested against mine. We looked at each other, breathed each other's scent. Good God! Here she was. I wanted to take her, there, that instant, belly and all. And in the next it occurred to me that if I married her, she would twine herself around me and never leave, a prospect that made me crackle with dread and desire. But I could still say no, leave there, and not look back, go on being who I was.

I gripped her hand so hard she winced. "A shotgun wedding, would that really satisfy you? Tell me once and for all. Is the baby mine? Can you swear it to me? Because if you have the smallest doubt . . ."

Her eyes had taken on a mirror shine in the firelight. Her lips curled with disgust, unmoving as she groaned, "You are insulting me."

She closed her eyes and seemed to collect herself with great effort.

Coldly her lips said, "Be at the house on Thursday at five o'clock. We will be married then." And she left the room, not giving me another glance.

Thoughts like black crows flapped around my head. Be at the house, at *Richard's* house, so I could be saddled with his sister and her baby, who might not be mine? A wife I could not trust, from a family I despised?

I closed my eyes and tried to clear my head, leave Richard out of it. What if she had told the truth? I felt a whisper of belief, and what if the child was born and looked like me? Could I forget the rest, her visits to Tim alone and that day in the sleigh? The sleigh was almost the worst, and it made me shudder with lust and disgust. She might speak the truth, but she was not chaste, and I did not know if I could live with her.

I went back to the fire and husked corn furiously, pulling deep on the whiskey jug when it came my way. It warmed my chest, and I tried not to think.

After a while, Smithson sidled up to me. "You're getting into trouble, aren't you, friend?"

Not answering, I threw husks on the fire, corn over my shoulder to the pile.

He went on with pretense at his usual geniality. "*She* seems to think you are, at least. And how much longer till the whole world knows? Until the birth, I mean?"

I yanked a husk free in one pull. "How should I know? I suppose, from the look of her, six or eight weeks. Look, I'm sorry for her trouble, but I'm not sure I deserve the blame."

"She says you do. Are you going to do right by her?"

"I'm in no condition to marry, if that's what you mean. Certainly not a woman used to being kept as well as she."

Smithson's voice went hard. "It's not about her keep, now, is it? I hear you wouldn't have to lift a hand to help her there. Her mother will do that."

So he knew the plan hatched out by Mrs. Cairnes and had helped to spring the trap. I felt a flash of rage. "Is that why you asked me here? It is, isn't it? And you sent word to her that I had come. This whole thing's a damn conspiracy!"

"A conspiracy for your own good, perhaps. Think, man. Do you know what will happen if you don't marry her? She'll be disgraced forever. No one will ever marry her. Her mother may throw her out, and what will happen to her then? Where will she go? She could end up in a workhouse, or worse. She could end up in a brothel with your baby, too. Don't you even care?"

I felt an urge to weep or throw myself onto the fire and just have done with it. My voice was choked. "Of course I do. You know I never loved another woman half so well."

But the image of her in a brothel was too easy to see, for reasons Smithson did not know. And I knew she could end up in a prison, too, if the baby was a shade too dark.

Now Smithson sounded shocked. "It's not because of what they're saying about—about that Negro of hers?" His voice trailed off, as if unable to go on.

At least I could keep the wolves from tearing her apart just yet, until the thing was proved. "Of course not. That's a filthy slander and should not be mentioned in my presence."

But as soon as I said it, I was disgusted with myself and her and Smithson, too. He looked at me like he was more than puzzled—he looked hurt and suspicious now.

"Then what is it, man? What is it?"

The ear in my hand was just half-husked, but I threw the whole thing in the fire. The hell with him. The hell with everyone.

"I'll tell you what, not that it's your business. Anything but marrying for me."

And with that I stalked off to the barn, tacked up Jack, and rode the long way home through frozen night—tempted to think I could just hide out in my mountain aerie and not see anyone from that accursed place again. I could be free.

BUT WHEN THURSDAY CAME, I knew I had to go. Like one condemned to hang, I washed and shaved with shaking hands and dressed in my best suit of clothes, fumbled in frustration with my tie, pulled it off, and tried again. The day was gray and frigid, the ground frozen hard and snow turning to ice, with flurries blowing sideways, rather like that day I made the first mistake, riding to her home holding a turkey's claws. I wished I could go back and change the order of the thing, but I could not. Well, I probably would not anyway. My days with her had been the best thing in my life, and I expected nothing more as good, truly. Exasperated, I yanked off the tie and stuffed it in my pocket, tacked up my horse, and started to ride.

The cold was brutal and the ride felt twice as long as usual. Dark shut down cruelly early, as if to proclaim the foolishness of marrying on such a day. My spirits were as black as the sky, when I began to recognize the roads that led to Jarrettsville. As I made my way close to the lands owned by G. Richard Cairnes, it seemed a wise precaution somehow to take a shortcut past some Negro cabins to Smithson's place. I could put up Jack in comfort in the stable kept for the patrons' use, and no one would notice if I left him there awhile.

It was an easy quarter mile through woods to Richard's barley fields, the dirt track between them lit by starlight, amplified by snow, and I followed it down toward the house, close enough to see the candles all ablaze inside, the parlor made festive with evergreens and white ribbons. Both of our families had gathered from the farms around, sleighs crowded together near the barn while horses warmed inside. The women wore plaid dresses for the season, their hoops bulging, glasses of sherry warming them, a fire in the hearth. Any normal man would have gone in and warmed himself and done the right thing by the girl, especially with her mother's promise that he only needed to do that and then be free to go.

But something in me was not normal anymore. I suppose it had been beaten out of me, though that's a poor excuse. If I walked into the house, it would feel like I was offering my wrists to be clapped in irons. Like that pup—that *pup!*—could throw me down and bullwhip me again.

Instead I turned up to the barn, into the hayloft where she had once lain with me to whisper and kiss. The loft was ours—the house was not. If only she could come up here to me, freely, on her own, I would take her in my arms and spirit her away. I would! Or so I told myself.

The hay was stacked high, still green and sticky from the recent harvest and piled up nearly to the barn's peaked roof. I climbed it to the very top, up bales stacked like steps in terraces, until I reached the open triangle under the roof's peak, where I could lean and gaze down the slope toward the house. A few more sleds arrived, men and women bundled in their winter best hurrying inside, pulling off gloves.

Then nothing happened for a long while. Cold crept into me, and I hunched in a ball on a bale, not knowing what I was waiting for. If I could not go down there now, I should go home. What did I think, that she would divine my presence and come up to me?

I closed my eyes, tried to imagine her—not as she was this fall, but her warm, slender, laughing self, racing away from me uphill above where the two rivers met, the night shrill with summer frogs, the stars fat and low. If I could go back to that night, what would I do?

A door slammed down at the house, and two men came running up the lane, a lantern swinging in between, its beams glancing, magnified by snow. Both of them shouted at once.

"I'll kill him!" yelled a voice I knew, hoarse and ragged. "I'll kill him!"

All on its own, my body dropped onto the hay and curled up against the wall, covering its white face to leave nothing showing in the dark. The loft door rumbled back, and I could hear them clearly now, her brother and my own.

"What good would that do your sister?" Alex puffed, out of breath from running even so short a distance. "Don't worry. We'll find him. We'll take a preacher to him. We'll wed them in irons if need be."

"Not if I kill him first!" cried Richard, who threw his saddle on his horse, leapt on, and shouted, "Hah!" to make it gallop off into the night.

"You think you'll find him by yourself?" yelled Alex, groaning as he heaved himself into the saddle, the leather creaking loud. His horse wanted to take off behind the other, its hooves drumming on the wood floor till he let it gallop out.

When they were gone, I lay listening to my racing heart, my mind scurrying along their likely route. Even galloping, they would have snow to slow them on the long ride north, and it made my hackles rise to think of Richard knowing where my home was.

But when they did not find me there, or at the Dutchman's Arms, they might circle back and look more locally, perhaps even at Smithson's place, where they might see my horse or hear from someone in the bar that it was there. But until they did, this loft might be the safest place on earth, because who would think of looking for me here?

A commotion from the house made me stand up and peer out through the frozen gap under the eaves. Women screamed, a door banged, and something raced across the snow, around the back. It seemed to be a ghost, a figure all in white against the snow.

But she passed a lit window, and it showed a circlet of white roses on her darker hair, thorns against the scalp, a white dress bulging at the belly, gleaming hoops held up to let her run flat out. Two men ran fast behind her, followed by a stream of women calling frantically.

"Martha, no! Stop her, someone!"

She crossed the yard, making for the barn, and for one wild second I thought she was coming to escape with me. I stood up taller, half wanting to signal her.

But she ran into the orchard, where the trees were bare, and I could see her racing toward the pump. What did she mean to do? The pump was iron, its top pipe hard and menacing, and I had a vision of her impaled on it. I tried to move but could not, like an awful dream.

One of the men pursuing caught her just in time and wrapped his arms around her from behind. She shrieked and tried to shrug him off, but the second man arrived to grab her round the legs and lift her up. I could not clearly see the men, but the first was tall and might be Isie's husband, Cairnes. The other looked young and uncertain, fumbling, and might have been G. A.

Her voice rose in a howl, no words distinguishable, and she struggled as they carried her back toward the house. Several women rushed to throw their shawls around her, exclaiming and murmuring. Soon they took her carefully into the house, and I had turned into a salt pillar, condemned to stand there through eternity.

BEFORE DAWN I SLUNK to Smithson's, got my horse, and rode back slowly on roads not often used, until I reached my rocky fields. Snow in the lane showed new hoofprints, but no one was at the house or barn to greet me but my hungry dogs and sheep. I fed them and waited for whatever vigilante posse might come now, aching hard one minute, feeling relief the next.

But that day passed, and so did the next, and then a week. Two weeks, three, and no one came. I tried not to think of her on Thanksgiving or weeks later on Christmas Day. I was invited to have meals with several Quaker families, but for a penance I stayed home and ate the thin soup the Irishwoman had produced for me. As New Year's approached, she offered straight out to relieve me of what longing I might feel for womankind. I suppose she must have felt sorry for me, but it made me feel encroached upon, and I gave her an extra month's wages and let her go.

I made do for a while, eating my own crude cooking, boiled eggs, potatoes, and cabbage, bread and cheese I bought from a neighbor's farm. I calculated profits and losses from the sheep, made myself a budget, read the *Sheepman's Journal* for tips. Evenings more than ever I would venture to the Dutchman's Arms to drink a pint or two and have a pleasant chat with other men. When the old sheep men were in town, I listened to them carefully, absorbing all they knew.

But it was clear that I could not go on forever on my own, and Sunday mornings at the Quaker meetinghouse, I allowed my eyes to wander, take in the eligible girls. One attracted me, a pretty, modest, fair-haired girl, just eighteen, almost half my age. I had no idea why she would want me, and yet she seemed to seek me out after the meeting several Sundays in a row. Her conversation was not stimulating, but she had been educated well, and she seemed to have a gentle spirit. She had never gotten on a horse or roamed free on her own.

January settled cold and bleak, with not much work to do, and eligible bachelors went courting then. But I did not call on her or anyone. I still had a sense of waiting for something that had to be played through. Waiting, in silence, not speculating, not wondering. Just waiting.

One clear, cold afternoon, the sky so blue that it looked stretched, my brother came on Honest Abe with the Harford County sheriff beside him on a piebald horse, a heavy, holstered man picking his brown teeth. I went out to meet them in the snow. I suppose I had expected the sheriff, known he would come eventually to charge me with the child, take some of my scarce income for its upkeep, whether it was mine or not. I supposed this meant the baby had been born, and in spite of everything, my breath came slightly fast. The sheriff tipped his hat but left it on.

"Sheriff," I said. "Would you care to come inside and rest awhile?" My feet were starting to go numb inside my boots, sunk deep in the snow.

"No need. I expect you are familiar with the bastardy statutes of the state of Maryland?"

I nodded, my mouth dry. "I am. Though I am a citizen of Pennsylvania now."

"No matter. I can take you back to Bel Air forcibly, if need be. And if you don't pay, your brother will. You wouldn't want to pass that burden on to him, now would you?"

I glanced at Alex, who looked mortified to be related to such a miscreant as me.

"Of course I won't do that. I expect you have papers to serve on me."

The sheriff handed down a heavy parchment, furled, and my hands trembled as I unrolled it:

SUIT TO MAINTAIN THE MALE CHILD BORN TO
MARTHA JANE CAIRNES, SPINSTER, ON JANUARY 1, 1869.

The spinster names as father Nicholas McComas, formerly of Black Horse, current whereabouts unknown. The state of Maryland charges him, and in his absence, his brother, Alexander McComas, with the upkeep of the Child, in the sum of $80 Due Immediately and $30 Per Annum until the Child is grown. Failure to pay will result in a misdemeanor charge, punishable by a prison term of undetermined length.

I blinked rapidly, blurring the page, eyes dazzled by sun flashing on snow. A son. Martha had a son. Possibly mine. Or not. The crowd of black crows flew into my head, cawing and flapping.

I squinted up at the sheriff. "Have you seen the child?"

His chin tripled as he gazed down at me sternly. "No, sir. Miss Cairnes is greatly respected in the county where I serve, by some of us at least. I took her at her word."

My head went light and I closed my eyes, requested that my heart send blood back to my brain. Maybe, if I could see the baby for myself? And if it looked like me? Could I still marry her and bring her to my rocky fortress, keep her and the baby safe? My heart, for answer, gave another leap. I would have to think it over carefully.

Meanwhile, I did the decent thing, took the document inside and tried to give it a signature worthy of the heavy parchment, with homemade ink and a quill pen. I had the $80 from the wool, though I would be hard-pressed to make it through the winter comfortably without it. I wrote out the draft in Martha's name and took it and the parchment back outside.

"Do me a favor," I said to the sheriff, though he had no reason to agree. "Don't give this to her brother. Leave him out of it. Can you do that? I have made it out to her. I want her to know I have agreed to say the child is mine. But not one cent of this is for Richard Cairnes. If you can't promise that, then I won't pay and you can take me into jail."

He held up pudgy hands in haste. "I don't want to hear no particulars. I got your signature and that's enough. But I will give the draft to her if you like. You'll owe another thirty this time next year. You can send it to her direct. But if I hear different, if I hear you don't send the money proper-like, I'll have to ride up here again and take you in. You hear?"

I heard, and soon he and Alex left, pausing only to water their horses with the snow I had melted for my own.

When they were gone, a strange elation gripped me, of unknown origin. I would be poorer. It would have cost me less to marry her, and she would have done the housework, which I could not afford to pay for anymore. So that would be the final laugh on me.

And yet, at that moment, money was not my worst regret. Right then I wished that I had asked the baby's name.

I HEARD NOTHING after that for months, all through the long and lonely winter, my existence fairly miserable as a solitary shepherd and barfly. I suppose I missed the Irishwoman, that bit of human contact in the day, and I was beat down by the cold. It was close to Maryland, but these hills felt more like Maine. Every day I dressed in long johns, wool pants, and shirt, two jackets, hat, gloves, and a wool scarf around my face, and when I walked to the barn, my nose running and freezing hard inside the scarf, I checked the maple in the yard. It had tight leaf buds, hard as horn, and they stayed that way, refusing to promise anything.

But one morning I was arrested by a purple crocus poking through the snow, followed the next day by more, then a whole flock of daffodils in the sheep meadow. No daffodils had bloomed out there the year before, killed by the late blizzard probably, and I took these hearty yellow bells as a good omen. Pussywillows soon fuzzed out, and the leaf buds on the maples swelled with a rush I felt in my own body, knew too well. Snow vanished. Creeks swelled bright and cold. Soon pink apple and white pear blossoms blew on every breeze, and the whole damn spring began again. The sky remained uncertain, cold showers chasing thin sunlight, the ground still frozen at grave-depth. But each day the sweetness grew, and I felt unworthy of it all, a man who brought lambs into the world and not much else. Though I might have a son.

Slowly I became resolved to see the baby, speak to Martha Jane, and settle that somehow. The boy would be several months old now, old enough for me to see if he resembled anyone I knew. I knew she would not want to speak to me, so I approached her warily, with a letter first to Isie.

Isie wrote back.

"I don't know why I'm writing to you, after what you did to her. Her confinement was so awful she can't even walk yet! And she won't look at the baby. She just lies there and cries and won't eat. Everyone thinks she might die of grief. Her own mother hopes she will! And that's because of you. You should hear the ugly lies people say about her! Here, I'll send you a sample. This is all your fault!!!! Nobody would have said those things if you had married her! Her life is ruined thanks to you. You disgusting man, did you really think she could give herself to a black Negro? That's the most disgusting thing I ever heard! I'm warning you, if I ever see you, I can't be responsible for what I do."

She had enclosed a piece of newsprint, a transcript of a sermon by a local minister.

THREATS TO TRUE WOMANHOOD

It has come to our attention that a woman, a supposed lady of respectable standing, has been brought low in a town near us, and while one must condemn the men accused with her, in this case it seems the manner of her upbringing must also be brought into question. She was known to ride out on a horse alone and traipse around the countryside at all hours. She had learned to fire a rifle and was observed to read more than the Bible without assistance from her father or brother.

Hark, God-fearing men! Women are weak creatures, not governed by reason, and we must protect them every second of their lives. To this lady's sad story there is more, much more, and worse. This woman, this "lady" of fine manner—this supposed virgin and pious church-member—has been observed on several occasions to show undue interest in African servants. Some say that has led her into the most deplorable unchastity of which a lady can ever been accused. And she has brought a child into the world from this unchastity. The soul quakes to think of such a godless, heathen act!

Her family has so far shown restraint in not ejecting her from their home. Yet the question must be raised: Might not a woman so polluted damage the innocents exposed to her? Should this contagion be allowed to fester in our midst, perhaps to spread?

I threw the paper on the fire, feeling great relief at having escaped all that myself.

Then guilt shot through me like a flaming arrow. I had to know about that baby boy. No one seemed brave enough to mention how he looked. If he was white—and if he looked like me—then I would either have to marry her or go through life with that arrow in my heart.

I wrote to Isie and Alex's wife Hannah, telling both of them I would make the return trip to Jarrettsville for Appomattox Day, and begging them to help me speak to Martha and see the child. The thought of the parade was terrible, exposure in that public way right in the heart of Jarrettsville. And yet I would be surrounded by a hundred other men in blue, hidden in my uniform as well as any sheep inside its flock. But if Isie or Hannah would tell Martha Jane, she might recognize me in the herd. "If Martha is well enough to come see the parade, I would be abjectly grateful to see her. I won't go to her brother's farm, and you have to believe me, I do have good reason for that, reasons that are not my fault. But I need to see her and especially the child, if there is any way to manage it."

THE DAY OF THE PARADE, I did the prudent thing and packed a Colt's pistol in the pocket of my militia uniform, knowing every man in Harford County would be armed. I had to saddle Jack and set off before dawn to make it there in time, and the air was still so frigid in the dark, I could not move my fingers, the first few miles extremely long and cold.

But as I crossed the Susquehanna, the sun rose, and soon it was high and hot. Cardinals and robins sang out joyfully in woods made dense with laurel shrubs in bud. The smell of fresh-turned dirt hung in the air, creeks high with snowmelt leaping cold and bright, a sense of new beginning everywhere.

Near Jarrettsville I took the King's Road to the pasture where I knew Federal veterans and militiamen would mass, and sure enough, as I crested a hill, I could see a field full of blue uniforms. It was tufted with new grass, and on it soldiers were assembling rank by rank for the parade. I arrived and joined the cavalry unobtrusively, but many fellows there had not seen me for a while, and they called out with yelps of surprise.

"Why, it's McComas, I'll be bound!"

"Nick! As I live and breathe, it's you!"

"You old miscreant, where have you been?"

They teased me about absconding from the scene of my many crimes, and I was grateful when they did not mention Martha's name—or, God forbid, Sophie's. Someone passed a flask, and the whiskey warmed me deeply going down. Jack was excited by the crowd, and he pranced, showing off, as we waited our turn to ride out.

At last the signal came, a round of volleys fired to the sky from the infantry in front, and flag bearers marched out smartly with drummer boys, piccolos, and trumpets to a huge cheer from the crowd. Gold sun slanted at my eyes, and as we first began to trot, I couldn't see, afraid to trample on the haunches of the horse in front of me.

Then I remembered—if you turn away from the sun, you'll see which way to go. It was a small thing, but it heartened me, and I turned my head and watched the rows of marching men and ranks of cavalry peel out the gates onto the road, allowing me to join them easily, Jack prancing side to side as I kept a rein on him.

The crowd cheered tirelessly along the road, women standing up in open carriages and waving handkerchiefs, a few young girls dashing forward to hand a man a pink magnolia bloom. I scanned each face intently, looking for Martha, but she was not there. We rode past Jarrettsville to its far side, wheeled in fine style to drumbeats and trumpet blasts, and marched back the way we came, like an exercise in futility, trotting toward the pasture where we had begun.

When the infantry was in the pasture, out of our way, and we were moving fast, the men in front starting to gallop, I saw a flash of white, a girl in white wool rushing toward my horse, holding something up, and my heart sprang high.

But it was not she, just a girl I hardly knew, extending a white rosebud to me. I barely managed to grab it. "A rosebud in April!" I cried. "Where did you ever get it?"

She did not answer, only flushed and stumbled as she whirled back to a pack of her girlfriends, all of whom squealed gleefully.

The bud had a long stem, and I had to put it in my teeth to hold the reins, letting the thorns prick me lightly as Jack burst to a gallop and we streamed into the pasture, rank by rank. This time the crowd followed us, breathless for the military exhibition still to come. I put the rosebud in my buttonhole to be a boutonniere.

I had not been to the rehearsals that year, but it all came back to me, and I rode out with my comrades as they galloped in figure eights, whole platoons at once, missing each other by inches as we crossed the middle. The crowd screamed with delight and we pranced through mock battles, jumping over obstacles with torches in our hands.

By the time we finished, the spring dusk had started, the sky turquoise with pink clouds. The field emptied, leaving the grass trampled, one small banner stuck to flutter in the ground, and I followed the others wistfully, sure now that I would not see her that day. Maybe she was ill, or angry, and I knew I did not deserve to look at her or her son. Maybe I would never be allowed to see his face or lay my fears to rest.

Somewhat disconsolate, I followed the other men to Jarrettsville, where lamps were being lit in the few houses. At the hotel I untacked Jack in the stable and saw that he had good bedding and lots of hay, since he would need a good meal and a rest after all he'd done that day.

A crowd of men in blue coats milled inside the hotel and spilled onto the lawn and porch, already deaf with whiskey. They all shouted at once, made up stories about war and other forms of manliness, roars of laughter rising at the slightest opportunity.

"And then there was the day I bagged that bear. Darned if it warn't ten feet tall, I swear, and black as hell! It just stood there and roared, and my horse dumped me and galloped off, he was so scared. But I got him with one shot, right between the eyes."

Men laughed and clinked glasses, and it made me feel much older than the rest of them. I fought my way up to the bar and secured a large double whiskey—possibly produced by G. Richard Cairnes, a thought that made it almost too bitter to drink, but not quite.

The men of my militia lounged around the porch outside, and I stepped out to join them there. But just outside the door I was accosted by Frank Street, a young man I had never met, though I knew he was a Rebel hotblood and a bully. He walked right up to me and gave me a shove on one shoulder, as if to push me back into the bar.

"You got nerve coming here," he said low and sinister, "after what you done. Ruined any ladies lately? Or is it true what people say, the nigra had her first, you couldn't manage it? Damn, thought I smelled a rat out here. Shoulda brought my rat-shooter."

Laughter stopped around us, like they thought we might fight. With an icy feeling round my heart, I wondered if Frank Street had been among the ruffians who held me down across a bale the night Richard Cairnes flayed and sliced my back for bacon strips.

But I was a Quaker now, and I walked calmly past him to one of the pillars holding up the porch roof. I was a little rattled, with a rushing in my arms and legs like they might shake, and I leaned against the pillar to steady myself, relieved when Street gave up staring at me and stepped through the doorway, back into the bar.

I stood somewhat apart from the men I had served with, but near enough to hear them lie and tease each other like schoolboys. There must have been fifty men out there with glasses in their hands, all shouting at once in the pink sunset light, holding whiskey up against the western sky to see it glow.

"Good Gawd, that day at Bull Run, you remember it? Galloped out of there so fast my clothes flew off, they did. Looked down and darned if I warn't buck naked!"

"Oh, go on, and how many Rebs you shoot that day buck naked, did you say?"

"You think I'm lying? I'll bet you anything!"

A commotion in the bar distracted me, made me look that way, and I wondered if it was Street again. The roar in the bar stopped abruptly, except for a few sharp shouts and gasps.

And without warning, there she was. My own dear girl, my Martha Jane! Slender again, in her blue velvet riding suit, looking, if anything, more beautiful than she had ever been. The sight of her electrified me, stole my breath. At last, here was another chance to make it right!

I rose from the rail and reached for her, and she reached a hand toward me, her arm straight out, her eyes on mine. Something bright shone in her hand, but I did not look at it—her eyes shone large, clear, pale, her cheeks rosy pink. My girl. My girl!

"Run! Run!" men yelled, as they all cowered behind pillars or ducked through the parlor door. But what was there to fear? My girl, my Martha Jane?

Something burst inside my chest, a miracle of love and heat that lifted me off the floor and set me back against the pillar. A clap of silence fell.

She spoke in a clear voice. "Gentlemen, you all know what it's done for."

Her arm stayed straight out, and now I could see it, yes, it was a Colt's revolver, engraved all over with twirling vines and flowers, its nose eight inches long, too heavy for a girl to lift. Yet she could, she did, and fired it perfectly into my chest again.

This time the beautiful explosion knocked me off the rail and over backwards into air. It seemed that I could fly. I landed lightly in the gravel yard below.

I lay there on my side, the way I used to lie beside her on the grass beneath the apple trees, on hay or straw, or on the grassy hill-side with two rivers meeting down below. Something red and white lay in the gravel a few inches from my eyes, and I examined it with curiosity, unable to move my head. Ah, it was the white rosebud, lately dipped in someone's blood.

She came down the steps to join me there, stood over me, and fired straight down. That one flattened me onto my back, and I was glad, since now I could see her, as she stood above me like she meant to lie on top of me and dally in the evening light. She shot again, and the bullet moved so slow I felt it carve up through my thigh muscle, not pain but heat, a trail of glory that made gold shimmer before my eyes.

Somewhere in the yard a man's voice shouted, frantic, incensed.

"Come on here and get on your horse! Come on here, get on your horse!"

She did not seem to hear it. Moving like an angel, she knelt and took my head into her lap and smoothed my hair. Her face twisted with grief, and her tears dropped on my cheeks.

I tried to speak, but blood filled my mouth. I spit it out, but it filled again. I wanted to explain, to tell her everything, to say that I had always loved her, always would, and she would be my wife. She would. Death would not part us. She would be my wife on Earth and in heaven, forever and ever, world without end.

But I could only say it with my eyes, as her dear face dimmed, and beyond her face, the sapphire sky.

IV.

We the People

APRIL–MAY 1869

It was a pretty Sunday morning in Bel Air. Church bells ringing. Clear blue sky. Birds. You never heard so many singing their heads off.

No one was in the jail, so I could make the wife happy and go to church. She liked it better if I stayed awake, and I did not succeed this time. But that made the sermon mercifully brief. A rousing hymn woke me, and soon they let us out.

It was a while to dinner yet, and I took the wife home in the buggy. The side of beef my brother gave us was holding up well in the ice cellar, and I cut her a good roast and made sure she got the cookstove fired before I left to see if anything had happened at the jail.

You never knew what Johnny Reb would get up to when good Union men marched out to celebrate that happy day four years ago and mourn its aftermath, when our president was shot. The Rebs had their own parade now, not for Appomattox but the firing on Fort Sumter, and they would swagger their puny selves in every little town and praise their hero, John Wilkes Booth, the low cur who had blackened the name of this fair town. Both days, men would get all liquored up, and anything could happen. Someone could get shot.

This place, you wouldn't know it from ten years ago. Or twenty anyway. It used to be a sleepy spot where peace officers never had a thing to do. Sometimes we had to round up drunken Negroes on a Saturday, throw them in the clink, and let them sleep it off.

The most exciting thing I had to do back then was help to throw an ox. Belonging to Will Cairnes, it was, and it had stepped on a porcupine, got quills rammed up through its hoof real bad. It took six of us to throw it on its side. You tie a rope around it, and five men haul it over while someone mans the horns and twists them down. Damned if those quills weren't in deep, too, wouldn't budge. They can break off inside and make the animal useless. Had to get old Dr. Jarrett Sr. over there to do a surgery. And what do you think he used? A shell case. Shoved it in around each quill and cut it free. A bloody business, but Jarrett didn't mind. He had hands like a lathe. That day Will Cairnes broke out the whiskey, and no one talked politics.

The fifties changed all that. In the fifties half those fellows stopped speaking to the other half. Some of them got shot. Some in your basic barnyard murder. Some in that big barnyard murder they called the Rebel Insurrection. Those years, every meeting turned into a brawl. Men killed their neighbors with bare hands. The paper sent out messages in code to signal all the damn Dragoons and Rifles that it was time to blast a railroad bridge. Half the men in town got rounded up and thrown in stir until the war was done. Only place where you could trust a one of them. But they were out now, on the loose. Some said the war had never stopped and never would.

But today it was spring, and I had seen most of those miscreants in church. It was a good day for peace. I wanted to enjoy it more, so I turned the horse out to graze and strolled downtown on foot. Bel Air wasn't big, but it had two wide avenues lined with tall houses and church spires and the courthouse in the square. Whistling as I went, I touched my hat to ladies in spring dresses, their hoopskirts sweeping the cobblestones. My, yes, spring was a fine time.

In the square, the usual collection of Negro ragamuffins dawdled by the courthouse in ragged pants and no shoes. One had a man's felt hat so big, it dropped over his ears. Another had a gray Confederate jacket down to his knees. I gave them a good once-over with my eyes to let them know I was watching them. They all looked at the ground.

"Eustace, Jimbo, Vance. You boys been good today?"

"Yes, sir, Sheriff," all three of them said quietly.

"Good. Now you just keep it that way." I crossed the street toward the jail.

I was almost there when I saw a pretty girl in a blue riding suit, striding at me like she meant to do something for sure. I knew who she was, daughter of poor George Cairnes. A spirited girl. I looked around for her brother or uncle, but she seemed to be alone.

"Why, Miss Martha, what brings you here all by yourself? Everything all right at home?"

It shot into my head—of course, nothing was all right at home. The last time I saw her she had seemed broken, lying in a dark bedroom that smelled of blood. Day after she was delivered of a bastard child, poor thing. I had to go in there and get the father's name from her own lips. She was almost too weak to speak. I had to ask her twice and bend my head down close to where she lay. I was careful to keep my eyes down and not look at her, for decency's sake.

I have to say, there was no child in evidence. Gossips in the neighborhood made out it had been born a shade too dark, if you take my meaning, and the Negro midwife took it off to be her own. If it was really black, I knew I would have to arrest Miss Martha sooner or later.

But in this great country, we allow as how a person is innocent till proven otherwise, and that day I gave her the chance to confess or tell me different. And the name she whispered was no black man's. Once I heard it, I got out of there fast as I could.

But now she looked herself again. Same girl I called to account for disturbing the peace, galloping her horse through Jarrettsville. Boys in the saloon had a good laugh over that one. The memory made me grin at her, though she did not smile back. And what had she just said?

"What, miss? What did you say?"

She looked exasperated, face going red, then pale. "I tell you, I have killed a man. Arrest me now. I must be hung. I want those to be the last words I ever have to say."

I thought it was a joke. I chuckled. "Why, Miss Cairnes, that's quite a thing to tell a man of a Sunday morning. Have you been to church?" You might wonder why I asked that. Maybe just to change the subject. Get back on familiar ground.

But she waved her hands impatiently. "I tell you, sir, I killed Nicholas McComas last night in Jarrettsville at the hotel. Fifty men saw what I did. You have to hang me now."

The name shot through me. McComas—why, was that the name she gave as father of her bastard? My feet realized it first, and they could not hold still. They shuffled side to side and kicked around like some sort of dance. Like a woodcock showing off for his ladies. I tried to make them stop. But they didn't. I took her arm and steered her toward the jail, hopping and skipping like a little girl. I tried to get hold of myself.

"Dead, you say? How many witnesses? And you freely admit . . ."

I led her through the heavy oak door to the jail, past the wooden counter to a bench in front of the three cells. She tried to go in one, but I hauled her out.

"Now, hold your horses. You stay out of there."

I led her to my office and offered her a chair. "Just sit quiet here."

She stayed stiffly on her feet. "Put me behind bars. I demand it."

Exasperated, I began to laugh. This was a new one on me. I tipped my hat back, thought better of it, and took it off. She was still a lady, so far as I knew.

"Can't do that. Got no warrant to arrest you. Ain't no one brought this in yet."

She gave a little cry. "But I have brought it in! I admit to what I've done. I demand to hang right now!"

I could not locate my desk, I felt so turned around. When I found it, I did a fast look through the papers there, to see if the bailiff might have heard of it and left a note for me. But I saw nothing of the sort. I squared my shoulders. Time to take this here situation in hand.

"There'll be no talk of hanging yet. First thing, I gotta have a warrant in my hand and I don't yet. Hasn't never been a lady in this jail. We need to get a place to keep you proper. Nobody's in here right now but you never know. Sometimes we get drunks and Negro thieves. Folks round here wouldn't put up with that, a lady in the jail with Negro thieves. We have a reputation to keep up, here in Bel Air. Now, you stay right here. I got to find a judge."

I took off so smartly, glancing back to make sure she would not move, that I whacked my head against the edge of the open door and reeled back, seeing stars. Now that was some dignified exit.

Why didn't I bring my horse? There was a judge who lived a few blocks off, but I arrived there in a sweat and found him at his dinner.

He kept me waiting on the porch awhile before he came out, napkin in hand, and looked at me over his glasses. "What is it now, Sheriff?"

I told him the unlikely events of the morning, and his brow wrinkled.

"Pity. I know Miss Cairnes, poor girl. I knew her father. Her mother should take better care of her. She must have gotten up too early from her confinement. Some of them go mad afterward. Let's hope she didn't do as she says. Is her brother with her? No? Well, send for him to take her back. I can't do a thing on a Sunday, not on just her word. We need witnesses."

"Yes, sir, I was pretty sure of that. But she keeps saying she wants to get hung today."

He scowled over his glasses. "Then she is demented. Get her family."

When I got back to the jail I could not find her at first, and that was a relief—maybe she had thought better of it all and gone away.

But I heard a rustle from the cells, and sure enough, that's where she was, lying on the hard wood bed in one, arm over her face. She had pulled the door closed, and it had latched itself. It was sickening to see her through the bars.

"Now, miss, you know you can't lie there. You got to come on out and go back home. Tell me, where's your brother at?"

She sat up, ignoring what I said. "Did you get the warrant?"

"No, miss, can't do it today. Judge said your own word is not enough. You have to go back home and wait till you get fetched. No one's told us about a shooting."

She shouted like I had tried her patience to the limit. "But I'm here! I'm telling you!"

I felt grim getting my keys and unlocking the cell. I thought she might refuse to get up and I would never get her out. But she surprised me. Got right up and marched back to my office. Sat there with a look that said she would not budge until I brought the noose.

Henry Farnandis, Esquire
Attorney at Law

IT WAS A DELIGHTFUL SUNDAY, Mrs. Farnandis supervising in the kitchen as the cooks prepared a lovely meal for all our children and grandchildren. Before we sat down to it, I gathered everyone into the parlor to listen as I read the Word of God. The servants gathered, too, as they did every Sunday, standing around the walls, all of us in harmony, bowing our heads.

But what was that sound? A low rumble like cavalry, and it seemed to come right up our lane and onto our front lawn. Someone pounded the door, and I was disinclined to stop. I read the passage to the end and told everyone to go into the dining room and start to serve, since I would not be long. Folding my spectacles into my watch pocket, I went out to the porch.

I knew at once something was wrong. It was a strange tableau, young Richard Cairnes on his red horse, guarded by more than a dozen of the county's best-known citizens, Harford Rifles and Light Dragoons. You must understand, they could all have been Knights of the Round Table, and if they were sent to retrieve the Holy Grail, we would have it today. Like me, they had been at Sunday services or dinner, all of them superbly dressed in black jackets, white shirts, clean cravats, and black striped pants. I knew that whatever emergency had taken them out of houses of worship or their homes was something I had to hear.

Colonel Stump rode out in front, right to the porch, and I stepped down to meet him. Stump was the most heroic of them all, excepting perhaps John Wilkes Booth, whose loss we all still mourned. Booth had been our eyes and ears, and once saved Stump himself from capture by the Federals. He had escorted a young lady to her home after a ball and remained there for the night, and when word spread next morning that the troops were after him, only Booth knew where Stump was and got to him in time.

Stump stayed on his horse but leaned his powerful torso down so he could speak low.

"There has been an incident at Jarrettsville, and we need your assistance to save one of the noblest ladies in our land. If you will have your carriage brought out, Richard Cairnes will ride with you and tell you what has occurred. We may need the carriage to bring the lady home. She has gone to the sheriff herself, and we must ride to town and speak to him."

I wasted no time and ordered my carriage brought around, and young Richard joined me in it as the knights escorted us on horseback, guns stuck in their belts and spurs clinking. Twenty horses strong, in a tight phalanx, we galloped toward town.

Inside the swaying carriage, Richard was flushed and beady-eyed with concentration. "We have to spirit her away. They'll hang her if she stays! We have people in Virginia we can take her to, where she'll be safe. If you'll lend us the carriage, we will take her from the sheriff and head south. I will be so much indebted to you."

I gave his knee a gentle pat. "Spoken like the loving brother I am sure you are, young friend. But we cannot do that. The lady has turned herself in to the law and taken that decision from our hands. Due process must be served now at its own pace. Put your faith in me. I will never let them hang a lady, and especially not one who has been so terribly wronged."

Richard was sweating visibly, his eyes gone wild. "Tell them I did it. Say I shot him through the window from the bar! She is completely innocent!"

I scrutinized him, weighing his idea. "Dear boy. I am proud of you for such a noble gesture. But do not give ideas to the prosecution. We will have enough trouble from them. Let us wait and see what we must do."

Outside the jail, humble townsfolk rushed to help us with the horses so the gallant militiamen could surround me and Richard as we stepped into the jail.

It was a shock to see Miss Cairnes in such a sordid place. Perfect bud of Southern womanhood, she looked far too delicate to endure such injury to her nature. I went to where she sat and sank onto one knee, lifted her soft hand to my lips, and spoke for all of us.

"Here is beauty wronged and innocence so pure it consecrates this godless place."

The men packed in the room murmured assent, and even the sheriff seemed to stand taller, exuding peacefulness, despite his bulk and his unseemly bulging guns.

Her voice was light and low, a lady's through and through. "If you would do me any service, sir, you will have them bring a rope without delay. I do not wish to see another night."

I bowed my head. "A noble sentiment, precisely what one would expect from a heart so fine and pure. You prove your innocence with every word, and gentlemen can only fall upon their knees to honor you. We shall shelter you and give you all our care."

She stifled a cry, pressing an embroidered linen handkerchief to her lips.

"Please, Mr. Farnandis, try to understand. I want no help. I'm guilty, and I want to hang. I will not leave here alive. I've killed a man in cold blood."

She turned to face the men, and they all closed their mouths and stared.

"You Dragoons and Rifles. You know it was a private matter between me and Mr. McComas. It had nothing to do with you nor with any disagreement between the states. You know the law says I must hang."

I felt a flood of pity at her certainty. What must have been done to such a sweet lady that she now preferred death to her life?

I signaled to the others that I wished to rise, and several Dragoons assisted me. Gently I placed my palms on both her cheeks. "The shock has been too much for your tender constitution, and one would expect no less. You must let steadier minds decide for you and see that justice is done. What good would come of another death? You have done a greater good than you can know. If it is true a crime has been committed, and there is a trial, I will defend you with every power the good Lord has given me. Now, come, my dear, we'll take you home."

I took her hand and tucked her arm through mine, not giving in to her feeble tugs. The men surrounded us, and we swept out in a pack to the closed carriage, where I helped her in and drove her home, Dragoons and Rifles on every side. Richard rode his own horse, leading her tawny mare, and through that whole long ride, I had to face her by myself. And I can tell you that she argued with me as eloquently as the finest lawyer might, and a weaker man might have given in and let her have her wish. But the Lord was on my side, as I hoped he would be at her trial, and I kept to my position that she should live.

At young Cairnes's farm, I left Colonel Stump in charge, and he positioned men around the house, where they would bivouac in shifts until the danger of reprisals passed.

Isabelle Cairnes Kirkwood
Mother of Seven

THE NERVE OF THAT MAN, sending me a letter! When I saw his writing on the second one, all big and flourished like he thought he was some kind of king—a goddamn king in exile—I chucked it in the fire. Whatever else he had to say, I didn't care. He was a silver-tongued devil, that was sure. That tongue had cozened Martha, but it wasn't getting me, no sirree. That was one good thing about losing your respectability at seventeen: You learned some things. You did not give a good goddamn what other people thought, and you knew a bad man when you looked at him and a good one, too. You knew a dear, truehearted friend like Martha Jane.

Cairnes was not a drinking man, so he had not been at the hotel that Saturday, and it was Sunday night before word got to us, when Martin Jarrett came to bleed me as usual. He insisted I had caught poor Sam's consumption, and that my little Becky had it, too. If it was Sam's, then I was honored to have it, that's all I had to say. But I could not stand it that my little Becky could be sick so young. She was just two, an angel, and all smiles. I did not want her to become a real angel yet (if there were real angels), and the sight of Dr. Jarrett always set my worry off.

But when he told me what Martha Jane had done, all other thoughts deserted me. I lumbered to my feet as fast as possible, which was pretty slow by then.

"I have to go to her. You'll take me there, won't you?"

I left the children with Cairnes's mother across the lane, my mind in an awful whirl. How could she have killed Nick, not letting on that she would, even to me? It made me feel odd, like she was someone else and not the best friend I had always known and loved.

She was the one person who had stood by me, even when my mother and grandmother turned their backs. No one was closer to me on this earth, not even my dear Cairnes. We were closer than sisters, which we almost were. Our fathers were brothers and our mothers first cousins, and we were also kin about twelve other ways. I mean, how many ways did you have to be related to a person before you would not marry him? Let's just say no one in this family liked the word "incest" much.

Martha had always loved it when I said naughty things like that. We had spent our childhoods together, climbing trees, teasing about "bottom burping" when one of us had gas. We never played with dolls or other sissy stuff, not when we could climb up in a hayloft and pitch tiny stones at our brothers till they figured out where they were coming from and took off after us. We liked to hitch up our skirts and climb on a pony, though we would catch it if anyone saw that—both of us on one pony, bareback, one holding the other's waist, till we started laughing too hard and fell off.

That summer when Cairnes chose me, Martha was my coconspirator. She let me stay with her and share her bed and acted like she didn't notice when I snuck out at night to meet him on some lawn and get all wet with dew. One morning I was standing in her room naked, sunlight shimmering on the water in the china basin, and she stepped up beside me, chuckling.

"What's this?" she said and pressed a cool finger to my neck.

"What?" I said, already giggling. She handed me her silver mirror.

On my neck was a mark like a composite flower, tiny purple buds hanging on to each other for dear life. I covered it with the washcloth, but she pulled it off and studied the mark.

"Why, look at that. I think someone has branded you. I can just make it out. It says GCK! George Cairnes Kirkwood, could it be?"

Cairnes was twenty-one then, I was just sixteen, and neither of us knew how serious it was, what we were doing. I planned never to let my girls out of sight when they got to be that age. Not that I was some kind of hypocrite. No. It was because I knew what it led to, for me and Martha both. If it was true she had shot Nick, then anyone who slipped out to meet a lover in the night was asking for her life to end. It might end with a noose or with drudgery like mine, but end it would.

Dr. Jarrett took me to her in his buggy, and as we rolled in the lane, we saw a lantern on the front porch of the house and two young men standing guard.

One of them was Jarrett's younger brother, and he must have recognized the buggy. But when we got out, he drew himself up tall and fired a warning shot over our heads.

"Who goes there?" he shouted. "Halt right where you are!"

Dr. Jarrett did not even slow his walk. "Evening, Josh, George Andrew."

He went in the front door, and I followed him. We found Martha flushed and feverish in black mourning dress, sitting by the front door like she was waiting to be lynched.

I brought another chair, sat down beside her, and took her hand.

But she leapt up and clutched Dr. Jarrett's arms. "Martin! Tell me quickly. What did you do with Nick?"

He gave her an astonished look. "Don't speak of that. Be quiet now."

But she wouldn't let him go. "Why can't I know, Martin? It's just a little thing. I'll be dead in a few days. Why won't anyone tell me? Just say it—did they carry him inside and wash him and lay him out? Where is he now?"

The doctor's face softened—he seemed to understand. "He's in heaven if he's anywhere. But we took his body in and laid him on the bar, and I attended him. He was already dead. Mrs. Street washed him, and we got him a clean uniform. His brother took him to his mother's house. They'll bury him at Bethel, I expect, where his people are. There now, I hope you're satisfied."

She collapsed, weeping, and the doctor caught her as her knees gave way.

"You should be in bed. Isabelle, can you stay with her? She shouldn't be alone. Take away her ribbons and laces, anything that she could use to hang herself. I'll give her something, and I'll leave more in case she needs it."

He got a glass of water from the kitchen, poured a packet of white powder in, stirred it up, and handed it to her. "This will put your mind at ease."

We almost had to force her to drink it down, but finally she did, and he left.

Martha would not go upstairs. She went on sitting grimly by the door, though I told her no one would come that night. It was already late, no sound in the house except the ticking of the tall grandfather clocks and the stately *bong, bong, bongs* every hour. The one in the entry hall would work itself up, whirring, then let loose. When all was quiet, the silence would be interrupted by the one at the top of the staircase, *bong, bong, bong* again.

Martha said wistfully, "I'll miss these clocks. They have never agreed."

I clutched her hand and studied her face, trying to decide how odd it was that she could talk about the clocks at a time like this. "Are you all right?"

"Of course," she said impatiently.

I touched her forehead, and it was hot. "Don't you get sick, too."

It felt good to pretend nothing had changed. But I could feel a bad dream gape around us. Where was the baby? He would be four months old, and even with a black wet nurse, he should be here in the house, shouldn't he? In my house, someone was always crying, and you could smell milk and baby pee and poop as you came in the door. But there was no sign of a baby here. Had she sent him away to hide the color of his skin?

Finally the sedative hit her, and she let me coax her up the stairs and into bed. I got in with her, and when she began to drift to sleep, I looked in other rooms upstairs, but found no trace of the baby. I was ashamed for not having been there since it was born. But her mother, my aunt, had made clear for years I was not welcome there, and I could just imagine what she thought should happen to the child. I was glad now she lay prostrate in her bed, attended by a freedwoman I did not know. I was willing to wager it was she who had sent the baby off and not Martha Jane.

In the morning, Martha dressed and sat beside the door again. I went to her, took her hands, and looked into her eyes. "Where is your baby?" I whispered low.

She looked at me wildly, like she had misplaced it. Her head quivered on her neck like a person with the shakes. "He's all right," she murmured finally.

I was glad to hear she knew that much, that it was a boy. "Who is taking care of him?"

Her head trembled violently, then stopped. "Not here. But he's all right."

I had to be content with that and cook dinner for the militiamen on guard.

Richard lived across the lane now with his wife, but he preferred to swagger through his mother's kitchen with two pistols in his belt, accepting coffee or a light for his cigar. Sometimes he seemed older, aged by marriage. But the next second he would be thirteen again, keeping his broad hat on even indoors, as if his business were too pressing to allow for niceties. He seemed happy, like he had done something grand, when so far as I knew, it had all been Martha's doing, and it wasn't grand. She had removed her only chance at happiness, and now she would be hung.

That day a late blizzard blew up and buried everything under two feet of snow, and the sheriff did not come. I missed my children and Cairnes with something like a physical hunger. But so long as she was here, at the mercy of so many armed men and others on their way, I had to stay.

Tuesday morning the sun rose bright, ice gleaming in lace patterns on every windowpane. Across the lane, where the pink magnolia had already burst in bloom, its petals now hung as brown and limp as old banana skins. Every daffodil had frozen paper-thin, and when Dragoons and Rifles stamped in to warm themselves at the cookstove, icicles hung suspended from their mustaches. I took a breakfast tray to Martha as she sat in mourning dress beside the door, but she would not look at it. She sat there all day. But no one broke the ice crust on the snowy lane, and I slept over a third night.

At last, Wednesday morning, the sheriff's black sleigh plowed in, and he took us both to Bel Air, wrapped in rugs against the cold and escorted by Dragoons and Rifles on horseback. The sheriff had secured a private room at Glenn's Hotel to serve as Martha's jail. It was a pleasant upstairs room with a fire in the hearth and a goose-down bed with ruffled canopy, nicer than either of us had at home. She took one look at it and tried to leave.

"Please take me to the gallows," she said in a firm but gentle voice.

The sheriff checked the position of his gun and swelled his chest, as if proud of how he was facing up to her, the dangerous murderess. "That's for the jury to decide. Now, you gotta stay here, miss. I gotta post a guard. You can't leave, but you can move about the place. Folks can come and sit with you, and you can eat your dinner in the dining room downstairs."

He placed a young man with a rifle on the porch, despite (or maybe because of?) the Dragoons and Rifles swarming in the halls, at least two outside her doorway at all times. Inside she lay on the bed, her eyes closed, and would not say a word or sit up to eat.

On our second day Richard pounded on the door and let in an Irishwoman with a tray.

"You eat every bit of that," he said sternly and pointed at the food.

Martha did not even open her eyes.

He shook a finger at the tray. "You're going to eat that and I'm going to watch."

But he faltered when it came to forcing her, and soon I took the tray away, half the food consumed by me, the other half untouched. It went on that way for days. I never saw her eat or sleep, though she would drink milk if I held it to her lips, and she may have slept when I did, so I did not notice it.

I fretted for my own children, and my breasts ached, hard with milk, like a poor cow impatient at the gate. Their grandmother could not nurse the youngest, but I knew she would manage somehow, and it did not seem safe to leave Martha yet, when she wanted so much to die. I put off going home from day to day and sheltered her from things she should not hear. Every morning now brought piles of newspapers, delivered to us by the staff of the hotel.

In Maryland and Washington, papers carried headlines such as THE TRAGEDY AT JARRETTSVILLE, and the front page of the *New York Times* proclaimed YOUNG LADY SHOOTS HER SEDUCER IN MARYLAND. Reporters were dispatched from New York, Boston, Philadelphia, Atlanta, and as far away as Maine and Florida. Every day they tried to speak to Martha, but the militiamen had orders from her lawyers to turn them away. Richard moved freely about the town and reported tourists showing up in droves, riding past in carriages to get a glimpse of the hotel and feel the thrill.

Mail started to arrive, basketsful of white and blue and ecru envelopes, often scented, the notes inside them penned in trembling floral script by women neither one of us had ever met. Martha wouldn't look at them, but I sat on the sofa in her room and opened every one.

"From a Miss Harriet Adams, of Boston, Massachusetts," I read out to her. "Miss Adams writes that all her friends have wept and prayed for you both day and night. They feel that when you are hanged, God will know the difference between your soul and those of ordinary criminals, and He will take you into Paradise. And here is one from Atlanta. Miss Alice Gagnier sends deep sorrow on your behalf and only wishes she had known you in your life."

Some sent gifts: a black silk veil, handkerchiefs with black borders, a flat black hat and black silk gloves, yards and yards of fine black silk.

The donor of the silk wrote, "You must have a new mourning dress made up in the latest form," and when the wife of a local statesman heard of it, she paid her own dressmaker to come and measure Martha for the dress.

Others sent hot pies—mincemeat, pumpkin, apple—from fruits put up the fall before, though Martha would eat nothing, and they fell to the Dragoons. As the days grew warmer, more blooms poked up through Harford County dirt, and one morning the hotel doorman carried in an armload of peonies, ruffled red and white and pink. Martha seemed distressed by the sight of them.

"Please take them to the orphans' home. They're mistaken if they think I am innocent."

But the doorman left them, and I went downstairs to find vases enough for all of them.

One day, as usual, I read out the names on envelopes to her.

"Then, let's see, Mrs. Allen Granger of Richmond. Miss Carrie Newton of Wichita, Kansas. Miss Ida Green of the city of New York. And I think this one's from a man. Mr. Timothy C. Lincoln of Philadelphia. Is he the first man you've heard from?"

Martha surprised me by sitting up and reaching out to take that one from me.

"Is he someone you know?" I asked, puzzled, having never heard of him, and surely I knew everyone she knew.

She flushed and did not answer me but ripped it open and read, and when she was finished, she handed it silently to me. The envelope was made of butcher paper, sealed with flour paste, the ink a cheap, watery blue, already fading. The writing was awkward, printed, not in script, and some letters were backward. But I puzzled it out.

Missy,

Heard of your trouble, afraid they gone hang you so had to right. You brung me them books back then and all. I heard what bad folks been saying down there. Folks hadnt oughta listen to such truck.

Been working at blacksmiths, learning some. Got Ma here and Sophie too. Had to go. It was too bad there.

*Well, ain't no good at righting. Just want to say May God
Help You.*

Yours & co,

Timothy C. Lincoln

"I think it's Tim," she whispered. "Maybe he calls himself
Lincoln now. But I bet the C is for Cairnes. He might have kept it.
That used to be his name, when he was ours."

I could not imagine who she meant. "Tim? Tim Cairnes? Who
is that?"

Then I knew: black Tim, from her place, the man who had
made the chair for Sam. And I flushed, too, remembering the talk.
I gave her a hard stare.

She held my look. "What? Are you thinking that filthy talk is
true?"

My face got hotter, because I supposed I was. I could not stop
myself from asking her again.

"Where is the baby?" I whispered. "What have you done with
him?"

She looked at me a long while, and I could tell she was hurt.
"He lives with his nurse, in a cabin in our woods. Remember the
one we used to think was haunted, near the white pines we used to
climb? Well, he lives there with her. I often visit them."

"Is his nurse black?" I asked, as if that were proof he would
be black himself.

Her chin went hard, like she would not say any more.

But instead it trembled, and her face broke into tears. "Oh,
Isie, I can't stand it if you doubt me, too. Please say you don't. If
you could see him, you would know. He is the image of my Nick.
His eyes. I can't stand to look at him, his eyes are so like Nick's. Do
you think I wanted to kill Nick? I loved him. I still do."

In a rush she told me about giving books to Tim, and how she had met his sister one day as she was riding to my place, on a wood's trail. She took his sister on her horse to Tim's cabin in Nick's woods, where she learned he had been beaten so badly he was almost killed.

"I rode back the next day and changed his bandages and took them food. It was winter, and they didn't have enough. It's vile that anyone could make that into something lewd."

I embraced her and told her I had never doubted her really. I hoped she would believe me, and she seemed to, though after that I felt a certain coolness between us and took it hard.

Finally, one day Richard came to the room to say Mr. Farnandis wanted to speak with Martha in the private parlor down the hall. She stood up as tall as she could and refused.

"I don't want to speak to him unless he means to have me hung at once."

"You will stop saying that," said Richard through tight lips. "You are not going to hang. You will have the best lawyers in the state. Now come and talk to their chief."

I helped her stand and kept one arm tightly around her waist, the other clutching her hand. Like that we walked to the parlor, our black hoopskirts bulging together side to side.

Mr. Farnandis was a tall man with a white planter's beard and mane, high white collar, dove-gray coat, and fine manners. Peering from the nest of his white hair were leopard's eyes, bright green, alert.

"Mrs. Kirkwood," he said and bowed over my hand. To Martha, he held out a bouquet of white lilies of the valley. "Miss Cairnes, these flowers cannot half betoken all the purity that's in your heart, and we will prove it to the world."

She would not take the bouquet, so he handed it to me. She turned away slightly, as if to deflect the power of his voice and eyes. "Good sir, I know you mean well, but I am neither pure nor innocent. If you feel you have to say I am, I'll ask you not to plead my case. I have committed murder, and I wish to die. I am afraid of it, but I have killed a man, and I am not a child. I am a responsible adult, and I have a conscience."

Mr. Farnandis revealed no impatience, but I had heard her say it now too many times, and I gave her a hard pinch. She did not even look at me as she bowed her head to him, wished him good day, and slipped out of my grip. I caught up with her outside the door.

"How can you keep saying that?" I hissed. "You can't abandon your own baby! Would you abandon *me*? I've got the damn consumption, and I'll be leaving seven children!" *Or six*, I thought and started to cry, for my little Becky and myself and Martha, too. "*They* need you to live and take my place. You could raise your boy with them."

She did not say another word that day. Her face appeared closed off, as if behind a mask, and I was afraid.

But Richard was not finished with her yet. Next day he walked into our room carrying a baby, and from ten feet away, I could see it had Nick's eyes. Nick's eyes! Clear gray and slightly droopy, with a soft wide nose and light pink lips. I gave a cry of relief and joy and held out my arms. He was no blacker than Martha Jane or me.

"Is this your little boy? What a perfect little man! Give him to me!"

I took him, and he felt sweet and warm and heavy. I squeezed his chubby thighs. He wore a long white dress like for a christening, and he smelled of milk and roses—his nurse must have washed him just before they left. I held him up to look him in the face, and he gazed back sweet and solemn, drowsy from the drive.

But when he saw Martha he stared so hard he almost went cross-eyed and broke into a toothless grin. So I knew it was true, that she had often been to visit him, not letting on to me.

She reached for him, and I let him go. She held him close and kissed his head over and over. Like all my children at that age, he was trying to make his hands work for him. He wrapped his fingers around hers, waved the other hand around, and when it caught her hair, it pulled free a long shaft and he grinned.

Richard was watching her. "Now go ahead and say you want his mother dead. You can keep him and raise him yourself if you say you're innocent."

The blood beat up in her face, but she held tight to the boy. "That's ridiculous. I will not say I'm innocent. You can't make me."

Richard beamed as if she had agreed to something. "Then we won't ask for your opinion. You won't testify. Just let them see your face and don't speak up, no matter what gets said."

"I won't let anyone say I'm innocent, no matter who."

He turned to me and gave me a long look, like he was charging me to change her mind.

"I'll let you and Isie think on it. Meanwhile, we're going to move the baby and the nurse in here, so you can be with him. I want you to remember, every day, that all you have to do is let Farnandis and the others work for you, for the sake of your son. We'll do the rest."

Martha's eyes told me she would hear no more of Richard's plan. But I knew the baby would do more for her than I ever could. He was playing with her hair now and making little crowing cries. He tried to kiss her back, slobbering on her chin.

After a while the black nurse came in shyly and stood by, waiting for Martha to tire of the boy. She was young and rather pretty, and I wondered if she had been forced to leave her own children to come here—well, one of us had to be here, and her bringing the baby might save Martha's life. But before Richard took me home to my own children, I found a coin in my pocket and pressed it in the nurse's hand.

THE TRIAL BEGAN one sunny Wednesday in May. Hailstones had rattled roofs the day before, but now the sky stretched blue, and when I got to the hotel, Martha had on the new black silk dress and veil. When she stepped out of doors for the first time in weeks, she threw back her veil to breathe the new-made morning air.

But spectators had lined the street, and as soon as she saw them, she flipped it back over her face. They stared in silence as she and I climbed in the sheriff's buggy, Richard and a posse of Rifles and Dragoons closing around it on horseback. Women pressed handkerchiefs to mouths as if afraid to breathe the air that Martha did. As we began to roll away, the silence broke.

"Murderess!" bawled a red-faced man in a top hat, sitting his bay horse to watch her pass. "Look on the day for the last time!"

Another man's voice sneered. "Look at her, she's cold as ice. She'd mow you down as soon as look at you."

Martha shrank into a corner of the buggy and sounded like she was in tears behind the veil. "Who are all these people? Have they come to see me put to death?"

"Pay them no nevermind," Richard called boldly from out-side the buggy, and the sheriff slapped reins on the horse's back to make it trot faster, as our escort posse began to canter alongside. Creaking and shuddering, the buggy groaned around a corner. But more people lined that road, and many hissed and whistled as we passed.

The sheriff gave gruff commentary. "Darned if it didn't take all day yesterday to get us twelve good men who hadn't plumb made up their minds and get them in the jury box. Some said we oughta hang you right off. Then some said you had a right. Seemed like nobody wanted a trial. But we're going to have one, by God. And everybody wants to take a gander at you first."

I held Martha's hand tight, trying not to think about the gallows, her chair on a trap door. How did it feel when they let the trapdoor go, the rope shutting off your breath? I hoped it would break her neck outright, make it quick. I hardly prayed anymore, but I could pray for that.

The crowd thickened near the courthouse square, and an awful noise burst out, people screaming, shouting, running toward the buggy. When the sheriff stopped in front of the courthouse, Richard and the others dismounted and closed in to surround us as we stepped down.

Inside the crowd it smelled of sweat, tobacco, cow manure. People stood in front of her and leered, one red face at a time.

"Make way, make way!" the sheriff cried and gripped her arm to tow her through, me clinging to her other side, as Dragoons and Rifles jostled a narrow opening.

Up the front stairs we went, across a lobby crowded with rough men, farmhands and laborers in work clothes, then through the high doors to the court, where rows of well-dressed, upright citizens had secured seats. High in the galleries sat ladies in fine attire, whispering to each other behind their fans and staring down at my dear, disgraced friend. The prisoner's dock was set where it was visible to all, a box of polished oak, and I walked right in ahead of Martha.

"Now, Mrs. Kirkwood," the sheriff said nervously, starting to sweat. "You can't go in there. You come on out now. Come on."

I did not let go of her, but I did come out as she went in. Our two sets of hoops would have been too big for the box in any case, and the sheriff let me set a chair against the box, close enough to hold her hand. When our girl cousins in the gallery saw me there, several of them flounced straight down and flanked us on either side.

Dragoons and Rifles fanned out along the walls, watching the crowd, and the sheriff stood beside the dock, his elbows bent and hands held ready near his guns.

In the front row of spectators sat all the living men in Martha's family, older than when I last saw most of them. Our uncle Will scowled in black. Richard was unusually well groomed (by his wife, I felt sure) and almost dapper in a gray suit. Martha's older brothers sat beside him, the Reverend William bony and forbidding in a black jacket and white clerical collar, Jimmy humbler in brown serge. Jimmy gazed at Martha's veiled form with kind eyes and looked as if he wished he could be somewhere else, the collar of his starched shirt tight. He had begun to lose his hair, and the new pink pate made him look like a baby. No one knew for sure how much he understood, since he had never been able to speak or hear.

"Look, Jimmy's here," I whispered. "Does he even know what's going to happen?"

She looked and gasped. "Oh, God, I hope not. How cruel of them to bring him!"

"Rest your eyes on him," I whispered. "He's the only person here who won't know what is said, and you won't have to see it in his face."

She seemed to do it, though her pulse beat so fast and hard against my fingers, laced in hers, that I could feel it through both of our gloves.

At a table in front of the family sat her lawyers, four men in black coats and elegant striped pants, all of whom I knew from poor Sam's funeral. Colonel Stump was the youngest, handsome, tall, and fair, and when he stood up and walked toward the prisoner's box, every eye in the courtroom followed him. He bowed in front of Martha and murmured low.

"Dear Miss Cairnes, please remove your veil. Your face alone will convince the jury."

Alarmed, my eyes flew across the floor—there they were, railed off, twelve mustached, bearded men. They all looked prosperous and starched, pink cheeked. Some I thought I might have seen before, most not. Would those men send her to the gallows by day's end?

Martha's hands were shaking, and she made no move to lift the veil. Mine trembled, too, but I pulled off each finger of my gloves, unpinned her veil, and folded it into my lap. Martha turned red, then pale. But surely the sight of her, still young, her beauty softened by motherhood, would work its way under the skin of any man! And one thing I knew for sure: The twelve jurors in that box were men.

Stump bent close to her again and spoke low. "You are our Joan of Arc. You are the noblest woman I have ever seen."

With a proud tread and his head held high, he walked back to his seat.

A murmur rippled through the court, as heads craned to gape cruelly at her naked face.

"Remember, stare at Jimmy." I squeezed her hand hard till she obeyed.

But the look he gave her was too close and eloquent, his eyes going red. Maybe they had somehow taught him to read at his deaf school. He might have seen the newspapers.

"Deceptively small stature," a man's voice said clearly nearby.

"Don't believe it," another answered. "She's strong as an ox. And a crack shot, too."

I turned toward the sound of their voices and glared. On our right was a long bench equipped with slanted writing desks and inkwells, and it was packed with men in cheap check suits or worn tweed jackets, giving off a mixed scent of cigars, whiskey, coffee, sweat, mothballs, and ink as they scratched their pens on cheap foolscap. A man with a sketchpad walked a few steps out onto the floor, the better to study Martha's face as he made swift charcoal strokes.

I closed my eyes to him, sorry I had taken off her veil. If only he could see how well she had been drawn, how many times, by a far better and more loving hand!

But Martha could not stand it. All refuge gone, she covered her face with her palms. I put my arms around her, shielded her, and rocked her back and forth.

Finally she seemed to resign herself. Sitting up, she fixed her eyes on the broad expanse of polished floor.

Thomas Archer
Member of the Jury

I WINCED TO SEE that poor girl's face. Some things should not be brought into the light where anyone can gape at them. It was clear she had been lovely once, but now she looked like something hatched too soon or something flayed. She had been exposed enough. Where were the men who should have sheltered her? Where were her brothers? It was a disgrace, letting a girl take up a gun to defend her own honor.

But I hoped no one expected me to pity her, when she had taken up a loaded gun and killed a man. It hurt my chest to think of it. No family hereabouts could spare a son, because sons took over what aged fathers had to let go. They led and protected their women and children and put food on the table for grandparents and unwed sisters and aunts. No, sir, here in Harford County we had no such thing as idle men. And God knew, of bloodshed and lost sons, we had seen enough.

Some might say that I should not be seated in the jury box, with three members of my family serving as lawyers for the defense. But you could not throw a rock in Bel Air without hitting an Archer, and the jury would not have represented this fine place without one of us. My people had founded this town, with a few other old Scots and Englishmen, and they had kept out the Romanists, despite the name the state got saddled with, for Queen Mary, the bloody Catholic. That lady also had a drink named after her, and that might have told you a few things you needed to know about this state.

Not that we were drunkards, no sir, not me by a long shot, and not Catholic either. But no state was more divided than this one—not even Kansas, where white men had scalped each other, pitchforked women, and burned homesteads to decide if they would cleave unto the North or South. Half the young men here had signed their lives away for States' Rights, and the other half had done the same for the trumped-up sovereign in Washington. Right here in the jury box were turncoat Yankees sitting cheek by jowl with Southern loyalists. I myself was of the latter camp, my own brother a colonel in Lee's army. Our first cousin was the general who had led the Rebel charge at Gettysburg, fired the first shots, and sacrificed his life.

So there we sat, unhappily, twelve men in a box, facing the prisoner. At right angles to us, the judges' bench stood like an altar, high as organ pipes, the lawyers' tables straight across from it.

And you should have seen the firepower lined up at the lawyers' tables on both sides. On the prosecution side, the state had sent its heaviest artillery, the attorney general himself, Isaac D. Jones, backed by the state's attorney, P. H. Rutledge. Both of them were well-groomed men in formal morning coats and crisp white stocks, and they sat with papers stacked in front of them and their elbows on the table as they whispered to each other behind their hands. They looked brisk and confident, like they thought to wrap this skirmish up by dinnertime.

But if they thought that, they were not counting the cannons on the other side. Leading the charge for the defense would be my cousin Henry Archer, brother to both the great general and to Stevenson Archer, former secretary of the Peace Party, which had selected Henry Archer as its candidate for governor. After him would come the great Secessionist statesman Henry Farnandis, and bringing up the rear would be two younger advocates, my cousins Archer Jarrett and Herman Stump, both of them large in local lore, legends as big as their mustaches.

In fact, all four of the defense lawyers were local Rebel heroes, most with recent bounties on their heads, and I wondered if it was quite wise to have deployed them all so visibly. I did not know the prosecution lawyers, but the government of Maryland had been forced to make accommodations with the military rulers we were subject to for four long years and with the Federals in Washington since then. Situated as they were inside the government, Jones and Rutledge had probably been Union men. Idly I wondered if that meant we would replay the War Between the States right here. It made me queasy just to think of it.

But I had no time to think about that now. A murmur swept the crowd as the court crier strode onto the floor and rapped his staff. The clamor in the courtroom stilled.

"All rise!" he proclaimed. With a great *phawhump*, several hundred people stood.

The door behind the bench opened, and three balding judges paced out in swaying velvet robes and climbed the steps to sit up high behind their bench, their faces expressionless. The judge in charge would be His Honor Richard Grason, a white-haired man with a round, smooth, hairless face like a moon rising over the bench. I knew nothing of his politics, and I wondered why three judges had been sent. What kind of stake did the state have here?

Grason declared the court in session, and the lawyers started opening remarks in solemn tones that sometimes rose to sermon pitch. Attorney General Jones stood first. He wore a short gray beard and moved with calm precision till he stood in front of us, exactly at the center of the jury box. He claimed to feel sorrow at this terrible event, though he did not look sad.

"You all must know how little wish I have to speak of it. And yet it must be said, a murder was committed, and the state will show that blood was cold when it was done. No passion could excuse this act, and of passion there was none. The defense may attempt to show that the prisoner's mind was deranged at the time the act was committed and that she is therefore not responsible. But I must caution the jury not to listen to a word of that kind. The state is sympathetic toward the injuries done the accused, but from all evidence the prisoner was of sound mind and cool the day she committed this awful act. The state will also show that the defendant's brother Richard Cairnes was accessory, and his assistance was premeditated and therefore murder of the most awful kind. The jury may decide to deal with mercy toward the tender nature of the accused and hold her brother culpable instead."

Well! That was more like it! *Had* her brother tried to protect her? I turned to look and spotted him with ease, his hair an uncompromising red, the only splotch of color in the surrounding black of morning coats. His eyes shone bright, and he looked young, too young to know what he was doing, and quite proud of himself. I felt uneasy for him. If he had tried to protect her, he certainly did not succeed. What good would it do now for him to throw his life away?

But a commotion in the courtroom drew my attention to the prisoner in the dock, who had shot to her feet and seemed to want to speak. I shrank back in alarm.

"Watch out, she's trying to escape!" a man murmured behind me.

"Does she have a gun?" another whispered urgently, as if in fear for his own life.

The sheriff stood up and blocked her way, both hands on the pistols at his sides.

Her voice rang out raggedly. "I want to speak to my lawyers!"

The sheriff shook his head and said something I could not hear. But I saw Mr. Farnandis gaze at her and press one hand toward the table, as if trying to press her back into her chair.

She seemed to straighten up as tall she could get, though she was quite small.

"Give me something to write with!" she cried.

Grason tapped his gavel and leaned far over the bench as if addressing a small child. "Miss Cairnes, you are not to speak unless called upon. You will sit down and be silent."

She sank into the chair and glared at the floor, and I wondered what she would have said if she were allowed. Did she dislike the imputation that she had not acted by herself? I wondered if she had no modesty at all. But she was brave, I had to give her that.

Henry Archer stood up next to state the case for the defense. He was a thoughtful man and had been a thoughtful boy, or so had seemed to me. He used to lie in the shade and read while all the rest of us were galloping our ponies or catching frogs. The corners of his eyes drooped down, as did my own and those of several other members of the family. It gave us all a look of sorrow, like retrievers begging humankind for food.

"Your Honors," he began. "Esteemed gentlemen, the defense will show that this defendant's name is purity itself to all who know of her. Here is beauty wronged, and no force on Earth can find her guilty when all heaven has proclaimed her innocence. We are confident the jury will acquit their duty and find her act entirely justified. However, should any of them feel a qualm at this defense, we'll further show beyond a doubt that the defendant was not of her normal mind when the act occurred, as many subsequent attendant facts will show. So the good gentlemen may put their minds at ease, assured that they will have an easy choice, with two clear routes to proclaim innocence where innocence can never be in doubt."

I wondered why he did not take the lead the state had given him, of deflecting blame onto the brother, where it might belong. Surely they ought to address it, if the state pursued the lad.

Opening arguments done, the prosecution began to make its case.

The first witness called was a Union veteran named John Ware, a red-faced young man with a mighty beard. Ware kept his wool coat buttoned to the throat, though it was too warm for the day, and rivulets of sweat coursed down his broad forehead.

"Where were you on the evening of April tenth?" Mr. Jones asked him.

"At the hotel in Jarrettsville," Ware said. "I was standing on the porch right by the door. And I saw a woman cross the barroom and run through the door."

"Where exactly were you on the porch?"

"I guess about six feet to the left of the door."

"And did you know who the woman was?" Jones asked in the silence of the court.

"It was Miss Cairnes, but I didn't rightly know her at first."

"Did she have a gun?"

"I didn't see it good at first, but then I did. It was a big Colt's, too big for a lady's hand."

Someone said low behind me, "Maybe too big for *some* ladies' hands."

Jones raised his voice. "What happened then?"

Ware looked rattled, and his eyes went red. But he took a long breath and told the story levelly. "When she got out the door, she put her hand right up, and that's when I saw the gun. And she just fired straight off. Then she looked shocked, like she didn't know what she did. But darned if she didn't look like she was going to shoot again."

"And did she fire a second time?"

"Yes, sir, you bet. Five more times in all."

I could hear whispers fly around the crowd. Six shots! The three robed judges looked stern, gazing around, and the room went still again.

Jones went on. "Did you hear her say anything?"

"Yes, sir, I did. She said, 'Now I'm gonna shoot you dead.'"

I could hear the crowd squirm now.

"The hussy bragged the moment she shot him!" a voice hissed behind me.

"Did you try to stop her?" Jones asked.

The witness's eyes widened. "No, sir, I didn't think to. I jumped off the porch and crouched down low."

"Why did you do that?"

"Well, I was trying not to get shot at the time."

Low laughter greeted this—the man had run.

"And did you know anyone was hit?"

"No, sir. I did not. Well, we all knew who she was shooting at, I guess. I told him, 'Run! Run for your life!' But he just fell off the porch. And she wouldn't let him go, no, sir. Darned if she didn't chase him down to the yard. She slammed them balls right into him real fast, *blam blam blam blam blam blam*. Just like that."

The witness seemed agitated and held his fingers like a gun, imitating what she'd done.

A few ladies in the courtroom let out fainting sounds.

The judge broke in again. "That will do, Mr. Ware. Just answer the questions."

Jones waited while several ladies were escorted out into the air. In a hushed voice he asked where the victim had stood, the distance of the fall, how she had followed him.

"Could you have interposed to prevent her from firing her weapon?"

"No, sir. I don't believe so. I was much excited myself."

"And Miss Cairnes? Was she excited?"

Ware wiped his wet eyes frankly with the back of his hand. "No, sir. She was not. She was considerable more calm than any soldier in an affray where life got took."

Farnandis rose to cross-examine, and he had a very pleasing voice, almost like the operatic baritone I heard once in Baltimore. "Let me ask you something, sir, concerning one of your last statements. Have you been in an affray where life was taken?"

The witness looked stubborn, his beard jutting from his chin. "I served my country putting down the Insurrection." He savored the word, one letter at a time.

A murmur of assent went round. But Mr. Farnandis wasn't satisfied.

"Yes, but were you ever actually in an affray where life was taken?"

Ware's face flushed almost purple, and I felt sorry for him. Why humiliate him further?

"No, sir, not but this one time. But life got taken there, you may be sure of it."

I was embarrassed for the man, he had so little shame.

But he had certainly done nothing to deflect guilt from the girl, and when the laugh wore off, I felt disturbed. Ware had seen her kill a man, and even now he seemed deathly afraid of her. If he was to be believed, she had dispatched her victim coldly, calmly, single-mindedly. She did not hesitate or show remorse, and that thought made my belly sink and took me down with it.

Would we really have to send her to the gallows by tonight?

G. Richard Cairnes
Distiller of Fine Whiskey

I LOOKED AT MY SISTER, who was dead pale and seemed to weave as she sat. It would not hurt a thing if she were to faint, and I looked at Isie with approval when she began to wave a good black mourning fan at her. Our prettiest cousin went out and came back with a glass of water and a cold cloth for my sister's head, attracting the crowd's attention to her delicacy. All to the good. That sniveling Yankee Ware had done us damage, but it might not ruin all our plans.

The year before, I had told my darling Belle we should not marry yet, because I might be hanged soon and I could not bear to leave her alone, so young, perhaps with child by then. But she was so brave, she humbled me. She would not hear of a delay.

"I will be your wife and worship you, whatever comes," she said the night I first proposed, as she knelt before me, her sweet face glowing pink in the firelight. "I will stand with you and pro-claim to everyone that you are right. They think the war is over, but they're wrong. The South will never die. And if you need to raise your gun for it, I will stand by your side. I want to have the right to stand there, and for that I need to be your wife."

I had not said what might end my life, but there was no need. She knew. Everyone knew, whose minds were set like ours, back to the grand traditions of the past. Seducers of chaste women had to die. It was a brother's duty to kill the man and save his sister's honor and his own. My two older brothers were unfit for it, one a man of the cloth and the other sealed inside of silence, knowing nothing—though if he had seen our sister big with child and still at home, he might have understood.

No, it was mine to do, and I had planned it for the day after the child was born.

But a month before that, my sister had faced me, trying to look fierce despite the comic belly she had then, her small stature leaving it nowhere to go but straight out. Really, she looked like a prime turkey fattened for the county fair. But what she said made me cease to laugh.

"You are not to lay a finger on him. You hear me? It is none of your affair. I will shoot you if you try to do it first."

This was just bluster, and it made me laugh again. "And if I kill him, do you think they'll let me live for long? One way or the other, I'll be dead. And so will he."

Her eyes had blazed up at me, ice blue. "But not at your hand. Do you think you are more wronged than me? Marry Belle and keep her safe. You have to live for her and your children. I have only one thing left to do, and when it's done, I don't want to see another day. I'll wait my chance to do it in front of witnesses who have no sympathy for me. I want to be hanged."

I was so surprised, I could not speak at first. "What about your baby?"

She blanched and whispered, "It should die with its father. I wish it would."

"You don't mean that. No woman ever thought like that. Heaven's sake, Belle and I will take the child. But wait till it's born, woman. You'll change your mind."

Her face had crumpled into tears, and I knew I was right.

But still she killed the man, and when she did it, damn! It was a sight to see. She did not hesitate. She was pure action of a kind any man could hope to show. It made me proud. My sister, brave and true. She would hate to hear me say it, but the honor she reclaimed was not only her own. She had given back a bit of honor to the South, what had been sold out by the traitor Robert E. Lee for thirty pieces of silver. She got it back, for a minute, in that place and time. What could I do but follow her example now?

True, she had usurped my brotherly prerogative, but that no longer bothered me. After all, I had settled with the man already, him and all his kin. Not only his fat brother the Federal and his foolish father—sure, I had dealt with them. I had yet to settle with his cousin, March McComas, who had scouted for the Federals and led them into Bel Air, where they helped enslave the county, trying to make us all sing "The Star *Strangled* Banner" forever and ever.

Compared to them, Nick was puny, vermin. But I had still settled up with him when he had the impudence to think he could steal my servants for life, three members of my family, and then spread slurs against my character. As if he were the champion of benevolence to Negroes, when it was all a lie.

I'll tell you what. It's nobody's business what I did with the girl Sophie. She was mine, always had been, from birth, or at least since my father's death. When my father died—when Lincoln killed him, the day he seized the sovereignty of Maryland—the care of Sophie and her family fell to me. I took my father's place, and she was mine, as was her whole family. We belonged to each other. It was the way things were. We served each other, each in our own way. It was theirs to serve and please me, and mine to shelter and protect them. It was no one else's place to ask what we did. That fool, that scoundrel, had no right to take her or her brother or their mother from my home. I had sheltered and protected them, and they had served me, every way they could. He had no right to them.

Bad enough that he slid into my home like a viper and thought to take my sister, too. She at least had some say of her own. She was a person of free will. And I blame her for that. I could not entirely forbid her contact with him, any more than Adam could chase the snake out of the garden. But my sister was a being almost like myself, made from my rib. And it has always been a flaw in the divine order, woman's weakness for the snake. I could not stop her when she took the fatal steps, far from my protecting hand.

As for the others—Tim and Sophie and Creolia—well, Negroes were not like us. They were not endowed with godlike reason or free will. God gave me dominion over my land, my flocks, my fields, my forests, my womenfolk, and all of my Negroes. Negroes were like children, and like children they needed to be nurtured and held to my bosom. I would have fed and clothed and housed them and all of their issue all their lives, if McComas had not taken them. Taken Sophie in every sense of the word, and for that he would burn in hell. Oh, yes. The man had a long record of indecency. Age thirty-five and never had a wife? No, he preferred to steal his pleasures, seduce the wives and slaves of other men. When he did it to a man's own virgin sister and left her standing at the altar big with child—well, anyone could see he ought to die.

And now at last the time had come for me to rise up and restore my sister's honor. Before the trial began, I had already set the wheels in motion to sacrifice my life while saving hers.

Mr. Jones called up Frank Street, and I sat back with pleasure to watch the wheels turn. Street knew his job, and in the first ten seconds, he had cast doubt on whether Martha could have fired all six shots by herself.

"She didn't have a pistol in her hand till after the second shot," he said with confidence. "But I saw Richard Cairnes hold a pistol out the window. He pointed it straight out."

Pleasure sent a warm flush up my neck. The crowd whispered like a breeze and only quieted when gavels fell and criers cried.

Farnandis rose to cross-examine Frank. He took his time, serene, pausing to peruse his pocket watch. "And where exactly did you first see Richard Cairnes that day?"

"I saw him come into the bar. He come in first, ahead of Miss Cairnes."

Oh, this was good. It wasn't true, but it was good. I was a man of honor, and I had promised my sister I would not fire first. I intended to finish him if need be, though I doubted I would have to, knowing her. And in the event, I had not had to do that.

Street's eyes shone with sincerity as he gazed at Farnandis, never wavering.

"Where did he come from?"

"He came along the passage from the door outside, a bit before she come through."

"And did he have a gun in his hand?"

"No, sir. I didn't remark it at that time."

"When did you notice it?"

"I saw it after the first shot, just after it. The one that killed the man. Hers all went wild."

"Mr. Street!" the judge said sharply. "Don't give us your opinion unless we ask for it. You are to answer each question as simply as you can."

The witness closed his lips with a knowing look and passed a hand over the lock of brown hair that hung on his forehead. "Yes, sir."

Farnandis went on patiently. "And what did you see exactly, after the first shot?"

"I saw Richard Cairnes stand at the window of the barroom with a pistol in his hand."

"What was he doing with it?"

"He was lowering it with his arm out straight."

"Did you see him fire the gun at anyone?"

"He had been pointing it out the window at Nick McComas."

"Did you see him fire?" Mr. Farnandis asked.

"I saw him bring his arm down. It were raised out straight and I saw him bring it down."

He seemed to want to say more, but the lawyers didn't ask him to, and the judge had an eye on him. As he left the stand I saw him throw a mild look of contempt at Martha, as if she had over-stepped herself to say she killed a man. He did not know her and had never seen her shoot. But when his eyes met mine as he went back to his seat, I gave him the smallest nod of thanks.

Now Martin Jarrett took the stand and spoke at length about the wounds.

"One ball penetrated about the center of the breast bone, two inches above the stomach, about opposite the fifth and sixth ribs." He gestured with his lean, tanned fingers as if poking in the wounds. "The ball entered obliquely to the left and probably passed through the left lung. Another ball struck the thigh in the vicinity of the femoral artery and in all probability struck another artery nearly as large. Death might have been produced from either."

Jones looked calm, his face outlined by his trim beard. "And in your opinion, from what angle was the first bullet fired?"

"From the direction of the doorway to the bar."

"Might it have come from the window next to it instead?"

That made the crowd buzz like yellow jackets in a jar.

"Silence, please!" the crier called.

Grason banged his gavel down. "Ladies and gentlemen, the court is aware of the intense interest in this case. However, no breach of decorum will be tolerated. You will listen in silence. The witness will answer the question posed."

Jarrett looked wary. "I suppose the first shot might have been fired from the window. It's close enough to the doorway there."

The crowd buzzed anew, and calm had not yet been restored when Farnandis rose to cross-examine him. But they soon quieted. Farnandis had always been worth listening to.

"We all appreciate your expert testimony, Dr. Jarrett. If you would be so good, there are a few more things we need to know. The deceased was found to have a pistol in his own pocket at the time of his death, isn't that so?"

"It is."

"And in your opinion, would it have been possible for him to have fired off the pistol in his pocket and inflicted on himself the fatal wound to his own thigh?"

The crowd gasped, apparently outraged, maybe because Jarrett had been called to help the prosecution, not the defense. I could make out some muttering.

"What did you expect? The man's a known Secesh. He was CSA!"

"Two-faced traitor!"

"What side's he on?"

Jones stood up to object. "The state questions the propriety of the defense carrying their inquiry into probabilities only admissible in the examination of a witness for the prisoner."

The three judges bent their heads together and conferred at length.

"Objection overruled," Grason said. "Witness will answer the question."

Jarrett looked relieved. "No, it isn't possible. The pistol in his pocket would have made an entry wound quite opposite from that inflicted. The wound to the thigh was consistent with having been shot by a gun held by a standing person a yard away, when the victim lay on his back on the ground."

Jones's face betrayed no excitement when he was allowed to counter-question after the defense. "So, Doctor, is it your opinion that either wound could have been inflicted in any other way than from a gun held by Miss Cairnes?"

The crowd seemed to hold its breath.

Jarrett's voice quavered slightly. "Do you mean, do I think she inflicted the fatal wound? Why, yes, I think she did. She certainly intended to. And she does know how to shoot."

I was disappointed with old Jarrett here, but had better hopes when the prosecution called his youngest brother next. Joshua was one of us, and he knew the plan. In the daylight he looked something like his older brother, only skinny and freckled, with the expression of a curious colt.

Jones asked him to describe the shooting, and he obliged with great enthusiasm, then told how he had followed Martha on George Andrew's horse.

Jones asked, "Did she say anything to you?"

"Yes, sir. She said, 'I told him I'd do it, and I done it.'"

This was not at all what he had agreed to say, and I glared at him. He was clearly making that up, and I hoped the jury could hear it, too. If Martha had ever said "I done it" in her life, our mother would have made her write it out correctly two hundred times.

"After the first shot, how did the victim look to you?"

"He looked pale and had the appearance about the eyes of a dying man."

"Did you see Richard Cairnes?"

"I did. He was at the window from the barroom, looking out onto the porch. I didn't notice him particular at first. But he had a gun, all right."

"And what was he doing with the gun?"

"Why, he was pointing it right out the window to the porch."

"And did you see him fire it?"

Josh sat with his mouth open and glanced at me. I gazed back and willed him to be brave.

"Why—why—yes, I did," he finally said, as if out of breath.

A small commotion made me glance toward Martha. She was standing up again, shaking off Isie's hands and glaring hard at Farnandis, her demeanor demanding he stand up also and do something. But Farnandis only gestured at her to sit down, though she did not until the sheriff stood in front of her, his hands on the pistols in his belt.

The prosecution called the wife of the innkeeper at the Jarrettsville Hotel. She was our cousin, an easygoing, plump woman, but she seemed nervous now, glancing at Martha and the jury. She twisted her handkerchief and looked ready to sob.

"Mrs. Street, tell us exactly what you saw."

Her voice was almost inaudible. "I saw Martha gallop to the front door."

"Please speak up, Mrs. Street, so we can hear you properly," the judge admonished her.

She looked cornered, but spoke louder. "I saw Martha gallop to the front door, and her brother pulled her off her horse. She flung the reins at him and climbed the steps into the ladies' parlor, and I met her there. I tried to stop her going in the bar, because I knew Nick was there."

"What did you say to her?"

"I said, 'This is no place for you.' But she didn't listen. 'Where is Nick McComas?' she said."

"What did you do then?"

"I went into the bar to find my husband, and he tried to stop her going in the bar. He's a big man, and he blocked the doorway from the ladies' parlor. But she faced up to him and said, 'It's Nick McComas I've come to see.'"

"What did your husband say to that?"

"He said, 'Nick was here, but he's gone away.'"

"What happened then?"

"She just shoved by him, and she was taking out the Colt's. It was in the pocket of her dress, and she held it out and ran through the bar onto the porch."

"Did you see what happened out there on the porch?"

"I did," she said too quietly. Grason asked her to speak up again.

She looked terrified. "I saw Nick McComas sitting on the rail in his blue uniform. The sunset was almost over, and it was pretty dark out there. But I saw him see her as she came through the door, and he stood up to greet her. She held out one arm—I thought she might be reaching out to him. But then I saw the powder flash. It was all over in a second."

"Where was the powder flash exactly?"

"It came from in front of her. In front of Martha Jane."

"And how did McComas look to you then?"

"I saw him—I saw him leaning back against a pillar."

"And how did he appear to you?"

"Why—why, he looked like a man who climbs up a silo and can't find a handhold at the top. He knew he was going to fall. And then he did. He fell backwards off the porch."

"Did you see Richard Cairnes?"

"No, sir. I did not see him at all, after he pulled her off the horse."

"Did you see him fire a gun out of the window of the bar?"

"No, sir, I did not."

Damn! I was worried now. Why didn't I talk to her before the trial? It had never occurred to me that they would call a woman up to testify, with so many men who saw it all more clearly from the porch and lawn outside.

But, thank God, Jones called her husband, Tom Street, next. Street was a large man with a steady, rocking gait. Jones asked if he had seen me in the window of the bar.

A muscle twitched in Street's jaw, and he may have glanced toward where his wife was sitting, back in the audience. "Yes, I did. I saw him in the window of the bar, and I saw him shoot his Colt's." He seemed compelled to repeat it to make sure, his eyes round. "He was there—he was there, all right—in the window, in the window, yes, and he fired his gun straight out toward where McComas stood."

"Did it seem to you that his shot hit its mark? Did it hit McComas?"

"Why, yes, I think it did. I think it hit him before he fell back off the porch."

That was better, and for the first time I felt a finger of cold fear. *Was* this going to work?

I glanced around quickly, hoping to see Belle, and there she was, beside my mother in the front row of the gallery. Her sweet young face beamed down at me, surrounded by gold banana curls, a locket brooch with my photo and a lock of my hair clasped at her high lace collar. She had asked for the hair to wear against her throat always when I was gone, and her eyes seemed to send a beam of pure blue strength to me. I fastened mine on hers. Yes. This was what heroes felt, what Stonewall Jackson knew before he died, what Jeb Stuart and Henry Kyd Douglas had felt. John Pelham had been only twenty-three when he died for his beliefs, and I could, too.

The traitor, Jones, announced, "The state calls Shadrach Street."

Shadrach was a farmer getting on in years, and he owned land near mine, beside the fork for Jarrettsville, and lived with his sister there. He described how he had seen me on the day of the parade, riding past with a little girl behind me on the horse.

"And did you see Richard Cairnes again that day?"

Street looked across the room to where I sat, his eyes rheumy and red, and I held his gaze so he would not falter with the tale.

His voice dropped low and tremulous. "Yes, I did."

"What was he doing then?"

He had to breathe a few times before he could speak. "I saw him gallop toward his own place, with his wife's brother, Charles Nelson."

"And after Cairnes and Nelson rode by your place, did you see what happened next?"

Street nodded and seemed to be panting. "I saw them meet his sister Martha on the road. She was walking quite fast toward Jarrettsville. They spoke to her, then galloped away toward Richard's place, fetched her horse, and galloped back."

He paused and did not seem to want to go on.

"Then what happened?" Jones asked gently.

"Richard got off his horse and threw her up on hers, and they all galloped off toward Jarrettsville. Miss Cairnes galloped off first. The last I saw of them, she was in the lead."

This remark prompted some snickering from the row of journalists, as if they thought she had humiliated me with her superior riding, and I felt two spots of heat bloom on my cheeks. Damn them anyway. Damn all of them. They would see what kind of dignity a hero had.

"And what time would you say that was, when they galloped off?"

"I remember particular. I looked at my pocket watch. It was about half past five o'clock. Not twenty minutes before the shots were fired, and they were headed there all right, to Jarrettsville, deliberate-like."

A murmur rose at this, like a flock of sparrows rising in delight, and I sat back, pleased. I might as well enjoy this, I thought suddenly, since it might be the last thing I would ever see.

Jones cocked his head thoughtfully at Shadrach Street. "From what you could see, did it appear to be Miss Cairnes's own idea to go to town? Or was it Richard Cairnes who told her to do that?"

Old Street could not look at me now. He sat breathing with his mouth open as he stared at the floor. Sweat shone on his balding pate. "She was headed there already, on foot. I saw her walking there quite fast before he came along."

"So in your opinion Miss Cairnes was already on her way to town, and her brother only brought her horse to get her there faster?"

Street nodded, now quite pale. "And maybe to help her get away after."

Jones thanked him, let him go, and called his sister, Hannah Street. Old Miss Street repeated all that he had said, almost word for word, but with none of his hesitation.

"They took her off pell-mell. Just that fast, pell-mell," she said and lifted a liver-spotted hand to snap her fingers.

"And did you think that they were taking her somewhere against her will, or was it, in your opinion, where she meant to go?"

"Oh, no doubt about it," she said enthusiastically. "She was already headed there. It was her own idea, I would say it was. She's not the sort of person who needs her brother's direction to go anyplace, no sir. She's not like that at all. She's a firecracker, that girl is."

At that she seemed to look toward the prisoner's dock, and Martha Jane and our girl cousins all gazed back at her as if they understood each other in some witches' pact. I looked from them to Farnandis to see if he had caught that, too. Good God, couldn't he do something?

But Farnandis did not cross-examine either aged Street, and Jones next called a local bachelor farmer, John Deets. Deets lived farther west, past Jarrettsville, and he testified that less than an hour before the shooting, he saw me ride past on the King's Road with a little girl behind me on my horse. Prompted by questions, Deets told the tale.

"I saw Charles Nelson catch up to Richard Cairnes, and they went up King's Road a bit and stopped a minute. Nelson seemed to say something to Richard Cairnes that made him ride back to the crossroads by my house and wait. He sat on his horse at the fork just by, with the little girl behind him holding on. And sure enough, pretty soon I saw Nick McComas ride past on his horse toward Jarrettsville. He was with a pack of other men in uniform, for the celebration, you know, and he didn't seem to notice Richard Cairnes there waiting, and Richard turned and followed him from a distance."

Now this was more like it. That scene shone in my memory, that beautiful sunset when the sky glowed like my wife's eyes, and how easy it had been to ride two hundred yards behind that swine, knowing I could have galloped at him with my pistol out!

Jones went on unperturbed, "Did you see Richard Cairnes again that night?"

"Yes, I did," Deets said. "Richard rode back and continued on where he left off, toward the west, and some minutes later he came galloping back toward Jarrettsville, fast as you please. No one was with him then. He'd put the girl off by that time."

Jones thanked Deets and recalled Joshua Jarrett, and I looked at Josh sharply. What was he doing, testifying twice for Jones? His first time on the stand had been a near debacle, and I was not eager to hear him put his boot into his mouth again.

But in response to what Jones asked, Josh said that he had seen the same scene from a distance, and he added one new, wonderful detail: "That little girl was on Richard's horse when he met Nelson there at the crossroads. She heard what was said."

Jones regarded him with intensity, as if he had not thought of this before. "Do you know the identity of the little girl?"

"No, sir," said Joshua as if pleased with himself, and shook his head briskly.

A low rumble rose out of the crowd and particularly from the newsmen on my left.

"Call the girl!" most of them said.

"She'll know what was said, all right. That'll prove premeditation, right there."

Grason tapped his gavel lightly once. "Does anyone know the little girl's identity?"

I thought fast, wondering if I should answer. The girl was my cousin Ella Hope, Isie's half sister, from her mother's second marriage, and she had come to visit our farm for a few days. I had been taking her home to Hope Place, a few miles west of Jarrettsville. I suppose she did hear what Nelson said to me, though she was only seven and might not recall it well. Nelson had been excited, and he had shouted that McComas was there and headed to the hotel.

There had been no need to say more, since Nelson knew of Martha's plan—our plan, that is, because it was mine, too. His color was high, exhilarated, as we raced each other back toward my place. We almost galloped right by Martha, who was on the road, half running toward the hotel. Somehow she knew, as if an angel had appeared to her. I had given her a Colt's Navy revolver and taught her to load and use it, and she had it in her skirt pocket.

Now, damn! What a chance missed to teach little Ella what to say and have her say it here! It would prove premeditation and that the gun was mine, not Martha's.

But we had not thought of that in time, and Ella was a child and might say the wrong thing. So I did not speak up. I glanced at Martha to see if she would. But Martha knew Ella might help to send me to the gallows in her place, and she firmly closed her lips.

At last the prosecution thought to call John Deets back up and ask him if he knew.

"Why, sure, it was the little Hope girl, Ella, I think it is. Father's James Hope. Mother was widow to one of the Cairnes men, and she married Hope later on and had the girl. Hope Place is down the road a piece from mine. That must be where Richard Cairnes was taking her."

Jones conferred with Rutledge before he turned to the judge. "Your Honor, the prosecution asks to be allowed to call Ella Hope, and to summon her if she is not in the court."

Grason tapped his gavel. "The court calls Ella Hope."

"Ella Hope!" the crowd said low at first, then loud. "Where's Ella Hope?"

I had no more need to look at Martha Jane. My heart was a hawk that soared above the courthouse, taking in the view, horizons shining blue and brilliant. Did she really think she could take all the glory and the blame?

Mary Ann Bay Cairnes
Mother of the Accused

My son was a fool. Sometimes in ways you could forgive, like his father at his best, so sure that he could mend the world and that it would not swallow him.

But now Richard thought to sacrifice his life to save that chimera, the South, its honor and its chivalry—in the person of that bigger fool, my daughter. I had chosen her name, but I would not say it again. For her he meant to leave his dear young wife and me with no man to watch over us and earn our daily bread?

My Richard, my George Richard. I had named him for his father and grandfather, who was one of the great men who had led our clan out of barren Scotland to the rich soil of this promised land. I had chosen to sit in the gallery, where I might be less subject to the stares of strangers, and from where I sat I could see my three sons below. They were all handsome, decent men. James, my first and tallest, had a sweetness in his nature that made you wonder if God blessed those he had afflicted most. He had been blessed, too, in his wife, a resourceful widow who had removed him to her farm and made it possible for him to run it as well as any man. My William sat next to them, clean and upright in clerical garb, and what mother was not proud to have a son called to God? But God was a tough master and had taken William far from home.

So I had one son left to be my comfort in old age. No, Richard should not pay for what she did. Why then was he sitting there with flashing eyes, like he could see a host of angels coming down for him?

Beside me in the front row of the gallery, his young wife gazed at him like she could see the angels, too. I wanted to shake her. Did it occur to her that they might hang Richard and Martha both, brother and sister side by side, or imprison both and throw away the key, dooming us to poverty, to taking in embroidery and lace-work? Ladies could not stoop to taking in laundry, and how else would we eat?

I could see that thought in other ladies' eyes, up in the gallery, their looks slicing cruelly to where I sat. I should not have come, and indeed I had not asked to. It was Henry Farnandis who said I must so that everyone could see I still believed in her. As if I did!

"I would rather see you in your grave than pregnant and un-wed," my own mother had said to me, and it still chilled my heart. But I should have said it to that foolish girl. Perhaps it would have saved her from a ruin more complete than ever a lady suffered or allowed.

Oh! She made me wish she were the one who had gone to an early grave, instead of my Rebecca, who had not lived to see three years. Rebecca had flown straight to heaven, a place her sister would never see. The night that scoundrel left her at the altar, I told her that.

"I wish you were never born," I said as she sat weeping in her wedding dress at midnight, all the guests gone home. We had not spoken since.

A rumble from the crowd below made me sit up. It seemed no one was coming forward with Ella, and the whole crowd was muttering.

"They're trying to hide her! Ella Hope! Get Ella Hope!"

Even the judge seemed caught up in the question and did not silence them.

The state's attorney rose. Mr. Rutledge was a less impressive figure than Mr. Jones, thin and clean-shaven and stoop-shouldered as if he were afraid to take up space. But he had a surprising voice, deep and firm. "Your Honor, the state asks the indulgence of the court. We have only become cognizant today of additional facts we wish to prove and have immediately issued subpoenas. We're not to blame, and we suggest the case go over till tomorrow."

Judge Grason scowled. "The court cannot allow the case to go over. The life of the prisoner is involved, and witnesses should not be detained here at this busy season of the year. We must proceed to the defense so as to conclude today."

Mr. Rutledge sat down to confer with Mr. Jones, hands shielding their mouths from view.

Mr. Rutledge stood back up. "Then, Your Honor, we suppose the state must close its case, though we beg further consideration if the trial goes over for another day."

It was midday already, and the court recessed for dinner. When Richard came up to the gallery for Belle and me, I put a hand on his arm and reached up to move a stray red lock off his cheek, as high as I could reach. "I am afraid for you. Don't do that for her."

He shook his hair back the way it had been, his eyes so bright it was like looking at the sun. "Won't you come back to the hotel and dine with us, Mother? Please. It will do you good."

I declined, having no desire to eat or see my daughter there. When I was sure they had both gone, I went downstairs to look for Henry Farnandis. The bailiff said the lawyers had all gone to dinner. Mr. Farnandis had been a friend to my dear husband, and I begged a scrap of paper and a quill and jotted a note to him.

"I must speak with you before the court resumes. If you have any care for my family, you will come and listen to me."

The church across the street was Presbyterian, and I said I would wait there for him.

The bailiff said he would deliver it, and I retreated to the tall church, its spire stretched to the sky, like a conduit to carry up my prayers. It was cool inside, and no one was there. I chose a pew in the middle of the vast space, in view of the altar and the beautiful stained glass above.

Presbyterians do not kneel in church, but I felt a need for it, and I pressed my knees to the cold floor, closed my eyes against my clasped hands, and put myself into the space of prayer, allowing my thoughts to lift up as they would. I thought of my husband and my parents and Creolia and my little girl who died. When your loved ones have betrayed you or left the earth, what is left? There is truth and justice, honor and purity, and Jesus Christ. There is forgiveness, which my daughter should have given that poor man. She should have stayed pure and let the peace that passes understanding enter her and give her rest.

And would I have to forgive even her? A tear squeezed from my eyes and wet my hands. I supposed so, but I did not have the strength. I supposed I ought to ask for it. I said the Lord's Prayer and the Nicene Creed and let my mind go silent, listening. Forgive, because His Son died. That was the mystery, as if it paid for every wrong.

But what of *my* son? Why did he have to die to save that wretched girl?

Unwillingly, I saw her as a baby. She had been tiny, wiry, energetic, and demanding, early to do everything. She had been so bent on keeping up with her big brothers James and William, she stood up by herself at six months old and walked two months later, a peanut of a thing with tiny legs. She would dash after the boys, themselves just two and four years old, James's affliction then becoming clear, though we denied it for another year. Some restless spirit seemed to have possessed her, and her father used to laugh and say it was a Cherokee maiden we had borne, not a real Scot like us. She never grew as tall as me, or filled out, womanly, even after the child. She had always been extremely odd, a girl who wanted to ride ponies bareback with her legs hanging on both sides, bloomers exposed. She climbed trees, swam rivers, ice-skated on ponds at breakneck speed. She never gave way to the boys, never let them win at shooting matches, footraces, croquet, or twenty questions, careless of what they thought.

How had I spawned this pint-sized Amazon? I had never been the slightest bit like that. From an early age I had tried to speak softly, do fine embroidery, make pies with flaky crusts, and tat lace by hand with pins to show off on my collars and cuffs to beguile some worthy man.

And that I had done, but never touched so much as his hand until my wedding night. Even after that, I was a lady, and a lady's blood runs cool. Of course I did my wifely duty, as my bearing five children would attest. I loved him as a wife should, and I mourned him still.

But I could not imagine what possessed a woman to behave in such a lewd, lascivious fashion as my daughter had, the like of which had never been seen in our whole county, much less in our own family. I knew what people said, how they defamed the South and said our bloodlines were all mixed because of lewd behavior by our men. I did not doubt it had occurred on plantations with five hundred slaves, masters and foremen swaggering with drink and lust, corrupted by their power over so much human flesh. Those places must have been like sultans' harems, down in the deep South in all that sultry air and even in the low-lying cotton-growing region on our eastern shore.

But here on the Maryland Piedmont, we breathed a cooler air. Our farms were small, and of the few slaves we had ever owned, most were freed ahead of the decree. It enraged me how Northerners assumed it must be Mississippi here, as soon as you crossed the Mason-Dixon Line. My brothers, my father, my grandfather, my uncles, my husband and his father and grandfather? All of them were upright men, God-fearing, their eyes on heaven rather than on the flesh. Our family was far too proud to risk disgrace, and how was it that my girl was not? She seemed to have run straight at it, arms open to embrace.

Now the spirit of forgiveness had deserted me, and I felt no peace. Lifting my eyes, I mopped my face until my handkerchief was wet. I heard someone clear his throat.

Surprised, I turned to see Henry Farnandis, looking reflective as he waited at the end of the pew. I slid back onto the seat and beckoned him to come to me.

"I am sorry. I did not realize you were here."

He sat beside me and folded my hands into his. "Dear Mrs. Cairnes, I would not have disturbed you for the world, in this holy place. Is there some service I can do for you?"

"There is." I started to weep again, my soggy hanky useless now.

Mr. Farnandis offered me his, of fine linen embroidered with his initials and pressed by his loving spouse or faithful servant, two advantages I no longer had, and I cried harder at that.

"Please, you must stop them from pursuing Richard. It was my daughter's doing all alone. Ask anyone who knows her. She is a better shot than Richard! She meant to shoot that man, and I am sure she did. I know Richard wants to sacrifice himself for her, and that is a noble wish. But he is not guilty, and he is all I have left. If they take him from me, I will have nothing, and neither will his young wife. We may starve."

Mr. Farnandis nodded. "Let me take you in our confidence. We think Richard may get off for insufficient evidence. But that isn't true in your daughter's case. She has given them all of the evidence that anyone could want. If the prosecution wants to cast doubt on her guilt and deflect it onto Richard, we ought to let it happen. It may be her only chance."

"I won't have him risked to save her. She alone must bear what she has done."

He bowed his head as if in prayer, and when he lifted it, his bright green eyes searched mine. "Do you realize your daughter will be hanged?"

My heart stumbled, but I kept my eyes on his. "I do realize that. But it is what she deserves, and what she wishes for. I do not see what life is left for her, after what she did. But my Richard! You know him. He has been young and impulsive, but always with good cause. Can you say anything so good of my daughter? I cannot. I would wish she had never been disgraced or moved to this extreme. But since she has been, I think justice must be done."

Mr. Farnandis sighed. "Let us pray on it a moment. All right?"

I agreed, and we both bowed our heads. I could not pray, afraid to open my mind to it, when I had just pronounced my daughter's death sentence.

Overhead in the steeple, slow, ponderous bells began to swing, bonging out the hour when the trial would resume. We lifted our heads.

Mr. Farnandis took my hands again. "I will try to save your girl. But I cannot promise anything. And if we stop the prosecution from pursuing Richard, I will have to ask you to take the stand in her defense. You must pour out your mother-love in all its purity and let them feel it in their hearts, especially those twelve good men charged to put your child to death."

The thought made me sick. To be pilloried on the witness stand, exposed in front of everyone as the mother of that awful girl!

"More than love I should have given her, that much is sure," I said with bitterness. And yet my heart began to beat more calmly at this inkling I had won. "She can't be saved, Mr. Farnandis, no matter what you do."

He gave me a sad look. "Dear lady, I only hope you will be half so eloquent in your daughter's defense. This is a tragic day indeed. But I will speak to Mr. Jones and see if he can be persuaded to pursue another course."

Rising, he took my arm and escorted me across the street, into the courthouse gallery, where I took my seat with more hope than before, feeling as if my chest were scoured out. It would be horrible, what was to come that day. But at least my Richard would be spared.

The afternoon was warm, and cicadas vibrated in trees outside. The courtroom windows had been raised up high, and sun streamed in, the air sweet with bloom. The defense lawyers began to call on upright citizens to praise my daughter's virtues, piety, and preference for good works. My brother had long served as a judge in the Orphans' Court, and they called him first.

"I've known her all her life," he said, gazing up to where I sat as if to reassure me. "She is my niece, of the highest social standing and of blameless character."

When my brother was dismissed, Mr. Farnandis called on two well-respected ministers who said they knew her well. That they did, but only on her best behavior, in church.

"Her general character is as good as can be in every respect," said Reverend Abraham Gladden. "There is no young lady of superior social standing in her neighborhood. She is very modest and retiring. There is no levity in her manner or cruelty in her disposition. She is kind and gentle and charitable, particularly so. She has always been very active in cases of sickness, death, and Sunday school celebrations."

Our own Reverend Cathcart said the same. "I have never seen any vicious propensities in her such as ill will, resentment, or levity. I've never heard a word uttered against her. She studied in my school, and she has been exemplary for her good conduct all the time I've known her. No one stands higher than Miss Cairnes or more respected for her virtue and excellence."

Mr. Jones stood up to cross-examine him. "How long did she go to school to you?"

Reverend Cathcart's eyes were small and jittery behind his spectacles. "Oh, it was a considerable time. A year or two, or even longer."

"Yes, and look where it got her!" someone muttered behind me, and my face burned.

"No good comes of sending them to school!"

"Hush!" several voices said, and the muttering died down.

The next witness called was Gabriel Smithson, and as he plodded to the stand, the crowd around me squirmed in anticipation, as if sure he would know something, tavern-keeper that he was, and so close to our farm.

It was Henry Archer's turn to do the questioning, and you could not help but admire his dignified bearing. He looked like who he was, nearly elected governor, and brother to a great Confederate general. A statesmanlike figure, tall, broad-shouldered, he had been handsome in his youth, though his fair hair had retreated and the pale skin of his forehead now covered his pate, and his dark eyes drooped as if with great sorrow. He asked Smithson about my daughter's reputation, and he agreed with the others. But Mr. Archer wanted something more.

"What did you see the night of April tenth at the hotel in Jarrettsville?"

Smithson told his view of the events with evident gusto. "I was on my horse in the act of going away and had ridden from the stable in the direction of the porch, when I saw Miss Cairnes appear from the parlor and shoot instantly. She looked pale, and her manner appeared wild and resolute. Her expression was quite different from what it formerly had been. The whole affair didn't occupy a minute—not half a minute. I could not have done it so quick."

Some laughed at that, and the judges gave warning glances around the room.

"And did you hear her say anything at that time?"

Smithson nodded. "She said something, but I couldn't make it out. Some said later—"

Mr. Jones sprang to his feet. "Objection. Hearsay testimony has no relevancy."

Judge Grason agreed. "Objection sustained."

"But did you hear her say anything yourself?" Mr. Archer asked again.

Smithson hesitated. "I didn't rightly hear, no. But I must say, she seemed quite insane, and I thought to myself, *She'll be a corpse before morning.*"

The courtroom went still, and even I felt chilled. Was I glad she had not killed herself? I did not want to look at her but could not help it. My eyes turned toward her fleetingly, through the rail of the gallery. She stared straight ahead, her face uncovered and so vulnerable, it made me wince. I looked back to the witness, determined not to care. She had borne a bastard and committed murder, and she alone must pay for it.

Mr. Jones stood up to cross-examine Smithson. "Were you acquainted with the victim?"

Smithson's eyes went red, and he blinked rapidly. "I had been with him a great deal. He was my friend, from boyhood till his death."

"What was your object in riding back to the porch?"

Smithson seemed to haul in a big breath before he could speak. "My object was to have some words with him before I left, on a particular subject."

"What was the subject?"

"When he first landed on the porch, he had a little altercation with Frank Street, and I rode up to see if I could help. But my attention was attracted by the appearance of the lady and the flash of the pistol. She fired wildly, and I wheeled the horse about."

"Why did you wheel?"

Smithson gave a sheepish grin. "The action was too hot for me."

Some in the court guffawed, though others shushed them, and I felt all eyes slide toward the prisoner's dock. I had to look again. Was her bare face contrite? It certainly was not. A spark seemed to light her big bold eyes—she almost laughed. Oh! To think I had almost forgiven her!

Belle took hold of me. "Are you all right?"

I nodded and pulled myself upright. I had to stand it now.

Mr. Jones went on evenly. "Tell us about Nick McComas's altercation with Frank Street. What was the subject of their dispute?"

Smithson flushed deep red and looked unwilling to go on. The crowd leaned forward. He was under oath, and he would have to say.

"It was about some talk going round the neighborhood."

"Go on. What was the talk?"

"Talk touching Miss Cairnes."

"What sort of talk?"

"It's too indelicate to say."

"I think you can go on in general terms. What did the talk concern?"

With a great flounce and rustle, several ladies rose and bolted from the gallery, as did several from the floor below. Some men eyed their womenfolk and seemed to wonder if they ought to take them out. For a few minutes the room was in chaos, the faint-hearted making for the doors. I had blamed her one minute before, but now I hated those who left for their certainty that such a thing could not happen to them and that my daughter's story might sully them.

"Silence! Silence!" called the court crier.

Judge Grason rapped his gavel hard three times. "Ladies and gentlemen, I must warn you once again. All those making indecorous exclamations will be expelled from this courtroom. Silence is the only acceptable course for you."

The witness waited until all who could not bear to hear had left the room.

Looking down, he spoke softly. "Talk touching her and a black man. It was all over the county by that time, and many believed it. Nick had told me there was no truth in it, and it was low and slanderous. He always defended her, and she killed him anyway."

He lifted hot blue eyes toward the dock, where for once my daughter had the decency to sit with eyes cast down, all laughter gone.

When Mr. Smithson was dismissed, the prisoner seemed to waver as she sat, and a lady stepped boldly across the hardwood floor, a glass of water in her hand. With her back to me, I did not know her, but she was tall and graceful, her mass of white hair elegantly dressed, rows of black lace flounces on her skirt, a black lace cap and gloves. The sheriff tried to stop her but she went on to the dock, held out the glass. Judge, jury, lawyers, and audience alike went still, and even the reporters stopped scratching to watch.

Leaning down, she said something my daughter, who shook her head as if to refuse the glass. But the lady persisted, and my daughter took it and drank. When the lady turned to walk back to her seat, I saw she was Mrs. Stevenson Archer, sister-in-law of the Confederate general and a great lady in Bel Air. Even in old age she was quite beautiful, with soft turquoise eyes and a famous heart-shaped face.

But what was that Mr. Farnandis had just announced in his clear voice? All eyes on the floor and in the gallery had turned to gaze at me. Down on the floor, Farnandis beckoned, but I sat frozen in my seat.

Belle took my elbow. "It's time. They have called you up, dearest. Here, lean on me."

My legs trembled so hard, I did not think that I could stand. A woman I did not even know rose to take my elbow on the other side, and she and Belle assisted me out of the gallery and to the stairway down.

There I was met by Colonel Stump, tall and mighty with a gentle face, and he supported not only my arm but also my waist, so I felt lifted off the floor. Belle went with me anyway, down to the gate into the court. I wanted to hold on to her like Naomi embracing Ruth.

Colonel Stump half carried me across the floor to the witness stand, and I fought off the panicked feeling that it was *me* they meant to hang or stone or drown as a witch, humiliate me any way they could, show that some flaw in my soul had made me spawn a murderess.

But it was far worse when I turned and faced their eyes. Never had so many people stared at me. My wedding had been small, just family, and it was my back they watched that day. That day at the altar, I had been asked only one question, and anyone could answer that.

But here? What would they ask?

"Dear Mrs. Cairnes," Colonel Stump said gently and held a Bible toward me, asked me to put my left hand on it and raise the right. "Do you promise to tell the truth, the whole truth, and nothing but the truth, so help you God?"

I nodded but knew that was not enough.

"I do," I whispered, just as I had that far-off day in church, and Stump withdrew.

Mr. Archer had been selected to question me, as if his mournful looks would only be appropriate, and when he spoke it was with noticeable gentleness.

"Mrs. Cairnes, could you describe your relationship with the prisoner?"

My voice almost vanished in the droning afternoon, and the crowd went extremely still, leaning forward to catch my quiet words. "I am her mother."

"Does she reside with you?"

"She has always lived at home."

"And what was your relationship with the deceased?"

The crowd shifted uneasily, as if it were indecent to question me about the man my child had killed. I closed my eyes. "I had known him for several years."

"In what capacity?"

I shuddered. But I knew I had to gather my resolve, and my
voice came out stronger. "My daughter and he were engaged to be
married."

"Objection," the attorney general said, and rose. "Deposing
to the declarations of the deceased does not tend to show the guilt
or innocence of the prisoner. The state contends that no excuse can
justify deliberate killing, and no provocation within the range of
imagination can be adduced as justification for that act. If the other
side intends to argue that this lady, when she violated the laws of
God and man, was not in her right mind, then the only evidence
allowed should be to that effect."

The witness box stood so close to the judges' bench that I
could hear Judge Grason's chair creak and his robes rustle as he
leaned forward to look over his spectacles at Mr. Archer.

"Counsel for the defense will explain his line of questioning."

Mr. Archer's sad eyes sagged with unusual fervor. "The question asked was meant to show the intimate relations between the
deceased and the prisoner. The state has the right to go back to
prove malice, and the defense has the same right to go back to
prove friendly feeling."

But the attorney general stayed on his feet. "The state submits
that the evidence should be confined to the condition of the prisoner's mind at the time of the occurrence."

More creaking and rustling as the three judges bent their heads
together for a long minute. Judge Grason lifted his head. "The
court has decided that, according to custom, the antecedent relations existing between the parties may be brought in evidence."

A mutter rose around the room, as if "antecedent relations"
were too nice a way of putting it, and my face flamed. The judge
glared and scattered his disapproval like buckshot around the

room. Ladies opened fans and rapidly agitated the warm, charged air.

"Did you give consent to the marriage?" Mr. Archer asked with a hint of accusation.

"He had asked for and obtained it," I said curtly.

"And when exactly did he ask for it?"

"In November 1865, a Sunday afternoon."

"Did he set a date for the wedding?"

I lifted my chin. Let them accuse me, but I had done everything I could. "There was a sense that it would happen before spring. We had the wedding clothes made up."

"But was a firm date set, in fact?"

I pressed my lips together, but I knew I had to say. "Several dates were set at various times. But he always delayed it."

I could see bonnets bobbing in the gallery, and ladies eyed each other with significance. I knew what they thought, because I had thought it, too: A long engagement might mean patience in a man, but eagerness showed more virtue. All over the courtroom, heads nodded with satisfaction, and fans twitched back and forth like a flock of wings.

"And if a date was set, why did the wedding not occur?"

If they ever let me off this stand, I might never speak again. "He put it off from month to month on one pretext or another."

"And was the engagement ever broken off?"

"It most certainly was not. We merely heard that he had left the neighborhood."

A hiss of whispers issued from the gallery, and men of every description, young and old, in farmers' clothes or lawyers' suits, looked disengaged as if they were not in the room as the ladies all absorbed the fact that Nick had run. Mothers raised eyebrows at daughters, as if to say, "You see, that's what a man can do." For some reason, that heartened me.

The attorney general half-rose from his seat, mildly. "Objection. Hearsay evidence."

This time Judge Grason did not consult the others. "Objection overruled."

"When was the last time fixed for the wedding?" Mr. Archer asked gently, and the courtroom held its breath to hear the gruesome particulars of my daughter's disgrace.

"The last time fixed for the marriage was last November," I said in a low voice, the silence now so deep it seemed to carry to the rafters. "But he did not appear on the day set for the wedding. We had everything prepared, with family and friends assembled there as witnesses, but he never came to our house that day or ever again. My daughter sat up past midnight to wait for him, and since that time she has hardly left her bed."

"And why was she put to bed for so long?"

I closed my eyes. "She was confined not long after he failed to appear, and she did not get up again until last month."

Mr. Archer prompted me almost in a whisper. "Why was she confined?"

I glared at him for asking what everyone in that room knew. My voice came in a singsong, like a nursery rhyme. "She was confined to childbed. She is now the mother of a little child. Mr. McComas knew she would be when he last promised to marry her."

The silence was broken only by the pen strokes of the newsmen, so quiet that I could hear hooves clop around the square outside and birds whistling in trees.

"Did he recognize himself as the father of that child?" Mr. Archer asked and brushed a hand before his face, as if to shoo a fly.

"Objection," Mr. Jones called and stood up. "The defense may not show by the declarations of the deceased that this intimacy was immoral."

From behind his round glasses, Judge Grason fixed a long, disappointed look on the attorney general. "Objection not sustained. Witness must answer the question."

"He agreed to its keep. And before that he said he would marry her." I could not bring myself to glance toward her, but I gestured that way. "He gave her a wedding ring. It was his grandmother's. It's on her finger now."

All eyes turned to look at her, a general rustling on all sides. Helpless to stop myself, I glanced quickly, and there it was, a gold ring catching afternoon sunlight and glinting on her finger. But she bowed her head and covered it with her other hand, as if to save it from their sight. For some reason I felt tears spring to my eyes.

"No further questions, Your Honor," Mr. Archer said and retired to his seat.

The attorney general stood up to cross-examine me, and he greeted me pleasantly. "Tell me, Mrs. Cairnes, did your daughter enjoy the company of the deceased?"

This reeked of suggestion, as if agreement might prove she had asked for everything he did, and I took offense. Icy cold around my heart, I felt all these men were arrayed against me and my daughter, wanting to kill us both. My voice quavered out.

"She was always cheerful in his company, and as cheerful as could be expected in the company of others. But she has shown great distress of mind for the past fifteen months."

Mr. Jones's measured voice continued in a cheerful way. "Did she ever object to his attentions or try to discourage them?"

I could see where this was going, and I glowered in silence.

"Please, Mrs. Cairnes," Judge Grason said. "Just answer yes or no."

I could not help it, and my voice came hot. "Of course she did not. My daughter cared for him. She was engaged to marry him."

Ladies shot startled looks in the direction of the dock, and I wanted to shake them. What, had they thought she was just lewd? Born debased, of tainted blood? No. Look at her. Look at her! She had loved the man. There was a time when she was innocent!

Mr. Jones's face remained quite bland. "And did she ever encourage the attentions of any other gentleman, or of any man that you know of, of whatever degree?"

This was so offensive that my head went light, and I slumped back with a cry. Oh, they really might kill me!

Something rustled toward me, and my eyelids flew up in alarm. Two ladies I had never seen before advanced boldly across the floor, shrugging off the bailiff, the sheriff, and the crier. One held out smelling salts, the other a fan to cool my face. I closed my eyes and breathed the bracing scent and the cool air, so grateful that tears surged out. My head began to clear, and they returned to their seats. Around the room the general satisfied flapping of fans picked up.

"Mrs. Cairnes," Judge Grason said gently from a few feet above. "Do you feel well enough to continue?"

"I suppose so," I said, not bothering to cloak my resentment, as I frankly dabbed a hankie at my eyes. "And yes, I remember what this man had the impudence to ask. No, sir, my daughter never encouraged the attentions of any other man, of whatever degree, as you so delicately put it. No man but Nick McComas, not in all her life. I have often accused her of chasing suitors off. She could have had a lot of beaus, some of them far better men."

I threw a look at Martin Jarrett, blaming him. Why couldn't he have won her over? I knew there was a time when he had wanted to.

"And why did she not choose a better man?" Jones had the temerity to ask.

"Because she never wanted anyone but him. And she was always a headstrong girl."

I heard how I had said that, as if she were already dead, and new tears slipped out. There seemed no direction I could turn that would not make me weep.

Blue evening light shone in the windows when I was finally dismissed, so wrung out that I could not have climbed the stairs without the arm of Colonel Stump. I thought I might have to go lie down, and I fretted, unwilling to leave. Enduring all those eyes had changed something. Was it because I had sat in her place? I wanted to stop everything and just say *Wait*. It was sickening to feel the trial rush forward, out of my control.

But it was now so late, the judges were forced to hold it over another day.

Mr. Jones stood up, looking pleased. "And will Your Honors allow the prosecution to call more witnesses?"

"So be it," Judge Grason said and declared a recess until morning.

"Stand back! Make way!" the sheriff and the bailiff cried as they closed around the prisoner to lead her out. Men pressed close to her, some leering, faces red with drink.

Shuddering, I waited till the court had cleared before I let Belle lead me out.

My older sons and their wives were staying at my house, and I rode home in James's buggy, grateful for once that he could not speak. My three daughters-in-law set to work on supper, but I was exhausted and had no desire to eat.

"Thank you, dear girls, but I'll say goodnight. I want tomorrow to come quickly." I kissed them and my sons, and thanked God again for each of them.

But Richard jerked his head away, hand on the pistol in his belt. He looked as if he'd like to swear but didn't have the nerve with William standing as stern as Cotton Mather next to him.

"Why did you stop them blaming me?"

I touched his face. "Dearest, you are a noble boy. But think of your wife. She cannot do without you, and neither can I. We can only hope God will forgive your sister."

William put his hands on both our arms. "We'll say a prayer." He waited till all our heads were bowed. "Heavenly Father, we know we have trespassed against Your law in more ways than we can enumerate. But we ask forgiveness on our souls, if not our bodies here on Earth. Our poor, weak, suffering sister will soon pass to Your Kingdom, and we humbly entreat you, in the name of Your Only Son, Jesus Christ Our Lord, who suffered on the cross and died for us, that You show her more mercy than she has earned. We ask in the name of the Father and the Son and the Holy Ghost, amen."

That night oblivion seized me, and I did not wake till dawn, when I heard my sons' wives downstairs in the kitchen, clanking pots, stoking the cast-iron stove. It was a beautiful spring morning, but nothing could prepare me for what that day would bring. I brushed my hair and coiled it in a bun, put on my corset and my widow's weeds, and draped a black veil on my head. I had done my part, and I did not have to let the rabble look at me.

At the courthouse, the lawyers seemed refreshed, pink cheeked and clean, ready to spar, and both sides had heavy law books on the tables next to them. Mr. Jones sat at the prosecutors' table, confidently writing notes and dispatching them with runners, as if new information had come his way and he needed even more new witnesses.

Meanwhile, the defense resumed briskly, calling the dressmakers we had hired to make the wedding clothes. Mrs. Morse was middle-aged and plump, her young assistant, Mrs. Curry, thin and meager next to her. Mrs. Curry went up first, twisting her thin hands and looking scared.

"Oh, she's the very first in society," she said. "The very first."

Mrs. Morse was more restrained. She paraded to the stand in a grand dress of dark blue serge and a wide hat topped with a bluebird in its nest, her face flushed as red as a rash.

"Miss Cairnes was a most kindhearted and amiable lady," she said with dignity. "We helped in preparations for the wedding more than one time. Several times it was, over the years."

She threw a glance across the room as if to apologize to the prisoner.

Mr. Rutledge took the floor, standing humbly stooped as he cross-examined her.

"Mrs. Morse, you are one of the only defense witnesses not related to the Cairnes family, and we count on you to tell the truth to this court. Did Mr. McComas ever speak of marriage to Miss Cairnes when you were present?"

"No, sir, he did not."

"So your information in regard to a promise of marriage was from the prisoner herself?"

"Yes, it was, and from her mother, Mrs. Cairnes."

"And you never heard anyone speak of it in the presence of Mr. McComas?"

"No, sir, I did not."

Mr. Rutledge stepped down, and Mr. Archer rose up briskly to counter-question her.

"Did you ever see Mr. McComas and Miss Cairnes in company?"

"Yes, sir, I did, several times at church and once at a church picnic up to Painted Rocks."

"And what was his manner toward her?"

"He was marked in his attentions toward her."

Mr. Archer thanked Mrs. Morse and let her parade back to her seat before he recalled Gabriel Smithson, who looked wary as he returned to the witness stand.

"Mr. Smithson, did you ever hear your friend Nick McComas speak of marriage?"

Mr. Smithson looked embarrassed, his blue eyes going flat. "Well, not before last November. But I had some conversation with him on the subject then."

"And what do you recall about that conversation, exactly?"

"Well, I told him I thought he was getting into trouble. He denied it, and I said, 'Yes, you are.' He finally agreed he was. No names were mentioned, but I told him he had better marry the girl in question. I'm afraid he didn't give me much satisfaction."

"What exactly did he say?"

"He said he didn't care for himself that he was getting into difficulties, but he cared for her trouble. He said he wasn't fit to have a wife, but that he loved her better than any woman he had ever known. He was very much affected. I asked him how long before this thing would be proved for itself?—meaning the child, of course. He said in six or eight weeks. I tried to persuade him to marry her. I told him the consequences, and he burst into tears. He wept quite bitterly."

I tried to recall that night at Mr. Smithson's when we had accosted Nick. Had he shed the smallest tear? No. His eyes had shone, perhaps, but that was all.

"Were the two of you alone when you had this conversation?" Mr. Archer asked.

"A number of people were at my house for a corn husking, and Miss Cairnes and her mother came to speak to him. That was the night we talked, after they left. But I don't think we were overheard by anyone. The subject was so delicate. And then . . ." Mr. Smithson hesitated, and his round fair cheeks went red.

"Go on, Mr. Smithson."

"Well, I pressed him for the reasons he refused to marry her, and I alluded to that slanderous talk I've mentioned."

Some in the audience groaned. "Not again!"

Mr. Archer only looked more mournful. "What did he have to say on the subject?"

Smithson looked relieved at this chance to answer. "He said, 'No one must say anything against her.' He utterly denied the language and said it shouldn't be said in his presence. So you see, he was not the one who promoted that talk."

"And did he ever give you a reason for why he would not marry her?"

"Well, no, sir. I tried to convince him several times, but it did no good. I told him the girl stood high, and if he didn't marry her he'd better stay out of the neighborhood."

"What did he say to that?"

Smithson seemed to freeze in place, holding his head stiff to stare ahead. His eyes shone, and it was clear he could remember something, but he did not want to say.

"Witness will answer the question," Judge Grason said.

Smithson's face burned red, and he looked up at the judge defiantly.

"I would rather not say, Your Honor. It was a most unsatisfactory answer."

"Let me remind you, sir, that you are under oath," the judge said calmly.

Smithson sighed and closed his eyes. "He said, 'Anything but marrying for me.'"

A gasp greeted this, and I felt a small thrill in my chest. Had Nick really been the monster the defense made out? Had it really not been Martha's fault?

Soon it was noon, church bells ringing in Bel Air. The judge adjourned the court for dinner, and Richard and Mr. Farnandis rushed out together as if it was prearranged.

"Where are they going?" I asked Belle beside me, and she patted my hand.

"I'm sure it's nothing. Won't you come to dinner at the hotel?"

I could not face the crowds and said I would prefer to stay inside the building, away from prying eyes. Colonel Stump arranged for me to lie on a sofa in a private room, and Belle loosened my stays and took off my boots, helped me to lie down.

After she left, I tried to sleep, but my mind was too much disturbed. Tonight or tomorrow, all those hateful staring eyes might watch my daughter die. *I wish you were never born*—what kind of mother says a thing like that? Filled with misgiving, I could not close my eyes, and I did up my own laces, put my boots back on.

Belle took me back up to the gallery, and soon we heard cheers and catcalls outside on the square, as happened every time the sheriff brought my daughter back. I dropped my face into my hands and plugged my ears and wondered how it sounded to her on the inside of that crowd. The roar increased as she passed through the lobby, and soon she emerged onto the floor below, looking pale and worn, resigned, and surrounded by the sheriff and his men. When she was in the dock, the judges asked the defense to resume.

Martin Jarrett was recalled and asked if he thought she was insane that night in Jarrettsville, and he offered his opinion at length.

"Dementia can be caused by childbirth in the best of circumstances, and especially outside of wedlock when the attendant griefs of childbirth are accompanied by shame and rejection from all who could offer support. Even when pregnancy does not occur, dementia can result from seduction and frequently does. The disruption of a pure lady's modesty causes incalculable damage, since such excitations are unnatural in women of pure character. Medical authorities have dwelt on the perilous conditions that result from such unnatural feelings."

He mentioned several authorities by name and quoted passages he'd memorized.

Mr. Rutledge rose to cross-examine him. "How frequently does childbirth result in insanity, would you say?"

Dr. Jarrett had to tell the truth, and it was obvious that he wished otherwise. "Well, postpartum dementia is the exception rather than the rule. But it's more frequent in the case of spinster birth. And, as I say, the excitations resultant from seduction alone can produce insanity."

"Did you attend Miss Cairnes in childbed last winter?"

"I did."

"And how did she seem to you then?"

"Objection!" Colonel Stump was on his feet, and I gazed at him, grateful for this intervention to protect my daughter's modesty.

But the judge overruled it, and poor Dr. Jarrett was compelled to answer. He loosened his collar with one finger. "She seemed unbalanced then and had for several months before her confinement.

My father was their family doctor for years, and I could only wish I had his wisdom in the face of such terrible harm done to a pure lady. It was not her fault. She had been driven insane, and I had no choice but to treat her for it at the time of her confinement."

"And of what did that treatment consist?"

I did not want to hear this. I dropped my head back onto the chair, hoping to faint. But dear Belle, meaning well, held the smelling salts up to my nose, so I had to hear.

"Medical practice dictates a simple operation as the most efficacious step, when a lady has been seduced and driven mad. The procedure relieves her of the burden of desire and restores her chastity."

Good God—what had he done to her? I had never heard of such a thing, and he had certainly not asked me if he could. I suppose he meant in some way he had rendered her incapable of repeating the offense. But how? It made me feel afraid.

The court was now so quiet you could have heard an evil thought scratching its way across the ceiling. Mr. Rutledge's next question was as quiet as a breath.

"And did you perform it on Miss Cairnes?"

Martin nodded and visibly exhaled. "I did when she swooned after the birth."

"And did it help her?"

"I would say so. She showed immediate improvement."

"So is it your position that Miss Cairnes was sane after the operation, including four months later at the time of the murder?"

The court murmured at the lawyer's cleverness, as if he had caught the doctor in a trap.

Martin seemed to squirm uncomfortably. "I believe the reappearance of her seducer in her neighborhood may have unbalanced her again."

Rutledge would not let that rest. "Has Miss Cairnes seemed sane to you since that time?"

"Far from it. She has lain weeping in a darkened room. She has been so low in spirits for so long, I have been afraid she might not live."

"So would you agree that the operation you gave her was not a success?"

"I think it was. But she's a delicate and tenderhearted lady, and the excitations she has endured the past year would have unbalanced anyone. I believe in time she will prove sane."

Mr. Rutledge looked skeptical. "How long have you been acquainted with the prisoner?"

"Most of our lives, since we were children. Over twenty years."

"And was she ever inclined to mental disturbances before this past year?"

Martin was slow to answer. "No. She's always been sensible and forthright, remarkably so. But, as I say, this past year or two has put extraordinary pressure on her delicate nature."

Mr. Rutledge pressed his palms together and tapped his fingertips against his chin as if deep in thought. "Let us return for a moment to the child. How did it appear to you?"

"It was a healthy boy."

"And of what race did it appear to be?"

"Objection!" bawled all four defense attorneys, springing to their feet, and I almost wept with gratitude.

But again the judge was hard, and he seemed to want to satisfy the lowest curiosity. "Objection overruled. Witness will answer the question posed."

Martin answered slowly. "I have never delivered a black child, so I am not an expert on their looks. What hair it had looked straight, and when I held it by the feet and swatted it to make it cry out and clear its lungs, it flushed a hard dark red."

"Have you had the opportunity to see the child since then?"

"I have not. It was given immediately to a black wet nurse, who took it from the house."

I felt uneasy, remembering the wet nurse I had hired. A cousin of Creolia's, she had a good reputation, and I had paid her handsomely to take the baby off as soon as it was born—hoping she might take it as her own and I would never hear of it again. I spent the holidays with cousins down in Baltimore, and apparently the birth occurred on New Year's Day, no sign of the infant in the house when I returned. But since then the wet nurse had come twice to ask for more money, and I feared she might threaten to exhibit it in public unless I paid her more.

Dr. Jarrett was soon allowed to step down, and the defense called John Hutchins, a prosperous farmer who was distantly connected to our family. He wore big red muttonchop whiskers and a tailored brown suit with a brocade vest, and I hoped he was not there to reveal more to my daughter's shame.

Instead Mr. Archer asked him to describe what he had seen the night of the murder, and I groaned inwardly. How many repetitions of that night could be endured?

Hutchins spoke with eyes fixed as if still afraid. "I was inside the bar, within two feet of the door to the porch, and I saw all but the first fire. I heard the report of the pistol and saw a woman step back toward the door. She then advanced back onto the porch and fired a second time wildly. By this time McComas had reeled to a post."

"And did you know the woman?"

Sudden commotion broke through from the rough crowd in the lobby, startled shouts and cries so loud, everyone paused and turned that way. The courtroom door flew open, and Richard burst in, leading a modestly clothed black woman who held a white baby in a long white dress. Was that the woman I had hired? It seemed to be, and Richard marched her to the prisoner's dock, where Martha leapt up with a little cry and held out her arms.

A chorus of shocked voices asked, "Is that the child? Is that her boy?"

I sat stunned—from where I sat, the child appeared to have fine pale hair, combed up like a rooster's crest, and large, pale eyes. It wore what looked like Richard's white baptismal gown, with lace tatting at the collar I had done myself.

But could it possibly be Martha's own? They might have borrowed someone else's, as a stunt. Richard was not past that, and surely it was ill-advised. Yet the baby seemed to know her. As she took him, his small face broke into a grin, arms waving happily around.

"Pure Caucasian blood!" called rough male voices below, from the reporters' bench. "Pure Caucasian blood. Get it on the wire!"

Paper was ripped from pads, and runners scrambled out with telegrams to send.

I sat feeling accused, my heart flapping like a flag in a stiff wind. The child was still a bastard, wasn't it? I had not been wrong to hide it, to salvage what I could of my daughter's reputation, not that anything was left. But surely it had been a prudent step.

And yet, and yet—it meant she had told the truth, and Nick was wrong, the liars all exposed. I could not help it, I felt a burning mix of guilt and vindication in my chest.

The judges were not even gaveling—they stared down from on high as if they'd never seen an infant in their lives. Martha kissed the baby, settled him onto her lap, and smoothed his fine hair, which stood up all the more as her hand passed. I recalled the year she had played Mary in the Christmas crèche, kneeling in a blue hooded robe, holding a doll.

"We could have searched all over the world and not have found a more perfect Madonna," someone had said to me when services were done, and I had been so proud.

Now here she was again, the focus of all eyes. When the trial resumed, she turned the baby to her shoulder and he fell asleep, sprawled like a shield across her chest, and her face relaxed, as if holding him made other feelings dissipate. Yes, let them look at her. Let them see the baby and his mother holding him. The jury, judges and attorneys, all the farmers, all their happy married wives, would see the baby and the murderess, and then they would decide.

Mr. Archer had to retrace and make Mr. Hutchins tell again what he had seen.

"And did you know the woman with the gun?"

"Why, yes. It was Miss Cairnes, there in the dock." But he could not look at her, and he sounded ashamed to say it now, as she sat with her child.

"And did you know her before that night?"

"Yes, sir. I've known her by sight for twenty years. I've never been in her company nor conversed with her, but I have seen her at Bethel Church and met her on the road."

"And how did she appear to you that night at the hotel?"

"When she came on the porch I thought she was crazy and had escaped from an asylum, and I got out of the way for fear of being shot. I didn't know who she was shooting at. But I was certain she was crazy from her manner. As I was going home a neighbor told me—"

Mr. Rutledge bolted up. "Objection. Hearsay evidence is not admissible."

"Sustained," Judge Grason said.

Mr. Archer looked only at the witness. "Mr. Hutchins, have you seen cases of insanity?"

The attorney general himself shot from his seat with uncharacteristic agitation.

"I object to these questions. The witness has no knowledge upon which to justify his opinion, and hypothetical facts are not evidence of insanity. No one but medical experts can give an opinion upon hypothetical cases."

Mr. Archer countered him earnestly. "Your Honor, this is not a hypothetical case. It is not necessary to be a medical man to know conditions of the mind. Anger, passion, and excitement will change the expression of the countenance, and any man seeing the demeanor, manner, and appearance of a party can form a judgment and state his impressions. It is for the jury to decide."

The attorney general refused to sit. "My learned friend and I are at direct issue. The law requires that a higher degree of insanity should be proved as an excuse for the crime of murder, being an act of God in taking away the reason of a person." He lifted a heavy book and read the statutes that applied, which said the mere opinion of a person not an expert could not be taken as evidence. "The law presumes a man to be sane until he can be proven otherwise."

Mr. Archer waited, and his manner radiated calm. "There are settled cases in which the state has been obliged to show the sanity of the prisoner to prove him guilty, as well as the defense to show the prisoner insane at the time of the occurrence."

He too lifted a heavy book and read authorities to show that Mr. Hutchins's views should be allowed as evidence. Mr. Jones replied to him, and the argument went on for quite some time.

Heat lay heavy on the room, all the more with so many people packed inside. Yet only the baby in the dock appeared to drowse, because the battle on the floor seemed like the last hope to save my daughter's life. In the gallery, some women wept openly, clutching handkerchiefs.

At last Judge Grason intervened. "The defense may ask the witness about his opinion."

Mr. Archer looked quite pleased despite his drooping eyes, and prompted Mr. Hutchins.

"The night of the occurrence, I didn't know who she was at first," Hutchins said. "I thought she was a crazy woman. I didn't know who she was shooting at until after the first shot, when I saw McComas throw up his hands and say, 'Oh!' Another shot was fired and it went up into the roof, and I recognized the side of her face. She was firing wild, but she got two shots aimed right at him and I saw one strike him. He fell off the porch, but she followed him down to the yard and went on firing at his body on the ground."

"If you had known the relations between the parties and all that had transpired previous to this occurrence, would you still have thought she was crazy?" Mr. Archer asked.

"Yes, sir, I would. She seemed deranged."

Down in the dock, the baby stirred, lifted his head, and made a fretful noise—all heads turned to watch. My daughter kissed his head and rocked him, but his cry grew stronger and the lawyers stopped to wait while she gave him to the nurse to take away.

When he was gone, her eyes filled with tears, and the stares of the whole courtroom recorded it, some shaking their heads as if she were an actress playing on their sympathies.

Mr. Archer watched her as the baby's cry receded from the room. "Your Honor, this concludes the examination in chief on the part of the defense." He took his seat.

The courtroom went still, like a huge waiting animal about to spring, and no one seemed to breathe. Would it be over now?

But the attorney general straightened his cuffs and rose. "Your Honor, the state requests permission to call witnesses to respond to the new line brought forth today by the defense."

Judge Grason consulted the other judges briefly. "Granted."

Slowly, like a fever dream, it all began again.

A young man was called up to the stand, and I was so tired by that time, I did not catch his name. He wore blue uniform pants with a plain blue jacket, and his hair stood frizzed around his head like a swarm of gnats. He had been on the hotel porch, and while he spoke he stared straight at the dock, the whites of his eyes exposed all around.

"Why, she was cool and reasonable as anyone I ever saw. She was right haughty and resolute. I've never seen her look any other way. After she killed the man, she looked around at us and said, cool as you please, 'Gentlemen, y'all know why I did it.' Never saw the like. Well, her brother thought she was quite cool himself."

"How did he show that he thought that?" asked Mr. Jones.

"Why, after the shooting he asked her to come get on her horse, like she was just gossiping after church and keeping him waiting."

Mr. Archer stood up. "Objection. What is the object of these questions?"

Mr. Jones raised his eyebrows. "To prove that her brother did not regard her as insane but addressed her as a reasonable person."

Judge Grason's round face remained expressionless. "The prosecution may proceed."

Mrs. Street was called back up, grimacing with nerves. "Why, yes, I think she was quite sane. I wish I could say otherwise, but she looked the same as always. She's my cousin, and I've known her a long time. She didn't seem different to me."

Our neighbor Mr. Ayres was called up next, and he strode resolutely to the stand, looking gaunt and uncomfortable in a faded green wool jacket. He clenched and unclenched his big worn hands as he answered each question, his cuffs too short, exposing big-boned wrists with more hair on them than on his head. Gradually Mr. Jones persuaded him to tell his story.

"I saw Miss Cairnes that night, all right," he said gruffly. "She came to my house just after dark. She was on foot and no one with her. I went on in to supper and spoke to her and she answered in the usual manner, the way she always has. I've known her more than twenty years, since she was a child. I asked her how she did and I think she replied, 'I am well.' There was nothing strange in her manner from what it previously was, and I had not the slightest idea that anything had happened. My wife spoke to her, too, and saw nothing different about her. I asked Miss Cairnes some questions about her brother, who was digging a well and so forth, and she answered as usual. There was nothing to indicate she was insane. Then my youngest son came home from the village and told his mother what had happened, and my wife got very much excited. Finally, Miss Cairnes's brother and her cousin came to my house to get her. She was there about an hour and left between eight and nine o'clock."

Mr. Archer cross-examined him. "Could you describe her manner for the court?"

Mr. Ayres stuck out his thin gray beard and worked his jaw. "I tell ye, it was the same as it has always been and not two hours after the shooting. There was nothing to show anything unusual. It's ridiculous to say she was insane."

A rumble from the crowd agreed.

"Silence!" the court crier called. This time a few members of the audience joined in.

"Be quiet!"

"Keep your opinions to yourself!"

Soon the judge's gavel pounded to silence the silencers.

Mr. Jones called Asbury Ayres to tell his part. He was an ordinary-looking young man with heavy cheeks and bark-brown muttonchops, his clothes serviceable brown except for the looping blue silk tie he had put on, I suppose to show his Union sympathies.

His face went fish-pale as he described how my daughter had looked to him in his mother's kitchen, and he could hardly speak for stuttering. "Th-th-there she was—c-c-cool as you p-p-please and all—c-c-covered in his b-b-blood."

I winced. Had there really been blood on her dress?

Mr. Archer declined to cross-examine Asbury, perhaps to stop him saying more about the blood. Dismissed, he walked quickly up the aisle and out the door, as if afraid to be in the same room with her.

"Your Honor, we have no more witnesses," Mr. Jones announced.

But the defense was allowed to make a rebuttal, and Mr. Archer called his famous cousin, Dr. George Archer, a physician respected all over the state. Everyone craned their necks to get a look at him. He was a thin man with a long white beard and kindly round blue eyes.

"I've been a practicing physician for twenty years," he said. "And I have to say, from my experience, the fact of the girl's having been collected and calm an hour or two after the shooting would be no indication of soundness of mind—rather, the reverse. Women's minds are extremely fragile, and they are always delicately balanced over the abyss. They should be thought of as more fragile than infants and more prone to unbalancing when violation touches them. A complete collapse of reason may be expected anytime such a thing occurs."

A cloud seemed to settle on the judges and the jury, all of them frowning at such contradictory evidence. The prosecution waived its right to cross-examine Dr. Archer, and it soon became evident that neither side had further witnesses to call. The audience held its breath, consulted watches on fobs. Could it really be almost over with?

At long last, the judge declared it time to make the closing arguments. The prosecution would begin and end the summaries, with the defense lawyers sandwiched between.

Mr. Rutledge stood up first for the state. He seemed reasonable and methodical as he laid forth the case in his deep, soothing voice. Point by point he showed her act was willful and premeditated, her mind quite sane, and therefore she would have to hang.

"I remind the jury that with the alleged crimes and wrongdoings committed by the deceased we have nothing to do. Rather, we are here to vindicate the insulted majesty of the law. No grounds can excuse outright killing, except for self-defense, which no one has argued in this case. The state freely admits that Nicholas McComas committed a great wrong against the prisoner, but this does not justify her becoming the avenger. McComas was a decent son and brother, and for years he was the only support of an aged mother, an aunt, and three delicate sisters. The only error he seems ever to have committed was in regard to Miss Cairnes, and when the state brought suit against him for the upkeep of the child, he agreed to pay for it, tacitly admitting it was his.

"What more properly concerns us is that Miss Cairnes's premeditation is quite clear. The prisoner inquiring for McComas when she came to Jarrettsville, her cool manner while she shot him, and the declaration she made afterward all show she planned to kill. And if the jury sees there was a plan, then that disproves the idea she was insane. Every man is presumed sane until proven otherwise, and has there been sufficient proof of insanity in this case? Some witnesses have said that she was wild and excited, but others noticed she was singularly calm, and she spoke to the bystanders the moment she first shot in a way that shows her mind was clear and that the act was done in revenge, which makes it murder under the law. The defense has not been able to find a single witness to give evidence of her insanity prior to the shooting, and the conclusion must follow, there is no such evidence. Therefore she is guilty of murder."

The audience nodded like a wheat field in the wind, and my daughter nodded, too, closing her eyes, as if they were right to convict her. Behind her, the reporters shook out their cramped hands and prepared to write again, recording the next flow of words.

Colonel Stump had been saved for just this moment. Preening his mustaches, he strode with gravity into the center of the open floor, where he stood with warrior calm and no notes.

"It is an honor to be called upon to defend such innocence," he said softly. "The deceased was an enemy to the human race, deliberately marking his prey, deceiving the trusting girl. He was worse than the serpent that entered Eden. There is a written law, but there is also a law in the human breast. I myself believe the act was justified and that the prisoner is guilty of no crime under heaven. But if the jury differs from me, then the evidence will show the prisoner was knocked from her ordinary orbit by his perfidy, and she was not responsible for her actions at the time. The prisoner is now in the felon's dock, but she has made it almost sacred by her presence there. Virtue and chastity sit on either side of her. Gentlemen of the jury, I appeal to you to bring in a verdict that will be a protection to your own homes and firesides, give assurances to every mother, and be a shield to every daughter."

He went on to enumerate my daughter's virtues for an hour. When he stopped, cheers rang out from the lobby, and someone raised his voice into the eerie ululation of the Rebel yell.

"Bailiff, find the man making that awful caterwaul and arrest him," Judge Grason said calmly. "Ladies and gentlemen, allow me to remind you that no demonstrations of enthusiasm will be tolerated in this court. If necessary, I will clear the room."

A hush fell, since no one wished to miss the efforts of the speakers still to come, especially now that the grand white visage of Mr. Farnandis was rising into view.

So great was his renown that ladies put away their fans to help keep silence, and some rough men from the lobby crowded in, removing hats and holding them as they stood along the walls. Farnandis made his way toward the jury box, where he stood humbly and spread his hands. His great voice began quite low.

"I find myself somewhat embarrassed, because the awesome duty laid upon me here has nearly paralyzed my energies. My friend the attorney general stands first in the brotherhood of the bar, but by the merits of this cause I advocate, I can only hope the pebble will weigh against the boulder. I am not here to invoke your mercy. I will make no appeal to your feelings. All that the defense wants is the truth. I know the learned attorney general. I know that while his head is full of legal lore, his heart is full of manly impulses, and no money could have induced him to appear here in the capacity of prosecutor if his official duty had not called him.

"Gentlemen of the jury, the prisoner before you has suffered the worst wrong a woman can, worse than can be suffered under any circumstances by any man, and when she acted, it was with no wickedness of heart. If you can find it in your consciences to trench the rigid bearing of the law, you will bring in a verdict pleasing to men and angels. Treat this girl as if you were her father. What father, if his home had been invaded in this manner and his daughter made a social outcast, would not have shot down the destroyer as a dog?"

Applause rippled from the lobby, and Judge Grason banged his gavel. But even he leaned forward, listening. Mr. Farnandis looked exhilarated and a patch of pink crept into his aging cheeks.

"God knows I hate to contemplate such a contingency in my life, but had it happened to me, good citizen as I endeavor to be, venerator of the law as I am, I would have had his heart, or my own life would have been offered up."

Louder applause from the lobby, and the gavel banged again. But Farnandis did not stop.

"Do you recollect the case of Virginia, whose own father stabbed her in the heart to save her from the ravisher Appius Claudius? The Roman people gathered around that poor father and overturned the government. Are we at this advanced age and in this Christian land to say he was a murderer? May a man enter your home and steal not your gold, but what is of far more value: the choicest jewel of your heart?

"If you find in your hearts that this girl deserves to die, then say the word. I have seen fairer women than she, and younger, but I have turned from them in loathing because all was rotten within. I have never yet offered my hand to one I deemed dishonored. But the moment you pronounce this girl guilty, I will take her by the hand and say, 'I think you as pure and true as woman can be.'"

Handkerchiefs flapped open in the gallery, and I caught a whiff of smelling salts.

But Mr. Farnandis was still warming up, and his voice swelled, consuming all the space, melodious, for two more hours. Gradually the courtroom walls glowed pink with sunset light, then blue, and evening freshness breathed in from the fields. Lamps were lit along the walls, and dark consumed the world outside, before Judge Grason interrupted him.

"The court regrets we must recess for the day. If it will please Mr. Farnandis to continue in the morning, the trial will be held over yet another day. But I tell you now, we will make an end before tomorrow afternoon."

A sigh from the whole courtroom seemed to sweep the gavel down, and cold fear shot down my spine. Tomorrow. The lovely speeches had lulled me all afternoon, as if it could go on like this, nothing but words. I had only wanted her to suffer, be humiliated, and understand how wrong she had been, why she should have listened to me more. But that was all. I did not want to hear a verdict! How long could it be till she was hung?

The sheriff rushed her out, all three of her brothers and their wives close behind. They seemed to have forgotten me, and I got caught in the crowd leaving the gallery. Some of them stared at me with presumptuous hot eyes, and I fell back, letting them go. My daughter was gone before I got downstairs, and it made me feel helpless. I felt a sob well up.

Immediately someone held me, and I looked up to see Mrs. Stevenson Archer, the vision in black lace. "Come with me, dear Mrs. Cairnes," she said softly.

She led me to the room where I had rested that day at noon. She brought me a glass of water and a cool cloth to wipe my face. She pulled a chair up close to mine and took my hands.

"There is something we must do to save your girl. Mr. Archer says there is just one way she will survive. The law is—it seems it's quite inflexible, and she will hang unless we can convince the jury that she is deranged, or that it's possible for her. He says it is the only way they can acquit her. He says they may *want* to acquit her, but they have to have a legal reason. They can't make it manslaughter, because Mr. Deets saw Richard in the crossroads, and Richard followed Nick, and Joshua Jarrett saw it, too. And the Streets saw her walking toward town already, and they saw Richard dash off and get her horse. So, either way, she knew McComas was there. It was not the impulse of a moment. It was planned murder, so there's no chance of acquittal now unless she was of unsound mind. We must convince her to walk into that court tomorrow morning and do something wild, just for a minute. She could shriek and tear her hair, or dance a caper and sing. If she does not, they will hang her."

Her eyes searched mine, but seeing only bewilderment there, she closed hers a moment, as if to gather courage to go on. "They have already built the gallows behind the jail. The sentence can be carried out before this time tomorrow night."

Something hot rushed in my breast, something I had squashed out of myself.

"Can you take me to Glenn's Hotel?" I cried, leaping up, ragged and thoughtless.

"My carriage is outside. I'll go with you."

She whisked me to the hotel, where we had to fight our way inside, reporters catching at my arms. "Miz Cairnes! Mary Ann Bay Cairnes! Won't you speak to us a moment? Please?"

Dragoons and Rifles choked the stairs, but I spied Colonel Stump up at the top and called to him, my voice strong and clear. He looked down, saw my distress, and ordered his men to clear a path for us, men parting like the Red Sea.

Once at the top, Stump took my arm, Mrs. Archer on my other side, and they swept me to a door I knew must be the prisoner's, because the sheriff stood outside.

"I will speak with my daughter," I told Mr. Bouldin quietly.

His face closed like a bulldog's, eyes focused above our heads. He adjusted his holster on his girth. "Miz Cairnes, Miz Archer, I am sorry. She says she won't see anyone tonight."

"I am *her mother*. Tell her I am here. She has to speak to me."

He seemed to know I would not go away, and he gave up and gave the door a timid rap.

"Miz Cairnes? Your mother wants to speak to you. Can she come in?"

She did not answer, but I had had enough. The door was unlocked, and I strode right in, leaving Mrs. Archer in the hall. The room was dark, and in the faint light from the hallway it took a moment to make out my daughter, lying on the bed, one arm over her eyes. She seemed to be fully clothed, even her shoes on, as if ready to depart. The nurse and baby were not there.

"Where is my grandson?" I demanded.

She bolted upright with a cry. "Who let you in here? Please leave at once!"

I stopped, stunned. "Dear girl, I am your mother."

I could not see her face, but her voice was hard. "Not anymore. You said you were sorry I was born. And as for my son being your grandson, that certainly never occurred to you before. You couldn't wait to get rid of him!"

I had forgotten how prickly and unpleasant she could be.

But I would still fight to save her, and we had so little time. "Of course I'm sorry that you bore a bastard, but he's still my grandson and you are still my little girl."

She flung herself back on the bed. "Not for long. Isie took Orlind home. She'll take care of him when I am gone."

So she had named the boy and not told me. Well, why should she? My knees felt weak, and I sat abruptly on the sofa. Isie, poor disgraced Isie, would take another child for her?

"You know I would raise him," I said faintly. "Who did you name him for?"

She gave a harsh laugh. "Who did I name him for? No one in this family. He is not one of you. He never will be. Now go home, please, and leave me be."

If I had not known before that she was lost to me, I knew it now. I suppose I had wanted her to be lost, preferably somewhere else. But not dead! Not dead! I never wanted that.

I started to cry like I might never stop, went to the bedside, and got down on my knees. She lay still with her eyes covered, and if she knew I was there, she did not let on.

"I don't blame you for hating me. So I'm not asking for myself. But there is something you must do, for yourself and your little boy."

I repeated everything Mrs. Archer had told me.

"You could spit on someone, anyone you like! Spit on that awful, cold-blooded Mr. Jones. Or spit on me! Sing and dance around the room! Anything, so long as they think you are mad, or that you could have been that night."

Martha bolted to her feet and paced away, as if she could not stand to be so close to me.

"My mind was clear enough. I knew I was doing wrong. I meant it to be the last thing I ever did. You taught us not to lie. Is life worth so much that it is all right to lie, just to hang on to it? And to steal? I would have to steal my life back from the state of Maryland."

"No!" I cried. "They haven't taken it yet. They don't want to! You were desperate. It was like being crazy, wasn't it? Can't you let them think it just this once? Everyone knows you're not crazy now. But if you could just show them it was possible—"

Her voice was gentler now. "I am sorry, Mother."

I cried with so much bitterness that I could not say more, and soon I left the room.

MARTHA JANE CAIRNES
The Accused

ON THE LAST DAY of my life, I woke early. It was dark still, and I lay and thought about the baby, as I always did first thing. Isie would have put him in a cradle, and he would be on his stomach, hunched up on his knees, his cheek pressed down, one great lump. His breath would move as quiet as a mole under the grass, while his heart *thump-thumped*. He had not been there a year before, and he began from nothing, from a moment's touch. Where had he been before? Where was Nick now? I saw him in the sheep meadow on a spring day. He gave me a lively, laughing glance and looked away.

My window faced the east, and it grew faint gray, then slowly pink. Outside of it a treetop showed new tender leaves, faint green. Something in my mind began to sing.

> For the beauty of the earth,
> For the beauty of the skies,
> For the love which from our birth
> Over and around us lies.

Did I believe in God? If I did, I did not feel much benefit from it. Someone or something made the world deliberately—it was too beautiful to be an accident. But whatever it was, it did not care for you or listen when you called, and there was no use in looking to the sky.

Yet the hymn had risen by itself and made me calm. It was not the Savior holding out His arms, forgiving me and granting me eternal life. It was not clouds parting, God's hand reaching down to lift me up. But I still felt a certain peace. Whatever came this day would be all right.

A hotel servant brought a tray, and it seemed like I was tasting coffee for the first instead of the last time. The oranges smelled sweet, and I was happy they were there. I held one in my hand, though I had no need to eat nor ever would again.

I put on clean underthings, the black silk dress. The hoops would hide the tremor in my legs, and it would do to die in public, scrutinized. I wondered idly where the hanged were buried. Probably not in the graveyard of their ancestral church. I would not have cared, except that Nick was in the ground there now, and I would have liked to lie by him.

I brushed my hair, not sure how I should do it up. How did a murderer arrange her hair? If I knew, I would do it that way in a minute to convince them it was true. I settled on a tight, neat wrap anchored with pins, no tendrils hanging down, nothing to soften it. I would sit like stone, like those eyeless figures Nick had shown me, carved in rock, their blank faces turned up to the sky.

But I could not face the street without a veil, and I threw on a black one and secured it with a flat black hat.

Did the Dragoons and Rifles never sleep? They were packed along the hall, looking brushed and clean and half-ready to weep. I did not know how much to blame on them, and it did not matter anymore. They had protected me in my last days, and as I passed I took the hand of each one, no one saying anything.

The sheriff took me to his buggy, where we climbed inside and waited while the men mounted around us before we started a last rocking drive along the now familiar streets.

A few ladies stood out in their yards in black dresses to watch me go. A few blocks from the courthouse, a young girl in white rushed at the buggy, lifted her arm, and pitched something straight at me—I flinched, sure it was a rock.

But it landed harmlessly in my lap, a small bouquet of lilies of the valley tied with white ribbon. I turned to look back, and the girl was standing in the street with her hands hanging down, gazing after me. I did not wave.

Outside the courthouse, the rows of spectators were silent now, solemn and respectful, though every one of them had come to see me die. More of them had filled the lobby and the courtroom and the gallery, hundreds of citizens, and all so quiet I could hear my bootsteps on the hardwood floor. Isie was already in her chair beside the dock, and I settled beside her gratefully.

"Make way, make way," voices called out from the lobby, and the courtroom door opened to let in Mr. Archer with a huge bouquet, long-stemmed white calla lilies and star lilies and peonies tied with excessive quantities of white ribbon that fluttered to the floor, opulent enough to be a bride's. A rustle rippled through the crowd as he bowed and held them out to me.

"Prepared by the hands of Mrs. Stevenson Archer," he said.

My hands shook as I took them, thanking him. I held them up under my veil so I could breathe their fresh and dusky scents.

When the judges processed in for the last time, Mr. Farnandis paced out to the center of the floor, and all waited for him to continue where he had left off the night before.

But he looked at me and gave the smallest gesture toward his own forehead. I knew he meant I should remove my veil, but I had no desire to feel a courtroom full of hostile eyes.

I felt Isie's gentle fingers at my temples, unpinning it, and saw she was already weeping silently. I kept my senses trained on the sweet, fragile bouquet rioting across my lap, as preposterous claims were made on my behalf, words thrown up like castles in the air.

"Here is a girl of great tenderness and mercy, as good and pure a mother as the world will ever see," Mr. Farnandis proclaimed in his lush voice. "Her seducer was a monster of lust and cruelty, an artful, lazy, practiced seducer and a blight on human society. Pure hearts know that the tender girl he so injured is already forgiven under the eye of heaven."

He went on at least two hours more about my supposed gentleness and purity, and when he stopped, applause and cheers burst out, despite the gavel banging down. It lasted so long, Mr. Farnandis had to stand and bow, accept the ovation while he waved at the crowd to stop.

Then it was Mr. Archer's turn to round out the case for my defense.

"Under common law," he began, "not all killing is considered murder, and when the heat of blood is present, such charges are always reduced. But our plea is not guilty. We have established her insanity without doubt. We have seen the causes operating upon the mind of the young lady while in a delicate condition. We have the nights of anguish and tears, the false vows of her lover, her seclusion from society. We see a young girl who has never hurt a worm, who rushes hastily and hurriedly upon a scene and comports herself in such a way that she convinces bystanders she was insane. Do you suppose it possible that a young girl, tenderly nurtured, brought up as she was, could shoot down a man and an hour afterwards go to a neighbor's on a friendly visit and talk as if nothing had occurred? Could any sane woman even witness such a scene and an hour afterwards show herself unmoved? She committed the act without any attempt at concealment. She saw only one man, while all present saw her."

He went on to denounce the prosecution for trying to connect Richard with the affair, when there was not one word of proof. "A man may take the law into his own hands to protect his home, his honor, and his property. It is right to protect our homes against

invasion, whether that invasion be by force or comes in the clothing of a sheep to take that which is most precious. If a father may
protect his child, if a mother may protect her daughter, if a brother
may protect his sister, may not a fatherless girl protect her own
rights?"

Out in the lobby cheers broke out, and the bailiff went to silence them. But even he could not stay away while eloquence was
being lavished on the air. It went on for hours and became almost
a game, bursts of applause in the lobby and the bailiff rushing out,
then quickly stepping back inside the court. Then more demonstrations of enthusiasm in the lobby.

It was noon before Mr. Archer made an end and returned to
his seat.

An electric feeling charged me, dread and excitement both.
The time had come for the attorney general to have the last word,
calling for my death. Neat and compact as always, he rose and
spoke in crisp and reasonable tones.

"Your Honors, ladies and gentlemen, gentlemen of the jury. I
do not complain of the bias displayed by the counsels for the other
side, and I find my task here unpleasant. But it must be recalled
that we have to do here with the conscious, calculated murder of
an industrious and hardworking man. Nicholas McComas was just
thirty-five years old, a fine example of sobriety and a faithful son
who helped support his mother, an aunt, and three sisters, and all
will miss him sorely now. She shot him in a public place, with no
attempt at concealment, exactly as the beloved president of this
great Union was killed four years ago, and I must strenuously protest against the invocation of some 'Higher Law' to which the jury
might appeal to acquit her. 'Higher Law' was the doctrine that
drenched this country in blood, when some men claimed it sanc-
tioned keeping other men as slaves. That supposed 'Higher Law'

tore our Union asunder and forced us into a conflict that stained our soil forever. Are we ready to listen to those words again, so soon after that awful war? I appeal to you in the name of all that's right. The only law we must obey is that laid down by our great forebears, by Washington and Jefferson and Abraham Lincoln. For God, for Union, for justice, I charge you to honor them and bring in a verdict of *guilty*."

Only silence issued from the lobby, but a rustle of applause swept round the courtroom, and Mr. Jones held up a restraining hand—he was not finished, and the crowd quieted. He apologized for the attempt to implicate Richard.

"I am sorry her brother's name has been brought into this case. I have not one harsh word to say of him, and he will not be charged before you with any offense. Nevertheless the evidence concerning him shows that Miss Cairnes knew her victim would be in the town, and she went deliberately to kill him. Therefore you must find her guilty of premeditated murder."

I felt Isie shudder next to me, and I gripped her hand and looked into her eyes.

"It's all right," I whispered. "It's the truth. It's what I want."

Isie stared at the ceiling, not bothering to wipe the tears that streaked her wan cheeks.

"I submit, furthermore," said Mr. Jones, "she was in full possession of her faculties. No evidence has proved her otherwise. The jury must understand that no excuse for murder can be offered except self-defense or insanity, and there is no evidence of either. It should be noted that the prisoner's mother was not even asked to attest to her insanity, and it can be deduced that she could not have done so. Her daughter has lived at home all her life, and her mother knows she has never been insane. This act was conscious, cold, premeditated, and therefore homicide. If the jury would be so unreasonable as to find against the evidence, the only verdict of acquittal they might bring in is 'not guilty by reason of insanity.' But the duty of the jury is to find in accordance with the evidence. And since her mind was clear, I very much regret to say it, but your only choice is to bring in a verdict of *guilty*."

Gravely Mr. Jones paced back to his seat.

Judge Grason seemed to sigh and shake himself. In a quiet voice, he charged the jury with their task, and when the jury stood to leave the room, they looked so solemn, they might have been a dozen pallbearers with a coffin on their shoulders.

Beside me, Isie gasped for breath, her hot fingers now like part of my own.

"That can't be it," she cried. "They can't go out on that note!"

But the sheriff was already there, jail keys clanking on his belt.

"She's gotta come with me, now. Just her, not you," he told Isie, who wailed.

"Where are you taking her?"

The sheriff's jaw set grim. "She's gotta come across the street with me."

Isie clung to me like eelgrass in a riverbed. But the bailiff disentangled her, and he and the sheriff took my arms and hustled me away so fast, I dropped the bouquet and had no time to find the veil. It didn't matter. Let them see my face.

My head up, eyes toward the sky, I saw nothing as they pulled me through the crowd outside and across the street, into the jail. The sheriff no longer seemed afraid to put me in a cell, and he clanged the iron door shut behind me and walked away.

The cell was a relief at first, no eyes. Mortar crumbled between the stones in the walls, and the floor gave off a smell of lye. Nearby someone whistled a sad tune, notes echoing, though I could not see who it was.

After a while, the cold of the stones began to creep into me, and I knew it was true: Stark wood already stood behind this building, holding up a rope. My heart skittered, and I tried to regain my resolution.

Instead I felt an urge to press up through the ceiling, see the sky and breathe the air, like a crocus poking up through snow. Stepping to the bars, I wrapped them in my hands—cold iron, like the bars of the calfpens, that day when Tim and I had let them out. I pulled on the door but it did not give.

The low ceiling started closing over me. I lay down on the bench and closed my eyes. I knew I only had to get through a few hours. It was my punishment to feel this way, more than my death would be. My breath came loud, and dirt seemed heaped into my mouth. My lids flew up. Dear God! Would someone make sure I was dead before they buried me?

I calmed myself. When I was dead, nothing would matter anymore. Far better death than to go on living. If I had to live, a thousand days would ooze by, one by one, another thousand after that. Never to kiss Nick or even to look at him—always to see him gaze across the porch at me. Having to live cloistered, alone and in disgrace. Always to be a murderer.

But I could not breathe, thinking of the rope. I knew this was the worst, imagining before the fact. When the thing occurred, it would be less than I thought now. I would lift my chin to help them slip the noose over my head. I would smell tobacco and the fear felt by the Negroes who had died before me on the rope. Would I pray? I could pray like Anne Boleyn: "Father, into Thy hands I deliver my soul to be a perfect living sacrifice to Thee." But so much about that was a lie, my soul not perfect and my death no sacrifice.

No, the prayer I had to pray was far more difficult. "Forgive us our trespasses as we forgive those who trespass against us"— could I say that? It might be an easy thing to say I had forgiven Nick, now that I had shot him dead.

But I could not ask forgiveness for myself nor forgive those who had told those awful lies about me nor my first forefather who ever bought a slave. Imagine a world where slavery had never been! No humans sold like meat, no Rebellion, no War Between the States. Nick and Richard not so bitterly opposed. My family's prosperity was all mixed up in it, a knotted web, and there was no going back to where forgiveness might be real for any one of us.

The sheriff trod back heavily, and this time he kept his hat on. His lower lip trembled, and for a moment his scarred face looked kind. He had brought the pimply guard from the hotel, and the boy stood by holding a rifle.

The sheriff unlocked the cell door. "The jury's come back in. You gotta come to court."

I touched his arm. "Mr. Bouldin, I want you to know that I forgive you in advance for whatever you have to do to me."

He looked ashamed, and sweat trickled down his temples. "Thank you, miss. Now, you come quietly."

The walk was cruel, across the sunlit street and up the stairs and back in through the throng. Pink faces leered at me, some sad, some ready to jeer, all with leaping eyes.

The twelve gentlemen sat tall in their box, the three judges high up on their bench, the room as full of people as the walls could bear. The judges waited till I went inside the dock. Isie had been removed somewhere, and I did not sit down.

"The accused will stand to hear the verdict of the jury," Judge Grason said and peered at me over his spectacles, as if he thought I might sneak down into my seat.

"I am standing, Your Honor," I said clear and strong, and a few people laughed.

Judge Grason nodded in acknowledgment and turned to examine the spectators all around. "Let me remind you all, no demonstrations will be tolerated either way. If necessary, arrests will be made." He glared around the room, but no one even seemed to breathe. He nodded. "All right. The clerk will poll the jury."

The court clerk stood, a fair, balding man dressed in black and wearing wire spectacles. He had to clear his throat three times before he read out the names of the jury.

"John D. Alderson."

The answer came from one of the fresh-scrubbed, bearded men seated in the jury box.

"Present."

"Do you freely agree with the verdict rendered?"

"I do."

"Thomas G. Archer."

"Here."

"Do you freely agree with the verdict rendered?"

"I do."

One by one he asked them all.

"Andrew Boyle."

"Isaac W. Coale."

"Albert Davis."

"William H. Harward."

"William B. Hopkins."

"Owen Michael."

"Henry Osthine."

"Edward Scarborough."

"Henry A. Silver."

"J. Crawford Thompson."

"Present," each one said, and then, "I do."

Judge Grason asked the foreman to stand. He was the small-est of the twelve, a man perhaps forty-five years old, with fine white hands and neat gray hair and trimmed mustache, no beard. He wore a dark blue jacket, unlike all the rest, whose coats were brown or black. I wondered, with an odd joy in simply being able to think, why the other gentlemen had picked this man.

"How does the jury find?" Judge Grason said.

The small neat man in blue looked nowhere but at Judge Grason. "Not guilty."

A roar swept over me. Too much light rushed in my face. I seemed to fall through space. Screams came from the gallery, but the judge silenced them.

"Not guilty on what grounds?"

The foreman paused, and his eyes seemed to fill. He seemed to steel himself.

"Not guilty on grounds of justifiable homicide."

The attorney general and the state's attorney shot out of their chairs as if to shout *objection* one last time. The audience was on its feet shouting. Voices bellowed.

"Why did they even need to leave the room?"

"They should have said that in five minutes from the jury box!"

Judge Grason banged and banged his gavel, barely getting back control. "The court thanks the members of the jury for their service, and they are dismissed." He turned to me. "The prisoner is free to go." The gavel tapped. "Court is adjourned."

Cheers filled the hall, and from the lobby came a massive screech of the Rebel yell. "Hooooooooooah-hoooooooooooool!"

"No!" I cried. "No! Not that!"

Isie fought her way to me, sobbing, and clamped hold of my arm. "Don't think. Walk."

Colonel Stump immediately grabbed my other arm. "There's a back door out. This way."

It couldn't possibly be true that I could go.

Stump hauled us past the judges' bench, along a dark passage, and out a door that opened on a miracle of a May afternoon. The sky was blue, the sunlight gold, picket fences white. Small pink roses twined up trellises, peonies nearby in frilly bloom. The air smelled of cut grass, horse manure, fried chicken.

Above my head, Isie and Herman Stump said bright, gay words, but I could not hear.

Stunned, I found myself at the hotel, where Stump guarded the door and Isie folded my things into a trunk. I stood where she had left me in the middle of the room, as if I had no will to move my feet. Coming toward me, I could see a slow drip of days, empty, miserable, nights so empty I wanted to end my life.

But then I remembered Orlind, how his smooth baby cheeks had crumpled into tears as his nurse carried him away from me. My chest felt filled with dying coals buried in ash, but now a door flew open, air rushed in and made the flames ignite. Orlind would be *mine*, and I could keep him with me openly. What did it matter if he had Nick's eyes? I could not wait to hold his sweet weight in my arms.

Hastily I scooped up stockings, slips, and camisoles and threw them in the trunk. "Never mind all this, we need to leave quickly, before Richard comes. We'll find someone to take us to your place."

I had made up my mind—I would not sleep another night inside my mother's house. I would go to Isie's, but it was too crowded there to stay for long, and too close to Richard's place. My brother the reverend lived the farthest from Jarrettsville, up in Pennsylvania, but I doubted life with him would be supportable. Jimmy's farm was inside Maryland, but well to the west, and I would ask his wife to take us in.

With the heavy trunk between us, we were maneuvering the hotel hall when Richard burst up the stairs, grinning with exhilaration. "Mrs. Archer sent her carriage to take us home. Come on now. Mother's waiting, and she's been through a great deal."

Isie and I exchanged a rapid glance, and I nodded—it would be all right. When we got to Richard's farm, we would collect my things and take the carriage on ourselves, alone. It was a closed landau, and my mother sat inside, closely veiled. Isie joined her there as Richard stowed the trunk behind and climbed up to drive the horses.

I paused a moment on the grass to regard the outside of the hotel, a place I hoped never to see again. In the distance something thumped in cheerful rhythm and a trumpet blared, as if for a parade. The sheriff's boy came running toward me across the lawn, and I turned to him, spared of my mother's company for a few seconds more.

"Miss Cairnes," he cried, excited, "the Bel Air band is marching here to play for you! They done collected a purse of money, too. They want to give it to you now!"

A band to play for me as if it were a thing to celebrate? A gift of money like you'd give a bride? Quickly I stepped into the carriage, to the corner farthest from my mother's veiled form.

The boy jumped on the running board and shoved his eager spotted face inside. "Ain't you gonna stay for them?"

"I murdered him," I breathed.

The boy gaped with lips ajar, until my mother's arm jerked out and took the door handle, the boy springing free just in time.

"No one will ever forget that," she said and slammed the door.

Epilogue

MARTHA MOVED IN with her brother Jimmy and his wife in Hereford. Her son's full name was Chester Orlind Cairnes, and in the census of 1870 he is listed as a member of James Cairnes's household, but as a girl named Orlinda, probably because, like most baby boys of the day, he wore a dress. Court records of the time show the bastardy charges against Martha and the suit brought against Nick, and both say the child was male.

Martha raised her son on Jimmy's farm until her mother's death, when she returned to the farm where she grew up. She never married, and she died at fifty-two of the tuberculosis brought home by Sam. When Chester Orlind Cairnes grew up, he moved to Baltimore, where he eventually owned a restaurant, his existence never acknowledged by most of the family.

A few months after the trial, Isabelle and her daughter Rebecca both died of Sam's tuberculosis, leaving Isie's husband Cairnes Kirkwood with six young children. He left them with his parents and went to Iowa to seek his fortune, and eventually he set off to return to Maryland to bring the children west. But on his way to the train station, he was murdered, his body left in a ditch. He and Isie have many descendents.

G. Richard Cairnes and his wife Annabelle had three daughters, one of whom died young, and the others never wed.

Alex and Hannah Cairnes McComas produced seven children, six of whom lived, and they have many descendents.

George Andrew Cairnes eventually married Cornelia Slee Haile of Baltimore, and they had eight children, the oldest of whom became the father of my mother. My mother's family was so proud of itself that my mother always said to me as I was walking out the door, "Remember, your mother was a Cairnes," and the family buried all traces of Martha Jane's story.

But in the 1950s, it appeared in *Ripley's Believe It or Not*, and my mother and her brothers noticed it. They discovered Martha's name on the family tree, though not her son's, except in one family Bible, where he is listed as a son of G. Richard Cairnes.

Soon they discovered that the trial was covered in detail by the *New York Times*, the *Baltimore Sun*, and the *Bel Air Aegis*. Some records report her name as Martha Jean (instead of Jane), Jeanette having been the name of one of my great-great-great-grandmothers, who first emigrated from Scotland, and Jean being my mother's name. (And by pure coincidence, my father, Harold Nixon, was always known as Nick.)

My mother waited till I was sixteen before she told me Martha's story. We were flying back to California, where we lived, after a visit to the family farms in Maryland, and a purple sunset preceded us for hours out the window of the plane, as we leaned together whispering and speculating about what the story meant. She wanted me to write it, but she died before I mustered up the nerve to try.

Eventually I inherited family papers that include a photograph of Martha Jane, a pretty young woman in shining silk, scowling at the camera. The photo was printed in sepia tones, but before it came to me someone took a red crayon to her lace collar and cuffs, perhaps to show she was a scarlet woman. The papers include those of my mother's grandmother, who was not a Cairnes but a Robinson. Rebecca Robinson lived on a farm near Jarrettsville and was a friend to Martha Jane, and Chester Orlind Cairnes once wrote to her. She apparently had written to tell him of his mother's death and ask if he would like to have her possessions. Chester Orlind Cairnes wrote back on the stationery of his restaurant and thanked her but declined his mother's things.

Near Jarrettsville, in the cemetery of Bethel Church, stands a gravestone of creamy marble, engraved with a weeping willow, eight lines of rhymed verse and the words:

In the memory of our murdered friend,
Nicholas McComas
who was murdered April 10, 1869
in the 36th year of his age

Just a few yards to the west of it stands a white marker of such porous rock that by the twenty-first century the words have nearly worn away. It says:

Martha Jane Cairnes
Born Jan. 16, 1841
Died May 23, 1893
At Rest

333

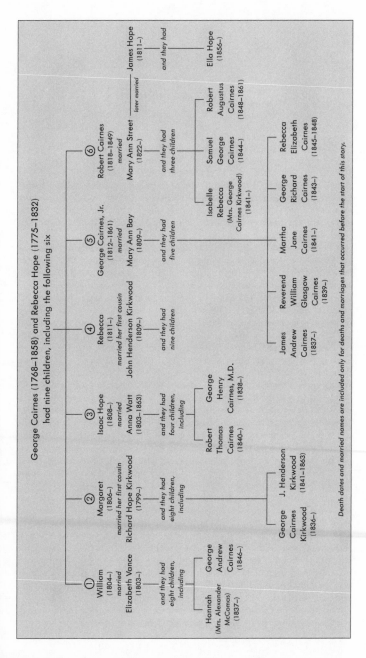

George Cairnes (1768–1858) and Rebecca Hope (1775–1832) had nine children, including the following six

James Hope
(1811–)

and they had

Ella Hope
(1856–)

① William
(1804–)
married
Elizabeth Vance
McComas

and they had
eight children,
including

Hannah
(Mrs. Alexander
McComas)
(1837–)

George
Andrew
Cairnes
(1846–)

② Margaret
(1806–)
married her first cousin
Richard Hope Kirkwood
(1799–)

and they had
eight children,
including

George
Cairnes
Kirkwood
(1836–)

J. Henderson
Kirkwood
(1841–1863)

③ Isaac Hope
(1808–)
married
Anna Watt
(1803–1863)

and they had
four children,
including

Robert
Thomas
Cairnes
(1840–)

George
Henry
Cairnes, M.D.
(1838–)

④ Rebecca
(1811–)
married her first cousin
John Henderson Kirkwood
(1809–)

and they had
nine children

⑤ George Cairnes, Jr.
(1812–1861)
married
Mary Ann Bay
(1809–)

and they had
five children

⑥ Robert Cairnes
(1818–1849)
married
Mary Ann Street
(1822–)
later married

and they had
three children

James
Andrew
Cairnes
(1837–)

Reverend
William
Glasgow
Cairnes
(1839–)

Martha
Jane
Cairnes
(1841–)

Isabelle
Rebecca
(Mrs. George
Cairnes Kirkwood)
(1841–)

George
Richard
Cairnes
(1843–)

Samuel
George
Cairnes
(1844–)

Rebecca
Elizabeth
Cairnes
(1845–1848)

Robert
Augustus
Cairnes
(1848–1861)

Death dates and married names are included only for deaths and marriages that occurred before the start of this story.

THE NEW YORK TIMES

MAY 9, 1869

THE MARYLAND HOMICIDE

Trial of Miss Carnes for the Murder of her Alleged Betrayer

Correspondence of the Baltimore Sun
Belair, Hartford Co., Md., Thursday May 6.

The trial of Miss Martha J. Cairnes for the murder of Nicholas McComas, her alleged seducer, on the 10th of April last, at Jarrettsville, commenced here yesterday. From the large number of talesmen summoned and the regular jurors, (after the rejection of a good many on account of having formed an opinion,) a jury was impaneled. The prisoner, a good-looking woman about 28 or 30 years of age, pleaded not guilty.

Attorney-General Jones opened the case for prosecution, setting forth the facts expected to be proved as establishing the crime of murder. Henry W. Archer, for the defence, then addressed some general and pathetic remarks to the Court and jury on the peculiar character of the case.

The first witness called was John Ware, who testified that he had been acquainted with McComas, but not with Miss Cairnes, though he knew her by sight; while at Jarrettsville, on the 10th of April, he saw her cross the bar-room and come rapidly to the door, looking upon the porch where he and McComas both were; the latter was about ten feet to the right of the door, and Miss Cairnes, leveling a revolver which she held in her hand, fired in the direction of McComas; then stepping backward, and apparently preparing to fire again, said: "Gentlemen, you all know what it's done for;" did not know McComas was shot; witness told McComas to run, but he staggered backward, catching hold of an upright of the porch, he grew pale, his eyes glazed, and he soon had the appearance of a dying man; Miss Cairnes advanced and fired a second time, when McComas fell off the porch, and while he was lying upon the ground she fired two more shots at him; she then passed into the bar-room; witness helped take McComas up; they carried him into the house, but never heard him speak after the firing commenced; it was found that one ball had penetrated the left breast, near the heart, and another the upper portion of the thigh.

John T. Street, sworn—Resides at Jarrettsville; knew Miss Cairnes and McComas; was at home when McComas died; it occurred at my house; she asked me if McComas was there; I told her I thought not; she sad, "Yes he is;" when I left the parlor, I went into the dining-room and stood at the table until several shots were fired; I then walked out, and some one said, "He is a dead man;" the time of the shooting was not one minute from the time I saw her until it took place; when I got out of the door of the dining-room into the bar-room, McComas was lying on the ground; he was picked up and taken into the parlor; I was too much confused to recollect anything about the windows.

Several other witnesses who were eye-witnesses of the occurrence were called, but their testimony disclosed nothing not heretofore elicited.

The case for the prosecution was closed this morning, and the examination of witnesses for the defence was commenced. Abraham Gladden testified that he has known Miss Cairnes intimately ever since she was born; her general character is as good as can be in every respect; her social position is very good; never heard of any complaints; thinks she has no superior in the neighborhood; that she is kind and gentle and modest and charitable, and very active in cases of sickness, death, and Sunday School celebrations.

Thomas M. Catheart also testified as to the good character of the prisoner.

Thomas M. Bay testified—Live in the neighborhood of Miss Cairnes; have known here all her life; am a connection of her family; she is the daughter of my niece; our families have been somewhat together; know her intimately; her character is very respectable; never heard a word derogatory to her character until this came out; she was remarked as a modest young lady; never heard of her being other than charitable and kind in disposition; she has lived with her mother since her father's death; was still living there up to this occurrence.

Thomas Hope, Rev. Thomas Myers, Rev T.S.C. Smith, William Hope, John Rush Street and several others testified to the good character of the prisoner, her mildness, amiability, and zealousness in the works of charity, &c.

Gabriel Smithson sworn—I have known Miss Cairnes intimately for about twenty years; she visited my daughters frequently, her mother's house being only half a mile from mine; I never heard her general reputation questioned; I was at Jarrettsville at the time of the occurrence and saw the firing; saw McComas on the porch; saw Miss Cairnes appear at the door and shout instantly; she looked pale, and her manner appeared wild and resolute; her expression was quite different from what it formerly had been; after the thing was over, I told the people I thought she was crazy. And would take her own life before morning; the whole affair occupied only half a minute.

Mrs. Mary A. Cairnes, mother of the prisoner, sworn—Knew Nicholas McComas for seven years: he was engaged to be married to my daughter, applied normally to witness for her consent to the engagement.

The State here objected to the witness deposing to the declarations of McComas, as not tending to show the guilt or innocence of the prisoner.

After discussion, the Court decided that the antecedent relations of the parties could be given as evidence, and Mrs. Cairnes continues: McComas was received into the family as an accepted suitor; dresses were made up and other preparations made for the marriage; no time was set; McComas put it off on various frivolous pretexts from one time to another; McComas finally appointed a day in November last for the marriage, but never came to the house afterward; my daughter suffered much distress of mind in consequence of this action; wept and shed tears; witness' daughter is now the mother of a child; McComas was aware of the fact when he last promised to marry her; witness inquired of McComas what he was going to do; he said it was all his fault; that he would take care of her; witness said, "You marry her, and I will take care of her;" McComas said, "Don't you blame Martha Jane;" I said, "I will not throw her out of the doors;" finally he promised to marry her on the next Thursday; his calculation was to go to Baltimore and be married, but he never came, and Martha Jane sat up until 4 o'clock, waiting for him, and then went to bed weeping; she was confined on the 1st day of January last; Dr. Martin Jarrett attended her; there was a wedding-dress and a wedding-ring, and it is on her finger now.

336

Third Day's Proceedings.
Belair, Md., Friday May 7.

This morning after two or three ladies had testified to the good character of Miss Cairnes, and to the fact that she was making her wedding clothes in the winter of 1867-8, *Gabriel Smithson* was recalled and testified: Heard part of Mrs. Cairne's testimony; heard Mrs. Cairnes speak of a promise made by McComas to marry her daughter; had some conversation with N. McComas the same night; he was at my house; I told him I thought he was about getting into difficulties: he denied it; said he didn't know; I said, "you are;" at last he agreed he was, and burst into tears; he said, "it is my fault;" no names were mentioned; he did not mention Miss Cairne's name; I told him he had better marry her; he did not give me much satisfaction; he said she was a fine girl and a lady; I did not understand him as refusing to marry her; he did not agree to marry her; I persuaded him to do so; told him of the consequences; he spoke very highly of her as a lady; and it was his fault, and wept bitterly; McComas was 35 or 40 years of age; had but little property; he lived with his mother and three sisters, one of whom is very delicate, the other two strong and healthy girls; McComas' father died suddenly, fell off his horse; McComas' mother and sisters were dependent upon him for support; his brothers are married men, have families; they are of limited means; on the night of his conversation with McComas alluded to above, there was a corn husking at his house; word was sent out to the pile for him and McComas to come in the house; witness went in and found Mrs. Cairnes there, and as he had nothing to do with it, he left; the thing had come out then; knowing that neither McComas nor Mrs. Cairnes wanted him, witness left them alone; it was after this that witness had the conversation with McComas; Comas said he loved the girl better than any woman he ever knew, but said he was not fit to marry; witness did not now what McComas meant by this; he always spoke in the highest terms of the girl, said she was a lady; afterward, at Jarrettsville, McComas called witness out and told him that they had brought suit against him for the maintenance of the child, and said that he was willing to pay for it; McComas then alluded to some slanderous talk which had been going around the neighborhood; that the child was either a married man's or a black man's; McComas said this was all wrong; did not deny the paternity of the child, but said that they could not prove that he had promised to marry her; witness then told him that he better leave the neighborhood; that the girl stood high; that the thing would not die out, and people would not let him alone; this was the last conversation witness had with McComas.

John Hutchins sworn—Was within two feet of the bar-room door when the shooting took place; saw it all after the first shot; saw the woman in the door firing; did not know who she was, but thought she was crazy, and had escaped from a madhouse; did not know who she was shooting at, and got out of the way; her eyes were glaring, and her whole appearance was that of a raving maniac. Attorney-General Jones objected to taking the testimony of this witness as to the sanity or insanity of the accused, claiming that under the law and precedents the opinion only of medical experts could be taken on such a point and asked that this evidence be ruled out. After considerable argument, Chief Justice Grason delivered the opinion of the Court that the opinion of the witness on the point could be received.

Witness had known Miss Cairnes by sight for the last twenty years, but was never in her company, had seen her at Bethel Church and on the road; had never spoken to her; did not know who she was on the day of the firing until after she turned to go back; only thought the woman was crazy because of her actions at the time; knew nothing of her movements or actions before or since; if he had he would not have altered his opinion—would still have thought she was a crazy woman. [At this point the accused smiled, and there was partial applause in the lobby.]

The cross-examination of this witness having been concluded, Mr. Archer stated that the defense had no further evidence to offer.

James Woods recalled by the prosecution.—When Miss Cairnes came through the dining-room after the shooting, her brother said to her twice, "Come on here, and get on your horse."

Mr. Farnandis—What is the object of this?

Attorney-General Jones—To prove that her brother did not regard her as insane, but addressed her as a reasonable person.

Judge Jarrett[1] recalled by the prosecution—Did not see Miss Cairnes ride off from the hotel; was asked by her brother to ride home with her; overtook her about a quarter of a mile from Jarrettsville, when she said: "I told him I would do it, and I have done it."[2]

Charles Ayres sworn: Is well acquainted with Miss Cairnes; known her for twenty-five years; Miss Cairnes, on the night of the 10th of April, came to his house alone with her infant in her arms; Miss Cairnes spoke in the usual way; the ordinary civilities passed between them; her manner did not strike him as being anything out of the usual way; had no idea that anything had happened; saw nothing in her to make him suppose anything had happened; her replies were as sensible as they always had been.

Dr. George Archer called by defence—Has been a practicing physician for twenty years; gave his opinion that the fact of the girl being collected and calm an hour or two after the occurance would be no indication of soundness of mind, but rather the reverse.

The case was then closed on both sides. P.H. Rutledge, Esq., State's Attorney, commenced the closing argument on the part of the prosecution, first reminding the jury that with the alleged crimes and wrong doing of Nicholas McComas they had nothing whatever to do, but to vindicate the insulted majesty of the law. After reading from various authorities, he claimed that the killing of McComas was a deliberately planned and premeditated murder; that her brother, Richard Cairnes, was accessory before the fact, and contending that the plea of insanity could not be sustained.

Herman Stump, Jr., Esq., on the part of the defence, then spoke of the pride which he felt in having been chosen as one of the defenders of innocence; that there was a written law, but there was also a law within the human breast, which had been affirmed and reaffirmed by the verdicts of juries in many similar cases; that the jury could temper the written law, and so alleviate it. He spoke of the wrongs suffered by the prisoner, and added to the jury that not only the eyes of the assembled concourse were upon them, but also the eyes of the whole community. He spoke feelingly of the modesty, kindness, amiability and excellence of character of the prisoner, as clearly shown by the evidence of many witnesses.

Mr. Stump was still speaking when this report closed, at 4 P.M.

1. The witness is Joshua Jarrett, not Judge Jarrett. —C.N.
2. Coverage in the *Bel Air Aegis* has it printed as "I done it." —C.N.

*Sympathy for the Prisoner—She is furnished Rooms at a Hotel—
Her Appearance and Demeanor.*

Correspondence of the Baltimore Gazette.
Belair, Md., Thursday, May 6, 1869

As a single, and, perhaps, remarkable illustration of the moral strength of the
sympathy of the people for the unfortunate young woman, it may be mentioned
that when she gave herself up to the authorities, some three weeks ago, no one
imagined, for a moment, that she was to be incarcerated like a felon. Had she been
imprisoned in the county jail, it is possible, indignation would have arrayed itself
alongside of sympathy and something might have occurred to the detriment of the
county's excellent repute for peace and order. But no such emergency was presented. The county jail, occupied chiefly by negro thieves, and containing besides
some few white culprits of the lowest riff-raff, was not considered a proper place
for a lady, and the term lady is applied to the unfortunate with honest earnestness
by all who know her. The Sheriff consequently assumed the responsibility of pro-
viding more becoming accommodations for her, and she was quartered accord-
ingly at Glenn's Hotel. Here she has the liberty of the hotel, receives her friends
and relatives at pleasure, and appears, unostentatiously, at the public tables.

Miss Cairnes is quite engaging, some say pretty in appearance. Her figure is
exceedingly slight. She is rather tall; has a small face, regular in outline, light com-
plexion, dark eyes and hair, and possesses a quiet, modest expression, which is in
keeping with her general demeanor. It will not be deemed carrying details too far,
when for the sake of more perfectly portraying her personnel it is remarked that
her physical weight, according to her own testimony in casual conversation with
friends, does not exceed ninety-seven pounds. Such points of observation might be
deemed trifling under ordinary circumstances, but it is well to take advantage of
even little things to correct an erroneous impression which has originated in this
case among hearsay attestators. It is reported by some who have even seen her,
but who cannot resist the impulse to invest the lady with heroic attributes that she
is of muscular frame, resolute and haughty in appearance, and quite a fitting character for just such a tragedy as that in which an unhappy fate has involved her.

During her nominal imprisonment at the Glenn House, Miss Cairnes has had
the companionship of her widowed mother most of the time, and has been frequently called upon by her brothers and other relatives and friends. The family,
which has always been in excellent circumstances, and enjoyed the respect and es-
teem of the community, still possesses its hold upon the hearts of its friends, rather
strengthened, if possible, by the affliction into which it has been plunged. And, on
the other hand, the soft voice of sympathy is not unheard beneath the roof that
sheltered the betrayer. There, too, a widowed mother mourns; and brothers and
sisters, bitterly grieved at the mortal ending of a brother's error, lack in their grief
nothing that a general condolence can yield to assuage it.

Thus far, the demeanor of Miss Cairnes in Court has been remarkably calm.
She appears to be entirely self-possessed, but there is an evidence of sadness in her
look which gives expression to the "brooding sorrow" that even sated vengeance
and public sympathy cannot expel.

Acknowledgments

This novel is a work of fiction. It was inspired by true events, but it remains imaginary, and some characters and scenes were invented.

Nevertheless, I am grateful for the inspiration I found in the work of scholars, painters, and writers, including Russell Banks, Ken Burns, Mary Chesnut, Bram Dijkstra, Lorna Duffin, Barbara Jeanne Fields, Eric Foner, Shelby Foote, Elizabeth Fox-Genovese, Charles Frazier, David Golightly Harris, Winslow Homer, Frances P. O'Neill, Henry C. Peden, Madge Preston, Michael Shaara, Daniel Carroll Toomey, Charles L. Wagandt, Bertram Wyatt-Brown, Jay Winik, Mary Cassatt, and James McNeill Whistler. I would also like to thank the American Antiquarian Society, the Maryland Historical Society, the Historical Society of Harford County, and Mills College for their invaluable assistance.

This book would not have been written without the help and encouragement of my aunt and uncle Ralph and Cornelia Galbreath Sloan, who gave me the materials they had, or of Wendy Weil, who made me take courage and get it written. Great thanks also to my editor, Adam Krefman, for his brilliant suggestions, and to these friends and early readers: Robert Hass, Brenda Hillman, Patricia Dailey, Deebie Symmes, Emily Forland, Emma Patterson, Jack Shoemaker, and Dean Young.

About the Author

Cornelia Nixon has written two novels, *Now You See It* and *Angels Go Naked,* as well as a book of literary criticism. She has won the O. Henry Award First Prize, two Pushcart Prizes, a Nelson Algren Prize, and the Carl Sandburg Award for Fiction. She lives in Berkeley, California.